SPLIT INDECISION®

SPLIT INDECISION®

PIERRE BATEAU

iUniverse, Inc.
New York Lincoln Shanghai

Split Indecision®

iUniverse books may be ordered through booksellers or by contacting:

iUniverse
2021 Pine Lake Road, Suite 100
Lincoln, NE 68512
www.iuniverse.com
1-800-Authors (1-800-288-4677)

ISBN-13: 978-0-595-38187-6 (pbk)
ISBN-13: 978-0-595-82556-1 (ebk)
ISBN-10: 0-595-38187-1 (pbk)
ISBN-10: 0-595-82556-7 (ebk)

Printed in the United States of America

Acknowledgements

In life there are many people who help you with your travels.

The road on which I walked to complete the journey that ultimately became this book was a long one.

I would like to take this time to openly thank the people who made me realize this dream.

First and foremost I will thank the GOD within me. Lord you gave me strength when I had none, time when I needed some, and in the end…space to bring this adventure to a close. Thank you for your many blessings.

Maxine, you are my coach and teacher. I could not have begun this journey without you.

To my family; and my niece Chantal, who has contributed much to my twisted mind, if anyone wants to know where I got my ideas, it was them.

To my great friends Jay, Richie, Angela, and Penny: There are no words to express the Love in my heart for you taking care of me in times when my heart fell out of my chest, and my brain fell out of my head. Thank you for being there when I needed you.

To my unofficial editors Anissa, Deliah, Janet and Dell: You guys are the best, and have better eyes than I will ever have. Thanks for putting up with my mistakes.

Lastly, to all the people I have met along the way that I hold a special feeling for, Thank you for showing up in my life when I needed you.

PPP

Prologue

The Beginning

This is weird; it's dark…I must be dreaming; my whole life seems like it's always part of a dream. I've been here before; I remember…It was like I was dying. There is so much in this life I have to do still. I'm gonna be twenty-five tomorrow. I can't disappoint Dad by not being here. Sometimes I just don't know where I'm going in this life.

Dad used to say that life was a journey that grows the self. Have I grown? I don't know; I don't even know who I am anymore. All I know is that there's something I gotta do, but what is it? Oh, no! I know what it is…I have to tell her; all this time, I never realized! Oh God, what have I done? It may not be too late.

"She's gonna hurt her! I have to stop her. God…I can't move!"

"Jacob…Jacob!" I heard the doctor's voice say softly. "When I count to three, you're going to wake up. You will rise slowly from where you are and wake to a warm place. Come back slowly and you will feel refreshed. You will feel the best you have felt in your life. Think back to a time when you were your happiest."

"They're gonna kill them!"

"Jacob…Listen to me…"

"Oh, my God!"

"Jacob, you are okay. There is no one there. Go back into the closet…"

"Okay…Okay, I'm back!" I sighed.

"Lie back down and close your eyes."

"Okay…" I had to concentrate to slow my breathing. "I'm back."

"I'm going to count to three now, and you're going to wake up and feel refreshed; one…two…three."

* * *

Hours earlier

"Oh! You scared me!" Startled, I jumped at the sight of a stranger.

"I'm sorry," the man replied.

I looked at my watch. "You're much too early for any appointment. It's barely seven a.m.," I said. My name is AJ Taylor, and I'm a clinical psychologist. I usually get to work a little early so I can prepare for the day's schedule. I wasn't prepared to see anyone in the lobby this early; I generally have this floor to myself at this time of the morning.

The stranger stood roughly 6'2" with short, wavy hair brushed to the back. He was well-kept, but very nervous. When he spoke, he shifted his glance to the floor as if ashamed. "I'm sorry." His voice was a low whisper. "I'm not good with time…I simply knew that today was the day. Today is the day. The day…"

"The day for what?" I interrupted. "Never mind; you obviously think you are supposed to be here at some point in time today. So, I need to know who you are so we can find out why you're here."

As I spoke to him, I walked over to the desk opposite us and logged on to my assistant's computer.

"Hello!" the computer blurted as it wound up with a whir.

I jumped at the greeting.

"I'll never get used to that noise!" Then I grabbed the mouse, wiggled it, and waited briefly as "Welcome to Macintosh" flashed across the screen. Once the system came up, I double clicked on the appointments icon.

"What is your name, sir?" I asked.

"Uh…Livingston…uh, Jacob Livingston."

"Okay, Mr. Livingston, let's see if, indeed, you are scheduled for today." I grabbed the microphone positioned by the monitor and spoke into it. "Appointment schedule."

Almost immediately the computer replied, "Voice print recognized. Good morning, Dr. Taylor. You're early as usual."

Amazing! A computer with a personality. What will Apple think of next?

"It talks?" Jacob said, amazed.

"Yes, my assistant, Cheryl, and her talking stuff. It's funny; if it wasn't for her, I'd still be using a pencil and a ledger to do appointments."

"She sounds really smart." He folded his arms as he spoke and rubbed his chin.

"Oh, that she is! She's about as smart as they come. I don't know what I'd do without her. She spends a lot of her time doing music and art on her computer.

I never really could see what the big deal was in the beginning, but now with the Mac on my desk, I see a big difference from the computer I used to use."

"I...I have one of those."

"An iMac like this one?" I asked.

"N...no, I have a Powerbook," Jacob replied.

That's right girl, keep him talking...

"Oh! I have one of those, too. Cheryl talked me into that one as well. She had a friend that got both this and my laptop for next to nothing. You can't argue with that."

"New or upcoming appointments?" the soft male voice of the computer asked.

"Upcoming."

"Displaying today's schedule."

Sure enough, Jacob Livingston was the first appointment in my new client's schedule.

"Well, Mr. Jacob Livingston." I looked up at him to see he was preoccupied with a picture of Cheryl and me on the desk. "Ahem..." I cleared my throat. "Your appointment isn't until ten, but you're in the right place. My name is Dr. Taylor."

I extended my hand to Jacob. He looked alarmed at my extended hand, but I stood firm and held it there until he took it in his own. I kept my eyes on his. He had warm brown eyes; they were friendly, but he looked a little wired, like he was on drugs or something. He reached forward and as the sleeve of his coat drew back, I noticed a very expensive watch on his wrist.

"That's quite a watch for someone who isn't good with time."

"It...it is, but I would trade twelve diamonds for one to twelve in numbers any day. I get so confused sometimes!"

"I see; well, do you know what time it is now?"

"I...I know I'm early," he admitted.

"You don't know do you? Hmmm..." I looked around on Cheryl's desk. "Ah-ha!"

I reached for a small, black object on the corner of the desk and pushed the button located in the center of it and the box came alive.

"It is now seven-oh-five," the little box chirped.

Jacob's face lit up in awe of the sound. "Wow!" he remarked.

"Yes, I know," I smiled. "As I said before, my assistant has an affinity for talking objects. She thinks it makes everything in the world more human or something."

"Would you trade that for this watch?" He started towards me and reached to unfasten the gold clasp.

"Stop!" I nearly yelled.

This man has issues! I guess I'm gonna have to be a little tough with him.

"You have three hours before your appointment, Mr. Livingston. I'm sure my assistant won't mind if you hold on to it until then." *I better be right about that one!* "Do you know where the café is, Mr. Livingston?"

"Yes! They have pie there!"

Okay…This guy is a live one.

"Okay, you can wait there until it's time for your appointment."

"I will."

He took the timepiece from my hands. "Ten o'clock!" I reminded him as I closed out the appointment page on the computer. I looked up to see that I was speaking to his back as he headed toward the elevator.

"It is now seven-oh-seven," the little box kept repeating over and over, fading down the hall.

"Jesus! It's gonna take me until ten to prepare for this one!"

I went into my office and put my briefcase down. My office is a second home for me. I have a closet to put a change of clothes and a bathroom complete with a shower for those power workers that hit the gym for lunch. I am *not* one of those people. Cheryl, on the other hand, worked out a lot and made good use of both the closet and the shower. The interior of my office is cozy, with plenty of wood all around it. I've always loved the look and feel of dark cherry oak furniture. My office walls were decorated with cherry oak frames and little knickknacks I managed to pick up on different trips I'd been on.

I looked around the office for a minute, then made my way back to my desk and sat down in the oversized chair that swallowed my slim 5'5" frame. I looked at the work I left for myself the night before and instinctively fell right back into the job and went right to work. After about twenty minutes, I looked up and threw my pen down, frustrated.

"Oh, you're never gonna get this right!"

I've always talked to myself when working. I'd done the same thing as a child. I used to hold entire conversations while sitting alone in my room having tea with my stuffed animals. Mamma told me that she used to watch me during my little tea parties, and she would notice how intense the look on my face was when I would ask my bear a question. Then I would answer for him, of course, with a precise, well thought out reply.

She said she considered taking me to a psychologist to make sure there were no problems, but when she went to go visit one to ask a few questions, an hour later she realized he was already recommending long-term treatment and pulling out insurance forms. By that time, she felt that I was safer in my world than on the outside with that maniac.

I was trying to put the finishing touches on a speech that I was going to give at a graduation ceremony for a class at a local college before Cheryl came in at 9:00. That way, I could hand it off to her and get ready to write it again after she took her red pen to it. As well as I did in English, Cheryl was just better at realizing what I wanted to say. Eventually, I usually got it right. Deep down, I hated the idea that anyone knew me better than I do, but I had to concede to Cheryl's uncanny ability to bring the real AJ out. For a psychologist, that could be rather threatening.

After some thought, I picked my pen back up and closed the speech out. *There! I'm finished.*

I put down my pen, sat back for a minute, and thought. I wonder how she does it. If I knew my clients like Cheryl knows people, I would be a millionaire! I've always wondered about her; she's been working here for like two years. I've never seen a person more dedicated to a job than her, and I know I'm not easy to work for! I can remember times when that girl wouldn't go home until I had finished every ounce of what I was working on, even if I didn't need her help. She would just sit quietly for a while and when it got too quiet, she would perk up and say the funniest thing. Not just a little chuckler either, but a fall-down-on-the-floor laugh until you can't breathe anymore type of thing that just made us both feel good.

There's just this odd thing about her. She always knows the right thing to say. She's just so comforting and so understanding. You know, AJ, she'd make someone an awesome husb…Ahh! I mean wife!

I had to shake my head.

Too many thoughts!

I stacked my speech together and put it in my outbox in my customary fashion. Then I grabbed the remote for my computer/TV (another one of Cheryl's feats) and tuned in to CNN to catch the morning news.

Cheryl

"It's six-o-clock in the morning, Los Angeles. Wake up! Wake up! Wake—*bam!*" I swung at the radio with a blind hand, but it didn't do the trick. Instead of turning off the alarm clock, I managed to hit the radio's volume knob. BLAH BLAH BLAH! The radio continued to blare until I reached down and violently snatched the cord from the wall. The clock went along with it, tumbling as it bounced against the wall and went end over end onto the floor.

"Ooooh!" Never enough hours in the night! That was one hell of a night. I haven't been out like that in I can't remember how long. Oh, my God, though. Man, what did I do? It all happened so fast. I know full well I shouldn't have lay down with that...Damn, Cheryl...I don't even want to think about it anymore! Now I gotta worry about more phone calls and like dinner or something. Man, you really blew it! But it was a whole lotta fun, though; I gotta admit that. Whoo!

My name is Cheryl Gooden. I'd spent the entire night out club-hopping with a new friend. That wasn't the norm for me, but somehow I became involved with this person in an all-of-a-sudden way. I mean, I thought it was what I needed. Slowly I'm beginning to realize that maybe it wasn't. The experience of a new relationship is always good in the beginning, but you can get caught up in the moment and not realize what you are doing. I grew up kind of lonely, and I guess I've been trying to make up for that ever since. What I really want is love in my life; real love. I have no idea what a sista has to do to get it.

"Okay, get it together, girl," I grumbled to myself. "Wake up, so you can put your face on and go to work."

I rolled out of bed and stepped into my favorite bunny slippers, dragged my feet into the bathroom, and leaned onto the large, black, marble top of the vanity below the bathroom mirror.

When I looked into the mirror, I realized I was tired!

Awe, man! There are enough bags under my eyes to supply all of Wal-Mart! I've been trying to make a change in my life forever now, Lord. I keep thinking that when the time comes, I'll know it. Now I gotta deal with this mess I got myself into last night. Ugh! I need help, Lord! I can't keep goin' down this road.

There were some good things that came out of the journey, but life was not totally the way that I wanted for myself. Personally, I just don't feel good about myself. Low self-esteem is something I swore to leave in the past, but in the fight to stay in control of my life, it seems to creep up every so often. I had to force myself to deal with it by motivating myself to get it done—whatever the task, just get it done.

"Okay, let's go!"

I kicked my bunnies off and started on my morning ritual to make myself what I liked to call, "socially acceptable." I stand a lengthy 5'10", with a body that looks as if it were carved from mahogany. I have to admit, I am a beautiful woman. I have the same hips as my mother, who was a dancer. I wish I'd known her better. Her full hips and long legs simply defied her small waist size. It was almost unreal how her body just fit so right. She gave that all to me, and what I hadn't inherited from her, I went out and made at the gym.

It was no secret to anyone now that I looked good. I had spent years as that knobby-kneed, tall girl too clumsy to walk. None of the boys would ever talk to me because I was so tall and so richly covered in dark skin. I remember I would cry alone for hours in the room I shared with my two sisters, Kiana (Ki Ki) and Jasmine (Jazz), wondering why God had made me so different.

For years I endured loose friendships. I intimidated guys and women were openly scared of me. It was ridiculous! It wasn't until later on in life, I realized that it was everyone else's insecurities that drove them away, and not me as I'd thought. It had little or nothing to do with who I was, so I learned to appreciate my differences and live the life that pleased me. I found that working out in the gym was an excellent outlet, so I decided that the skinny body that I walked in with over 10 years ago would become the masterpiece that I sported today. Every cut, every line, and every striation I created by pulling, lifting, and pushing this body to perfection.

I unbuttoned the top of my silk PJs, revealing a sleek body before the full-length bathroom mirror, and let them drop to the floor.

How dare they hurt me so bad when I was a kid. Yeah, if they could only see me now, every one of them little punks would be riding my bra straps!

I stood there for a minute looking at the results from my workouts. I did that every once in a while. It was the only way I could see the results of changes I made in my life. That let me know I had the power to make a change if I needed to. I grabbed a towel from the hook on the wall and wrapped up my hair; yep, *my* hair. I grew every inch of it, and it's down my back. Not that I'm hatin' on my sistas that wear weaves. I love them just the same. Even them sorry Bs that cut me ugly looks just 'cause I'm me. They need to know I'm not changing for them. I am very proud of my very muscular frame. I finally turned from the mirror and reached out to the glass door of the shower. Reaching in, I turned the large, single, ivory handle, which caused the shower to come alive with the sound of rushing water. When the temperature was just right, I stepped in, letting the warm blankets of water drape over my brown skin.

"Ahhhh!" I gasped as thousands of drops of water pelted my still-sleepy body. I took my body sponge from the shower caddy hanging from the showerhead. After squeezing a small amount of scented liquid soap on the sponge, I began to lather up. I touched a tender spot on my left breast and immediately, it took my mind to last night when me and my current lover made love for the first time together.

"Damn, you were good!"

I was still overwhelmed at the thought of my lover tracing the curves of my toned body, kissing my face, nibbling on my neck, twisting my right nipple gently while nursing the left with well-placed kisses.

"Oooh!" I gasped again as I remembered that biting down hard, but not too hard, then the sucking sounds. I couldn't forget the blowing of an ever-cool breath back and forth over my taut nipple. I'd moaned and writhed in ecstasy.

"Ooooh!"

Gentle kisses followed the centerline of my abs to the gold ring that adorned my navel. Oh, I cooed at the thought of my lover's face inching ever so slowly to my closely shaven, eagerly awaiting lips of passion, until that long awaited moment when...

"Ooooh!" The phone rang.

"Damn you phone; any other time, you'd sit your trifling self, quiet!"

My answering machine picked it up. There was a slight pause and then the soft voice of a woman simply said, "I just called to say I love you, and I can't wait to see you again."

"Girl, I know what you mean!"

I finished up in the shower and got dressed. When I got back into the room, I looked at the clock on the floor and shook my head, thought about it, and just left it there. I went over to the dresser to grab some business card samples I had printed for a consulting practice I wanted to start. I grabbed both them and my purse off of the dresser and tossed them in while my stomach was reminding me about breakfast.

No time to eat; I'll get something at the café.

The Devil Herself

"Eight o'clock. Eight o'clock...She said she would call at eight o'clock!"

"It is now eight-oh-one," the timepiece squawked.

"Oops! I must be late!"

"Shit!"

I openly jumped at the sound of her voice. *She's back again...*

She sat down opposite me and just looked me in the eyes. I looked down at the table for a moment, then looked up and smiled. "Today is the day!"

"Yes, it is, Jacob. Today is definitely the day." She kept her eyes on me, smiling a very evil, almost sinister smile. I just continued to look at her with an eager expression.

"What time is your appointment?" She looked at me like she knew the answer already.

"Ten o'clock!"

"It is now eight-oh-five!" the box piped up.

I knew that was a mistake. I can't seem to stop doing stupid things! She drew her head back in confusion, looking for where the sound came from. Then she saw the box in my hand.

"You've finally got that watch beat, huh? May I?"

I had to draw back—I mean, I'm scared of this woman. She held her hand out, bringing her joined fingers back and forth, indicating she wanted the box.

"Give it here!" she banged her fist on the table. A few people at tables near us glanced our way, but almost immediately returned to their own conversations. I was panic-stricken.

Reluctantly and with fear in my eyes, I obediently passed the timepiece over to her. She snatched it from my hands, her eyes glaring back with a look so mean, it seemed it would burn violently through anyone it focused on.

"I...I have to...I have to give it back!" I whined.

"Where did you get it?" her voice rose louder.

"She said her secretary wouldn't mind 'til ten!" I was nearly in tears.

"Her secretary?" Instantly the glare in her eyes disappeared. "I should have known."

She stroked the little box as if it were some kind of delicate animal, raised it to her face and took a deep breath, inhaling what little aroma she could. I watched her just coddle it like it was her favorite thing ever.

"It smells like…apple pie!" she frowned.

She then looked over at me and then down to the table where she could see what was left of a large piece of apple pie on a plate. What could I do but just look back at her with a sheepish grin?

"It doesn't matter." She sat back in her chair. "You make sure you return this!"

"I will, I will." I was relieved that she gave it back.

"Now, back to the matter at hand. Why are we here?"

I immediately sat up straight and answered, "I don't know you!" in the proudest voice I could. I couldn't wait for this; we practiced it over and over again.

She put her head down and shook it left to right. She then looked up, laughing.

"No, Jacob, you don't, but that's just for you to remember when you see me, not for you to say—okay?"

"Yes," I answered, smiling. I couldn't help it. I don't know what's wrong with me!

"You like this, don't you?" she smiled along with me.

"Yes!"

"Okay," she started again. "Why are you here?"

"I have problems!"

"Stop smiling!" she screamed at me. The look on her face switched from pleasant to evil in a split second. The café got deathly silent for a moment. She scanned the room and caught the eyes of many of the people there. No one held her stare for more than a fraction of time. The café went back to normal, and she turned her attention back to me. That woman could still the devil with her looks!

"Do you remember what happens when you cause me problems, Jacob?"

I sat back so far, trying to get away from that look, I was almost a part of the seat.

"Sit up and answer me!"

I felt like my whole world was about to end. I looked down at the table and opened my mouth to talk, but I couldn't form the words I wanted to speak.

"Never mind!" She slapped the tabletop with her hand and brought her face close to mine. "You just remember that when she asks you why you are there. Do you understand?"

"Yes." It was all I could say…

She reached out, stroking my face saying, "It's okay, baby brother. I love you." She paused and said, "You do know that don't you?"

"Yes…"

"Okay, now, you know what to do right?"

"I know what to do."

"I love you."

"I know…" I couldn't look her in the eyes. "I know…"

"It's time for me to go, baby brother."

"It is now eight-thirty," the little box piped up.

I looked towards her as she stood. "E—"

"SHHH!" she interrupted. "What did I tell you?"

I cringed in my seat. With that, she turned around and walked off.

The Way

As I backed out my garage, I reached for my favorite CD.

"Where is it?"

I looked through CD after CD, frustrated. Then I remembered. "Shit!"

I shut off the engine to my BMW and ran back into the house, going straight into my room to the stereo cabinet in the headrest of my bed. Then I pressed the eject button on the DVD player.

"There you are!"

I lifted the Lauryn Hill CD from the tray, pressed the close button, and ran back out of the house, locking the door behind me. Climbing back in my ride, I popped the CD in and said with a smile, "Let the journey begin."

With that, I backed from the garage, hit the button on the remote to close it, and began the 30-minute trek to work, singing out loud as the first programmed track started. I checked the rear view mirror to look at my face. I still looked tired.

But I look good, though!

I hit fifth gear heading onto the highway. My mind often wandered during the drive to work and home. You would think my little blue car knew its own way. A lot of times I'll look up and realize that I just parked at home or in my space at work. This time was no different.

I never really had a real man in my life, and after several disappointments, I turned into myself and started a regimen. Every day it became work, run at lunch, and off to the gym after work. At the gym, it was all *my* world. Weights, the pool, the dreaded Stairmaster; it was all my domain. I used to share my passion for working out with my former trainer, Tia. I hate to say it (actually, no, I don't), I no longer had a need for that bitch. Funny how it happens, however; Tia was not quite done with me. It was Tia who introduced me to my own passion and fucked my whole life up for me at the same time. She taught me things about myself that I never knew existed at the time. One night at Tia's house, she introduced me to a part of her life that changed my life forever:

I was sitting on the couch in Tia's living room. The couch was a warm red color with a large, pillowed backrest. Tia's house was modern, but very plush at the same time. Everything in it seemed to have a certain sensuousness about it. From the warm, glowing chandelier centered in the room, suspended from the ceiling, to the plush carpet that enveloped your feet as you walked across it. She had these long red curtains that matched the couch exactly! It just made you feel welcome with pleasure.

"Here, try this."

Tia had been giving me supplements since we met, so I didn't think twice about taking the pills from her.

"What are these?" I asked as I blindly popped them in my mouth and swallowed.

"It's called Herbal Ecstasy," she answered as she handed me a glass of post-workout glucose drink (or nasty Kool-Aid, as I like to call it). I was thirsty so I downed the liquid quickly, wrinkling my forehead.

"Herbal Ecstasy? That's one hell of a name for a workout pill!"

"Ha! It would be—if that's what it was."

"Well, what's it for?"

"Just relax, girl. I'll be back in a minute."

Tia walked to the back of the room and pulled her shirt over her head, revealing her very muscular back.

She has more definition than I do.

I really didn't know if that was true or not because at the time, I had made a point of never looking at myself in the mirror. It was a practice I learned long ago growing up.

"T!" I called after a few minutes.

"Yes, Ms. Thang?" she answered from the back.

"Do me a favor?"

"What?"

"Put on a suit and come here."

I almost couldn't believe I said it, but that is exactly what I wanted her to do. There was something different about the way I felt.

"I've got something better."

"I hope it's better than that Kool-Aid," I laughed. I was really feeling it now. I had no idea what it was, but I was hot and I could hear the blood rushing in my ears. About ten minutes later, Tia came back out, wearing a long T-shirt that went down to her ankles.

"You call that better?"

"Hush, girl," Tia started softly. "How do you feel?"

"Like a…I feel like a…" I couldn't get it out before Tia interrupted.

"Shhh!" Tia hushed, as she placed a finger on my lips. "Is it good or bad?"

"What?" I was zonked!

"How you feel?" she said, sitting down next to me. "Is it good or bad?"

"It's definitely not bad!" I said very loudly. I had to shout just to hear myself. Once again, Tia put a single finger to my lips.

Now, I am not used to people touching me at all, but all of a sudden, I just didn't mind. She got up and went to the entertainment center, flipped through a few CDs, pulled one out, and popped it into the CD player. Soon after that, the room came alive with the sound of Marvin Gay's "Let's Get It On." Tia then went to the dimmer on the wall and turned the lights up bright.

"Wow, girl, you almost need shades in here!"

"Not to see what I have to show you," she answered.

Tia went to the center of the living room and started to sway slowly, back and forth, to the music. I was mesmerized. All I could do was watch as she went to work. As she danced with that long shirt on, she held on to it at her waist and let it rise above her muscular calves. She moved with precision and like an ocean wave, going from one leg pose to another. She then reached across her body with her right hand, pulling her shirt bottom to the ground as she knelt. Then she raised her head and lifted the sleeve of her right arm up to reveal the solid muscular triceps peak and strain against her pose. Then in one motion, she stood and turned her back to me, lifting her shirt over her head and letting it slide to the ground to reveal her prized back, covered only at the edges by the silky ties of her newly designed lingerie.

"Wow!" I was amazed at the 5'8" frame of Tia's muscular body.

Tia turned and smiled as the song went off. "Do you like it?"

I just looked in amazement and said, "I love it! What do you call it?"

"I don't know," she shrugged. "I put a lot of thought into it, and it's pretty original."

She turned the music down with the remote as she talked when the next song on the CD started. Then she sat down next to me again, only this time, she leaned back so I could see her entire body. My dumb ass! I'd like to think I'd have caught on by then!

"What would you call it?" she asked me.

"With a body like that? I'd call it temporary!" I laughed at my own joke. Tia laughed too. All of a sudden, I was funny!

"You want something to drink?" Tia stood up to go to the bar.

"No! No, girl!" I waved her off. "That shit you gave me before is still working my nerves."

"Good." Tia poured herself a glass of Remy Martin and whisked it back, smiling, closing her eyes, and shaking her head at the same time. When the initial shock to her system passed, she poured herself a healthy glassful and came back to the couch.

"Girl, I could never wear that." I shook my head, putting my hand up in the air in a stopping motion.

"You don't like it!"

"No! I love it!" I reassured her. "I just don't look like you do."

"You're right!" She paused, "You look better than I do."

I was a little shocked. No one at that point had ever told me anything good about the way I looked.

"You would know that if you got rid of some of those old rags you wear." She looked at the baggy sweats I always wore. I loved those sweats!

"What? These are my workout clothes!"

"Girl, please! Those are your gym clothes, your mall clothes...Hell, you probably sleep in them, don't you?"

"Well...yeah!" I blushed (as much as one could tell). I was a little embarrassed.

"You need to show that body off, girl! You've been working on it long enough!"

"I...I...I..."

"Aye, Aye, Aye," Tia interrupted. "Is that all you can say? What are you wearing under that mess?"

I thought for a minute. "My favorite underwear."

"The ones that jerk bought you? What was his name...Julian?"

"Don't remind me," I frowned.

He did have good taste in drawers. I can say that much about him.

"He probably used to wear panties!" Tia laughed.

"Tsk, don't say that! That says a lot about me, doesn't it?"

"We both know about the men that you've dated."

"Oh, fuck men!"

"Here, here!" Tia raised her glass and looked right at me. She couldn't wait for me to say that.

"What's your favorite song, Cheryl?"

"I don't have one."

"Girl, please! Do I have to do everything for you?" With that, Tia got up and went back to the stereo. "Here!" I guess she found the right CD.

When the song came on, I immediately said, "Oh, no, you didn't put on that song!"

"My, My, My," by Johnny Gill, was one of my favorite songs, whether I knew it or not.

Tia pressed the stop button.

"Come here, Cheryl."

I stood up, a little woozy, but still in control and went to where Tia was standing. She grabbed me by my shoulders and moved me to the center of the room. Then she went and sat down on the couch where I had been sitting and pressed play on the remote.

"Now," Tia said, "pretend you're on stage before the whole world, close your eyes, and do what comes natural."

"I ca…"

"Ah ah ah," Tia interrupted and hit the pause button. "Dance, girl, and show off that body! C'mon, it's way too easy! Sing it with me. *Put on your red dress…*" Tia pressed the 'play' button again.

I was feeling very good by now, and it was on! It didn't take much for me to get into it once the music started. At the first note, I closed I my eyes and began to dance like I'd done a thousand times before in the privacy of my own house with the vacuum or in front of the mirror. I swayed to the music and sang along with the words. I can't tell you how good I felt. I quickly threw off my sweatshirt, letting it slide from an extended arm to the floor. It felt so good to get rid of that shirt, and I felt relieved by the cool air that hit my sweat-moistened skin. It was my turn to shock Tia. I just continued to do my thing while I danced in the light in my favorite lace bra. Then in quicker moves than before, I kicked off my shoes. I looked at the mirror on the wall as I turned away from Tia, flexing my back; it was *twice* as defined as Tia's.

"Take it off, girl!" I heard in the distance, but it seemed so far away.

I turned, facing her, showing off my well-defined abs. I pulled at the string of my sweats, and they slid down my thighs to my feet. I stepped out of them and flexed my thighs to show the power in my legs. I was already in a trance. By this time, I was absolutely lost to the world. I remember just swaying to the music, pausing every so often to strike a pose. In my mind, I was naked in a field without a care in the world. I was comfortable, and I felt good, as if for the first time in my life!

I felt a warm pair of hands reach around me from my back. I didn't even think about it. I didn't want anything to disturb the mood I was in. The hands pulled me closer to the body that they belonged to. They were warm and comforting. I placed my hands on top of them and caressed my body with them.

This is like a dream…

Together, my hands and the hands of another felt the wants and the needs that my body longed for. I needed to be free, to let go.

I was so deep into myself that I could no longer hear the music, but my body continued to sway to its own beat, intertwined with another. I knew it was there, but could not sacrifice the euphoria I felt long enough to think about it. I felt my bra come loose, and it made me feel better. Small kisses lit up my shoulders and neck. They made me shudder with delight.

I leaned back to feel the warmth of the body behind me, but I kept going and going as if floating to the ground. I felt the soft fibers of the carpet that once sat beneath my dancing feet. Then more kisses lit up my body, first on my forehead, my nose, and then my mouth! The lips were so soft, the smell so sweet. They followed a line straight down the center of my body and landed where no lips had ever been before. Oh, my body just exploded! I tore at the carpet with my outstretched hands.

This is what I've always wanted!

There was a rumble inside of me. It scared me at first, but I couldn't let go of the feeling so I reached for it inside of me. It started at my toes and rippled wildly through my entire body. I cried out like I was in pain, but pain was furthest from what I was feeling. My entire body was charged with an electric sensation. I saw vivid colors of red, yellow, and bright white beneath my closed eyelids. The feeling just got stronger and stronger. I had to cry out louder, not knowing if I could take it any longer! My mind and body were in a state of constant rage, like the water pounding the rocks at the base of a waterfall. Then just as I thought my body was just going to burst from its frame, the feeling subsided. It went away slowly just as it had started, draining away, taking all of my energy with it. I rolled onto my side and brought my knees together and just held myself. Tia's body joined with me, holding me tight until we both drifted off to sleep.

Déjà Vu

BEEEP! Once again I looked up, and I was pulling into the parking structure where I worked. I don't even remember the turn off of the highway. As I passed the ticket machine, it sounded off, reminding me to push the button for a ticket or punch in my code. I reached out of the window, punched in my code, and drove to my parking spot. When I reached, it I turned off the ignition, and then turned the key back so the music kept playing. I looked in the mirror, as I never used to do, and realized I had been crying. "When the time comes, you'll know it," a tiny voice said to me. "And I think that time is now. I really do."

The parking garage where the office was located was quiet for a weekday morning. I walked up to the elevator and was thinking just that. I reached out and pushed the call button for the elevator and waited. While waiting, my mind wandered.

If I would have only loved myself more; it's not fair!

Another tear rolled down my check. I went to wipe it away and a bell sounded. The elevator doors sprang open.

"Oh!"

I jumped, but the scared look on my face was met with an empty elevator.

"You're so silly!" I shook my head.

I walked into the elevator and reached into the miniature backpack I used for a purse, then pulled out a small makeup kit and a handkerchief. Once again, those tired eyes glanced back at me from yet another mirror. Only this time, I smiled.

"You're the one I really love."

I checked my makeup to see if it was still acceptable. While I fixed my face, the elevator doors closed. I turned to push the 1st floor button and said, "Lobby, please!" then held on as the elevator immediately began to move upward.

Hmmm.

I reached over and picked the elevator phone from its cradle and dialed four digits.

** AJ **

"Goodness! Every day it's the same old mess on the news. That fool over in the desert is acting up again. More Army guys are headed somewhere else. They need to give me a gun and one of those hard hats. The way I feel right now, I could solve all those problems over there. Nobody would be left standing...Humph, all this news is making me hungry. I wonder if Cher..."

Riiing! The phone interrupted my rambling thoughts. I pressed the speaker-phone button and said, "This is Dr. Taylor. How may I help you?"

"Are you hungry, boss lady?"

"Hey, girl! I was just thinking about you. You sound kind of distraught. What's the matter?"

"How do you get 'What's the matter?' out of 'Are you hungry?'" Cheryl asked.

"What do I do for a living?"

"Anyway!" Cheryl answered.

"And quit rollin' those big brown eyes. I can hear them from here all up in your head. Where are you anyway?"

"I'm in the elevator heading to the lobby! Breakfast, boss, how about it?"

"I am hungry. What are you getting?"

"Never mind, Dr. Feel-Good. I know a thing or two myself. I'll be up in a few so get ready."

"Great."

"Do we have time to eat?"

"I do need you," I winced.

"Okay, we'll make it a power breakfast. I'll be up soon."

"Okay; girl, you're so good to me."

"We're good for each other; see you in a little while."

** Cheryl **

I hung up the phone and the elevator came to a stop on the lobby floor.

As the elevator door opened, I got a strong feeling of déjà vu. It was a smell, a smell so strong in my mind, I had to close it to squeeze out the pain I knew would come with it. When the feeling passed, I realized I was holding onto the rail in the elevator.

Get it together, girl!

"Hold that door, please!"

I came to my senses and hit the door-open button as the door was about to close. The doors reopened, and then I realized that this was where I intended to get off.

"Thanks," a woman said, rushing up to the doors. She had her briefcase, some food, and a newspaper clutched to her chest with crossed hands to ensure she wouldn't lose them.

"Sure, I must have blacked out for a second. This is my stop." I stepped out into the lobby and looked toward the front entrance. *There's no way! Tighten up, girl, before you're no good to anyone.*

I had to conclude at the time that what I thought I saw was in my mind, and I was just caught up in that daydream from years back.

Food! That's what we need. I headed towards the café, but as much as I was hungry before, my appetite was really completely gone. I knew in my mind that what I thought I *saw* could not have been real.

They would put me away for sure!

My mind went back to a time when my life belonged to some other part of me. What I did, what I said, everything about me was much different in those days than it is now.

I won't go back. Never again! Not when I've finally made it, Lord. I…I just can't. AJ, I really need you now…

* * *

Two years back when I first came to AJ's office, it wasn't for a job. I had been contemplating seeing a psychologist for quite some time. I only made it as far as the café. AJ had just happened to walk in and since the café was full, she asked to sit with me. We had a good conversation. We talked about our youth and family. Things we liked and disliked. We hit it off great. When I found out later in the conversation that AJ was, indeed, a shrink, I quickly excused myself for a moment to make a phone call. The call I made was upstairs to a neighboring clinic where I had an appointment. I promptly canceled and apologized, then made my way back to the table where AJ was waiting.

"Girl, do you know how hard it is to find someone to talk to sometimes?" AJ asked.

"I would think that you would have that all the time in your job, don't you?"

"No, girl, not at all; the people that walk up in here sometimes, you would not believe. I get paid to listen, not to talk."

"Do you like what you do?"

"I love it; my only problem now is keeping my schedule straight. I lost my secretary yesterday, and I am not in the mood for a temp today."

"How do you do your schedules?"

"Right now, I'm totally manual. If my brother, the automation freak, found out I had a ledger and sharp pencils, he would have a cow!"

"I mean…I'm having a cow listening to you!" I retorted. "Listen, how much time do you have?"

"About an hour before my first client. I have a short schedule today."

"Let's take a walk and see."

"You think you can help?"

I just gave her the most comforting look and replied, "I can fix everything!"

Between the time we left the café and AJ's first patient (who cancelled, incidentally), AJ learned more about computers, networks, and me than she ever knew. I left knowing that I had a job the next day and maybe a friend that would do me a wealth of good. Things were really looking up for the first time in a long time.

"Now I'm doing something I should have done a long time ago." From that point, I took off on a journey that would start some real changes in my life.

* * *

I looked away from my preoccupation with the entrance and went straight to the Starbucks counter. The young lady behind the counter smiled as she saw me approaching.

"Good morning."

I looked up at the sound of her voice. I was still in a trance, trying to clear my mind of the thoughts invading it. "Hey," I finally answered.

"What can I get you?" the young lady asked.

"A pair of mocha lattés."

"What size would you like?"

"Both of them Grande, please."

That ought to get me started.

As the drinks arrived, I paid the woman and thanked her, then went over to the Bagel counter, where I ordered a small feast of breakfast bagels, fresh fruit salad, and yogurt. I had it all boxed up with the drinks and moved back to the elevator. Once inside, I hit the number five and watched the café disappear behind the doors.

Wouldn't it be neat if you could just leave your past behind by getting in an elevator and pushing the button to a new life?

I was so mad at me for allowing myself to forget what I'd been through. *Last night was a mistake!* I finally admitted to myself. *What the hell was I thinking?*

I was nearly in tears; it had been a long time since I had been involved with anyone. The woman I was with last night was new in my life. She just showed up as if she picked me out of a line-up and decided for both of us that we should be together. It had been nearly five years since that encounter with Tia. After that night, I never saw her again. I was so upset that Tia had violated my trust. And I was torn from the knowledge that I had been a part of a homosexual act and how pleasant it made me feel. What was worse, I really thought I saw her heading out of the front entrance of the building from the elevator after I caught a whiff of what I know was Tia's favorite perfume. It was a scent I had never experienced before and hadn't smelled it since then. Tia told me that she had made it herself and as special as it was back then, it was now a horrid reminder of what happened to me that night.

"It wasn't right! She had no fucking right to do that to me!"

Tears were freely flowing down my cheeks now. I couldn't help it. Somehow after all this time, that night that changed my life had taken its toll. I was bent over sobbing. The tears were soaking my blouse and the napkins on top of the box of food. When the elevator doors opened, I started running down the hall to the office. When I got there, I opened the door and dropped my purse, the box of food, and the drinks next to my computer.

Time takes its toll

** AJ **

"AJ!"

As soon as I heard Cheryl's voice, I knew something was wrong. I left my desk and went to the door. When I opened it, Cheryl was standing on the other side with her head down and her hands covering her face.

"Get in here!" I was almost in tears. There's something about friends when they cry. It's as if it's contagious and you have to cry with them. I struggled to help Cheryl over to the couch, almost carrying her full weight. She was weak from crying, with tears still flowing down her face.

I sat her down and sat down next to her. She had to gather herself before she spoke. While Cheryl openly sobbed, she reached out for me. For a good while, we just held each other. It was good for both of us. I had no one to really care about outside of my family, whom I hadn't seen a lot of lately. My job and Cheryl are my entire life outside of them. Funny, I didn't really know *how much* I cared about her until now.

Cheryl pulled away far enough to look me in the eyes. I could see the pain they held. It was tearing me apart to see her so hurt. I knew it was coming, though; there were too many things about Cheryl that I didn't understand. For me, that didn't make sense. People are my job. I know them inside and out. Strangely enough, Cheryl was different. In all actuality, it was my own denial that left me blind to Cheryl. It took me a long time to learn that.

For a person that listened so well, I seldom listened to myself. I have an emotional side that I keep in check. I don't pay any attention to it. I feel no need for it. It was taking over now. Cheryl's state had stripped me of my guard. For a brief second as we sat gazing into each other's eyes, Cheryl thinking she was now safe, and me realizing, just for the moment, I really *could* love someone. That was enough for me. I gently wiped the remnants of tears from her face. My hands were instantly soaked.

"Jesus, girl, you really had that coming!"

I reached over to the end table for a box of facial tissue and paused for a moment to realize what I had just felt. For the first time since I'd met Cheryl, I finally understood.

How could I have been so blind?

I had to gather my thoughts. I couldn't allow Cheryl to see the surprise of the discovery on my face. That single moment was the closest I would come to exploring that side of me that all people have. At the same time, that realization allowed me to see what the problem was before I had to ask. It was as if Cheryl just came right out and told me. I may not have known the details, but I knew I was definitely in the ballpark.

Cheryl finally spoke, "I'm so sorry." She cleaned up her face and sat back on the couch. "I'm not sure what to say. I never talk about my personal life. I mean…Not just my relationships, or lack thereof, but my real life. I really don't think I have actually lived for years. I can't talk about this now, but, AJ, there will be a time when I'm really going to need you. I mean *really*. I just need to know that I'm not wrong feeling that I can trust you to no end."

She looked up at me when she finished speaking. The look on her face was one of helplessness and hope.

"Cheryl, you may be the most important person in my life this moment, and I will tell you that I am here for you. I can't put into words how strongly I mean that. When the time comes, we will get through this *together*. This I promise."

"I love you so much," Cheryl said, reaching forward and hugging me "You are just too good to me."

"How are we doing?" I asked as she let go.

Cheryl just nodded her head to say okay.

"Oh my God; the food!" She got up and rushed out to the front. The box was there where she left it, right next to her iMac. She picked it up and brought it back into the office.

"Oh, I smell latté!"

"Yes, boss lady, just how you like it." Her face brightened up a bit as she let out a final sniffle. "I really just needed you at that moment, AJ. No one else would have done. You just have to understand that."

"It's okay, girl. I'm just glad I was here."

"Work!" Cheryl said, preparing for the morning ritual.

"Ah!" I cautioned with a single finger in the air. "Food! We need food."

"I'm so lucky to have you in my life," Cheryl said as she made a place to eat.

"And I'm just as lucky," I finished for her. "Now, let's eat."

With that, we both began breakfast and at the same time, Cheryl went over the speech with me I had been working on all morning to get the day started.

Close call

** Elizabeth **

Damn that was close! I'm sure she didn't see me. That would just fuck everything up. I need to get into the middle of this crowd just in case she saw me. It's been a while, but she will never forget my face. Pathetic human trash! These fucking people need to hurry up! Damn, if another one bumps into me while I'm trying to get past, I'm gonna slip a knife in her kidney as she passes! Bump into that, bitch!

"Never mind! I'm about to have it all."

I am Elizabeth Tianna Livingston. My story is that I have lived a hard life. I am the product of a relationship (if you can call it that) between my mother, Sheila Williams, and of Jacob Livingston Jr., the father of Jacob Livingston III, my 27-year-old half-brother. Mr. Livingston was on a business trip to Los Angeles back in 1976 when he met my mother at a bar where he was working on a deal with a banker to finance a project over at the local university. My mother was a waitress at the bar, trying to get through college on long hours and shitty tips. At the end of the business meeting, Mr. Livingston stuck around to have a few more drinks and to make plans for the project he was working on. My mother sat to talk with him and he seduced her, got her drunk, impregnated her, and the rest is standing today in the form of a twenty-seven-year old love child named Elizabeth—me.

** Jacob **

Damn, she was there; I heard her running through the house. I heard them laughing as they tore the place apart. They were after everything we owned. They killed my mom and dad! She was there with the people that killed mom and dad. She was there with Wayne. I know it. I know she was, and now she's here with me; but I'm not scared anymore, and she doesn't know I'm getting better. I can think straight. I don't swallow her drugs anymore. She doesn't even check anymore. She thinks I'm a lost cause. I have to find a way to stop her!

I was really getting better by the day. My crazy half-sister had kept me on a strict regimen of depressants, as well as a few homemade cosmetic drugs of her own to keep me like I've been—like a zombie. She walked into my life at the worst moment with every intention of killing me, but there was a letter that stopped her. It was sent to her mother, Sheila, who was at the same time in the same hospital, sick with cancer. The letter was a draft of the will that my mother had planned to show me on my 25th birthday.

The will stated that Elizabeth was a beneficiary of the Livingston estate. There was a clause in the will that stated that in the event that anything should happen to me and should my parents already be gone, that Elizabeth would become the heir to the entire Livingston estate. The clause also listed her as my next of kin.

She was supposed to be responsible for my well-being. What a joke! She was trying to kill me. I was worthless to the world after I got out of the hospital and I finally realized that my parents were gone. I was to be under her charge until a qualified psychiatric panel released me to carry on with no interference from outside help.

Elizabeth knew she had to keep me down until she could figure out a way to get rid of me. For the time being though, she had limited access to my father's money. It was all part of her elaborate plan to become the sole heir of not only the estate, but also the patents that she knew existed from the work that her mother did alongside my dad.

Now, this woman was no common thug. She was definitely a Livingston. She carried that gene that made school so easy for us. She majored in chemistry with minors in psychological biology and medicine. She was all but a certified chemist, and not far from a practicing physician. But her heart was as black as fallen trees after a forest fire. Her mother became sick some years back. Cancer was rampant within her body. To this day, Elizabeth attributed her mother's illness to the worry that she felt was inflicted by her affair with my father. She made a point to study and apply herself to finding relief.

** Elizabeth **

My mother is my entire world. For years I watched her try and find happiness in guy after guy. I knew I was in the way when I was little. Mamma never let me know it, but I always knew I was. She used to drop me off anywhere she could so that she could go out and hit the streets. That all stopped when she left me with a so-called trusted friend and wound up nearly killing him for raping me. I know that I never fully recovered from that experience. I stopped talking to anyone but my mother when I could get away with it. I avoided most adults and hated all men because of that experience. My mother was all I needed; she was all I wanted. I spent most of my time feeling really frustrated. I couldn't get the thought of him—*THAT MOTHERFUCKER!*—out of my head. Later on, I learned to work out at the gym to occupy what time I wasn't studying or reading some type of material. I had to find a way to help my mother get better. That habit grew into an obsession. My need to reach out to someone grew strongly, and just like I found my workout partner/trainee, Cheryl, I was found and showed a way of life that I came to hold onto as a sanctuary. I found a friend in a woman who was really soft spoken. She was easy to talk to. I would have never believed that I would have found myself being with a woman, but Charlotte, my mentor, took me in and made me feel safe from the world of men that I was just scared to death of. With Charlotte, I was safe from the world of men. They could never hurt me again as long as I was stronger, smarter, and she kept me safe from their grasp. Eventually, I was on my own as Charlotte moved away, and I got a job working at the gym that I used.

Since the day that Cheryl first walked into that gym, I had an eye on her. She was still kind of shy back then, but there was something about her that made me just *want* her. I watched her progress in her workouts. Cheryl was a maniac in the gym. It was as if she was punishing herself for some wrongdoing.

I remembered feeling like that. I wondered over and over again in my mind, trying to find out why I always felt so guilty whenever my mother looked at me. Inside, I was still a mess; my insides remained ripped apart. There was nothing I could have done then. He was much bigger than me, *THAT FUCKING MAN!* But now I take my frustrations out on myself by working out. I could see that look on her face; it was one of hurt, one of frustration. She was beautiful! I watched while she worked out her thighs on the thigh trainer. Now there weren't many men that used that part of the gym. I'm sure it was by someone's design that put that room together before I started working there. I don't know why anyone would face the thigh trainer towards the mirrored wall. It was probably some man with the idea he could walk through and catch one of us women on it as he looked at us while we opened and closed our legs, straining from the weight. I know we would never see him watching from an angle, not to mention our eyes are usually closed when we strain dealing with weights. I don't want to think about who did it or why, but I catch myself looking. I love the way Cheryl just fills up the chair. She is so tall and strong. She looks like she should be on TV on some Amazon show. I caught her eye one or twice. She had a great smile. I just had to meet her.

** Jacob **

My half-sister Elizabeth is freaking crazy! There's no doubt about that. She speaks with a lot of confidence when she's in total control, at least when she thinks she is. What she really doesn't know is that there are two more completely different parts of her who are barely aware of each other. Elizabeth was a hurt child who needed to feel safe in the world. She is barely a part of the life the rest of her is living. The other was Tia, a woman who needed love in her life and would die without it. You could tell when she was in charge because she just had this helpless "in love" look on her face all of the time. She used a lot of endearing terms like "baby" and "honey." The way she dressed showed off her face a lot, and she always wore her hair down, but out of her face. The last part of her was a jaded soul named Liz, who was fueled by hate and bent on destruction. Nothing in her path was safe. She wanted her way and would kill for it. I think Liz is the one I see the most. Whenever I start to call her Elizabeth, she goes really crazy. She puts her hands to her ears like it hurts to hear the name. Liz is all about body suits and showing off all of what she has. I think the idea is to get men to look. If they ever stepped to her, though, it would probably be the last day they were alive. Elizabeth is just lost on the inside and the other two personalities take her along for the ride, each one fighting for control of her mind. I rarely speak to her as Tia, but I've seen Tia in action. She loves to *Love*; you can hear it in her voice. She is cute and bouncy. Elizabeth has a body from hell. She has these huge breasts that just stick out in front of her. I can tell when she makes it back to the front of her mind and gets back in control. She cries a lot, and she always runs to the room and finds something big to put on to cover her body. She doesn't want to attract any attention to her figure at all. I think she's afraid that some guy will get close to her and try to hurt her again. Elizabeth will not talk to a man, even to save her own life. She is scared to death of men.

Both her other personalities were attracted to Cheryl. Tia was the patient one. She waited months before she approached Cheryl. She saw that Cheryl was at a point in her workouts that she was not progressing. Tia was an accomplished bodybuilder, and she knew exactly how to help Cheryl get back on track. Soon after, they would become friends and Tia empowered Cheryl with the knowledge of sculpting her body effectively. Cheryl empowered Tia with a bond that she desperately needed. Tia had a former lover who couldn't decide whether she wanted to be with women or men.

When Tia tried to convince her, she wound up in a confrontation with the woman's husband. Tia was so outraged when he put his hands on her that she snapped and Liz, the impatient, wild personality took over. Neither the man nor his wife lived to tell the story. The next day, Tia knew what had happened, but the enterprising mind of that half-sister of mine fixed everything. The headlines the next day read: *"MAN KILLS WIFE AND COMMITS SUICIDE IN DRUG INCIDENT."*

That wasn't the first of that type of encounter. The woman that showed Tia "the way," her name was Charlotte; well, she wanted space. Tia was not only attached to her, she was dependent on her, or at least she thought she was. When it came down to it, she didn't need her too bad because Charlotte finally got the space she was looking for. She was found by LAPD in a parking lot, the victim of an apparent drug overdose. That was Liz's specialty! Tia knew about that one, too. She felt the need to get away, so she left school and got a job at a local gym. That was when she found Cheryl. Now that she had Cheryl in her life, she needed to show Cheryl "the way." Tia was convinced that Cheryl was ready.

Ten O clock

** Cheryl **

"Okay, girl, I think that's enough," AJ said to me as we finished her speech. "I swear to you, Cheryl, I don't know what I would do without you."

"You would do just...You'd do just fine without me." I looked down at the ground shaking my head.

"Oh, Cheryl, girl, are you gonna be okay?"

"Boss, you are so important to me."

"Listen, you know I've always hated when you called me that."

"I know, but it's my right. As close as we are to each other, I'm still very much your employee."

"I could fix that you know," AJ said, smiling.

"You fire me? Please, girl, what would you do?"

"I know; right. I am so stuck with you. Hey, what do you say we take the rest of the day off and..."

"Hold that thought, boss. I think your ten o'clock is here."

"Damn, this is a live one, too. I don't think we can afford to let this one go."

"You can say that one again." I stopped as I was walking towards the door. "This one was paid for by wire transfer. Big dollas, girl."

"Well, alrighty, then," AJ smiled. "Let's do this."

I opened the door and stepped halfway out. "I'll give you a few minutes before I send him in."

"Hey, who's in charge here, anyway?" AJ called back.

"Gotcha," I smiled.

I closed the door quietly while AJ was still talking. She talks way too much sometimes. It's funny how she just has to be in charge. I love her for it though, 'cause sometimes, I really just like to be told what to do. Okay, let's see what's up with this guy. Mr. Big Money Transfer Man...He looks harmless. But, damn, the boy is cute!

** Jacob **

Inside of my mind there was turmoil, but day by day, I could feel myself getting better. I mean, I can remember a time growing up when I didn't have to care about anything! My mom and dad were the best! Although my dad was gone from time to time on business, I remember when I used to hear the tone from the alarm beep when he came home. I used to run through the house and greet him at the door like I was a puppy or something left in the house all day by myself. It was one fatal day that changed my entire life forever.

Prior to that day, I had just come from a local MENSA meeting. That's the club for misfits with high IQs. You should see the people who show up to these things. Some of them drive up on these loud Harley Davidson motorcycles. They come in the building smelling like they just burned a whole field of marijuana. Others are like these little nerdy people with some kind of book stuck permanently to their faces, behind some really thick glasses. I love the mix of people. I've learned a lot from them.

By the time I turned eighteen, I had obtained two masters degrees from the University of Southern California. The first was in computer engineering, and the other degree was in applied physics. Aside from math as a hobby (I took all of the math courses the school had to offer over summer vacations), I also studied people. That's why I loved my MENSA meetings so much.

With my own brand of psychology, I saw and took note of patterns in human behavior. All of which made me realize that there were only a few different types of people in the world. I could see distinguishing characteristics reoccur again and again in different people. I knew how many types there were and even gave them names. There were times when I would try and talk about my findings by asking people if they'd ever seen a person that just reminded them so much of someone else. The way they walked, the way they talked, as if they were the same person, but in a different body. Most would just entertain the question and listen to me. Every once in a while though, someone would have a profound insight on the subject, and I would pull out my mental pen and notepad and compare findings between the two of us.

The names I'd chosen for each of the different "types" of people I'd encountered were the first names of the people of the particular type I'd noticed first. There was Wayne and his counterpart, Mary. Wayne and Mary were kind of my rendition of Bonnie and Clyde, only with a twist. They were, in fact, two of a kind, separated only by gender. They were true psychopaths. They killed for fun. Although I had never personally encountered either of them, I felt the need to create them from the headlines that constantly portrayed them.

"MAN KILLS FOUR IN RESTAURANT SHOOTING, FLEES WITH FEMALE ACCOMPLICE."

I knew that these types of people operated from a different set of rules. There was no telling whether they had more information than so-called ordinary people (genetically speaking) or whether they were missing a crucial gene that normally proliferated a humanitarian sense of being. These were just passing thoughts until that one fatal day when my life was changed.

Revelations

"*Tell me the plan, Jacob!*" my sister yelled.

The thoughts echoed in my mind. I put my head down when she spoke. Part of me was scared to death of her. I knew deep down that she was up to no good. The plan was to get close enough to Cheryl to place one of Liz's special drugs into her drink, a drink that I was supposed to buy from the café after a few visits. I was also supposed to watch Cheryl enter and leave the building from the garage, follow where she went to lunch, and take note of which route she took to and from home and the gym. That part of the job I didn't mind so. Following Cheryl around helped me concentrate.

Cheryl was crazy punctual! She was also the type of person that took the term *meticulous* to new heights. She took the same routes everywhere she went. She ate at the same places on the same days of the week. She was a stalker's wet dream. She could almost be found in the same place at the same times daily. I am far from a stalker, but I was very intrigued by Cheryl's precise nature.

Cheryl is my model for the type of personality she possessed. Deep down, I knew I couldn't let anything happen to her, so I took it upon myself to purposely mislead Elizabeth of her actions, while at the same time, I studied her habits from a distance.

I was one with Cheryl for almost a year of studying her habits. All the while, Elizabeth thought I followed her instructions very well when they were given precisely. Daily, I would report to her about Cheryl's activities. Elizabeth would take this information and use it to construct a plan to get Cheryl back in her life.

There was something in Cheryl that Elizabeth, Liz, and Tia, in unison, had to have in order to have peace between them. When neither Tia nor Liz was the dominant personality, Elizabeth was probably a normal person, but I don't think she could fully function without one or the other half's assistance. Elizabeth was the little girl that was so brutally hurt all those years ago. Tia and Liz were the protection mechanisms that allowed her to continue living without breaking down. Elizabeth really didn't know that she was alive.

* * *

"Good morning, Mr. Livingston," Cheryl smiled as she approached me.

I was shaken for a second, still not fully in control. I immediately looked around, expecting to see my father answer her. It took a second, but I recovered and answered, "Good morning!" in the best voice I could manage. I really liked this girl!

It's funny; she like looked me up and down.

** Cheryl **

Damn, he's fine. Tall, good hair…Hmmm…Wow, if there was a time for change, this might just be it.

** Jacob **

Wow! She likes me, too! I can see it on her face. Okay…okay, don't mess this up.

"And your name is…?" I tried to get a little cocky. I could see that her mind was elsewhere.

** Cheryl **

I can really see my life starting over again today! I've come a long way, and I have to start to, at least try to, trust people again. I really messed up last night. I don't know how I wound up back where I was. I want a man in my life. I have to make a change. There was something about her! She reminded me so much of that first time, the way she spoke, the way she moved; it was almost as if she was the same person! I can't say I don't enjoy the touch of a woman, but I know it in my heart, it's because I've never been that close to any man!

** Jacob **

"That's about to change," she said softly, thinking out loud.

Whoa!

My whole world nearly stopped for a second. I couldn't believe what she'd said. "Marriage?"

I could barely form the words to speak; my whole world seemed at risk at that moment. "Ex…excuse me?" Cheryl said confused.

"You said your name was about to change. Are you getting married?"

"Huh?" Cheryl said, unable to connect. "Oh!" she finally caught on. "No! I'm…I'm sorry, let's start over. My name is Cheryl. I'm Dr. Taylor's administrative assistant."

"Jacob, Jacob Livingston III, to be exact."

"The third, huh? Where are the senior and junior hiding?"

Wow…She went there, didn't she?

"My father has passed, and I never knew my grandfather."

"I am so sorry!" *Damn it, girl, how could you be so dumb?*

"Don't be; there's no way you could have known." I could see she felt really bad and needed a quick escape to recover.

"Okaaay, Mr. Livingston."

"Please, call me Jacob."

"Okay, Jacob; if you will excuse me for a moment, I'll see if Dr. Taylor is ready for you. She turned around and took the shortest path to AJ's office door.

Good Lord, she has a nice butt!

She knocked and then went in.

** Cheryl **

"What's wrong?" AJ asked.

"Why is he here?"

"That's a strange question coming from you. His parents were murdered a few years ago, and he's in court-appointed therapy to determine his competence to handle his estate."

"Estate?"

"Yes, and from my research, I'd say his estate is about the size of Texas."

"Rich?"

"Have you lost your vocabulary, girl? What's with the one-liners? You look as if you're really disturbed. Did he say something wrong to you?"

My mind went back to that place far away in my head.

"Cheryl!"

I snapped out of it. "Um…No. No, boss, I was just thinking…Never mind. Are you ready for him?"

"Yep, send him on in."

"Can we talk later?"

"Of course! Let's do lunch after we wrap him up."

"Cool."

I turned towards the door and looked back before I opened it. "Thanks, boss."

"Anything for you," AJ replied.

** Jacob **

Knock knock!

AJ looked up from her desk. "Come in."

I stepped through the door looking a bit hesitant, I'm sure, but I was much more confident than earlier in the morning.

"Well, Mr. Livingston, I see we managed to make it on time."

I wondered if she normally took this tone with her patients or, in this particular case, she sensed a feeling of adolescence in me this morning that she felt needed attending to. "Y...yes, I...I..." I stopped for a moment and regrouped. "I did, thank you, and the credit goes to you."

Yeah, I got her with that one. I can see the look on her face...

She was really taken aback by my voice; I could tell I did a good job, not only on my voice, but also my confidence.

"Who am I speaking to?" I guess she had experiences with multiple personality disorders, not that this was the case, but she had to make sure.

"Your memory could not have failed you so quickly, Dr. Taylor," I answered. It was hard to stop from laughing.

"You're right. It's just that your level of confidence has risen tenfold since we last spoke."

I had to think about that for a moment. I knew that I was getting better by the day. I also was starting to remember more and more about Elizabeth's wrongdoing. She was bad, and I knew it. I couldn't understand how I hadn't the will or the strength to pull away from her for so long.

The fear I had felt at the time was real. I had no strength to fight her, nor did I have the inclination, but by the day, I was changing. Although I wasn't done mourning my parents' death, I was moving on in a more positive direction. I had a survivalist instinct, and it was rising to the top of my consciousness.

"I have a lot to talk about, Dr. Taylor."

I really just ignored what she said. I'm sure that's gonna piss her off. I had to fight to stray from all of the coaching Elizabeth gave me to prepare for this meeting.

"Do you now?" she said in a condescending way.

I don't think she meant any harm, but she was the one in control and she felt the need to maintain that control, if not for her own reasons, then for professional reasons alone.

Women…

"Do you want to wait for me to ask that you sit down and at least get comfortable?"

I just looked back at her with patient eyes.

"Have a seat, Mr. Livingston. And let's see why you're here."

Letting go

** Cheryl**

God, Cheryl, you have got to get a grip on yourself. I can't remember the last time I've gone through so many emotions in the same day. Just tell me he's not crazy, Lord; I think I can deal with anything but crazy. Oh, yeah, and he better be a MAN, too. My life is screwed up enough!

The phone interrupted my thoughts.

"Dr. Taylor's office. This is Cheryl speaking."

"Hey, baby!" a voice spoke softly.

"Hey," I said a little confused; it was Gina. "How did you get this number?"

"You left one of your business cards at my house."

"Oh." I knew there was a problem immediately. "Okay, so what's up?" I was interested in what was coming up next.

"Lunch, don't you remember?" She was getting a little excited, apparently, from me not remembering.

Damn! I have got to get rid of this girl!

"Oh…uh…hey! About lunch, we've got a ton of things to do today and almost no time to do them. Um…As a matter of fact, the whole week is going to be like that. You know what, girl? I'm going to tell you straight up. I think…No, I know I made a mistake last night. I'm sorry if you feel I led you on I…I just have to tell you that I can't see you again."

I never felt so good about saying anything in my life.

"You're kidding!" The voice on the other end went from soft to almost a shriek. "YOU CAN'T DO THIS TO ME!" she screamed.

I moved the phone away from my ear, but not before I heard the phone drop on the other end. I could hear her in the background.

"What am I going to do? She's gonna kill me!"

"Hello?" I said into the phone.

Gina picked up the phone. "Cheryl, baby, was it something I did, or did I say something wrong?" She seemed almost in a panic.

"No," I said calmly. "It hasn't got anything to do with you. I just had a lapse in the way I was thinking, and I made a mistake."

Ain't that the truth…

"I really don't think I'll be needing your kind of love or affection or…whatever it's called nowadays. I don't want it anymore!" I was getting a little frustrated.

I wasn't prepared to have this conversation yet. I had intended to talk to AJ first, so I could be sure of what I was going to say.

"I could be much better, baby!" Gina started again in a panic. "I can show you the way…Just like it was showed to me!"

Oooh, shit!

Now I was getting scared. When she said that shit, it threw me for a loop. Those were almost exactly the words Tia said to me as I stormed out of her house that morning while I was pulling my clothes on as I went.

"I can show you the way, baby, just like it was shown to me!"

My head was spinning. *This can't be happening!* Deep down, I knew it wasn't over.

"Lord, it really isn't over, is it?"

I was taken right back to the elevator ride up to the office this morning before I ran into AJ's office.

"Don't call back here!" I managed. "Don't you ever call me again!" I screamed just loud enough so that only Gina could hear me.

"NOBODY CAN SAVE YOU, BITCH!" the voice on the other end shrieked. "You've killed us both!"

The voice softened to a whimper. Then the line went dead with a loud click. I was beside myself. I knew I would have to be strong, but this was really big.

AJ, I really need you! Lord, stay with me. I can't do this without you!

Okay, I'll spend the next hour going over what I will talk about with AJ, and in the meantime, I'll work on feeling better by daydreaming about a rendezvous with Jacob.

Jacob Opens Up

I had a seat in the chair that the clients here had to love. It was a huge, comfortable place where people could relax in its depth. I guess it was meant to do just that, but I wasn't so relaxed. I sat on the edge of it with my hands together and my fingers interlaced with each other.

"Well, Mr. Livingston," AJ said behind her desk, "I don't mind telling you that I'm a bit concerned about your behavior this morning. So I'm going to start with a few basic questions to see where we stand."

"Fair enough."

The doctor just looked at me to see the expression on my face, only to realize that it was genuine. I'm sure she was thinking either I was very good at manipulating my demeanor or I was really crazy.

Here we go…

I sat back as patiently as I could and figured I'd put her where I wanted her to be. She was too bossy for me; I'm not putting up with that noise.

"First of all," she said, "do you remember this morning?"

"Very well," I answered flatly.

"Don't make this into a round of twenty questions, Mr. Livingston. I would appreciate fluid, well-defined answers to my questions. We have a lot of ground to cover in the next few hours," AJ demanded. "So let's try this again. Why were your actions so adolescent this morning since you claim to remember so well?"

"Truly, first of all, my name is Jacob; Mr. Livingston is a title I don't care to go by. Can we at least agree upon that before we really get started?"

I made sure she kept eye-to-eye contact with me while I spoke. My purposeful audacity was making her livid inside, but I guess she had a few tricks of her own up her sleeve. She wasn't about to fall for a tactic she used extensively herself.

"Sure, Jacob," she managed to squeak out amongst everything else she was holding back. "I'll take care to remember that as I respond to your *answers!*" She stood her ground. "Now, you were saying about this morning…?"

"This morning…Hmmm…Tsk." I sucked my teeth while preparing to answer. Then I took a deep breath and began, "I said I have a story to tell, and I hope you're ready for it. I can only ask that you listen to all the things I am about to tell you and keep your composure."

"I'm listening," AJ said impatiently.

"Okay, beginning with this morning…"

I began to explain why my behavior in the morning had been the norm for me for a very long time. AJ listened and her eyes widened after each word. I guess she was paying attention after all. I explained how I grew up in a very closed environment. I had two loving parents who were my whole world. My days were comprised of subject after subject of study material, papers on theory, and application of different computer models for encryption, languages, and countless other groundbreaking ideas which I gladly dedicated my time. I was a bona fide nerd!

My dad, at some point, realized that I never really had a childhood. I mean, I was a certified genius at a very early age. I had been published at the unheard of age of ten years old. I wrote a document that changed the face of the study of Chaos and fractals (at least for the professors I studied under). I realized that the mere concept of random anything was unlikely and proceeded to explain why, with complete confidence before a room of scientists with more years of experience in the subject matter than my years of being alive.

I explained to her that I was truly a gifted individual. When I turned twenty-five, I found out that I was to become a full partner in my dad's corporation. He expected me to share and continue his vision of the future of applied computer sciences for not only his company, but for the benefit of the world.

That all but ended on the day before my twenty-fifth birthday.

* * *

"Damn, gee!" I heard a woman's voice as she stepped over the headless body of my dad. "You took that mothafucka's head clean off!"

"All in a day's work," someone replied.

"I see you got the bitch, too; all right, take everything you can find. There ain't nothing in this house that don't cost a lot. What you can't take, tear the shit out of." I heard her laugh as she headed upstairs past the front closet.

I was lying on the floor behind the closet door in a pool of blood. I was barely conscious and struggled with my thoughts. I heard the sound of a woman's voice. *Mary*…It was the last thing I remembered before I passed out.

* * *

"I'll never forget the sound of that voice," I said, continuing with the story. "For the past two years since Elizabeth signed me out of the hospital, she has kept me in a crazy state. For the longest time, all I could feel was what I compare to a hot, wet, wool blanket holding me down. I couldn't think! All I could do was react. I never knew what it was until Elizabeth left town one week and left me with the wrong medication. For an entire week I could feel! I knew who I was, I knew where I was, and I realized that people were in danger.

"She told me to follow Cheryl wherever she went. It was a task that took me all across town. I was to report to her on what Cheryl did, when she did it, and where she went at any given time."

AJ was horrified at what she was hearing. I could tell she had to struggle to keep her composure.

"I remember when she brought Cheryl home and how excited she was. It was the only time she was truly alive; and then I saw them together."

"Together?" AJ finally spoke.

"Yes, together. Elizabeth gave her one of her drugs and they wound up on the floor together. I had never seen two people…two women, together like that. It really was beautiful. I never saw Elizabeth so happy. Deep down, I thought that was all Elizabeth ever wanted and everything was going to be okay from then on—until the next morning. I heard screaming and crying; it was Cheryl. She was upset. I didn't know what was wrong then, but Elizabeth kept saying over and over, 'It's okay, baby. It's what you needed. It was right for you. Don't worry. The first time is always difficult.'

"Cheryl was running around the house, trying to find her clothes. She ran right by me once. I was hiding in the back. She never saw me, though. She just kept running back and forth, and she kept screaming, saying, 'How could you! How could you do that to me! I'm not like that! I'm not like that!' I don't think she ever saw two women together like that either. Cheryl ran out of the house with her shoes in her hand and her clothes barely on."

** AJ **

My alarm went off and the session was supposed to be over. I'm sure it was the fastest two hours of my life. I had to think. What am I going to do? I can't call the police yet, and what about Cheryl?

Oh my God! I have to hear this whole story!

Taking Jacob back

** Jacob **

"There's a lot more to this story, Dr. Taylor. There are some parts that I can barely remember because I was so drugged at the time. I know that lately, she leaves it up to me to take my own pills now. I've found out that she makes the drugs herself. She keeps extensive notes on the effects of each drug she makes. Her research is every bit as thorough as I have ever seen it done. She's brilliant, Dr. Taylor. You have to help me stop her."

Dr. Taylor looked stunned. "O…okay." She started, "I have to take some time today to absorb what you have told me. I want you to see Cheryl on the way out and tell her to schedule you an appointment for first thing tomorrow morning. Do you have any objections to being hypnotized?"

"No, whatever it takes to put an end to this."

"Okay, I don't have to tell you how important it is for you to keep all of this you have told me under wraps until we can find out what to do about it, do I?" she asked.

"Not at all; I'll be back in the morning to continue this."

"Wait!"

Dr. Taylor looked at me and decided that this had to be done now. She got up and went to the door.

Cheryl looked back as the door opened. She looked distraught. I hate to see such a pretty face all frowned up.

"What does my schedule look like?" I asked Cheryl in a whisper. Cheryl told me that my next appointment rescheduled and that I had a later appointment in a few hours. I thanked her and stepped back in the room.

I was kind of tired after telling the doctor that story, and I was also tired of leaning back, too, so I laid back on the couch. It felt really good. The leather was cool against my skin for a second, and then warmed up to just the right temperature to put someone tired like me to sleep.

"We need to do this now!" the doctor said as she walked back in.

Damn! I really could have just dosed off.

"What do I need to do?"

AJ went to her desk and opened the largest drawer on the bottom. She reached in and pulled out a small velvet bag. She then wheeled her chair over by Jacob and left it for a moment. She walked over to the wall and dimmed the lights. "I need you to relax."

She pulled two objects from the small bag. One was a small laser pointer with a stand that she set on the edge of her desk a little bit away from her and Jacob. The other object was a small crystal, suspended from a long, black cord.

AJ pushed a button on the top of the small laser. It looked just like a laser pointer someone would do a presentation with, only the light that came from it was blue. I looked over at the wall where the blue dot fell. It was pretty neat, but I had no idea what she was up to.

She went back and turned the lights down in her office until it was almost dark. Afterwards, she came and sat back down near me and held the crystal up, moving it around until the blue dot from the laser hit it. The crystal exploded with light that cast dozens of brilliant beams that resembled stars in the night.

I was fascinated, all the while I was thinking I had to get my hands on whatever that was.

I could do some damage with that thing!

"Jacob," Dr. Taylor said in a soft voice.

My eyes were fixed on the object. Dr. Taylor held it in place, twisting the cord so that the stars moved about the room back and forth.

I had to take a mental break and look at this woman; I mean, *really* look at her. She was beautiful with that blue light cast upon her. But I thought for a minute as my eyes wandered beyond the base of her neck, that I could use this time to think about the other woman who was sitting right outside the door. I guess that's what got me because one second too long looking at that crystal, and it had me in its grasp.

"I want you to relax. Keep your eyes on the lights and become one with them. Move with them, Jacob, like you can float as free as they do."

I was completely lost in the brilliance of that crystal. I had been here before; my sister was a master of post-hypnotic suggestion. It's how she made sure I did certain things when she was not around. The doctor continued to take me under until I was lost in that in-between world called trance.

"Jacob, I want you to go back to the day before you met your sister, back to the time you told me about before."

I went down easily and slid through time, landing in the home I grew up in…

* * *

"Jacob, have you seen my favorite coat?"

"No, well, maybe, Mother. The cleaners dropped off some stuff yesterday. It might be in the downstairs walk-in."

"Which one?" my mother answered, walking out of the room.

"The one by the front entrance."

"Honey!" My dad called for his wife. He was a stout man in his forties and well-respected in the community. He walked upright and proud, as if the world knew just who he was.

"Yes, dear?"

"I need help with this damn tie!" He was obviously frustrated because he seldom used curse words.

"Here I come." My mother arrived in the room where my dad was standing before a behemoth mirror, fighting with his bow tie.

"Why can't I just wear a clip-on?"

"I threw that thing out with the powder-blue tux and white patent leather shoes!"

"I never!"

"Only because you married me! Now hold still." She reached up to his neck and effortlessly tied the bow tie in a neat knot and said, "There! Now you look like a multimillionaire."

"And that I am."

And that he was. My dad, Dr. Jacob Livingston Jr., was a banker extraordinaire. He also held various patents in encryption coding which he co-authored with none other than his son, Jacob III. Although I didn't really know this, my father used to give me problems for homework. Those problems were usually algorithms for a new kind of encryption that his company had been working on for months. I was the key to solving the code and, ultimately, completing the program. My dad felt it was only fair that I share the credit because of my accomplishments.

He walked down the wide upstairs hall of the house we called Livingston Manor to my room.

"Son, don't you make any plans for tomorrow."

I looked up to see my father decked out in a tuxedo, sticking his head through the doorway.

"Yeah, Dad. You have something very special to show me, right?" I mocked.

"That's right, son, not just something special, but several special things."

"I hate birthdays!"

"I know, son, but this one will be different, I promise."

"As long as you don't buy me a pony," I laughed.

"How 'bout a mustang?"

"Dad!"

"Okay, okay, we'll talk about it tomorrow."

"Okay, Dad."

"Honey, let's go. We're going to be late!" my mother pushed. "Jacob, honey, can you see if my coat is in the walk-in, please."

"The one by the door?" I said, making fun of her.

"Don't be a smart-ass!"

I kind of ambled down the stairs, with my parents close behind, opened the door to the walk-in closet, and pushed through the plastic-covered shirts, suits, and coats to find the coat my mother loved so much. Both of them stopped right behind the door to the open closet and continued to talk about the speech that dad was going to give that evening.

Then there was a knock at the door. "Who could that be, honey? Did you call for a limousine?" my mother asked.

"No…"

I found the coat she was looking for amongst the dozens of plastic-covered items and could hear them talking, so I headed back to the front of the huge closet to see them.

As my dad opened the front door, he was immediately met with a very large shotgun barrel.

"NOT A WORD!" the masked man bellowed from behind the trigger. That man walked forward into the house, leaving dad, who was too shocked to even think. Dad slowly backpedaled, step by step with the armed man. Just as the man cleared the front door, my mother realized what was happening and did what came natural. She took the deepest breath she'd ever taken and opened her mouth wide in sheer terror, but the scream was never heard. I made it back to the front of the closet and heard a horrendous explosion.

The body of my beloved mother was propelled backward into the closet door, slamming it shut and painting its surface with her blood and body. On the inside, the door met me right in the face, instantly splitting my right eyebrow and throwing me backward, where the back of my head met with the corner of an old oak trunk. The back of my head was no match for the brass-covered edges of the trunk. There was a loud crack, as my skull fractured on impact. I never saw what hit me.

"I said not a word, bitch!" the voice behind the mask said coldly. As fast as he turned the barrel of that shotgun away from Mr. Livingston, it was returned. Right before his nostrils, he could feel the heat from the freshly discharged weapon.

The smoke stung his nose and watered his eyes even more than the tears he had barely a chance to realize. In the back of his mind, during the split second when his wife was alive, he thought, *I must do something!* All of a sudden, in a rage he both thought and realized that everything he lived for was now gone. The killer must have seen it in his eyes because that was Mr. Livingston's last living thought. He saw a bright light, and then he saw nothing at all. His headless body wilted to the floor following the second discharge of the deadly shotgun.

"Pity you weren't fast enough," the killer said calmly.

He looked around and surveyed the damage to the front entrance.

"Not bad."

He pulled a two-way radio from his side. "All clear."

Within two minutes, the entrance to the Livingston home was full with masked people clad in black. There were six in all.

"Nice work!" said the last one through the door. "No alarm set; ol' doc and the wife are, let's say...indisposed."

"Damn, gee! You took that muthafucka's head clean off!"

"All in a day's work."

"I see you got the bitch, too; all right, take everything you can find. There ain't nothin' in this house that don't cost a lot. What you can't take, tear the shit out of."

"It's party time," the leader spoke with a cold, yet excited, almost exhilarating tone. "Take it all!"

They all dispersed into the house to plunder, to steal, to relieve us of our possessions.

* * *

"What was that?" I asked, still under.

"What happened?" AJ asked.

"All I can see is clouds." When I first came to after the murders, I thought I was dreaming.

This is a strange dream.

I remembered crawling from the closet. I could see only from one eye and could barely move. I pushed at the door, but something was blocking it. I pushed harder and as it slowly gave, the thick smell of copper filled the air. I crawled along the floor, and my heart stopped when I found the obstruction to the door's path. The pale, swollen face of my lifeless mother lay there in a pool of thickening blood. I tried to scream but couldn't. My mouth lay open with my tongue outstretched like I was gagging. I was delirious, but conscious enough to drag myself to the front door.

When I reached the door, I managed to stand and stretched out my hand and hit a single red button on the keypad on the wall. Out of energy, I melted back to the floor. I could barely breathe as my face lay on the hard wooden surface of the foyer. I could see my dad's body lying in front of me, and that tie he had struggled with so. But beyond that, I saw no more. It was too much for me to handle.

I was crying, still lost in the world of the past. Dr. Taylor studied me closely and wiped the tears from my face, being careful not to break the trance I was in.

* * *

"Jacob?" Dr. Taylor called, squirming a little bit. She was getting nervous.

I didn't answer. It seemed to her that my mind had shut out the outside world. She had seen this before and knew it was dangerous. She had to get me back to where she wanted me, to a place where I could be reached.

"Cheryl!" I screamed.

Cheryl actually came to the door and cracked it open. AJ waved her off. She quickly closed it.

I was dreaming now. I could see a bunch of men chasing Cheryl, with Elizabeth and some guy in front. She was running for her life. She looked just like the day I saw her running from the house with her clothes barely affixed to her body and her shoes in her hand.

"Cheryl!" I screamed again.

AJ couldn't stand it. She hadn't had time to get over the shock of the story I'd told her before. Now that she learned how my parents died, she realized how deeply troubled I really was. She knew she couldn't afford to make it worse by opening up old wounds too quickly.

"Jacob, think about your father before his death. Think about the things he used to tell you that made you closer to him. What did he say to you when you were lost and needed help?"

I stiffened up and spoke slowly. I had to struggle to keep my composure. It was like a bad dream.

"Dad used to say that life was a journey that grows the self. Have I grown? I don't know; I don't even know who I am anymore. All I know is that there's something I gotta do. But what is it? Oh, no! I know what it is…I have to tell her. All this time, I never realized! Oh, God, what have I done? It may not be too late. Mary!"

AJ had heard enough.

"Jacob…Jacob!" AJ's voice said softly. "When I count to three, you're going to wake up. You will rise slowly from where you are and wake to a warm place. Come back slowly, and you will feel refreshed. You will feel the best you have felt in your whole life. Think back to a time when you were happiest."

"They're gonna kill her!" I screamed.

"Jacob…Listen to me…"

"Oh my God!"

"Jacob, you are okay. There is no one there. Go back into the closet…"

Despite the chaos going on in my head, I heard her and my mind obediently listened. Instantly, I found myself on the floor of the closet. No blood, no nothing. It was calm, and I felt a lot better.

"Okay…Okay, I'm back!"

"Lie back down and close your eyes."

"Okay…" I had to concentrate to slow my breathing.

"I'm back…"

"I'm going to count to three now, and you are going to wake up and feel refreshed. One…two…three."

AJ got up and turned the lights back up as she counted. She hurried to her desk and gathered the light and the crystal that went with it. She put them both back in the velvet bag as she sat back down.

"How do you feel?" she asked me.

"I feel okay. Actually, I feel pretty relaxed. Did everything go okay?"

"You had me a little worried for a minute, I'll admit that."

I smiled at her; she looked like she really cared.

"O…okay. I have to take some time today to absorb what you have told me and we will talk about what just happened later. I want you to see Cheryl on the way out and tell her to schedule you an appointment for first thing tomorrow morning."

"Whatever it takes to put an end to this," I told her.

"Okay, once again, keep all of this to yourself, all right?"

"I will."

I got up from the chair and had to stretch. *Oh! That feels good!*

Then I made my way over to the door with my mind only really on Cheryl. As I was walking out, I could see out of the corner of my eye that Dr. Taylor put her head down on the desk and pushed her hair back. I knew she was disturbed. Elizabeth use to do the same thing when she got one of the headaches from the change she was about to go through. My attention was moved to what was in front of me, though. Right now, it was all about Cheryl, and as I opened the door, there she was. Cheryl looked back at me and smiled.

That is what I want!

AJ's Dilemma

"Oh, God! What am I going to do?"

I lifted my head from the desk and grabbed the phone. "Big brother, if I ever needed you, it's now. Please be there!"

"What are you doing right now?" I asked as he answered the phone.

"AJ? I'm in the middle of a tough one at the moment," he answered.

"Can you talk?"

"For a minute."

"No...no, that won't do! I need to sit down and really talk with you."

"Okay, this is where I ask the obligatory question—IS EVERYTHING OKAY?"

"I know, I know, but I really can't do this on the phone," I said, changing the tone of my voice.

"Are you pregnant?"

"Listen, brother, this is not the time."

"Then it is serious! Well, what do you need me to do?"

"Just let me know when we can meet. *Soon!* This thing is really big, Alonzo, and I do *not* know what to do."

"Wow! I don't think I've ever heard you say that, sis. Okay, listen. This is a multimillion dollar deal I have on the table. We have about another couple hours of haggling, and then it's contract talks. Tell me if I have to give up this contract."

My brother spoke slowly to me because I knew that there was nothing in the world he wouldn't do for me, even if it meant giving up the single largest deal his company had ever taken on.

"No!" I started almost in a panic. (I knew he meant it.) "I just had a problem with a client today and there's an incredible amount involved. Just let me know as soon as you're done, and I'll come see you, okay?"

"Sure, sis, I'll even try to push for an early end. We're almost there. From here on out, it's all fine print. I'll call you as soon as I can take off."

"Okay, I'm going out for a minute, but I'll have my phone."

"Okay, sis. I have to go," he said, as people were starting to filter back into the conference room. "I'll call you later. Better yet, hit my hip as soon as you get back so I'll know to hurry things up while you're waiting on me."

"It will be a couple hours."

"Cool!"

"In a minute."

"All right, sis."

After I hung up, I sat at my desk for about five minutes. I kept my head down and was oblivious to everything, including the knocking on the door when Cheryl came in.

"It couldn't have been that bad," Cheryl smiled.

She was still a little giddy from her last encounter with Jacob. I just sat there without moving, not hearing her.

"Boss!" she called, almost yelling.

I heard her this time, almost jumping through my skin.

"What's wrong, girl?"

"Hold on," I said, getting up and running to the bathroom.

I turned the water on full blast to make sure Cheryl couldn't hear me emptying the contents of my stomach. When I was sure I was done, I pulled a toothbrush from the cabinet and rid my mouth of the taste of regurgitated Mocha Latté and the rest of my breakfast.

Then I came back out to see that Cheryl was sitting on the corner of my desk. She sat there quietly and looked me in the face with an inquisitive look. Now Cheryl knew one thing was a constant in life, and that was that she was sure everyone had to die at some point. Another thing in life she came to realize was that there was one other person in her life that she could count on to be as strong as a rock when she needed Him. Cheryl's faith in God was strong and unnerving; He was first in her life. Cheryl's second outlet was her boss—me—AJ! The strongest female figure that she had ever come to know.

Without saying a word, Cheryl stood up and came to me with open arms. I accepted her offer and wrapped my arms around Cheryl tight, as if I were about to lose her. Cheryl knew at this point there was something seriously wrong. She didn't feel right trying to guess what the problem was, so she waited patiently until I pulled away.

When she did, I turned my head to hide the tears on my face. Now Cheryl was scared. Not two hours ago she was the one in tears, and I was the only one in the world that could help. Cheryl didn't know if she could be the rock that I obviously needed now.

Think, girl! What would AJ do if it were me in her place?

Cheryl was good at role-playing. It was something that I had taught her. This was no game, however. If there was ever a time where I seemed to be cashing in the first of those several million favors that Cheryl thought she owed me for the bad times I had helped her through, this seemed to be it.

I could see that Cheryl was intent on doing her best to be of some help. I walked over to the couch and sat down in an attempt to collect my nerves. Cheryl sat back down on the corner of the desk until I spoke. I took a deep breath and said, "Let's go to lunch."

"She speaks!" Cheryl said, doing her best AJ impression.

I managed a smile and reached in my pocket, pulling out a set of keys to a rental car. I had dropped my car off at the dealer early this morning, and they gave me a cute little convertible Audi.

"Come on," I said, almost running out the door.

I'd gotten off of the couch so fast, Cheryl almost didn't see me move. Before she knew it, I was out the door and down the hall.

"You coming?" I yelled down the hall. "Lock up for me, and I'll meet you at the garage!"

I can't let her see me like this much longer…

Head on trouble

** Cheryl **

I pushed the button to set the alarm on the pad on the wall of the office. If anyone had ever broken into this office, they would be met with a host of countermeasures. There was an electronic lock on all of the file cabinets that was almost impossible to negotiate, and while any perpetrator of a crime took the time to try, there were hidden cameras on all sides of the room.

As I set the alarm, I thought of how the tables turned on me today. I really felt good that there was a possibility she would need my help. I was excited at the possibility of being able to help. I finished by pulling the door shut and walked over to my computer. I leaned over to the microphone and spoke softly.

"Lunch."

The iMac on my desk spoke back in a cheerful voice, "Closing all open applications."

"Sleep well, baby."

I grabbed my purse from my desk.

"Silly, woman!" I realized that AJ ran off without her purse. I walked on down the hall towards the elevator.

This is going to be one hell of a day. I've got to tell AJ about my plans to change my life. I've already taken the first step.

The elevator opened. I got in and pushed the button for the garage level, where we had parking spaces. I had almost forgotten about that phone call I received earlier. I knew something was wrong immediately because Gina lied about having one of my business cards.

The cards I had were all samples that numbered four. I checked to make sure I had them earlier that morning when I grabbed my purse so I could take them back to the print shop to order the ones I wanted. That wasn't the thing, though. The cards were for my computer consulting business that I did on the side. The numbers on those cards were my cell phone and answering service.

The number to this job was *nowhere* on those cards. I had no idea how Gina had gotten my work number. I never told her where I worked.

This is getting to be too much.

AJ was parked right outside when the elevator doors opened. I got in without saying a word and she just drove off. I looked at the rear view mirror so I could see her face without openly staring at her. I could tell her mind was in another place.

Whatever it is, it couldn't possibly be as bad as what I have to tell her, but as strong as she is...hell, it may well be worse!

I couldn't even fathom the possibility of something worse. We would both probably have to take the week off. I sat back and just enjoyed the ride. It was good to be outside, and as we drove on, neither of us spoke a word.

** AJ **

Lunchtime traffic was always bad in L.A. It doesn't matter where you are in the city, everyone is headed somewhere all the time. As we drove down the street, it was quiet. I had in my favorite Sade CD, and it took me to a place of calm like it always did. Cheryl was actually asleep, with her head bouncing back and forth. I tried to watch the turns so I didn't decapitate her. Mostly I was deep in thought. I remembered whenever I was in trouble, I used to run straight to my twin brother, Alonzo. I had always thought that since we were twins, whatever I was feeling, he would have felt the same way, so I could ask him what he would do in a certain situation. He always used to come up with the right answers every time! I didn't know if he would have the right answers this time, but with his track record, it was well worth the try. I looked down to make sure I had my purse and realized that I left both it and my phone in my desk.

"Shit!"

I rarely cursed and the way I just shouted woke Cheryl up and made her jump.

"Girl, I left my purse in my desk!"

It had been twenty minutes since we had left the garage, and with all the silence, Cheryl was long asleep.

"I meant to tell you that before I got in," she said, rubbing her eyes.

"I don't have my ID or anything." I started slowing down.

"Never mind!" Cheryl said, placing her hand on top of mine, helping me shift back up to 3rd gear. "Lunch will be on me, and you ain't looking all that young today, so I would imagine you'll slip past at the margarita bar, too. And while you're at it, as long as you quit driving all crazy, you probably won't need your license either. Get it?" Cheryl flashed a smile.

"You're something else!" She must have forgot that she had a ton of bricks to drop on me.

"OH, SHIT!"

This time it was Cheryl's turn to curse and frighten both of us. I looked up from the road ahead and saw it too. A black car came charging right at us on Cheryl's side. There was nothing I could do to avoid it. It came smashing into the side of the little convertible and tossed it like an odd-shaped ball into the oncoming traffic of the next lane. There, we were hit by two other vehicles and were narrowly missed by a city bus.

The car came to a stop on its side, up against a building on the far side of the street from where we were driving. Both Cheryl and I were strapped in our seats, tangled and bloodied. The pungent smell of the air bags filled the mangled cab of the car. The smoke cleared quickly because the top of the convertible was folded over backward, exposing us to the outside air.

Somewhere in the background, a terrible explosion roared through the air. The car that hit us had gone up in thousands of tiny pieces. They came raining back down to the earth, some lighting fires as they lit upon flammable targets. One of which was a business card that sailed with the light breeze. It had come from Cheryl's open purse, which lay in the street with all of its contents emptied on the asphalt. A pair of transients raced over to the small treasure that was some snacks and her wallet. They quickly scooped up what they could and ducked out of sight, as if they were never there. A crowd gathered quickly once the danger of falling objects was gone. The once-busy street seemed to be dead silent, with an occasional horn beeping in the background.

"Somebody call 9-1-1!" a woman shouted.

"They're as good as dead if you are relying on a 9-1-1 call," an onlooker commented.

A short while passed while onlookers kept their distance, looking at the mess in the street. Someone must have called just as it had happened because the wail of the Fire Department's EMS truck and the fire truck along with it could be heard approaching through the street traffic. Cheryl and I lay atop each other, still strapped in, appearing to be lifeless to those who looked on. I could still hear what was going on, but I couldn't bring myself to move. All I could do was moan silently. The once-cute little Audi was no more the shiny showroom car that it had been. It now resembled something one would expect to see in a junkyard, pending recycle amongst a myriad of other mangled and twisted cars with no owners.

The ambulance and fire truck came screeching to a halt at the sight of the burning mass of metal that was the car that hit us. As the first fireman hopped from the truck, he pointed to the car up against the building. His name was Fred; he'd been doing this job for almost twenty years.

"Over there!" he motioned for the EMS truck. "No one could have lived through this."

"What do you think?" his partner Evan asked as he grabbed the hose.

"Any dummy can see that this car was bombed."

"That's what I was thinking, too."

"Let's get a line over here!" Fred shouted as he went to work as he had done so many times before. *What a way to go!* The hose filled up with water and he began to spray down the wreckage. The water from the hose batted the flames into submission, and in a matter of minutes, it was a smoldering mess.

Over at the other car, the rest of the fire crew and the EMS personnel were extracting me from the wreckage of the car we were in. They had to cut me out of my belt and slide me from under Cheryl. Once they got me on to a backboard, three of them whisked me away and strapped me in tight, with all kinds of medical tape.

"Get that hose over here; we've got a fuel lea—"

Even as Evan spoke, it was too late. From under the car, the fuel leaking directly from the gas tank had somehow ignited, and the tank blew away from the car, throwing it in the opposite direction, causing it to slam up against the building and settle upside down. It was so loud that it made my already-ringing ears ring more! James and Henry, the two firemen that were working on Cheryl, had yet to get her cut out of her belt, and they were now under the burning vehicle. Luckily, they had been slammed into the Audi's interior and merely slammed up against the soft leather seats.

While the hose made its way over to the burning car (lacking the gas tank), the two fire fighters quickly finished cutting Cheryl free and slid both themselves and her from under the car through a space where the door once used to be. Only fuel remnants were now burning on the underside of the car, which was on top because the car was upside down. Once they got her away from the burning car, another team of firefighters came with another backboard and quickly affixed a neck brace on her, then strapped her to the backboard. Once they were done, they put her in the same ambulance next to me.

"UCLA MED, this is Rescue One," the driver whose name was Horace said on the radio.

"Go ahead, Rescue One," a voice said on the other end.

"We are inbound with two victims of a T-A rollover…"

Horace went on to explain their injuries that were written on a strip of tape for him by the two that did the preliminary examinations of both of us. When the top of the car flipped back and the car went over on its side, I had hit my head on the concrete sidewalk, opening up my forehead.

The entire right side of my face was swollen because both Cheryl's and my face had collided with each other. The left side of her face was the same as the right side of mine. I also had broken bones in one of my legs, and my shoulder was badly bruised from the seatbelt. Cheryl suffered a bruised hip and several broken ribs. The medics worked on her constantly because one of the broken ribs had punctured a lung and she was barely hanging on. As the ambulance wailed through the city, the EMS crew in the back worked feverishly to stabilize both of our conditions. When we approached the Emergency Department at the UCLA Medical Center, a host of medical personnel clad in white met us at the automatic doors.

"Okay, Jane Doe One and Jane Doe Two—get them both over to OR Number 3 stat!" One doctor looked into Cheryl's eyes, holding them open and shining a penlight into them.

"Careful with this one. We have some cranial deviation and uneven pupils on Jane Doe Two. All right; get me the on-call neurologist and let's get ready to go to work, people. This is what it's all about—saving lives!" He pushed through the doors and got ready to scrub. "All in a day's work!" he went on, and with that, they went to work. Both Cheryl and I were oblivious to everything going on around us. Neither of us had expected that our day would turn out like this.

The Taxi Tail

** Jacob **

When I left the office, there was no doubt that there was a lot to think about. I've never told anyone about my situation. I really had never acknowledged it myself. But like I said, my mind was coming back to me, and things were becoming very matter-of-fact to me. The most important thing was that I had to be sure not to allow Elizabeth to know the truth. I'm no longer scared of her, but I have the awareness to know that she's as resourceful as I could be at any given time. So, if I were to go after her so she would pay for her crimes, I would have to be very methodical in my approach to alerting the authorities…

I've lost so much because of her. My life as I knew it in the past will never be the same. I had to piece together my entire life as the years went by since she killed my parents. I don't really know if it was actually her that did it, but I know she had to have something to do with it! Now to know the cause of all of my grief is here, back in my life, and she is only causing even more damage by milking my family's fortune by forcing me to have a court-appointed psychological evaluation is too much. As I exited the building, I realized as soon as the smell of the outdoors hit me that I was standing too erect.

Too confident.

I quickly relaxed into the slumped-over, sluggish persona I'd been used to actually being. Now it was an act; an act, incidentally, that I'd perpetuated as I got better. It's like I had a sixth sense. No sooner than I assumed my sluggish appearance, I saw Elizabeth drive by in that old, familiar Jaguar that used to grace the hallows of my father's huge garage. There were several cars that resided there.

I remembered that the Jaguar was one of my dad's favorites. Sometimes he would spend the whole day babying that car. Very seldom did it ever get past the driveway to go out of the gate. He only drove it on very special occasions. The last occasion was my parent's twenty-fifth anniversary. I remembered that night. I'd thought I'd never seen a happier couple on earth, which made me wonder just where my half-sister came from.

I knew that, legally, she was my next of kin. I also knew that she had living relatives that were not related to me in any way. I looked down the street and saw that Elizabeth had been stopped by a red light.

"Going somewhere, mister?" a cabbie asked as I was standing in front of his hack.

What an idea!

I'd spent countless days learning to be invisible in the streets when I followed Cheryl around town. This was a great opportunity to put my skills to work on something I felt I needed to know and that was, just who was Elizabeth Tianna Livingston?

"Can you follow that Jaguar, mister?"

"You're the boss!"

I was thinking that Elizabeth must have been waiting for me to leave so she could assure some part of her current plan was in place. *She won't be going home anytime soon.*

"Okay, sir!"

"That a friend of yours in the Jag?"

"No, it's my sister."

"Yeah, sure."

I could hear the tone of sarcasm and replied in a whisper, "She's driving Daddy's car."

"Oh! I get it. You've got a little blackmail thing going, huh?"

"Exactly! She can't know I'm back here. Daddy never drives that car, and he's not here to see her now. I've got to find out where she goes."

"She's as good as busted!" He was determined to do a good job at tailing the "suspect."

We drove for about ten minutes outside of downtown L.A. on the way to Watts. Then she turned into a neighborhood and slowed down.

"I'll pull over here; we don't want to blow our cover."

"Good thinking," I played along.

The cabbie was actually right. She pulled over in front of a quaint little house and got out. Walking to the front door, she opened it with a key.

"That her house?"

"No. I don't know who lives there."

"Well, she's not staying long."

"Why do you say that?" I asked a bit confused.

"Look," the cabbie said, pointing to the car. "She kept it running!" He laughed. "Now *that's* what I call being prepared!"

"For what?"

"A quickie!" he replied, looking very pleased with his observation.

I didn't know what to say to that.

"Here she comes!" the cabbie barked. "That's gotta be some kinda record!" he kept on. "Uh oh," he cautioned.

"What is it?"

"That bag she's carrying."

"What about it?"

"It's one of those personal belonging bags they give you over at the University Hospital."

"It could be just a bag."

"No," he continued. "That kind of bag they take back from you when you…When they…"

I waited patiently as he looked at the bag she was carrying. He could barely make out the letters UCLA written on the outside.

"My wife died in that hospital; they did all they could." A tear streaked down his cheek. "It was cancer, you know. They give me one of them their bags to get some clothes for her to, you know…look pretty in for one last time." He was fighting back sobs now.

"I'm really sorry."

"Don't be!" he perked back up. "That woman was the tightest bitch on earth, God bless her. She left me with a fortune. Since then, I quit my job and went to doin' somethin' I always dreamed of! Owning my own hack! Now all I do all day is ride around and meet all kinds of interesting people like yourself, mister." He went on, "I haven't had this much fun since I got to film two women doin' it right here in the back of my hack. And if that didn't beat all, they paid me fer it and sent me a copy of the whole movie it was in. I love this job!"

"I can see why."

"Here we go!" he said as she drove off.

Sure enough, as we continued to follow my sister, she got on the freeway, headed towards UCLA Medical Center. The cab driver talked the whole way, seemingly not even paying attention to me in the back. As we rode, my mind wandered. I remembered the last time I'd seen the medical center. That was where doctors called in the specialist that helped patch my skull back together. I could remember waking from the coma I was in to only be able to see a white haze. I had to undergo all kinds of therapy to help recover my motor skills. I was quite the celebrity during my last days staying in the hospital. As the cabbie drove into the parking lot, I could see Elizabeth hang a Handicap Parking permit on her rear view mirror.

"Well, this is the end of the road," the cabbie said, feeling a sense of accomplishment.

"Okay; how much do I owe you?"

"Are you kiddin'? This damn thing don't even work!"

He slapped the meter on the side. "I outta pay you just for the good day!"

"Well, thank you, sir."

I didn't have time to argue with him. Elizabeth was out of the car and on her way into the hospital. I bid the cabbie goodbye and hurried up to get to the building so I could at least catch a glimpse of where she was going.

"You need a ride?" I heard him say in the background.

The cabbie was on his way back to downtown L.A., with another potentially adventurous customer.

I cautiously approached the glass doors to the entrance and saw my sister headed to the elevators. I followed closely behind, making sure I had a place to duck behind if she happened to turn her head. She never did. Instead, she walked at a very determined pace and the elevator she was approaching opened just as she came to it. She walked straight to the back and pushed the number nine on the back wall opposite the door she walked in. I could see it clear as day.

"Jacob? Jacob Livingston?"

Oh my God, I know that voice!

I slowed to a crawl without turning around; the sound of that voice was like a knife cutting through the thin-threaded material of my life. I had to stop altogether while I closed my eyes for a moment, trying to remember. I knew that voice! I would swear to it I heard it in my dreams. Finally, after what seemed like an eternity, I slowly began to turn to see where the voice was coming from. I turned around and looked at the owner of that voice, vaguely remembering who she was. In fact, I almost didn't know who she was. I thought I was making a mistake, but she was calling me. She looked right at me with bright eyes. Oh, she looked good! She was tall and slender; she looked as if she played a part in a soap opera as a nurse. I had no idea real nurses looked like her.

"Wait, close your eyes," she hushed and covered my eyes with her hands.

I could smell the perfume on her hands. *Peaches!* I knew that smell from my dreams, too. Before I could say a word she spoke.

"Listen, no man is an island to himself, but Noman was. His only strengths were all his weaknesses..."

"Loneliness, apathy, and a total disregard for fellowship," I interrupted. "I wrote that!"

Although I hadn't heard the words in years, I knew them like the back of my hand. It was my first attempt at literature, a novel called *Noman the Island*. I decided I liked it so much, I had it printed and bound into a single copy.

"I read the whole thing to you when you were here in ICU," she said, removing her hands and moving to face me.

I wished she had kept her hands there. For the short amount of time she spoke in the darkness I experienced, I'd never felt so at ease. My eyes began to swell with tears. I don't understand why I'd become so emotional all of a sudden.

"Oh, my God, Jacob. I don't think you have ever seen my face before." She hugged me as she spoke. Now she was in tears.

"I need to sit." I was feeling faint. Whenever she spoke, it seemed to drain the energy from my legs. "I don't understand!" I felt frustrated and was getting angry.

"You remember, don't you?" the nurse said. "The pain, the frustration of trying to wake up. You had that same look on your face before you finally woke up."

That's what it was! I could remember her voice saying, *"Come on, baby, come on! I know you can hear me. Come back to the world!"* I could remember the dreams I had when she sat and talked with me almost daily. The machines that surrounded my hospital bed would light up like a Christmas tree whenever I heard her voice.

Night Nurse

** Stacy **

My name is Stacy Caugman. I met Jacob in this very place about two years ago, maybe a little longer. I was so intrigued when I went to visit him, and whenever I spoke to him, the machines in the room just went nuts! It happened the first time by accident. I was in my final year of clinicals in the nursing program, and I was doing rounds with the head neurologist when he took me into Jacob's room:

"This young man hasn't responded to any stimuli we've tried," Dr. Coleman explained. "He's still pretty wrapped up from plastic surgery. But he's in there pretty deep. Functionally, there is nothing wrong with him; he just seems to be off-line. It happens occasionally, but usually there is some type of response to outside stimuli."

"What's this?" I asked as I picked up a book that seemed out of place among the beeping medical equipment.

"It's evidentially a book that his father gave to him before his unfortunate demise," he explained.

"Demise?"

"It's a long story," the doctor said. "Come on, I'll explain over coffee."

I learned of Jacob's father's death and as much of the rest of the story that the doctor knew. He was actually a good friend of Jacob's father. In fact, he was one of the few whom Jacob's father let call him "Dr. Livingston," I learned. He despised the title "Dr." for himself. He may have earned it, but people respected his wishes and few called him that.

Well, I took it upon myself to go and visit Jacob one day on duty. I sat beside him and observed the helpless look on his face. The doctor may have suggested that he was just off-line, as if he were some type of computer or android or something, but I noticed small, insignificant movements made by him.

I placed a hand upon his now bandage-less face and saw his nostrils flare. He took a deep breath, as if he were simply asleep. I thought it was odd and spoke aloud, saying, "You're really in there, aren't you?"

No sooner than I opened my mouth, the machines in the room lit up like they had just been turned on. His pulse was up, his breathing quickened, and small beads of sweat started forming on his forehead. Thoughts in my mind became very blurred quickly, partly because of excitement, and a little bit of anticipation to see if he was going to come out of his coma of six or so weeks. My friend, Suzie, the floor nurse on duty at the time, came running in the room to make sure he was okay. I let her know that things were fine and that I was going to stick around to see if he was going to come to. She had another small emergency to take care of, so I told her I'd keep an eye on him. I really wanted to see him wake up. Soon I came to realize that he wasn't, but it put me on a mission to visit him daily in my off-time to see if I could affect his recovery.

I would come in daily, during work or off duty, it made no difference. There were times when I just knew he was going to come to. I would sit and talk to him, telling him about how my day went. Eventually, I became so used to just sitting and talking with him that I ended up talking about myself.

I talked about my dreams and ambitions as a little girl, about how I once stole a puppy from a neighbor's yard because I just felt sorry for it being tethered to a stake in the ground by a long leash. I kept it all day until my parents asked me where I had gotten it. Since I was a very honest little girl, I told them the truth. I said the puppy just looked at me with sad eyes, that all I could do was get him. I felt as if I had no choice.

My parents both took me back to the neighbor's, where I returned the puppy with tears in my eyes. I told Jacob that was the first thing I had ever loved. I also told him that he reminded me of that puppy in a way. I felt as if he called to me to help bring him back from the depths of the state he was in. For weeks, I came day in and day out. Then one day, I looked in a drawer next to his bed and recovered the book the doctor had spoken about. Its purpose there was to jog his memory in case he came out of the coma with amnesia.

I sat down and began to read it and realized after reading the inscription inside that Jacob was, in fact, the author. I didn't know what to think or feel. I was overwhelmed by emotion. I felt that this was a way that he could speak back to me. I also felt that maybe I could learn a little bit about him by his writing style. I decided to read it aloud like I used to do with some of my favorite magazine articles whenever I sat with Jacob on my lunch break. The book began with a quote from an unknown author summarized by Jacob himself.

"There is a saying that goes, 'No man is an island unto himself,' but Noman was. His only strengths were all his weaknesses: Loneliness, apathy, and a total disregard for fellowship. Noman needed no one, or so he thought. He learned a lesson we all must learn at some point in life—that everyone needs someone. Noman, however, would learn the hard way a valuable lesson, that there is a price one has to pay for solitude."

As I read and as had happened time and time before, the machines in the ICU that Jacob was attached to lit up and came alive. Only this time, it was different. As soon as I finished the words of the opening quote, Jacob moved!

This was a first. He had only subtle changes in his movements up to this point. But this time, at the sound of those words, he moaned and arched his back violently. When I stopped, he settled back down. I was so engrossed into what I was doing that I hadn't noticed that there was a figure standing behind me, a figure of a woman that faded back outside of the door she quietly stepped into. My concentration had me enveloped.

"Come on, Jacob! Come on back to the world where you belong. Come back, baby, come back! I know you can hear me. Concentrate, but relax, baby. It's just like when you're asleep and you think you're awake and can't move. Relax and it will all come to you. Relax your mind, but focus on waking up. You can do it, Jacob. You can do it!" I pushed with tears in my eyes. But it was to no avail. Jacob went back to his expressionless sleep, with no more indication that he would awaken that day.

** Jacob **

In my mind, there was a host of things going on. The comatose condition for me was an eventful situation. It was one big dream in which I'd gone deeper and deeper to find the answers I was looking for. I could feel the voice of the nurse who came to visit me daily. Soon after she started to visit, her voice had manifested itself into an image of a woman. It was just the kind of woman you want to show up in your dreams!

"You are the woman of my dreams," I said, upon seeing her for the first time. Yeah, I know, it may not have been the coolest thing to say, but I have my style. Although all she did was speak on the other side of my consciousness, in this world, she was silent. I would watch as she looked over me. The first time she touched my face, the smell of her perfume took over all of my senses. In this world, my rules of solitude didn't apply. I hadn't the strength to fight the pure emotion I was feeling. I could feel myself longing for her touch, the aroma of her perfume, and luminescence of her sparkling eyes. There was still a part of my subconscious that allowed me to play down the almost involuntary nature of my longing for what I was feeling. If it could be named, it would hold the title of Denial.

"I created you," it made me say. "You are a figment of my imagination because no one is as perfect as you."

The woman smiled and kissed me on the forehead. I could only see her eyes, just as I would look at someone normally when I spoke to them. I used to look directly in her eyes to see what she was thinking as she spoke. Her eyes would not let go of mine like others would. I knew that she could see into my mind, my thoughts, and my apprehension—most of all, what was really on my mind.

I was very driven to be the studious, straightforward, emotionless, and apathetic person to the outside world (meaning, those outside of my very tight circle). I'm a normal guy in my twenties. I have all the feelings and emotions and, most especially, the libido of any guy my age. I just don't have the nerve to use it. So I learned to suppress my feelings and desires for anything but my work. My work has never made me nervous or taken away my ability to speak. And so, everything else to me besides my work became a waste of very useful time.

Unfortunately, the subconscious doesn't play that mess. The entire concept of the word "horny" would be emphatically beyond me if you asked me about it in a court of law. In my dreams, though, I have done things I could never tell my mother about. In fact, I very liberally acted out in those situations that I would, under normal circumstances (real-life situations), completely avoid.

I knew I wanted this woman, and as she held my gazing eyes with hers, I knew the secret was out. I moved to shift my gaze from her eyes to where my mind really wanted to go, and the sky around us turned red. The peaceful place where we once stood became a violent storm of colors surrounding us. I could see the colors swishing to and fro. There were deep colors of reds and jagged yellows, bringing with them feelings of pain and anguish. My mind was in turmoil. Someone else was there. I could feel the presence of something evil. I could smell the bitterness of it fill my nostrils. The swirling colors around us were loud, and they smelled of blood. I could hear thunder crack and wicked laughter echoing in my ears.

I was scared to death. The threat from this thing was real, and I had no strength to fight it. It surrounded me and lifted me from my feet. I cried out loud and arched my back from the pain. I screamed like a child because it hurt so much. Then it was all gone. It was as if it were never there, and my dream mate was gone too. I was left alone in the darkness of my solitary confinement.

This is what I've done with my life…What have I done, Dad? What have I done?

*   *   *

I sat there in tears as I saw the pain and anguish leave from his face and turn into the expressionless face of what reminded me of death. The picture in my mind of him arching his back in what seemed as if something snatched him up from the bed would not leave. I then thought about the door. At some point, I thought I heard the door softly close, as if someone had been there and did not want to disturb us. There was a smell of perfume that was not mine, that had a creepy aroma to it. I felt I'd had enough for the day. I kissed Jacob on the forehead. "Rest well, baby." I had to leave. I was getting much too involved with his recovery.

For the Love of Mamma

** Elizabeth **

I waited patiently as the elevator approached the ninth floor. My plan to have Cheryl where I want her is on track.

On the next visit, that idiot half-brother of mine will have Cheryl drugged out of her mind. Then Gina will get her out of the building and down to the garage. That's when I'll see her again. She will love me again; I know she will. I just have to make her see, see how I can love her, too. No one can please her like I can. She belongs with me. She'll see.

The elevator finally came to a stop and the doors opened. My mother was in room 904b of the cancer ward. There was an eerie feeling of death on the 9th floor. As you passed people in the hall, you could tell they had either been crying, or they were still in tears. I hated coming up here. I wish my mother was the frisky, full-of-energy woman she used to be when I was young.

I knew that she loved me a lot, and my asshole of a father was the source of her problems. I walked down the long corridor and thought back about when I was a child, and the few times I could spend quality time with my mother. I had what was far from a normal childhood. Jacob's father set up a trust so that I could attend private schools. It also paid my way through college and graduate school.

Oddly enough, I partly blame the trust for the separation of me and my mother. My mother encouraged me to go and do well in school. I loved school and I did just that, but unlike Jacob, I had gotten on an educational track that spanned a decade.

No one really knew how smart I was. Most people felt I just had good study habits. Once my mother had gotten sick, I dedicated my course of study to the cure of certain kinds of cancer, and I did it all on my own time. That's where the trust really came in handy. Mr. Livingston had it set up so that any legitimate course of study would be funded. The funds were practically unlimited. The more I spent on equipment to help save my mother, the more I hated Mr.

Livingston. It was almost as if he were helping me help my mom. That was a contradiction that I could not handle.

I continued to walk down the hall until my head started to throb.

What is wrong with me…?

The pain was so great that I had to stop. "Argh!" I started to fade from existence, and I couldn't do anything about it.

"Not again! Where am I? Oh, I'm near mamma's room. I can see the knitted sign on the wall. I can't keep going through this. I have to finish my work on the bipolar drugs. I can't keep waking up in places I don't remember going. At least I'm wearing something halfway decent. I need to fix my hair before I go inside."

I fixed myself up as best I could and thought, Mr. Livingston told mamma that there was no way in the world that he could be a part of our lives. He promised to always provide for me, but that was where it had to end.

"I have too much to lose," he explained to her.

I had to be kept a secret as far as he was concerned, but he did a better job of keeping a secret from me. I didn't find out who my benefactor was until after Mamma had gotten sick. I was looking around for some legal documents in her closet, when I came across the trust agreement for my private education. Digging a little deeper, I found several letters that were addressed to Dr. Jacob Livingston, but were never sent. I opened one of them and had to sit down to avoid falling.

> Dear Jacob,
>
> It has been another year since the birth of our daughter. She is as beautiful as the sun. It seems she is getting smarter by the day. Now at the age of three, she has been talking for almost two years. I wish you could see her grow. I understand that you have another life with a loving wife and another child. I just wish it could have been different for both of us. I know I shouldn't have fallen in love with you. You were everything I ever wanted in a man. I thought I could convince you to stay, but I wasn't thinking about anything but me. I did take the time to put myself in your wife's position and think about what I was saying. I know it isn't fair what I'm asking. It's simply how I feel. It is every bit my fault as it is yours that we made the mistake we did. I knew what I was doing. We both knew we couldn't handle all that alcohol. Now we have a beautiful daughter together, and I am destined to raise her alone. I could never love another man.

> Nor could I ever let another man have me the way you did. Thank you, again, for the trust fund for her education. As I told you before, I don't need anything for myself. I do well enough with my position at the university. I will always love you, even if it is silently to myself. As long as I know you are in the world, I will love you. I pray that our daughter will learn to love you too.

I stopped reading with tears filling my eyes. This is the reason! I was furious. This is why you're so sick, Mamma! This fucking man has ruined your life! I sat and cried even harder.

Men had never been a positive experience in my life. After I was raped, Mamma took me away. We moved to the house where she stayed now. I must have just come from there because I have a bag with her clothes in it. I remember now, Mamma was about to be discharged. She was cleared for home care. Her cancer had stabilized, and her condition was holding.

The hospital cancer staff wanted to keep her on the ward for extended tests. They could not understand why she was getting better. I knew, though. I would see Mama every day so that I could learn the nurses' schedule. Then I arranged to have my own personal time with her so that we could be alone. When the coast was clear, I added my own drugs to her IV drip.

Sometimes I would change her IV with a bag that had a premixed solution created in the lab at the university. I always made sure that it resembled the exact solution that was prescribed by her doctor.

I used to also talk extensively with the charge nurse, Stacy Caugman, and when I could, the doctor on duty. I needed to find out what course they were taking in the fight of her cancer. I always carefully studied Mamma's chart so I could make sure nothing that I substituted would make her have a bad reaction.

The staff on the cancer and ICU floors came to know me well and almost expected to see me whenever they came to work during visiting hours. I was rarely kicked out when visiting hours were over. My plan for Mamma's recovery was working. I never thought that the research that I was doing could help anyone else. The only thought on my mind was that I wanted my Mamma back. I wanted her to live the life she always dreamed she would.

Soon, I thought as I stepped into the room. Soon you will be as good as new, Mamma.

The better Mamma had gotten, it seemed the worse I got. It was all the hate and frustration of my mother's sickness that was feeding my own problems. Mamma was part of the medicine I needed. Along with developing medicine for her, I developed a drug for myself in the lab at school. It was a drug that was meant to correct a bipolar deficiency. I worked on it feverishly day and night because I knew I had a problem. There were too many times I woke up wearing strange clothes and not being in the same place I last remembered. I don't know how the whole thing got started. I was working on a formula one day and one of the chemists in the lab commented on the drugs I had on the table. He mentioned that they would make a great cocktail for a crazy person. I don't even remember why I had them out, but since then, I have been trying to work on my problem along side of Mamma's cancer.

Seeing the Past

** Jacob **

I can't believe I'm talking with Nurse Caugman in the hospital lobby. I must be crazy standing out here in the open like this. Elizabeth could walk right back out of the elevator if she forgot something. I barely noticed the people walking by and around us. I was still feeling the ill affects from my initial encounter with the nurse. This had been a long and trying day for me so far, and I could see no end to the events that were constantly unfolding before me.

"This is so weird for you. I know it has to be." I moved to a chair off to the side and she followed. I hated to do it, but I had to put my head down for a second. I sat there in that position just long enough to keep her from talking.

Then I looked up and peered into her eyes. She smiled and just enjoyed the moment.

If I could have had that look just once. I would have paid more attention to the look on her face seeing the thoughts that crossed it, but I didn't have the patience for it at the moment. I had to find out who she was.

"I know your voice. I even know your eyes, but Miss, I have never seen you before."

"There is a reason for that. I want to tell you the story, but I don't have time. Plus I know you are here to see your sister."

"My sister? How do you know about my sister?" I asked somewhat alarmed.

"I just saw her get on the elevator before you walked in. Did you not know she was here?"

"No, no, I knew. I just don't know of many people who know I even have a sister."

"Oh, that's right. I forgot, she's really your half-sister. That's *her* mother up on nine West."

"Yeah, uh, how is she doing?" Now I knew why she was here! I tried to prod her for more information without letting on that I had no clue of what she was talking about.

"She's the talk of the whole floor! No one has ever seen that type of recovery from such a severe case of cancer. I mean, I've seen the test results myself! She seems to have a lot of tissue regeneration. That's unheard of in patients that were in her condition.

"Your sister has been pushing for her discharge, and it looks like she's finally gonna get it. I'm told she has like two more days before the hospital has to let her go. We all hate to see her go because she's so much of an inspiration to everyone else. But you have to know at the same time, we're all so happy for her. Jacob, you have to realize on nine West, it's one bad story after another. Most people show up breathing and leave with the sheets pulled over their head and the priest trailing behind them."

I sat back in the chair I was in, and she scooted next to me.

"Is there a restroom near here?"

"Right through there," Nurse Stacy pointed to some double doors. "Look, Jacob, I need to see you again."

"That's a good idea," I replied, looking at her.

"When can we meet?"

"I'm not sure. I have to leave for a while; that's why I'm here. I need to straighten out a few things with my sister before I go."

This was the first time I could remember lying to someone and it bothering me so. "Let me have your number, and I'll call you as soon as I get back."

"You promise?"

"Of course. I have a million questions for you."

"And I have the answers for you. Say hello to Mrs. Williams for me."

"Mrs. Williams?" I said, thinking quickly. I had to get her name. "No one calls her that!"

"Well, say hello to Sheila then."

Bingo!

"That's better. I don't even know what to call you!"

"Here!" She pulled a piece of paper out and scribbled on it, then handed it to me and smiled.

"My name is Stacy."

I took the paper from her.

"You can reach me at either of these numbers."

"Thanks. I'll call you as soon as I get back."

"Okay, I have to go, Jacob. It was so nice to see you up and walking around. I'll be waiting for your call!" She walked away and before I knew it, she was gone.

What else could happen today?

Two More Days

** Sheila **

"Oh, baby!" I saw my daughter emerge through the door. Her clothes were different again, but her hair is the same. "Did you hear? I may get to come home soon. The doctor said just a few more days!"

"Just *two* more days, Mamma. Just two."

My daughter gave me the biggest hug. "Look," she said, holding up the bag she was carrying. "I even brought you new clothes!"

My eyes lit up. New clothes had not been a part of my life in quite some time.

"Why did you put them in that old death bag?"

"Mamma, the reason for this bag is so that the nurse on duty won't try and inventory it whenever you come and go with it. It's something that is common with this floor," she explained.

"That ain't what I know it as! Every time I see that bag, it means I'm not going to see someone again soon."

"Well, you're not! You're bustin' out of the joint in a couple days!"

I had to smile at that. "Home," I murmured softly.

"Yes, Mamma, home."

"It's been so long since I've seen anything besides the plain walls of this hospital."

"Mamma, I'm so happy you're getting better!"

My baby had tears in her eyes. "We're going to talk about that when we get home."

"What?" Elizabeth smiled, trying to look as innocent as possible.

"We will talk, little girl!" Then I gave my daughter another hug.

Elizabeth filled my arms with herself and gave me another big hug. "I love you so much, Mamma."

"And I love you," I told her. "Now go on. I know you have things to do."

"I do; I'm already late. I'll be back tomorrow, Mamma." Then Elizabeth turned to walk out of the door.

My daughter has been through a lot. Sometimes I don't know that she knows who she really is. I pray to God that one day things will get better. She used to come up here and not even come see me. I'd see her on the floor in some kind of sexy somethin' outfit. I know all of her problems begin with me, and as soon as I leave this place, I will tend to them. I'm holdin' on, Lord. I'll see the task done as long as it's Your will.

I was full of energy as I went to sit on the bed. Then I turned on the TV to see what was on.

One more night in this place, and then it's home I go! I'll be able to watch my own TV.

I laughed at a funny commercial that was playing. I knew that my recovery was not as miraculous as the confused doctors were thinking. If it had been, I may have stayed for the benefit of the friends that I would soon be leaving. I knew Elizabeth was the reason for my recovery. What I didn't know was how.

I thought she was treating me with drugs from the university that were not allowed to be dispensed. So I couldn't bring it up until we were in the safety of our own home.

Home—the smell of fresh baked pies straight from the oven—oh, I can't wait.

Pies were one of my specialties. I could make a pie from scratch faster than most single people could thaw one out. My pies were always the best at the church fair.

** Jacob **

I walked through the double doors on the way to the restroom and spotted the sign for the males. Walking through the door, I went straight to the sink, twisted the knob for the cold water, and just looked in the mirror. It had been so long since I had taken the time to just look at myself. I used to do it regularly; it was my way of realizing where I was in my life.

I could take one look and tell if I was ill at ease without feeling it. Those telltale signs like bags under my eyes or just an overall tired look when I relaxed my face and just looked in the mirror allowed me to realize I needed to make a change. I could see that now. I had to put an end to this ordeal soon so that I could begin to have some semblance of a life.

I splashed cold water over my flushed face. It felt good. I had no idea what I was about to get into. I could see myself staring Elizabeth's mother in the face and saying, "She killed my father, you know."

I wasn't going to do that, but what I was going to do, I didn't know. I dried my face and threw the paper towel in the trash. Leaving the restroom, I thought, *I need a place to hide until she's gone.*

I cautiously opened the door and walked out into the lobby. Looking around, I saw several rows of chairs facing the entrance where I had came in. As fast as I could, I walked to the furthest row and sat in a chair that just allowed me to see the entrance. I reached over and grabbed a newspaper as I'd done many times before when I was in the same building as Cheryl, making sure I wasn't noticed.

I didn't have to wait long either. Elizabeth came walking through the lobby just a few minutes later, but there was something different about the way she was walking. It was more like she was meandering through the lobby, without a care in the world. I didn't know what to think. I have never seen her move like that before. She looked as if she had gotten hold of the pharmacy tech, who made her a cocktail to go. I knew better than that though. As crazy as she was, she never took any of the cosmetic drugs that she made.

There was a drug that I saw her take on several occasions that made me wonder though. Right after she took it, she was the most loving person to me. I knew whenever she called me "baby brother" in that soft, sisterly voice, that she had taken a dose of whatever-it-was. I can remember thinking often I had to find out what it was.

I even know where she keeps it. I don't know why I've never taken the time to look. Deep down, I could remember that every time she went near the cabinet where she kept drugs, I would lose sight of what I was doing and forget all about it. I watched as Elizabeth sort of sauntered out of the doors. She even waved to a nurse on the way out.

Wow!

I didn't take the time to finish the thought. I looked at my watch and realized that I had plenty of time. Deciding that I was hungry, I headed towards the cafeteria. Several doctors and staff rushed by me in a flurry of motion. I looked to see where they were going, and it appeared to be the Emergency Room. I could hear an ambulance as it drove up to the double doors to the Emergency Department.

That must happen all day, every day.

As I got to the doors the doctors and attendants had just rushed through, I could see the EMS crew pulling two gurneys from the rear of the ambulance. I could also see the tremendous amount of blood on the sheets that covered what appeared to be two women. I turned my head as they came toward the door and picked up my pace. I had seen enough already. They quickly came through the double doors and I could hear one of the doctors saying, "All in a day's work!"

It took my mind back to that day I woke up in the closet.

I wonder if when they wheeled me through those doors, if those doctors had felt the same way.

I continued on down the hall to the East wing elevators. I had a strange craving for a piece of pie. I didn't know why, but that was what I was after from the cafeteria. So food was a good thing for now. It would help me think more clearly.

Five O clock News

Mamma is looking better every day! But she sounds like she is suspicious of something. I wonder what? She seemed to know when I was coming, too. That is just so odd. One of these days, I'm going to look up and I'm going to be driving on the freeway and have a wreck from not knowing where I'm going. I have got to find a cure for what I have. And I need to get Mamma home. That's what I need to do. I can't wait until the day when we'll be walking side-by-side, enjoying the sidewalk entertainment at Venice Beach. We're going to do the rides at Magic Mountain and check out It's a Small World at Disneyland. I'm working hard for that day to come. Mamma deserves it.

I made my way outside of the hospital feeling pretty good about my day (as short as it's been). I wasn't in a hurry at all. But as soon as the sun hit my face, I felt a really sharp pain in my head.

"Argh!"

Bitch!

What the fuck was I doing here? I haven't seen this parking lot since I got that bastard Jacob out of the hospital. All this fuckin' hair in my face! I looked over at the Handicapped Parking section and saw the Jag I took from his father, the fucking, filthy-ass man! I hopped in the shiny green Jaguar that had been Mr. Livingston's favorite. I loved the color of this car; it fit me just right.

Damn; I've got to check on Gina. Gina's job was to make sure Cheryl made it back to me.

I feel like someone just popped me in the back of my head. Shit! My fuckin' head hurts. I need to get back to the house and get a bottle of the new drugs I just made. I can't tell if they're working or not. As long as I keep waking up in fuckin' strange places, I know I need to keep working on the formula. Since I started the daily doses of those drugs, the decisions that I made were mine. No more waking up in the morning in clothes I would never wear. I'd wake up in these big-ass sweaters that hid my titties. I'm not tryin' to hide shit! I want a man to come up to me and spit his game. That motherfucker won't be spittin' shit but teeth soon after. I can't figure out how after I do a job, I wake up all cleaned up and all the blood is gone. Cleaning up is my favorite part!

I have a following, too; a high-tech band of killin', thievin' motherfuckers that will do anything I ask. They never know when I will call, and they don't know how to reach me. I'm like the brilliant villain. My shit can be compared to comic book motherfuckers! The only thing I'm missin' is a fuckin' cape-n-sit to fly from building to building. These motherfuckers have no idea what they dealin' with!

What the fuck is goin' on here? Wow! That was a pretty nasty. I drove past what was *left of the scene of an accident.*

It's gonna be good to sit down finally and talk with you, Cheryl. You should have never left me. I forgive you, though. I need you as much as you need me.

I sure hope she sees things my way. I turned her ass out, and I know she stayed that way. Gina really works it out! She says Cheryl is as good as I was with her. Bitch wasn't supposed to have that much fun. But it's okay. I know what I needed to know now.

I wonder if Gina got the job done?

A little while later, I arrived at Gina's apartment. As I got out of the car, I knew something was wrong. The car she bought from a lemon lot to take Cheryl on her last ride if it came to that was missing. I told Gina's ass not to take that car anywhere until she got the word from me. I walked up the walkway to the first-floor apartment and saw the door wasn't closed all the way. I kicked it and it swung backward. The place was a fuckin' mess. It looked like Gina was looking for something unless the bitch got robbed. The furniture was all fucked-up, and shit was everywhere. A note was taped to the phone, and wouldn't you know, it had my fuckin' name on it. I snatched the note from the phone and read it slowly.

> I messed up really bad, and I know what I have to do. I love you, sister, and I know you once loved me. I know why you love Cheryl so much now, but I also know that she won't have either one of us. I know it's my fault, so I'll do what needs to be done. I'm sorry we couldn't be together. I'm sorry I couldn't make it right. If everything goes right, you should see that I solved all our problems. Cheryl and her friend should be dead, and I am probably gone with them. I'm sorry I couldn't be what you needed.—Gina

"What the fuck did you do, Gina?"

I had to sit down and think. I wasn't prepared to have Cheryl out of my life yet, and now Gina was gone too?

"Fuck!"

I looked over at the clock by the TV. "Five o' clock, I'm just in time."

I reached for the remote for the TV that was on the floor by my feet, turned on the set, and tuned to the evening news. Sure as shit, I saw what I was expecting.

> In a bizarre incident today, a car whose driver at this time is unidentified, came speeding across the intersection of Figueroa and Adams and plowed into another vehicle, hitting it squarely and sending it into the oncoming traffic, where it apparently was hit by at least two other vehicles, one of which sent the car flying onto the sidewalk, where it rolled onto its side and came to a rest against the side of a nearby building.
>
> Witnesses say that shortly after the first collision, the car of the unknown driver violently exploded, leaving nothing but a blazing, twisted metal frame of the car. Altogether, there were five cars involved in the accident. There was said to be at least two occupants in the car that was hit. The victims, who have yet to be identified, were taken to UCLA Medical Center and are reported to be in critical condition.

I turned the TV off. "Shit! Damn it, Gina! Why couldn't you have waited?" I knew that Gina was a smart girl. The fact that she went to such drastic means meant that she must have had no other choice.

"The world needs more women like you, Gina. Such loyalty is extremely hard to find. Now I need to find out whether or not they're going to live. I can't believe I was right there after it happened. What a fuckin' mess."

I got my shit together and left the apartment of my lover/soldier. I walked over to the green Jaguar and looked at my reflection in the tinted window.

"Only one thing to do now."

If Gina thought she had to kill Cheryl and her friend the shrink, then we must have somehow been found out. That meant I had to get to them before they had a chance to talk. They were very lucky to be alive. I'm sure Gina died instantly on impact. The bomb in the car was supposed to explode on impact also, but the chemical reaction must not have taken place soon enough. I made that bomb as a last resort if Cheryl didn't see things my fuckin' way. Gina didn't know it was there in the car. The whole purpose was to make it Cheryl's last ride with my dimwit half-brother riding along with her.

The bomb was designed to completely incinerate everything in the car, along with it. It should have left no traces for the police to investigate. The blast should have been so strong that there wouldn't be enough left on the inside to do a dental record check of the victims. Now that they survived the crash, getting to those two is gonna be hard as fuck! First, I gotta gain access to wherever they are, and then, somehow, get to their IVs. It didn't even matter if it appeared to be blatant murder, so long as I make it out of there without being seen.

I know that the only way I could pull it off is to be on the floor after visiting hours. That part was easy; the critical care ward was on the opposite side of the cancer ward. I had been up there after visiting hours many times to stay with Jacob. I probably still know all of the late-shift staff. I need to figure out a way to get in and out of Cheryl's room without being seen.

My mind went to work as I drove to the house to get prepared for that night's mission.

I haven't seen that idiot brother of mine all day.

I don't have time to fuck with him right now; I have a lot to do and only a short time to do it in. Planning with a short time till execution was one of my specialties. This time I had to be at my best because the slightest miscalculation would get me caught! I had to contact my gang. This is the official beginning of the end—right here! I remember when I first got a hold of my boys…

Roughnecks

I gained control of my band of thieves one day when I came across them in an alley. I walked alleyways on purpose because they were places that weak bitches would never go. I walked up on the group of roughnecks. I had just left the gym, and my shit was all poking out. I had my all-black body suit on with a red sash around my waist. And I had on a big white T-shirt to make motherfuckers wonder what was up underneath it. The leader of the group stepped in my path.

"What do we have here?" he said, a wry smile on his face. "A bitch on a stroll? You a long way from home, girl, ain't you?"

"You looking for trouble, punk?" I said to the thug with a smile.

"Trouble?" he repeated. "Trouble be what you found, bitch!"

"Well, what you got, big man?"

"Yo—get her, Big Dogg!" one of them piped up.

"Oh! You a smart bitch, huh? I got this big-ass dick!" he said as he grabbed his organ.

"That is so original," I laughed. "Big Dogg with the Big Dick."

A couple of the other gang members laughed.

"Oh, yeah?"

Most men hated to be ridiculed, as most bullies did. That's usually why most kids became that way. Violence commanded respect.

"How would you like to suck it?" he moved closer, zipped his pants down and let his organ fall out.

Awe, this is gonna be good! "Wow, I've seen bigger sticks in a pack of gum!" I laughed. "And what's with the hook?"

I couldn't take it. That was just too funny to me. By this time, several of the hoods were laughing, too. The more I taunted him, the smaller he got. Soon, he was barely sticking out of his oversized jeans.

"Man, grab that bitch!"

I didn't even fight. The two closest to him ran up to me and each grabbed an arm, almost picking me up. One of them noticed how solid my arms felt under my shirt.

"Careful, fellas," I smirked.

"You know why I like this spot?" he told me, rubbing on himself so that his length returned. "It's far from the street. So no one can hear your lil' bitch-ass scream. Hold her down!"

I went to my knees with little fight. As he got to my face, the punk on my right made his first mistake. He let go of my arm and put me in a headlock. When the leader's dick was just inches from my face, he said,

"Yeah, bitch, you gon' taste some of this here man, but you ain't biting me, bitch!"

"That was one too many bitches!" I said through my teeth.

Before they knew what happened, I flipped the two holding me forward and they went sprawling in different directions. Even faster than that, I stood and ol' Big Dogg found himself face to face with me.

"Now where were we?" I softly embraced him, my nose millimeters from his.

The rest of the gang was in awe. They were probably thinking that no one could be this lucky. I now stood looking the leader in the eyes and grinding my pelvis against his manhood.

"This is how I like it," I mused. "And most of all," I went on while the leader of the gang was beside himself, "I prefer it like this!"

I raised my voice when I spoke and at the same time, I raised the razor-sharp butterfly knife I pulled from my back with feline quickness. Yeah! Big Dogg felt a sharp pain that only lasted a second. Then it came back with a vengeance, and he really *was* beside himself. As he screamed from the pain, he looked down to see his prize lying by his feet with blood slowly draining from it. He went to grab himself at the point of severance, but, oops, all he felt was the zipper of his now blood-soaked jeans. From that point on, he was bent over in agony.

"Wow, I must have gotten it all!" I laughed, raising my knee so that it forcefully connected with his head.

The rest of the gang members couldn't believe their eyes. They had never seen anything like it in their lives. One of them tried to rush me from sheer fear of it happening to him. He let out some kind of battle cry and came at me with all his might. He was stopped short in his tracks by the heel of my Reebok. I pulled my foot back and lunged forward, dragging the knife across his throat. I stopped halfway through the cut, pulled downward, and snatched the knife back in the opposite direction from where I started, releasing his Adam's apple from its once-secure position. He made a gurgling sound and raised his hands to his throat to hold all the pieces in place. It wasn't working. He began to choke to death on his own blood.

The rest of the gang just ran. Big Dogg laid on the ground in shock, bleeding to death. His partner in crime lay next to him in convulsions, ready to die along with him. I managed to keep the blood from getting on my shoes, but my shirt was splattered with their blood. I reached into the pocket of the second punk and, luckily, found what I was looking for. I pulled my shirt over my head, being careful not to get the fresh blood on my face. I cleaned off the knife, then threw the shirt on the ground and set it on fire with the lighter I got from the second thug's pocket. After that, I set the lighter on top of the shirt so it would destroy itself in the flames. Finally, I checked myself to see if there was any evidence left on me. There wasn't.

"This is a nice day for a jog."

I placed the knife back in the small of my back under the sash and went for a run. With the body suit I was wearing, I was already dressed for the part, so I jogged out of the alley and made my way back to the street. I got a few miles in before going back to the car, which was parked near the gym. I went home and took a shower, as if nothing out of the ordinary had happened all day. That's the kind of day I live for!

A month later, I went back to that same alley. Only this time, I had a very large semi-automatic handgun.

Amazing!

Several gang members were there, just as before. Most of them were young, but they had a new leader. I walked up and saw one of them that was there before when I took out the last leader. He whispered in the new leader's ear, then found a spot as far from me as he could. I looked down on the ground and could see the fading outlines of the murder scene paint. In the center of them was a fresh spot of running liquid. I looked at the new leader and saw that he and a few others had been drinking beer from large bottles.

"Did I come in at a bad time?"

"Pourin' some out for the homey!" the smallest one said.

"He would have still been here if he knew how to treat a lady," I smiled wickedly.

"What you want, lady?" the new punk on the block asked, keeping an eye on my weapon.

"I've got a job for you fuckers. That is, if you can handle it..."

And that's how we got started. Most of them didn't make it through my probationary period. I had them breaking in houses that were heavy with security. There wasn't a system I couldn't bypass. I paid attention to how fast they were. If they weren't fast enough, they never left the house.

I armed them with high-tech weapons and communications. With a few additions, I had a crack team of thieves and killers. When I felt they were ready, I laid down a plan for a new hit. I had them watch a mansion in the richest part of town. It had a large gate at the entrance with a script L on each side of the gate. The Livingston Manor was next on the list, and they were ready to do dirt.

One Up Two Down

** Stacy **

Both Jane Does lay still on their gurneys, completely lost to their surroundings. Neither of them had any identification on them, so they were known to the staff for now as Jane Doe One and Jane Doe Two. Jane Doe One (the tall, dark one) was lifted up on the stainless steel operating table labeled OR#1 and Jane Doe Two (AJ) was put on OR#2 directly after.

They each had a team of doctors and staff from triage to themselves. They both required hours of attention. The doctors had to take twice as long as normal because they had to do tests to make sure that neither one of them were allergic to anything. By the time they were done, both of them were clad in bandages from head to toe.

They were both sent to ICU because their conditions, although stabilized, were still critical.

"Okay, we've got room in the 9 West ICU. Let's get these two up there and hooked in stat," the ER doctor stated as he washed up from his work. "Check with the duty nurse to make sure we're copasetic."

I was upstairs on a break when the phone rang. "This is Nurse Caugman," I answered.

The intern on the phone explained that there were two Jane Does on the way up to ICU and asked if everything was prepared for their arrival.

"Sure, I'll meet you there." I put my Tupperware bowl back in the refrigerator of the break room, and then I quickly washed my hands and dried them off.

Jacob Livingston. You know, I never thought I'd see you again. I would have given anything if I could have been there when you woke up.

When Jacob was still in a coma, Liz had come to realize that I kinda had more than tending to the sick and injured on my mind. She watched quietly on several occasions when I would sit and talk with Jacob for hours on end. I never found out until long after someone let it slip. I would be so engrossed in my one-way conversation that I failed to notice not only Liz when she was looking in on us, but also my own colleagues, who used to run around behind my back and talk about my activities with Jacob.

I had heard a little talk about it, but it didn't matter to me. Jacob was my short-term purpose in life. I felt a connection between us. I knew that no one could cause a reaction in him but me. The doctors all knew this too. That's the reason they allowed me so much leeway when it came to my visits. Liz didn't like it at all. She felt that I was weak. I could hear her now.

"The bitch can't find a man, so she's living out some kind of sick fantasy with a comatose patient!"

I had got into the habit of kissing Jacob on the cheek as I said goodbye. The last time I was with him, Liz was watching me during her daily ritual and after what she heard and saw, she had had enough.

"Jacob, I wish you were awake for what I have to tell you," I said to the motionless Jacob. "For the last few months, I've come here, hoping to see your eyes pop open and you just come alive. I know that these things can be very difficult at times, and patients come around on their own time. I've never really had anyone to call my own, but when I sit here and talk to you, it's as if we are together having a regular conversation.

"I know it sounds crazy, but I feel as if I know you and that you can hear me. Like you know my entire life story. I mean, I've told you things that I have never told anyone before. I spoke to you about things that I could never speak to anyone else about. I know it could be months or even longer before you wake up, but I just wanted to let you know…that I really think I love you."

I gently placed my hand over his sleeping face, then bent down and kissed him on his lips. At any other time, that kiss would have been meant to last, but under the circumstances, it couldn't last too long, but it was long enough for Liz to interrupt.

"Ahem!" she cleared her throat.

I wheeled around at the sound.

"How long have you been standing there?" I asked somewhat irritated, but mostly embarrassed.

"Long enough to hear you give your goodbye address!" Liz said in a way which I understood as this was the last time I would see him.

"I'm so sorry," I said as I gathered my things.

"This might be a good time for a vacation," Liz suggested as I brushed past her, heading out of the door in a hurry.

There was something about the way she looked at me that made me realize that she wasn't joking. I had come too far now to lose my job. So the next day, I came in and took what I described as a short leave of absence. I told the hospital administrator that I had been under a lot of stress lately, and that I needed some time off.

* * *

The next day, my replacement told me that Liz showed up to see that Jacob's daily visitor had not come. She was on the other side of the room, just like Liz had been when she was spying on me. She told me Liz walked into the room and noticed that the machines were a bit busier than normal. It was almost as if I was there because that was the only time they made such a commotion. Liz walked up to Jacob and sat beside him on the bed. She looked at the uneasiness in his face. Then she placed her hands at the sides of her temples and held her head as if it were going to split in two.

"Arggh!" she screamed out loud.

** Jacob **

I remember when I first came to from my coma. The last thing in my mind I saw was my nameless childhood friend, one I'd dreamed about as a child, waving goodbye, saying she would never forget me. And here she was, so I thought. She was sitting next to me. I hadn't even realized I was in the hospital. I just looked in her eyes. Those eyes were full of love; it was the first time I had ever seen Elizabeth. Her eyes longed for attention and understanding. It seemed an eternity as we stared at each other, like each of us knew that we needed each other. It was as if our minds collided into a single thought. Our lives depended on each other's existence.

I saw the transition from Elizabeth back to Liz right before my eyes. As I gazed into the eyes of the one whom I'd thought was the friend in my dreams, I reached an IV-laden hand to her face. A tear raced down the cheek of the woman staring back at me. Then she closed her eyes and screamed out in pain. I woke up completely. My eyes never left her face. She had placed her hands on her temples. I watched in horror, as my nightmare became a reality before my eyes.

She let out a growl as she moved her hands, pushing her hair back as she twisted her head side to side. I could hear the cracking sound her neck made as she twisted her head again. She tied her hair in a knot behind her head and opened her eyes. I was so scared, I couldn't release the scream lodged in my throat. The woman now looking me in the eyes was the devil. Again, it was too much for me. As I faded to black, there was a single, lingering thought in my mind. *Mary…*

** Stacy **

"All right, Jane Doe #1 on the left in bed A and Jane #2 goes straight across on B," I said, directing traffic for the newest additions to the room.

They were both banged up pretty good. They looked like science experiments. Both of them had wires and patches coming from them that made them look like some old movie where the mad scientist was trying to create life from the dead. That's how it is here, though. It always looks worse than it actually is. They were far from dead; both AJ and Cheryl were in good hands.

"Post the notice down at admitting and at the ER desk. These two belong to someone, and I'm sure they will be missed before long. I can't see how they both made it here with no identification." I walked away to set the schedules for their care.

"What a day!" I mumbled as I walked down the East wing of the ninth floor.

Today has been way too much! I can't believe all of these feelings that are coming back to me. I know he can't love me. He doesn't even know me. The blank look on his face when he first saw me was far from what I was hoping for when I was waiting for him to wake up. I don't know what to do about Jacob. I don't know if there is anything to do. I just hope he calls me when he gets back. I just feel so anxious!

"Come on now! It's already going to be a long night. When those two wake up, they're gonna feel every bit of that collision they were in."

Since the medical histories of Cheryl and AJ were not known at the moment, they had been given no drugs. Efforts to wake them were fruitless. They were both on artificial respiration throughout the setting of their broken bones. They were both given a temporary fix for their situations. MRI results showed fractures in both of their faces, and the casts they were clad in would need to be replaced with rods and pins in some of the bones that they were holding in place.

Pre-Game Warm-up

I ate well in the cafeteria. I hadn't eaten all day. I put down a large turkey sandwich with lettuce, tomatoes, and pickles piled on it and topped them with spicy mustard. I had to eat up! I was on my way up to the 9th floor, with absolutely no idea what I was about to do.

If she can't talk, she will just have to listen.

I didn't have a clue what her condition was. I got up from the table and dropped my trash in the can and then placed my tray on top of the counter it was sitting under. Walking out of the cafeteria, I reached the elevator, took a deep breath, and pushed the button. The door opened immediately, and I stepped in. I rode the elevator down and got out on the first floor.

I walked out to the hall that led back towards the emergency room. The ER was quiet this time. I didn't even glance toward the large double doors. I'd had enough blood for the day. I moved on to the West wing elevators and contemplated what I was going to say; that is, if I had the opportunity to speak to her. There were several people standing by the elevators, so I stood patiently with them. I couldn't tell if I was scared or excited. I just knew that this had to be done. I had to put the empty pieces of this puzzle together. Just who was the woman I only knew as my legal guardian, and how on earth could she be walking around as crazy as she was?

Crazy.

I knew better than to call her crazy. Crazy was a relative term, generally used by people who don't understand other people. Schizophrenic is the preferred term by Freudian psychologists. To me, both the terms were excuses for all who used them. I always felt that schizophrenia was a poor excuse for indecision. At one time when I was studying psychology, I told a professor just that. My professor scoffed at my blatant disregard for years of study on the subject. People have devoted their entire life to the study of multiple personalities.

"How could such a bright mind come up with such an incompetent position?" he asked me.

I simply smiled and said, "Because it's true." Then I walked away.

I knew that this would cause my professor at least a few sleepless nights, pondering my answer. I knew that most of the faculty I came into contact with hung onto my words. They all knew that I said few things for no reason. They also knew that I said even fewer things with the intent to pass on information. So if they were made aware of any new ideas by the boy wonder, there may have been a book in it for them. Fortunately, I knew that this professor wouldn't abandon his years of studying why everyone wants to have sex with his mother from the teachings of his deceased mentor, Sigmund Freud, to follow a course that would contradict his teachings.

There was a quiet *ding* as the 1st floor elevator to the West wing opened.

Here goes nothing, I thought as I shuffled in behind the people in front of me. I turned around in the double-sided elevator and pushed the button for the 9th floor. The door closed, and I was on my way. I had no idea what waited for me at the end of the elevator ride, but I was determined to find out.

Lucky

** Cheryl **

I could feel myself being moved as I was being lifted onto a new bed. I know my mind had turned into itself to protect me from the horror of the vehicle impact, but I wasn't so fortunate. In my mind, there was already too much hidden away. As the car came smashing into us, I saw everything. Aside from the look on the face of Gina, who I had barely known, I saw my entire life pass before me in slow motion.

I had just enough time to thank God for letting me come to terms with myself in the last milliseconds of my life. I saw the hate in the eyes of the woman whom I'd shared such an intimate time with. It consumed her, and it showed in her eyes. I don't know why she went so spastic on me. I knew at that time there was no escaping the wrath that had become Gina. *OH, SHIT!* rang the words in my mind over and over again.

** Stacy **

My two Jane Does have been here for a while now. This was one of my late nights, so I needed to make sure I checked on them often throughout the night. I walked over to Jane Doe 2. I could tell the girl was beautiful, even with all of the bruises and bandages on her face. She was really tall and built like a tank. I checked her pupil response and it was good; she was just taking a break from the world.

I wonder where you are in there. I hope you're not in any pain like Jacob was. You look kind of at peace.

I know now that when a person is in a coma, she is still very coherent in a mental sense. They were just off-line, like the doctor once told me about Jacob when I first came in contact with him. I felt the need to look behind me to make sure no one was watching me.

"I'll be talking to you, Miss Doe."

"Oh!" came a moan from across the room.

I hurried over to Jane Number One. The anesthetic was wearing off and she was beginning to feel the bumps and bruises from the collision. Tears were coming from her eyes.

"Well, hello there, lucky lady. Do you have a name?"

She tried to answer, but she couldn't open her swollen mouth enough to form the words to speak. I saw the difficulty that she was having and said, "Shh, never mind. Can you nod at all?"

She was still clad in a neck brace and had her head all taped up. She could, however, move her head enough to acknowledge a yes or no. She slowly moved her head up and down to let the me know she could.

"Can you shake your head no?"

She tried, but it was obvious that she couldn't.

"Okay, it looks like I have to ask all yes questions," I smiled.

She looked at me blankly and closed her eyes to force out the tears that were welling up in them.

"Are you in pain?"

She concentrated and nodded her head in such a way that I knew she was indeed in a lot of pain.

"Okay! One pain killer coming right up. We did run a lot of tests; if you are not allergic to anything, nod yes."

She let me know she wasn't. So I got on the intercom and called to the desk for a morphine drip. A few minutes later, an orderly came through the door wheeling in a strange-looking machine with him.

"Here we go, Stacy. The standard maximum dose per hour is set."

"Perfect! This one has got to be in some pain. She only had an endotracheal intubation done for surgery, so she is definitely feeling the effects of that metal rod in her leg, as well as all the other bumps and breaks she suffered." I spoke to him quietly so my patient couldn't hear me.

I attached the drip to the tube taped to her arm and then faced her to get her attention.

"Okay, Lucky, this is a morphine drip. Whenever the pain gets kind of bad, I want you to hit this button."

I placed the hand-held drip button in her hand and placed my thumb on top of hers and pushed the button with her. The machine immediately made a pumping sound and a small amount of the drug was dispensed into the IV drug access. I sat with her to see if the pain was residing; it wasn't. She looked at me with impatient eyes and moaned.

"It's not working is it, Lucky? Hmmm. That happens every once in a while. I'll tell you what. In extreme circumstances after we start a drip and the meds don't kick in, we give a patient something to help in the meantime. I'm going to do that for you, okay?"

I called the orderly back in and told him to get me a Demerol booster. He went and returned with a hypodermic and a small vial. By this time, Lucky was in extreme pain and she was fighting against it, but it was overwhelming her. She started to arch and buck, but she quickly stopped because that made the pain worse.

I had to imagine that her entire body was on fire. She not only felt where the surgeon drilled several holes in her left leg to insert an eight inch titanium rod that went from her knee, all the way down to her ankle. There were screws that were drilled through the side of her knee and through a spot just above her anklebone. There was also a four-inch patch of bone that was all but missing in the middle of her shin.

My friend Horace was one of the EMTs that brought her and her friend in. He told me that during the impact of the crash, AJ's legs became crossed. Her left leg was snapped in half over the right as it was slammed against the underside of the steering column. As she was forced forward by the momentum, the seat belt did its job and snatched her back, bruising her collar bone, and to seemingly add insult to injury, the airbag went off and slapped her in the face as it fully inflated with the force of a shotgun. She wasn't centered on it. She was completely to the side of it, so it pushed her head into the side window. The airbag didn't go off until a truck coming in the other direction hit them for the second time, head-on.

He was told by a cop that the driver of the SUV tried to avoid them, but he couldn't help slamming into them because it all just happened too fast. There was absolutely no reaction time for any involved.

"Here you go, Lucky."

I quickly administered the Demerol shot into the butterfly IV valve taped to the back of her hand. Almost immediately, she relaxed into a slump. The look of pain left her face and was replaced by one of relief.

"That better?"

She just lay there with a placid, thankful look in her eyes.

"Okay, then, we will see you on the hour, Lucky."

I gathered the remnants of needles and accompaniments and looked up at the monitors above her head that showed heart rate, respiration, and several other items of interest to the doctors. I then pointed to the camera next to it.

"I'll keep a good eye on you the whole night through. If you need anything at all, push that button on the rail." I pointed to the call button right next to AJ's hand.

She slowly nodded her head as if it took a lot of effort.

"You're feeling it now aren't you, Lucky?" Some of us have all the luck.

Problems Don't Get Better With Time

Whoa! Look at all of this stuff. Where am I? All of this stuff is mine from when I was a kid. Everything is here: my favorite doll, my first bicycle, and my favorite blue sweater I got for my fifth birthday.

Everything I could remember about my youth that was good was right there and noticeably out of place. I was standing in the room I shared with my sisters, Ki Ki and Jazz, but this time, it was different. Unlike the times I was here before, I had the room to myself. There were those rare occurrences when that would happen and when it did, I would always do the same thing.

I went to the open door of the room and closed it. At the same time, I closed my eyes and pretended to be a movie star. When I was young, I didn't know of any movie stars, but I knew that being a movie star meant being pretty and most everyone loved you. Just like I used to then, I opened my eyes to see the reflection of the most beautiful movie star of all.

If I was old enough, I would swear that the person that stared back at me in the mirror was dressed in a colorful outfit with the biggest hat and glasses. For just a brief moment, I was that person. I opened my eyes, but this time, I saw what I thought was a horrible image of myself as a child. My skin was dark as coal, and it was wrinkled and deformed. Before I knew what happened, the reflection in the mirror was no longer in the mirror; she stood before me.

Somehow I knew that this…thing was a reflection of how I felt about myself as a child. The sight of her pulled at a part of me. The deformed child just looked at me. She stood slumped over so that she didn't appear to be as tall as she was. She kept her head down, as if she were expecting to be hit at any moment. I looked on with awe. We just stared at each other in place.

I'd had enough. My feelings seemed to be tied directly to the sight of this little girl. As I felt worse, the appearance of the little girl worsened. I noticed it immediately. I remembered that this is how I felt I looked to the rest of the world.

"No, baby!" I said in tears.

I reached out and hugged the little girl, ignoring her deformities. I kissed her on the cheek and looked her right in the eyes.

"You're the most beautiful girl in the world!" I was barely able to speak. "Don't you ever let anyone tell you different. You are more beautiful than the best movie star in the whole world."

The little girl's eyes lit up, and she quickly took a deep breath, placing her hands in front of her mouth to hide behind her own mask of excitement. She seemed not to be able to speak, but she didn't have to. Just like me, she had never heard anyone say anything like that to her. She stepped back and before my eyes, transformed into a tall, beautiful little girl that reminded me of when I was eleven. With tears in her eyes, she mouthed the words, "Thank You." She then bent over and kneeled to the ground. A pair of wings grew from nowhere on her back. As the little girl stood, she rose from the floor and floated to where the ceiling should have been.

A little angel!

I looked up after her. All I could see was a bright, sunny sky, powdered with a few cotton ball clouds. I could feel the excitement from the look on the little girl's face. I understood. For someone to tell me that I was beautiful was all I needed as a child. It never happened. I felt as if I had just freed a part of myself that had been locked down inside of me. It was a part of me that had been confined to a life of misery inside of me, with no trial for reconciliation.

I had turned my back on those feelings instead of dealing with them. They had come back to remind me of days that I had not forgotten. I had just refused to acknowledge them. Forgotten problems don't go away. They must be dealt with while they freshly exist.

I was feeling pretty good at this point. A warm wind swirled around me as my surroundings changed from my room to a grassy field. It wasn't tall grass; it was more like the perfectly manicured grass on the green of a golf course, only a little taller, like the rough that lined a fairway. I had never seen so much grass. It just went on and on like the ocean. I looked down at myself and realized I was naked.

I panicked for a second, covering up with my hands and looking around to see if anyone could see me. As soon as I did, I found myself surrounded by people walking down a busy downtown street. No one paid me any attention. They just seemed to carry on with their daily grind like it was lunchtime and they were all in a hurry. They were too busy to notice me standing there naked.

I found it hard to move, like something was holding me back. The more frustrated I felt, the harder it was for me to move. I felt exhausted and had to sit.

To hell with all these people. I have to sit.

I moved my arms from covering my breasts and reached for the ground. As soon as my hands touched the sidewalk, it turned to grass, and as the rest of my body came into contact with the ground, I found myself back in the large grassy field.

The backyard of my world…

The sun burned bright in the sky, and it felt good on my skin. I brought my knees up to my chest and wiped the sweat down my legs. I loved this feeling. I looked around and saw the rolling hills of a land that I had never seen before, but it was strangely familiar. In the distance, I could see a bright object coming towards me. I stood to my feet and placed my hand over my eyes so that I could see better.

It was the child I'd spoken to before. She flew effortlessly to where I was standing and just hovered before me. She reached her hand out to me. I placed my hand in hers, and my feet rose from the ground. I had to concentrate to suppress my fear, but I was really comfortable. The warmth of the sun and wind hugged my body as we floated through the air. I had no idea where she was taking me, but I didn't care. I felt "Free" for the first time in my life. There were different levels of happiness that I was just discovering. I looked ahead and saw that the rolling grass hills had, indeed, an end. We were approaching a city covered by black clouds.

This can't be good.

We floated above the clouds, and I could see through some of the breaks in them. Each of the breaks seemed to hold a memory that I could see playing out before me. There were things I never wanted to remember, things that reminded me of the very life I hated. The more I saw, the colder I got.

There was a large break coming up and upon looking through, I saw the one thing I feared the most. I saw Tia on the floor, holding my naked body in hers. My feelings took over; I became very heavy all of a sudden and could no longer hold onto the hand of the little girl. I looked toward the little winged girl, only to discover that she was no longer there. I was immediately overcome with fear and began to fall. I screamed with all my might.

This is Your Life

** Stacy **

I was just at the end of my rounds when I heard the scream come from the ICU. I ran to the intercom at the desk and yelled for Grant, the orderly on duty. I continued on to ICU. As I came to the entrance of the room, I started to run straight to Lucky, but saw that she was okay. Immediately thereafter, though, I heard the heart monitor beeping erratically. Again, I reacted quickly and yelled into the intercom.

"This is Nurse Caugman. I need a crash cart in the ICU stat and get the on-call cardiologist!"

"This is not gonna be good, Jane Doe." I cut the bandages from around her chest.

She already had broken ribs. If the crash cart didn't get here soon enough while her heart was stopped, my efforts to revive her could kill her. I could hear feet running down the hall and, all of a sudden, both the doctor and several staff members came through the door with the crash cart. I stepped back and let them go to work. They were well trained and made a great team.

Lucky just lay there in her bed. Jane #2 woke her up when she screamed. I pulled her curtain to keep her from seeing too much. I didn't want to put her through any more trauma than I had to. Now she could only hear what was going on.

* * *

I landed hard after my fall from the sky. I could feel the pain all through my body. I felt all kinds of confusion around me. I felt as if I were fading in and out of two different realities.

"Is this real?"

It was cold and uncomfortable. I was wearing the same blue pantsuit I had put on this morning.

"What is it?"

I felt this uncanny presence that I knew very well. It was another one of those things inside of me that I learned to ignore. I was feeling an uneasiness that would never allow me to relax—like danger was lurking around every corner.

I was surrounded by buildings; they looked like an industrial plant of some kind. It was cold, dark, and lonely. I remembered that feeling well. I also remembered how the day came when that feeling went away.

"AJ?"

I didn't know how, but I knew she was there.

"AJ!" I called again.

Each time I called, I looked around to make sure I could see where my friend was when she answered. Up ahead, I saw the little girl again. She was standing before a large door. It was so tall that I couldn't see where the top ended. The little girl smiled an eleven-year-old smile and pulled the large door open. As the door swung outward, a bright light emanating from behind it filled the space that I was standing.

Think good thoughts Cheryl…

I walked to the door and looked at the little girl. She just pointed through the door without saying a word. I walked through the door and shielded my eyes from the light. There was a loud bang as the door behind me had slammed shut. An image emerged from the brightness that seemed to drown out the intense light with its shape. By the smell, I could tell who it was.

I held my head down and put my arm up so I could see. I thought about this situation, as well as the events that happened before. It was one big learning experience about my life and the decisions I made that controlled the environment around me. All of a sudden, I became very angry.

"Stay in control! She can't hurt you anymore."

"Did you really think you were gonna make it out of here without dealing with me?" the woman's voice boomed.

I looked up for the first time and put my arm back down. I found myself staring at someone who only looked like Tia.

"This is your life, bitch; answer me!" she demanded.

I looked at her and decided if I let this woman scare me, I would loose, so I stood my ground and bravely looked her up and down.

"My God!" I was losing ground already. "She's huge!" She seemed to be at least seven feet tall. It damn sure wasn't the five-foot-eight Tia that I used to train with.

I quickly gathered my senses and said, "I made you this big in my life."

Tia laughed loudly, so loud, in fact, it hurt my ears, but I stood my ground.

"Answer me!" she barked at me, putting her face directly in front of mine.

"I have to beat you. It's the only way I can ever be free to continue my life!"

"Life? I've already killed you!"

"No! I won't let you control my thoughts. You did that to me one time before, and I trusted you. You turned my life into something it was never meant to be! I hate you for that! If I had it in me, I would kill you right now!"

"Cheryl!" a voice from behind me called.

I whirled around; I knew who the voice belonged to.

"AJ?"

AJ stood on the other side of Tia, and beside her sat the little girl that brought me here.

"Would you kill the little boys that called you blackface?" AJ asked. "Would you end the lives of the little girls who ridiculed you for being tall?" she continued.

"I don't understand."

"I think you do," AJ said flatly in her usual, matter-of-fact tone.

I thought about it and realized I did understand. I turned around to find that the woman who looked like Tia didn't appear so large after all.

"I don't hate you," I told her. "In fact, I love you." I stepped towards her.

The look on Tia's face changed to everything but confident. I grabbed her and pulled her close.

"Is this what you want from me?" I said as I moved my hands through her hair. I placed my hands on either side of her face and pulled her lips to mine. "Is this what you want?" I gave her a long, wet kiss.

I pushed her away, then spat on the ground in front of her. "I'm taking my life back! I don't fear you. I don't want you, but I know you are a part of my life. If I hadn't ever met you, I wouldn't be the person I am today."

I turned to AJ. "If it hadn't been for those mean little boys and nasty little girls, I wouldn't be the woman I am today!"

AJ nodded in approval. I turned back to Tia, who appeared weak and stunned. "I no longer need you in my life. *My* life! You understand? I am in control now. You don't run shit for me!"

Tia's appearance began to change. Her hair fell down around her face, and then she pulled it back into a knot. Her face hardened, and then became soft with the look of an innocent, young girl. She screamed and placed both hands at her ears, as if she couldn't stand to hear herself.

"Cheryl!" AJ called again.

I turned to look at my friend.

"Remember what you have done and remember to think first. Things aren't always like they seem. Sometimes your enemies are victims themselves."

I didn't quite understand what AJ was saying, but before I could ask, I heard a little girl crying. I looked around to where Tia was standing and saw a little girl kneeling on the ground, crying. I bravely went to her and saw that it was a young Tia, or so she appeared to be.

"What's wrong, baby?"

The little girl just looked up with tears in her eyes and said, "Can't you help me?" She reached up and started to hug me, then grabbed me by the throat.

"I won't go away, you bitch! I won't go away until we both die!"

I couldn't breath. I was scared to death. I couldn't get the wicked little girl off of me. I tried to shake her off, but she wouldn't let go! I looked into the eyes of the little devil girl and saw the reflection of yet another little girl, kneeling on some rocks with her face covered by her hands. We fell over and I landed on my back. I could see both AJ and the first little girl floating through a hole in the black clouds above.

AJ must have died; she must have…

The accident! I realized as I fought with the little devil girl.

"Aaaaay Jaaaaaay!"

The Anti-Drug

** AJ **

My curtain had been drawn shut so I could only see people's feet as they brushed into it. The one thing I knew for sure now was that I was in a hospital. I had only just realized it. I had a dream about the accident and as the car struck us, I could hear Cheryl scream. Somehow, I knew that it was Cheryl on the other side of that curtain.

"God, what is happening?"

I was only somewhat coherent, but I distinctly heard the word "Clear!" and the associated thump that followed it. The long beep of the defibrillator as it was fully charged and the loud thump of someone's body landing back on the bed brought me back into a reality I wasn't ready for.

I couldn't move; my eyes streamed tears. I still had the morphine pump switch in my hand, and I was gripping it tightly. The machine beeped loudly and made a strange clacking sound. I saw the tube jerk twice as the machine malfunctioned and gave me two large doses of the drug ordinarily meant to be dispensed over a period of several hours. I faded to black, releasing the switch and fell limp. The last thing I remember was the sound of the switch hitting the floor.

** Stacy **

"She's back!" the doctor said with a sigh of relief.

"Oh, that was a close one!" I added.

Dr. Coleman and most of the staff were soaked in sweat from working to revive her.

"Pulse is steady as a rock. Good work, everyone! Welcome back to the world, Miss," the doctor told Cheryl.

"AJ!" she said as best she could. Her face was in tremendous pain. "Ow!" she cried from the pain. Then it all just hit her at once.

"Here we go again!" the nurse said. "Give me that morphine drip from across the room. Let's hope we have a bit more luck with this one." The orderly went to the other side of the room to disconnect Lucky from the machine.

"Doctor!" the orderly called from across the room.

Dr. Coleman and the staff rushed across the room to Lucky's side. In the commotion, no one could hear the respiratory alarm going off.

"Shit! Get me a six cc hypo of Narcan! She's going into respiratory arrest; it looks like an overdose!" Narcan was to drugs what gas is to fire, and fire is what it felt like when it rushed through your body, consuming and reacting to other drugs in your system.

I was off like a shot and soon after returned to see the doctor trying to wake AJ up as I prepared the Narcan solution and pushed the morphine drip to another staff member to administer to Jane # 2.

"AJ!" she called from across the room.

** AJ **

I was awaken from a dreamless sleep into a pit of hell! I gripped the sheets on the bed and just screamed uncontrollably. My eyes were bulging wide open as I looked around to see a bunch faces that surrounded me.

"This isn't real!"

The pain was horrific, but my mind was extremely clear. I watched the nurse slowly pushing a drug into my IV tube.

"Make her stop!" I screamed. I was in a complete panic, but my mind was still extremely clear.

"Whatever it is, it's too much!"

The more time that passed, the more intense the feeling was.

"Make her stop! It's too much!" I begged.

I looked at the nurse, who looked at the doctor for guidance. My attention shifted from her to the doctor.

"Make her stop!" I pleaded with him.

I had this intense feeling of falling, like I was on some terrible ride at an amusement park. The medicine burned so badly that I couldn't stand it. I swore I was on fire from the inside. It was like my blood was boiling.

No one could possibly take this much pain and live. I wanna die, Lord! Aggggh, I wanna die!

The doctor looked up at the monitor and my head moved up as far as it could, but I couldn't see anything, so my attention went back to the nurse.

"I'll rip it out!" I threatened, motioning to pull the IV from my hand.

The nurse quickly looked over to the doctor again. Just as before, I shifted my attention back to him. He just looked back at the nurse, and I followed his gaze back over to her. It was like a bad tennis match and all the while, the drug was screaming through my system like a lit fuse.

Finally the nurse was done pushing the drug. She replaced the syringe she had with a saline flush, but I didn't know the difference. I placed my head back on the pillow, tears streaming from my eyes. As my eyes closed, pushing more tears out as they shut, I could actually *see* the pain I was going through.

It was like a bad dream. I could see a tunnel of molten fiery rock. As I looked on, I saw several faces lining the black and orange burning rock that seemed to revolve into place. I didn't know why, but I felt as if these faces held the answers to life itself. Suddenly I seemed to be all-knowing. Then a calming sensation came over me, which made me realize that I knew. I knew all there was to know about life without even thinking about it. After that, a comforting breeze blew that made me very calm. But I could still hear myself screaming at the doctor and nurse on the other side.

What is going on?

The tunnel then turned into a hall of bright light.

I could feel myself being pulled and slipping at the same time. I was dying and I knew it. I saw the doctor and nurse standing on either side of me, like they were moving in slow motion, and all of a sudden, I was alien. I couldn't see my body. I felt as if I had left it. I screamed and could hear the harmonics of my voice breaking up, and it scared me even more. I sounded like a machine of some kind, malfunctioning.

I could feel my legs moving up and down, and each time, there was a piston-like sound that resembled a chamber being filled with air, followed by the air escaping. The whole situation was unnerving. The doctor looked at me with a look of pity, and I felt that I had to make a choice.

I had to decide whether the world I was living in was real, or if I was part of some super-huge falsehood and nothing in the world as I knew it was real. I had to make a choice, and I had to make it now. At this point, I realized that I had not been living this life. It seemed to me I was about to pay for that life of solitude.

Do I give up on this world and move on to the next one within it? Or do I stay and make the best of this one? I hear the question, Lord, but I'm so tired, I don't know what to do. I was wrong, Lord; I want to be human again, Lord. I'm not ready to go. I'm not ready, Lord. I'm not ready!

Each time I said it, I felt myself slipping more and more and the light of the tunnel became farther away. I could hear myself accusing the doctor of not knowing what he's done. I was screaming to the point of hoarseness. Soon, I was wide awake and the calm feeling completely subsided.

"I have to pee!" I pleaded.

"Get her a bed pan!"

The orderly left and immediately returned with a stainless steel pan for me.

"Out!" the nurse said to everyone as she prepared me to use the pan.

I winced in pain as I voided. The smelly urine was the stench of pure fear. It was thick with adrenaline. "You did this to me! Do you smell that? You did this to me!" I cried out as I finished.

The nurse cleaned me up and removed the bedpan. She held it away from her because the smell was overwhelming. She gave the pan to the orderly on the other side of the curtain, then she returned to me.

"I'm so sorry we had to put you through that, baby." She had tears in her eyes. "We almost lost you, and I just couldn't live with that. You weren't breathing so we had to bring you back."

She sat on the bed and stroked my half-bandaged face as she spoke. "I'm so sorry you had to go through that, but it was the only way."

I just lay back and took count of my faculties. I noticed that my head felt stuffy compared to the clear feeling I'd felt before. I understood that God had closed my mind to what I didn't need to know—which was everything I felt I knew or had just realized during the ordeal. I felt my legs still going up and down and heard the piston sound. I saw that my legs were in Velcro boots and there was a circulation device affixed to both of my feet to keep the blood flowing in my legs.

Was any of it real, Lord?

I guess that was the whole mystery of it all. I was supposed to decide whether I believed what I felt or not.

Thank you, Lord, for giving me the chance to live.

"Try and get some rest," the nurse said.

"I will."

"Sleep tight, you two," the nurse said as she left the room. She tried hard to hold back the tears that she knew were coming. "Sleep tight."

Ms. Sheila

The elevator to the nine West wing opened to an empty hall. I wasn't really trying to move too fast because I had no idea what I was getting into. I forced myself to put each step together. From behind me, there were several footsteps moving up quickly. I wasn't sure what was going on, but I knew to get out of the way. Two staff members and a doctor rushed down to one of the rooms. I was in the middle of trying to figure out what I was going to do, so I figured I'd stand in place for a minute. It wound up being more than a minute; in fact, it was more like ten minutes I'd been standing there. I hadn't realized how long I'd been standing in the same place until the same two staff members came back from down the hall.

"Can you believe that woman?" one of them said. "She gets a kick out of playing with the machines. The last time she pulled off her heart monitor, the whole floor ran down to her room, thinking flatline. When we got there, the wench was smiling at the doc, saying she wanted to see how fast everyone would come to see her croak. She actually said the word 'croak'!"

"She's not smiling now," the other man said.

"Yeah; it's a pity. You hate to see the live ones go," the first man laughed.

"These guys are too much!" I said under my breath as they passed by.

What if it's Mrs. Williams they are talking about?

I started walking faster. I thought that maybe since Elizabeth is off her rocker, she may have gotten it from her mother. If something were to happen to her before I had the chance to speak to her, I would be lost forever about my half-sister. This made me quicken my pace even more. Before I knew it, I came upon a room with an oversized crochet sign that said S. Williams on it. I stopped dead in my tracks as soon as I saw it. My heart felt like it was going to leap out of my chest.

Here goes nothing.

I knocked quietly on the door and walked in. "Hello?"

I cautiously stepped around the door.

The light is on but there is no one inside. She might BE just like her daughter judging from that!

The room was a small, two-patient room. There was only one occupant, I could tell, because the room had a lived-in appearance on only one side. There were pictures and little knickknacks all over on the other side. I knew I was in the right place as soon as I saw the first of the pictures. It was a picture of Elizabeth and her mother that was obviously taken years ago. The look on her face was one that I had never seen before.

"She just looks so…happy."

"And why shouldn't she?" a voice said from behind me.

I was completely rattled. I dropped the picture, but as luck would have it, the picture of Elizabeth and her mother landed on the bed. I quickly turned around, but instead of greeting my host, I unwittingly closed my eyes and was lost in the surprise of the moment.

"Jacob?"

Now I was even more rattled than before. I opened my eyes and as they readjusted to the light, my gaze fell upon a cheerful, beautiful woman in her forties. Again I was speechless.

"My Lord, it really is you." She had tears in her eyes.

She walked toward me and placed her hands on my face. I was still at a loss for words and just stood there like an old scarecrow. I had never seen this woman before in my life.

I'm tired of this!

There was no doubt that she was the mother of my half-sister; and there was no doubt what Elizabeth would look like in twenty or so years.

"You look so much like your father!" she said in a soft, motherly voice.

My mind was still out of whack. I tried my best to speak, but I couldn't form the words.

"Shhh. Don't say a word; sit down."

I had no problem with that request. She pulled out a chair for me. I was glad she was in control for the moment because I was still shook up from when she spoke to me the first time.

"That pretty nurse Stacy told me the story about a young man that was here in a coma a couple of years ago. She told me so much that I felt that I knew you as much as she did. It wasn't until some time later that I realized who you were. She had been telling me all about your sister and how she came to see you every day. She told me how she used to schedule her visits with you around your sister, my daughter, so that she could be alone with you. It was such a beautiful story of love. It reminded me of a Florence Nightingale story."

As she spoke, I just sat there and listened quietly. I knew now that I would learn everything I wanted to know, but I also realized that I might have to tell—no, I would *have* to tell—about who and what her daughter really was.

"She told me some things I expect also I will hear from you."

I couldn't take it anymore. It was bad enough that she was expecting me, and then all of the fretting I did down the hall about what I would say to her once I met her. Now only to have the control taken from me, and then she already knew what I was afraid to tell her! What could be worse? I was afraid to think of the possibility. I was not the confident shell of a person that I knew myself to be. It was time to take a stand, and I knew it. I had been in the room for nearly five minutes, and I had yet to say a word.

"Mrs. Williams…"

"Sheila," she told me.

"Sh…Sheila," I continued as I collected himself. "I had no idea what I was going to do once I got up here. In fact, I didn't even know you existed until earlier when I was downstairs and I ran into the nurse you were talking about. She came up to me and spoke as if we were long lost friends. I had never seen that woman, but I felt like I've known her for years." I took a deep breath.

"Take your time," she told me.

"Okay; first, the hard part. Your daughter suffers from a multiple personality disorder. I'm sure of it."

Damn! I can't believe I just said it!

As I spoke, Sheila sat down on the bed and picked up the picture of her and her daughter. Tears welled up in her eyes. It became difficult for her to breath.

"Are you okay?" I asked. "Do you need me to call someone?"

"It's all my fault, you know," she said flatly.

All of the life seemed to leave her face as she spoke. Her voice became very cold. I almost thought that she was about to change herself.

"My daughter was raped at a very young age, Jacob." Tears streamed from her eyes.

Damn, what did I do…

"I…" she paused for a second, then continued sobbing as she spoke.

I wanted to console her, but I wasn't good at those types of things. Judging people was the extent of my people skills. I awkwardly got up from my chair and sat down next to her on the bed. I didn't want to put my arm around her simply because I was scared to, so I thought quickly and decided to put my arm under hers and held the picture with her so she would remain focused, but at the same time, she would know that I was right there with her.

"When I was younger, I was very ambitious. I studied hard in the computer science department. We were working on a new form of encryption that would allow for more secure transfer of information across the Internet," she spoke slowly.

I could tell that this was very hard for her. I was shocked to realize that she wasn't just a regular ol' mom. I quickly realized that she was every bit as knowledgeable about encryption methods as I was.

"I met your father in a bar where I used to wait tables near the university. He had just spoken at a conference for new and upcoming computer technologies that the school was to fund for research. The encryption project was one of them. I kind of forced a meeting of my own on him after he had just had dinner with some of the finance executives for some of the projects. We sat and talked about encryption and money for the computer science wing.

"He invited me to dinner so we could talk some more. He said I had some good ideas and he would give me my own budget through the university. Well, we had dinner and I got him drinking this very strong wine that I knew about from working at a restaurant. I'll never forget. It was a bottle of Pineau Des Charentes Red. Two glasses usually put a person to sleep. We went through the whole bottle. The next thing we both knew, we woke up in each other's arms." She paused when she saw me react to what she said.

The whole time I had dealt with the issue of my sister, I never once thought of *how* she became my sister. In my mind, my parents had the perfect marriage. Never once did I think that it was possible that any infidelity could exist. Although I felt bad for her, I had to ask, "When is her birthday?" Then I pulled back a little.

"She was born on the fifth of July in 1966."

"That's not possible!" I said as I stood and walked to the other side of the room. I placed my hand over my mouth in surprise and disgust.

"It's not only possible, but it is very true. I pushed her out at 1:36 a.m. on the fifth of July."

"No! That is not true!" I shouted. I realized I was getting angry but didn't understand why. I knew, however, that I had to calm down. I mean, she started this story off with the rape of her daughter, and that she said it was her fault. I looked back at her to find that she had a very puzzled look on her face. She didn't understand why I was angry; yet really, neither did I.

"What do you know about me?" I asked her.

"Almost nothing at all," Sheila admitted. "I knew that your father had a son soon after I contacted him about the birth of our daughter," she answered.

I wished she would stop saying that! The thought of any reference to my father with someone else besides my mother ate at me.

"My birthday is the fifth of July 1966!" I told her.

I looked at her and could tell that she was completely shocked. Sheila didn't know what to think. It was, indeed, a very confusing fact, and it hurt for her to hear it. And I meant for it to hurt! Whenever she spoke of my father, I felt the need to strip some of that comfort away. This is where my people skills came in handy. For me, controlling a situation was mandatory when I was at a loss. Now was clearly a time where I felt that I was out of control, and I needed to keep it hidden. When I was on my way up, I felt sorry for her because I had horrible news to tell her. News, as a matter of fact, I had yet to begin to tell her.

"You were born on the same day?" she asked weakly. She cleared her throat as if she hadn't heard me correctly.

"We were born in the same *hour*, Mrs. Williams!"

"It's Ms. Williams!" she snapped back. "It always has been and will always be that way!"

I looked at her and saw that despite the way I was making her feel, she didn't have the energy to keep going back and forth like that. At the same time, I knew I was out of line. I usually had complete control over my emotions, and I was sorry I took her down that path. I thought of a way to reconcile the moment.

Triumph Gone Bad

"You said it was your fault?" I asked her in a much calmer voice. I had to get to the heart of this, but not at her expense. I felt that this was a story she had not told before and telling it would help her heal spiritually. I looked her in the eyes and said, "I'm sorry. This is hard for me, and I am positive it can't be any easier on you. Please forgive me for my insolence."

I sat down beside her again and took her hands in mine. "Tell me what happened."

Sheila was calm, but it was hard for her to tell the story that ultimately brought us together on this night. She sat back on the bed and took a deep breath. This was just as hard for me as I was realizing the true depth of her story.

"She was such a beautiful girl," Sheila started. "I was young and foolish. I spent so much time in the lab and then taking care of a growing little girl. I was jealous of my friends who did have a life. I used to hear them talk about the clubs in L.A., and I just wanted to be a part of something other than my work and my life as a single mom. Elizabeth went everywhere with me that I could take her, but I found a babysitter whenever I could.

"One night we were in the lab, and we made a breakthrough. The newest algorithm we had been testing worked. We broke through the 128 bit encryption barrier. We were all so excited. Even Elizabeth was jumping up for joy. She knew how important that project was to all of us. Well, we all decided to go out and celebrate…"

* * *

"We did it! Oh my God, I can't believe it!" I said to the group. "Baby, we did it; we really did it." I picked up my young Elizabeth. There was elation in the air; notes and all kinds of paperwork were strewn all over the lab! It was a time for celebration.

"You really did it, Mommy. Finally?"

"Yes, baby. After all this time, all of our hard work paid off, and you were right here with us the whole time."

Elizabeth smiled. She was proud to be considered one of the team. She wasn't at all a silent member. She used to help solve problems by asking simple questions that brought about answers. She was very instrumental in achieving the goals that the group reached for.

"Let's go celebrate!" Chuck, one of the guys on the team, said.

"Oh. Um. Guys, I would love to but me and the little one need to get home," I replied.

"Come on! It's such an important night; it calls for a celebration. Besides, you're always talking about how much you want to hang out with the crew. This is the perfect time," one of the interns said.

"I don't have a sitter," Sheila said.

"Nonsense!" the first guy named Fred spoke up. "Sam just got done telling you yesterday if you needed a sitter, he would be glad to help. Plus, he's got more games in the house than any kid could play in a lifetime."

"I don't know, guys," I said hesitantly.

"Mommy, I'll be okay. I can play him on the Play Station," Elizabeth said.

"Are you sure, baby?" I asked, kneeling before her.

"Yes, Mommy, go and have a good time; you deserve it."

I gave my daughter a big hug. "You are the greatest daughter a mommy could have!"

"I'll make the call," Fred said. "One babysitter coming up." He walked off to see Sam.

"Are you sure you're okay with this?" I said, handing Elizabeth her backpack once we got to Sam's house.

"Yes, Mommy, you look nice. Go out and have a good time."

I backed away from the door.

"Have a good time. We'll be just fine," Sam said, standing behind Elizabeth.

"Okay," I said as I hopped into the car with the rest of the gang.

I knew I could never really relax and have a good time, but I needed a night on the town. I had been working on this problem for more than a year. The team had seemed to be so close for so long, that it became a harrowing experience just coming to work every day.

By the end of the night, we were all exhausted. I had a great time. I hadn't had the opportunity to get out and do that sort of thing in a while. Elizabeth was my life, and there were times where she was all I knew. We headed back from the club. I had already been feeling a little guilty about letting my hair down and enjoying the night with my co-workers. Although I deserved it, it was tough juggling my time schedule between my daughter and my work.

Most of my co-workers were asleep in the car as we drove back, but I had an uneasy feeling about relaxing any more until my daughter was back in my arms. I didn't feel well at all, and I didn't know whether it was because of the alcohol or the worry.

It was usually the combination of the cigarette smoke and the alcohol that I hated when I was working in the bar where I met Jacob, Senior. The clubs in California are different now. Smoking is not allowed in any building. It was a welcome change for the nonsmokers once the legislation was passed. At the same time, the smokers had to either learn to cope or quit.

As we drove into the driveway, I found out that my fears were well-founded. It was 2 a.m., and the front door to Sam's house was wide open. As soon as I saw it, I quickly opened the door of the SUV and jumped out while the vehicle was still moving.

"Wait!" Fred yelled after me as he slammed the gearshift in park. The SUV jerked to a stop and all its occupants went back and forth with it, jarring them back into wakefulness.

"What is it?" one of the interns said, still half asleep.

Fred reached into his glove compartment for what a good percentage of all Californians have in their possession when they're driving the everyday streets, his very large gun. He jumped out and ran after me.

"Baby!" I yelled as I ran through the house.

"Mommy!" I heard my daughter scream from somewhere in the back of the house.

As I ran towards the back, I entered the living room and was shocked to see Sam hanging upside down with his leg caught and twisted between the slats in the stairwell. He was suspended about four feet off of the ground, wearing nothing but boxer shorts. His face was near purple from the blood pooling in his upper body, but he was clearly alive as you could hear his labored breathing.

"Mommeeee!" my baby screamed again.

I kept on going, ignoring Sam's lumbering breathing and headed towards the hallway closet, where I thought the sound had come from. I snatched the door open and saw my baby with her knees pulled to her chest and a distinct spot of blood at her bottom. I reached down and picked her up, almost immediately knowing what had happened. Fred came running up behind me. He saw the blood and replied, "Oh, God, no!"

I just kept repeating, "Oh, I'm so sorry, baby; I'm so sorry."

"Let's get her in the car!" Fred said to me.

"Mommy, he hurt me," Elizabeth managed to squeak out.

Her voice sounded sickly. I summoned up all of my strength and handed my child to Fred. I did it so quickly, he had almost no time to react. He opened his arms to receive her and in his haste, dropped his gun on the ground. I immediately picked it up and ran into the living room.

"Sheila, no!" Fred called after me, but he was helpless with Elizabeth in his arms.

"You son of a bitch!" I screamed.

I knew that if I shot him, it would have caused more agony in the end for both me and my daughter. I was no stranger to guns so I instinctively dropped the magazine from the huge Desert Eagle .50 caliber handgun and pushed the slide back, letting a chambered round fly to the ground. I then released the slide and grabbed the weapon by the barrel and used it as if it was a hammer and Sam was a loose plyboard on the wall. When it was all over, I woke up with blood all over me and a paramedic was shining a penlight in my eyes.

"My baby!" I screamed.

"Calm down, Miss. Your daughter is okay," the medical technician told me. "She's right outside in the ambulance and as soon as we're through looking at you, we're taking both of you in," he continued.

"He…He…" I stammered.

"He's still alive," the EMT finished for me. "The police have him in custody at the hospital as we speak. You were smart not to shoot him," he continued. "He will probably rot in jail for the rest of his short life."

I was only halfway present in my current state. I was in shock from both the tragedy of my daughter being raped at the hands of a so-called friend, as well as the experience of beating a man to within an inch of his life. When I was done with him, he looked like a freshly cut quarter of beef hanging from a hook. He came alive after the first blow, and I didn't stop until he stopped moving again. There was so much blood everywhere, one would have thought he had exploded.

A Voice in The Darkness

"...That was how it all started," Sheila said as she looked back from that horrid picture of the past.

I sat silent. All of a sudden, I felt so sorry for the two of them. I especially felt sorry because I hadn't even begun to tell her the story I came to tell. Then I thought about Elizabeth. Deep down, I loved the fact that I had a sister. Even deeper, however, lay the thoughts of my parents being slaughtered and the fact that Elizabeth, in whatever personality, had something to do with it.

I knew that, in a way, she was not responsible for what had happened. Even if she had pulled the trigger herself, the condition that she suffered from possibly made part of her unaware of it. I knew there would be a time when she would have to deal with it, but now, I needed to concentrate on the present.

"How much do you know about your daughter now, Mrs...." I stopped as she looked up and then caught myself before she had a chance to say it. "Miss Williams," I finally got out.

She looked at me with trusting eyes. "I know that my daughter is a very special person. I also know that if it were not for her, I probably would not be alive at the moment."

"How do you mean?" I asked.

Sheila put her head down and took a deep breath and let it out with a sigh. "The only reason I am in this room today instead of down the hall with all of my dying friends that I have here is because my daughter has created some kind of cure for what I had inside me."

"And that is...?" I edged her on.

"It *was* cancer, young man, but it isn't any longer," she told me with a sincere look on her face.

I looked at her, trying not to argue, but I felt I had to say it. "You're trying to tell me that your daughter has found a cure for cancer?" I asked without hiding the doubt on my face.

"Young man," Sheila started, "I find it hard to believe that she found anything. What was not there before, she created with the mind that the good Lord gave her. She came in here night after night with her own drugs and her own IV bags. She constantly watched over me. She took more blood from me than the doctors here did. And all the while she spent her time working on me. Day and night I was her only patient. I was her only worry. She didn't have any rounds to do, and she didn't look at me as if I were a thing of pity.

"She is my daughter, and she loves her mother. She took the gifts that God gave her and used them on an otherwise dying patient. I was not supposed to live with the amount of damaged tissue I had. Now my body is regenerating itself. I haven't felt this good in years. As a matter of fact, by this time in two days, I will be at home in my kitchen, baking as many apple pies that my oven will hold. I will be living my life once again. Elizabeth is the only reason that I can say that."

I had to think for a minute. How could such a twisted person bent on destroying people come close to the glowing description just given by this woman? I had a decision to make, and I knew that it would be one of the hardest of my entire life. I also knew that this was not the time to make it or even ponder it.

"Miss Williams," I began.

"Call me Sheila."

"Sheila," I continued, "I have to tell you something that will be very hard for you to take."

"As I said when you first came in, I suspect you will," she replied, bracing for the news. She didn't have a clue of what I was going to say, but she knew that it would hurt.

"My parents were killed two years ago in July." I had to pause, realizing that I had never actually told this story before to anyone. Everyone in my life that knew about my situation had been around me while I was in the hospital.

"They were murdered by a gang that invaded our home and who didn't give them a chance to live. I don't know why I am still alive today, but I would imagine it is because of what my family was…is worth today. It happened the day before my birthday. My father was going to receive an award at a banquet held in his honor that evening.

"My mother told me that he was going to tell me the next day for my birthday that all of the patents for the work he did on encryption were in my name.

She said that if it wasn't for the work that I did—the work that my father gave me to do—none of it would have been possible. He had created a foundation in my name, which gave me creative control over all of the work he had started. In essence, the company was mine. That was to be my birthday present."

I paused to collect myself and then continued. "He never got the chance to tell me himself," I said in tears. "All I remember was I was looking for my mother's favorite coat, and when I found it and was on my way out of the closet, I heard a loud explosion and the door slammed into me. I remember crawling on the ground. There was blood everywhere." I was openly crying by now. "He was there!" I sobbed. "He was there, and his head was gone!" I managed to get it out before I couldn't speak anymore.

Sheila pulled me closer and held me tight. I needed the affection, but I also needed to say what came next. I drew away from Sheila so I could look her in the face.

"Your daughter was there, Miss Sheila. She was there with the people who killed my mother and father!"

I had finally gotten it out. Sheila pulled me closer again, and this time I stayed, sobbing uncontrollably. I cried as I had never cried before. I'm guessing Sheila felt that she had to stay strong for both of us. She heard what I had said, and it had to lay heavy on her mind.

"Lord, I need you now like never before," she whispered.

She said she knew it would be bad. There was nothing she could do to prepare herself for this. It was going to be a long journey for all of us involved. She waited patiently while I cried in her arms.

"We will get through this, baby," she said to me, rocking me back and forth. "God willing, we will."

I didn't know what I was doing at the moment. This was not part of the plan. I had barely known this woman had existed until only moments ago, and now I was going through the most important part of my recovery from my incident with her. This would be the closure I most desperately needed. This would also be the moment where the driving forces of my emotional state would subside, and I would be able to utilize my strengths.

I had been a strong person before the untimely change in my persona. The tragic events that changed my life took me away from myself until now. For me, this hospital room would be the proverbial telephone booth in which I would change into my alter ego. My ego was forged by my strong belief in what I felt my purpose was in life. I spent many years studying people. My encounter with my sister in the state that I was in disallowed my ability to see her as she really was.

Even now as I came to the realization that I did not hate her for who she was, I did, however, feel tremendous conflict in knowing that if she had any part in my parents' demise, I could not altogether forgive her for it.

My parents may have died by this woman's daughter's hand.

Often times, I would have these "realizations" which seemed to be answers given to me by some higher force. I believed in God; my concept of the role that God actually played in the lives of everyday people was drastically different than that of anyone else. People use God as an excuse; they use Him as a reason; they use the name of God for any purpose that suits them. I took this very concept of people's adaptation of God's purpose in their lives as the reason *not* to be like the rest of them.

I took my ideas and subtly dropped them on people just to see what their reaction would be. If they looked at me as if I just opened the door to a new way of understanding for them, then I felt that I had done my job. On top of that, every time I got a reaction like that, it would reaffirm my belief that I was more right than wrong in my beliefs.

"God willing," I repeated after Sheila.

In my mind, this was my license to figure the whole thing out. I knew I not only had to figure out a way to stop my sister, but I had to find a way to get her back to her supposed normal self. Oddly enough, I did not know who she really was. There were several times when each of her personalities seemed to be perfectly blended. These were the times when I actually liked her.

I could remember the conflict in my mind about the way I acted in contrast to the way I had felt. I was extremely brave; yet, whenever Elizabeth, in the form of Liz, raised her voice, I would be forced by something beyond my comprehension to cower before her. I couldn't formulate the presence of mind to think about it then, but it was as if my mind held all of the events of the last few years in a preserved state for me to recall them at a later date. Those thoughts played themselves out like a movie in instant flashes. I could remember every conversation I'd had with all of Elizabeth's personalities.

I pulled away from Sheila and sat back. I was in a sort of trance. My mind was busy showing me everything I could not pay attention to in my lessened state. My body was whole. My feet felt the miles I'd walked when I couldn't drive. My ears took in the sounds that didn't register in my consciousness. My eyes never failed to see what I was blind to in my constant stupor. It was all coming back to me now.

Sheila looked at me as I went through this mental transformation, and I could tell she was scared. She saw the intense look in my eyes. It seemed as if I were peering into space, but concentrating so much that she could almost see something out of the nothing that was before me. I was sweating profusely. My eyebrows forced downward, almost meeting together in the center. Then all of a sudden, my face lit up and I relaxed. My eyes danced brightly, and my movements became much more animated.

I sat up, looked at Sheila, and said, "We will do the will of God." I thought that this would be the perfect thing to say in this time of action. I knew that I would need Sheila's help in bringing her daughter in so that I could figure out a way to get what I needed from her. I didn't feel that I was being blasphemous, because I really knew that this is what I felt God would want.

I would use Sheila's faith to do *my* bidding. This was the thing that I felt one day I would have to answer for. It was as if I were some kind of Moses and I was leading the people to some kind of promised land, but I would speak in the name of God what *I* felt needed to be said. If I were a king, I'm sure people would follow me. If I were an evangelist, I would have a huge congregation, but these weren't the things that I wanted.

All I wanted were for things in life to make sense. I knew the chaotic nature of life itself led to any number of possibilities for people and personalities, but I felt that there were rules that established very fundamental, very solid truths, that created solid parameters for humans to huddle between. In my mind, people had all of the answers they sought in life. Somehow humans have *learned* to place restrictions on their minds that hide their ability to "know" some things.

I knew in my heart that there was indeed something else out there in the fabric of space and time that created a crippling ability in people to shut their minds down. Scientists have long said that we use a very minute part of our brain in terms of its size. I felt that there were a few people on this earth that had the ability to lift the mask from the brain so that the rest of its abilities could be realized by their body. I didn't really feel that I was one of them, but I did, at least, understand the concept, and I felt I could see it in other people.

So I studied—man after man, woman after woman, and child after child. I observed them until I understood where they all fit in the larger scheme of things. This was the gift that I felt was given to me from a God that, to me, was very real. Only I felt that I knew Him so much more than most other people.

I never understood those who reveled in His supposed "grace," as if God were the shadow of the statue that was built in His honor in their minds. To me, God was "common sense," although if you were to ask me, I would tell you that there was no such thing as common sense. God was big in my life, so my convictions about the way His name was used would do battle with those of the members or heads of the religious hierarchy. All said and done, I would use the name of their Lord in vain to get them to do what I wanted them to do. This scared me, but I knew in my heart that it was the right thing to do.

"Jacob?" Sheila said.

I could see she was still a little leery about the way I had been acting before. I wanted her to think that I was having some type of divine vision. I slowly turned my head to the side as if I were studying her. I gazed into her eyes with a warm stare to let her know that there was no danger. Then I spoke with a slow, soft, deliberate tone.

"He told me what to do."

"He?" Sheila repeated after me.

Most people were taught since their youth about God and the Bible, but deep down they are skeptics when it came to modern-day miracles. I sensed her apprehension and asked, "You can understand the miracle of birth, yet this you cannot accept?"

Sheila looked dumbfounded. She didn't know what to think or what to feel. She merely looked at me for what seemed to be the first time. I looked at her reaction and thought to myself, *We will all get through this; I'll make sure of it.* I hadn't been my confident, almost cocky self in a long time.

I felt the control I once had. I felt the power I once had long ago. I thought about the different personalities that defined, yet separated, my half-sister. I knew how to deal with each of them. Hate, love, compassion—all of the emotions and feelings that are thrust upon us as humans, I would use to set things straight. I knew I would make some enemies along the way, but it was a means to an end that would be justified in time.

AJ's Independence

I still have no idea where I am and I was fading from the sight of the nurse that was walking away from me. I could swear I heard my brother Alonzo calling me.

"Angie!"

The only time he called me Angie is when he was scared or in trouble. I had to be dreaming. I could see scenes of the time Alonzo was stupid enough to walk on a narrow beam that went across this huge underground access for the city water utilities. He fell and wound up hanging from the beam. As he was holding on, he did the only thing he knew how. He looked for the only person who *always* made things better.

"Angie! Angie, help!"

It was all he could think of. He didn't even know where I was or if I heard him. As always, though, here I came to his rescue. I came running around the corner from behind him. I actually ran past him, not seeing him hanging from the beam.

"Angie!"

I stopped in my tracks and turned around to see him hanging on for his life. He didn't seem like he could hold on much longer. I looked around and saw this huge rock. He saw me pick it up and didn't know what to think.

"AJ?" he looked really confused.

For the moment, he forgot he was tired from hanging from that beam. He didn't take his eyes off of his sister or that rock. He looked kind of thoughtful, like he was thinking about the last time he got me in trouble or the last mean thing he said to me. He just prayed I wasn't mad at him at the moment. He watched in awe as I just looked at him and ran towards him with that big rock. When I got close enough, I lifted it over my head and let it fly.

"A…!"

He started to scream, thinking I was about to finish him off. Alonzo closed his eyes as the rock went way over his head and into a large window of an apartment behind him. As soon as the rock went crashing through the window, a booming voice came cursing through the curtain on the other side.

"I couldn't leave him, mister!" I cried to that voice.

When the man saw what the deal was, he went through the window himself, breaking it totally, the frame and all. He came right over to where Alonzo was and with one extended arm, grabbed and lifted him out of the hole. He sat him on the ground and lifted the heavy metal cover that was hinged to the beam, letting it slam shut.

"Don't worry about the window. Are you okay, son?"

Alonzo just nodded. He was still in tears. I helped him up from the ground and gave him the biggest hug a sister could give her brother. He was so surprised I didn't even yell at him. I just said, "Let's go see what's in the fridge." Then we walked home together.

I seemed to be at peace. I dreamt of things that made me happy. Drugs are funny that way. As bad as they are supposed to be for you, there isn't a person on earth who could dispute their benefit when used properly or in moderation. As complex as I like to think I am, the things in life that made me happy were simple. The way I lived my life had more to do with my determination to succeed than anything else. Those rare times when I actually had nothing to do (before I met Cheryl), I would go all-out to spoil myself by myself. I loved to take hot baths with essential oils and fragrances. I had a special bathtub installed in my master bathroom. It was huge by comparison with anything else in the house. When I originally saw it in a catalog, the first thoughts in my mind were those of eternal bliss, with a husband sharing my bath with me after a long day at work. Eventually, it came down to "I deserve this!" when I made the phone call to order it.

It didn't take long for that tub to become a big part of my life after work. Sometimes I would completely forget about the special meaning of the "tub experience" as I was always rushing to work, taking quick showers, and spending just enough time on my makeup to "qualify" myself as a grown-up. I think I look okay. I'm not close enough to anyone to have him kick me out of bed. People have told me that I was strikingly simple. I have to take that as a compliment, although it doesn't say much about me. I don't need makeup at all. I have natural brown skin that is flawless until you get to my knees. I mean, I'm definitely a part-time tomboy. That was one of those things that I thought added to my appeal.

When I was little, I had my dolls and my tea parties. I also had one of the meanest left hooks a girl was allowed to have. I was tough as nails on the outside. Since I grew up, I did as everyone eventually does—figured out that I had other needs that I couldn't fulfill without someone else. I learned quickly over time that being a strong woman was not always the most appealing thing to a man.

An independent woman seems to be a threat to men. I felt as if there was nothing I wouldn't do for the man in my life. There would be none of that drama that you always see in movies about people in love, but I didn't understand the concept of "in love."

For me, everything was a calculated decision. There was none of that spontaneity that would allow me to get flustered and lose my appetite. There were none of those heart-wrenching revelations that made me lose sleep or made me come to the conclusion that I couldn't live a moment without a certain someone. I just didn't get it. My lack of friends was part of the reason I didn't get it, I'm sure of that.

That was probably the reason I was so much better off than other women. I know I'm right; however, only half of my life was an ever-so-perfect saga of picture-perfect productivity. There was an entire other half of my life that was not only unfulfilled, it was downright ignored. "I didn't have time" was my favorite excuse whenever I was talking to Mamma about this very subject.

"Baby, you are gonna have to settle down one day," Mamma would tell me.

"It won't be anytime soon, Ma."

The only things that took my mind off of my work were Alonzo and Cheryl. I smiled in my mind as I dreamed of a past Christmas when I gave him a stuffed animal from the *Little Rascals* series.

"Look, you looked just like him when you came out," I laughed as family and friends sat around drinking eggnog and telling stories.

"I'll never forget when the doctor handed you to me for the first time," Mamma said. "I was worried about that mark around your eye, but the doctor said it would disappear before too long. He said you put up a heck of a fight to be born first," she laughed as she rocked in her favorite chair.

"I keep telling you guys I *let* him be born first!" I laughed.

"Is that even good English?" Alonzo asked me.

Deep down, I felt he always loved the name Pete. He really liked the dog, too, but when you've heard those stories as much as they had been told about me kicking his butt before he was actually born, I thought he might resent it a bit.

* * *

Cheryl, of all people, was the one whom I had the most in-depth conversations with about men. We were good for each other; each of us possessed an important piece of the puzzles in life that we were assembling as we grew. I had always thought that Cheryl was way too independent. The funny thing was that as independent as I was, I willingly depended on Cheryl to help me with little things that I wouldn't admit being bad at.

"Like it matters to a man if I can program a computer!" I said to Cheryl when she was teaching me about databases and how they could help me run my practice more efficiently.

"Could you imagine some guy walking up to me and me saying, 'Yo, my sista, come check out these databases I got! You know you wanna see them, I mean, that's all you think about, right?' Could you imagine that?" I laughed hard.

"What on earth would you know about what a man wants?" Cheryl asked me. "Girl, you might as well be a man as much as you don't make room for one in your life."

"Look who's talking!"

Oh, shit!

Deep down, I could look at her and tell she knew I found out about her *preference*, and we were friends enough to talk about it. As a matter of fact, she couldn't wait to tell me so that I could help her with her problem, but all of a sudden, this was not the time.

What a dream…

"What are you talking about?" Cheryl asked innocently.

"When is the last time you had a man tied to you?"

"Who has time?" Cheryl mocked me.

We sat and had a good laugh with each other.

"Sometimes you're all the medicine I need."

She gave me the biggest hug.

"You too?"

"They just don't make friends like you every day."

"No, God doesn't make friends like us everyday."

"They didn't have anything to do with it."

"Man! That was just too deep. Which 'they' are we talking about all of a sudden? Is it everyone else in the world who are not like us, or is it the famed other half of our species, who take credit for all of our accomplishments?" Cheryl said, starting back to her fits of laughter. "Didn't no man create this!" She did the *Price Is Right* wave as she displayed herself as the prize behind door number one.

"English, girl! English!" I fell over, holding my stomach. "'Didn't no man'? You think they really made it to the moon?" I managed to get out in between breaths.

"Girl, please! There are no gas stations between here and the moon for them not to ask for directions. They can't even make it up the street without getting lost."

I couldn't take it anymore. I fell off of the couch in her office onto the floor. Cheryl just put her hands over her face as if she were trying to hide her hysteria from the world. I picked myself up and sat down on the couch, leaning on her.

"Girl, we're perfect. How come we don't have men in our lives?"

"Cause that would negate our perfection," Cheryl said without looking up.

When she did look up, she regretted saying what she did because she could see that I was serious. Cheryl put her hands together and took a deep breath. Now is as good a time as any…

"I know, girl, it's tough," I said before Cheryl had the chance to speak.

If you only really knew…

* * *

I woke up from my dream and reached for a tear streaking from my eye. The movement was difficult and jerky. I really didn't think much of it because I was still half asleep with the thoughts that Cheryl had tried to tell me several times about her life and her choices. I found it amazing that I never saw it, until that morning when Cheryl came running into my office, crying. I hated when I didn't pay attention to subtle details that lead to a bigger picture. After all, it was my job to pay attention to the little things that we are so quick to take for granted. That was how I earned my pay.

You would be surprised to find out that people pay upwards of $400 an hour just so I could tell them that they needed to pay more attention to their spouse or to look closely into themselves and realize that all the answers are there. They just didn't pay attention to what their bodies and minds were telling them.

"When you ignore your mind," I would tell some of my patients, "it will fight back to make you pay attention. Give it a chance to let you know what you want, but use reason to quell any obsessions; your mind knows you better than you do. Listen to it on occasion."

I can remember saying this to several of my clients.

Why don't I listen to myself?

Somehow, I just realized where I was and I accepted it. I hate the smell of hospitals. I lay still and looked around the room with my eyes only. I could only see so much because the curtain around my bed was drawn most of the way. I could see the machine that was attached to the tubes that were taped to me, but not much else.

Down by my hand, I saw the call button had been re-attached to the rail of the bed. I went to reach for it with my free hand, and then I really noticed that I was in a bad way. Whenever I moved, I jerked as if I was being driven by some kind of bad rhythm. For the first time, I was really scared. I tried to sit up and found my entire body joined the fray. I was going into convulsions, but my mind was clear. It was like I was wearing my Sunday best and got into the raggediest car I could to drive to church. Everything on the inside was okay, but on the outside, I was shaking and jerking around like I was possessed. Whenever I went to move a body part, it just came alive on its own and shook and jerked along with the rest of me. Soon it became violent, and my body was lifting up and slamming back into the bed. I managed to grab hold of the call box and push the button as I blindly reached for it. Soon a nurse came running into the room and saw what was happening.

I couldn't tell what she was doing because my body was now shaking so violently. I could only ride it out. The nurse had called for an orderly and before I knew it, I was right back in the hell I was in before. It didn't last as long this time, but the Narcan still had the same burning effect in my veins as it raced through my system, looking for and reacting to any leftover drugs in it. Having been here once before, I just held on and cried out until the pain subsided. When it was all over, the convulsions were gone and all I could do was lay there half-conscious.

"It will be okay, Lucky," I heard the nurse say in the distance. "You're going through withdrawal. I hate to say it, but we gave you too much, and your body doesn't know how to handle it." She stroked my face. "Sleep tight, sister; it will all be better soon."

I'm guessing she got up to go have a look at Cheryl. She was in bad shape. After her heart attack, she just lay there in a peaceful sleep. She was being monitored as closely as possible. I was also being afforded the close watch of the night nurse. My pain was replaced by the serenity of my protective mind. I went from the pit of hell that the antinarcotic Narcan caused to the peaceful setting my mind allowed me to relax in. It was obvious that I had been through enough because of chemical-induced reactions caused by the human hand in the name of science.

I think it's funny how scientists allow people to go through experiences that they themselves would not be willing to go through. There are an abundance of drugs that are effective in the treatment of drug addiction. Somehow, doctors have come to the conclusion that if it is good for an addiction, then an overdose should be included in the category of possible uses for certain drugs. For a person who is at the mercy of whatever caregiver happens to over prescribe or who puts him in a situation where suddenly there are too many drugs available or too much of any particular drug in that person's system, the pain of the treatment far exceeds the limits of acceptability for the patient.

I had never taken any drugs that were not prescribed for me. On top of that, I took care of myself to the point where I very seldom ever got sick, so drugs of any kind were almost nonexistent in my life. When I received such a large dose of morphine, along with a large dose of Demerol, it was way too much for my system. I had been given more drugs than my body had ever experienced in its life. It should be understandable that my body went nuts to rid itself of the poison. I had the shakes for a good while. It was just one more thing to deal with. I lay there restless while the machines around me were alive with bright lights and sounds.

Me vs. Me

I had been half up for a good while during the night, thinking about my situation. I was somewhere in a hospital; I was more than sure that no one knew that I was there, and worst of all, my best friend was possibly across the room, and I didn't know what kind of shape she was in. I was hesitant to move. The shakes were bad enough, but the nurse on duty had been in there every hour on the hour to give me a shot to help rid my system of the residual drugs I was given. Despite my situation, I was in fairly good spirits. I was in a lot of pain, but I was the type of person to just put all things I had no control over behind me.

All of a sudden, I realized the extent of what I was thinking.

Mamma!

I have to let them know. I tried to move to push the call button, but soon realized instead of the jerky motion I had before, there was no motion at all. The worst immediately entered my mind.

Paralyzed? God, no!

Now, I was strong, but such a thought was entirely too much for me. I wanted to scream, but I couldn't feel anything, I couldn't do anything, and most of all, I couldn't say anything. My emotional state was fully intact, however; I went through the entire gamut of emotions in these few minutes. I started out just being glad to be alive, and then the physical pain set in, only to be followed up by the fear of being like this for the rest of my life.

"It's hard, isn't it?" a voice said from somewhere.

The next thing that happened scared me more than anything. As I turned my head to see where the voice came from, I realized that what I was seeing was not real, or at least, it wasn't what I thought it was. I had a mental picture of the view of the hospital room and that is what I'd been seeing. Now, it seems that I was dreaming instead of thinking. As I turned my head, the view of the hospital disappeared and what I saw nearly stopped my heart. I saw myself, or at least a very similar looking AJ, sitting upon a fire hydrant.

Behind me was an empty street with a burning mass of something that resembled what I could only imagine was left of a car. The other AJ pointed behind me. I instinctively looked around to see what was left of the little black car that was so shiny and new not so long ago, upside down against a building on the sidewalk.

"Tell the truth," she said.

I opened my mouth wide in an effort to see if I was going to be able to speak.

"You can speak just fine."

"Okay," I started. I immediately went into my "Let's rationalize this and make sense of it" mode.

"You are obviously some part of me which I have ignored, and you're here to take me back like Ebenezer Scrooge, am I right?" I asked, amazed at how well that came out.

She looked at me and just sat there for a minute.

"I'm supposed to get some kind of lesson from all of this, right?" I pushed.

She just continued to look at me with patient eyes. I realized after a moment that she was doing to me exactly what I did to my clients. There was something else, but before I could complete the thought, my new twin stepped off of the hydrant and reached out. The next thing I knew, I was flying backward after her hand met my face with a resounding SLAP! I felt every bit of the hand to my face, only I didn't get mad. I halfway expected it. It was exactly what I felt like doing whenever one my clients started running off at the mouth to challenge the very reason they were there for therapy.

"You see, that's what your fucking problem is!"

I quickly answered back saying, "I don't talk like that!"

"Are you ready to shut up and listen?" she asked.

I decided not to argue with my other self. I got this strange feeling that, although I could hear what the woman that looked like me was saying, I could more "feel" what she meant. It was frustrating because she seemed to be speaking through me. It was like the words were leaving my mind, and I could hear them. They whooshed either by or from my ears with a faint sound like rushing water or air blowing past me from behind. Then they would come back to me through the mouth of this "thing" standing in front of me. I understood it, but I was unable to concentrate on the fact that it was happening and hear what was being said. It was like I was being driven or forced to listen to the sound. I was extremely confused.

This is too real to be a dream.

"I love Richard Pryor," she said to me.

"Huh?" I replied; I didn't get it.

Again, the thoughts rushing from me before they manifest themselves into words revealed themselves before I heard her speak them. This time, I didn't hear the words spoken. I simply thought about how I used to sneak and listen to my father's old Richard Pryor albums. I loved to hear Richard Pryor talk; not only talk, but do what he did best. I loved to hear Richard Pryor curse.

There was something about the way he said "FUCK" that just made me laugh.

If Mamma would have known that I had a Richard Prior habit, it would have killed her. Mamma would have broken all of those records over my behind.

I was beginning to understand that this thing knew me, or quite possibly was me, and had all of the answers to my sarcastic inner self.

"You just think you are in total control, don't you?" she asked me.

I knew better than to answer this time. She looked me in the face and smiled.

"You ready to listen?"

"Tell me a story," I said to her.

"That's more like it! I asked you a question," she continued.

"You asked me, well, actually you said, 'It's hard, isn't it?' I guess I was supposed to say, 'What's hard?' and you were going to follow with…" I asked.

"Not being in control. You're a control freak. You think all of the strings need to be pulled by you, and all of the buttons pushed by you, don't you?"

I gave her the only answer I could. "Yes. That is a very accurate statement."

"I would never insult you by telling you that your ideas are way off base. In fact, you are the proud owner of what one might call a clue." She took my hand.

"Why, thank you!" I said, smiling. I was being sarcastic.

"You still don't get it!" She looked at me with disgust. "But you will."

Again, I didn't hear the words being spoken, but all of a sudden, I realized that I had been feeling her voice my entire life—every time I got smart with someone, or more so, whenever I had insulted a person and they weren't smart enough to realize it.

"My conscience?" I asked as I looked at the other me.

"Oh, but I'm so much more."

I was satisfied with that answer. I had always felt that there was a part of me, and other people, that is ignored from time to time. Almost like a person in the lives of people that is consulted only when it is convenient. Strangely enough, I had always felt that it would come back to haunt me.

"Ha!" I laughed aloud.

"Here's Johnny!" she said with a spooky look on her face.

In an effort to stay in total control, I took a look around so I could attempt to stay a step ahead of this thing. If there was a lesson to be learned, I was going to figure it out myself. I wasn't about to be held hostage by my inner self. That is precisely what I helped my clients fight on a daily basis.

"You can't live in both worlds," she said to me with a serious look on her face.

This was becoming too much for me. The look that she gave evoked a feeling that I usually felt when I was trying to convince a person of my sincerity. The feeling sometimes made me want to cry. Like the time that I tried my best to convince someone that I loved him, only to have my efforts and cries fall upon deaf ears. I felt volition and desperation intertwined with hope and anticipation, only to have my wishes dashed and dismissed as something that I felt alone and had no tangibility outside of my person. Men could be so cruel sometimes.

"I could push your emotional buttons all day and watch you melt away."

"What good would that do you?" I accepted the challenge.

"You are talking to yourself! Ask the question again, but pose it to yourself since you fail to realize you have already done it."

I thought about it and decided to do just that. "What good would becoming all emotional in any instance do me?" I asked aloud.

All of a sudden, I became overwhelmed with a feeling of guilt. I had to double over from its strength. I became delirious with it.

"I don't care!" I cried. "It's not my responsibility! You people are all wrong; you don't have a clue about what this life is all about!" I screamed to no one in particular.

"Poor Angela," she mocked. "She doesn't care. She feels the whole world is confused and she is the only one with the answers! But wait; she spends her every waking hour trying to help the masses get their oh-so-sorry lives together. Oh, and let's not forget that she makes a ton of money doing it, too. What do you think that will be worth when the Day of Judgment comes?" She stood over me as I cowered in the guilt of my supposed sin.

"Get up, girl!" she held her hand out to me.

I took her hand again and immediately felt better. "Those people couldn't do it alone! So you helped them get to a point where they could stand on their own two feet."

"I profit from people's suffering." I placed my hands on my face to hide from the moment.

"And what about your own suffering?"

"I…I…"

"What about my suffering?" she screamed at me.

I looked in the face of my inner self. She showed signs of severe fatigue. She was in pain.

"I would never let anyone see that!" I was getting angry.

"Where the fuck do you think it goes, Angie?" she spoke desperately.

She took me by the hand once more, and we continued to walk. I was worried by that statement. That's exactly what my brother said to me when I told him I couldn't fall in love again after I was tossed to the side by the man I loved. He said that just because you deny what you feel inside doesn't mean the feeling goes away.

"Things that you bury always come back up to haunt you, Angie. You have to confront what you feel and come to terms with it so that there's no need to bury it."

I never listened to that advice. I realized now that I should have. It made so much sense to me now, but then my judgment was clouded.

"Are you learning anything?" my other half asked me.

I was in a momentary trance. When I looked up, I was right back where we started, with the other AJ sitting atop that same fire hydrant.

"I wish you would just come right out and say what it is you want me to know."

She put her head down and shook it from side to side. She got up from the hydrant and, once again, took me by the hand and pulled me along. I was feeling rather self-righteous by now. I didn't see the point; better yet, I wasn't trying to see the point. I could feel a dull ache all over. She looked back at me and, once again as I felt it would happen, the back of her hand met my face hard. I fell back in extreme pain. She looked at me and then held out her hand.

I was furious, but I reached forward and took her hand. Once more, I felt instantly better. She pulled me along as we started to walk once more.

"All this walking and we're not going anywhere!" I complained. She pulled harder, yanking me along. I felt the frustration and snatched my hand back from the woman.

"No! I will listen to you, but I won't let you pull me along! I…I…"

It started to sink in. I felt the dull ache all over once more. And again, I was back where I started with my other self, sitting on the fire hydrant.

"Listen to my emotions, but don't let them lead my life," I said flatly.

"I always knew you were smart," she said as she once again got down from the hydrant. This time she walked away from me and said, "Remember what you feel."

The dull ache worsened. I could feel it all over. My surroundings began to fade away as I awoke from the dream and opened my eyes to the hospital room. I had no idea what time it was, but I could tell it was late. My body hurt all over. I thought about what I had just gone through. I could barely remember what it was about, but I could feel that I came to some kind of crossroad. An overwhelming feeling came over me. It had been forever since I'd felt it, but I knew exactly what it was, and I welcomed it. As the first tear streamed down my cheek, I just let go and cried a lifetime's worth of tears.

"I'm sorry, Lord," I prayed as I cried. "Sometimes I need help, too." I sobbed lightly and closed my eyes until I drifted off once again.

"It's gonna be okay, Lucky," the nurse said as she got up from the chair beside my bed.

"I hate this stuff," she said quietly, referring to the antinarcotics she had just given to me. "The dreams it must give you."

Liz Encounters Elizabeth & Tia

"Damn, I got a fuckin' headache! I gotta figure out a way to get to those two. They are just fuckin' up everything"

Like what?

"Who the fuck is that?"

You don't know why you hate them so much. Just thinking about it makes your head hurt, doesn't it?

"Where the fuck are you?" Ah! My ears are fucking ringing. I need to hurry.

You don't have much longer.

"You ain't shit, whoever you are." It was like a nagging voice that would not go away, only it wasn't a voice. It was more of a realization. It was a reality that I was ignoring. Just like any other problem, though, simply ignoring it would not make it go away.

"What is wrong with you?" I screamed.

I refused to give in. Consciously, I didn't even know that I was fighting. I could feel it, however; in my mind, I could feel a message trying to push itself through.

"I need to get back."

I drove for another twenty minutes and finally made it to the house. I don't know when I started coming here. It was an okay place, tucked in a cul-de-sac. The first time I saw it, Cheryl was here and running out of the door. I must have had her that night. She barely had any clothes on, running out the door. I remember picking up her lace bra and…"Argh! My fucking head!"

Once I hit the driveway, I quickly shut off the Jaguar motor and bolted into the house. Then I opened the front door and ran straight for the kitchen. Opening the cabinet over the sink, I remembered how I hypnotized Jacob and told him that every time he saw that door, he would think of something else, something that pleased him. Pie was the dimwit's favorite thing in the world at the time. He constantly thought of it, and I always made sure that there was plenty of it in the house.

I reached into the cabinet for the bottle of drugs. My head felt as if it were going to split open.

"Ahhh!"

The bottle slipped from my hand and hit the floor with a crash, and I followed it straight to the floor. Glass and pills surrounded my face as I lay there with my cheek on the cold surface of the kitchen floor.

"Got to take one." I fought to stay conscious.

I reached for my face, while dragging my hand on the ground, gathering both broken glass and pills mixed together.

Without even looking, I pushed a pile of dirt mixed with pills and glass fragments into my mouth. Then I began to chew. It became a muddy mix of blood, drugs, and glass. I didn't try to swallow; I didn't have to. The mixture was strong enough to reach my blood stream through the newly made cuts in my mouth.

I stopped chewing and spit the excess out, trying to get as much of the glass out as possible. Only a small amount was in my mouth, but it would be enough to cause internal problems if I swallowed it. My last conscious effort was to spit it all out while doing my best to keep a single capsule in. I did it and comforted with this, I stopped struggling and passed out.

I felt myself sinking in the darkness. It was an odd feeling. The farther I sank, the more the pain went away. Soon the pain was gone completely. When I opened my eyes, I was no longer on the floor. I was standing in my favorite black body suit with the red sash around my waist. Righteous!

"What the fuck is this?"

Deep down, I knew what it was. It was the very deep down itself that I was feeling. I was inside—not as an emotion as I was born—but as the very personality I was. I could feel the warmth of the walls like living tissue on my face. I could feel the frustration that allowed me to live.

The drugs I created were meant to seize the state my mind was in and elevate that part that was strongest. There is nothing stronger than me! I know I tended to change clothes without realizing it, but I did not know why I constantly tried to hide those pills in a different bottle so that they wouldn't catch the attention of whoever was borrowing my body.

You have something I want. I heard a voice say from somewhere.

"What the fuck? Did I hear that? Or did I feel it?"

I really didn't know. The truth was that the world I was now in belonged to Elizabeth's mind. Her real mind was taking back what it lost. It lost control years ago, but it was tired of taking a backseat to its emotional counterpart. The mind of Elizabeth pulled a fast one and emerged from the darkness as Elizabeth herself. In this state, it was tired of doing things the way that her emotional enemies did, which had caused so much trouble up to this point.

I looked around and realized that my movements were sluggish. I couldn't move like I did when she was on the outside, but I was still very aware. All of a sudden, the bitch that I always changed from her clothes appeared from nowhere. She looked just the way I hated her. Long hair that lay over half of her face, a dress that looked like it came out of a Walton's, or a *Little House on the Prairie* episode, and those little white tennis shoes that girls wear that are good for nothing but walking short distances before they have to sit down or fucking have someone carry you.

She seemed larger than life, too. Of course, I had never *seen* her, but my senses were on heightened alert and I was well aware of who she was in here.

"I'm Elizabeth."

"You're nothing without me!" I came back on the offensive.

"Wait, this is all wrong!" came yet another voice or another thought as near as I could figure. I was beginning to realize that maybe I never could actually *hear,* but I definitely understood that there was somebody else present.

"Who the fuck are you?" I asked.

"You can call me pride, but my name is Tia. All of that brute force that you have forced upon us has been to our detriment."

"What?"

"All of that killing and shit has got both of us in a heap of shit, if I must use language you can understand," Tia said to me.

I could see Tia and how she was portrayed. Feeling that I was without a physical form, I dare not provoke her because I knew of no defense. Tia showed as much body as I did. Only she was in a "pumped up" state. Her form was perfect. With one glance, I could see her entire body, front, back, top to bottom. She was a muscle goddess. I knew now how I forced Elizabeth into the gym to work out her body and her frustrations with them. What I didn't know was that once the frustration was gone, Tia took over automatically. When there was no need to feel superior, Elizabeth instinctively needed love. She needed something to solidify her existence. She needed comfort from someone who understood her. Tia's job was to find that love for her.

Deep down in here where we were, Elizabeth was scared of men. This place could be part of the soul. The soul went much deeper than the mind did. It was where the rules were really enforced. If the soul set the rules (which it seldom did), that was all that counted, as far as the rest of this body was concerned. There was no changing or manipulating them.

"I'm here to tell you two that your end is near," the mind said through Elizabeth. I could hear it in my head. "What you have done, I have, no doubt, in some way, asked you to do," she continued. "In here, the rules work much different. We are in the mind. On the outside where we have to deal with reality, you have seen and felt and touched. These are things you should know nothing about. You cannot survive on the outside without the mind, and the mind is rested. Live while you can," Elizabeth added. "Your end is near."

"No!" I raged.

By this time, I could only realize my thoughts, but I wasn't fucking done! I could still feel the frustration that allowed me to flourish. "I'll kill you all!" I went running and made my move back to the outside world.

The pill I took before I passed out was kicking in and by the second, I was getting stronger. Not only that, I now knew that there were two more adversaries that I had to deal with. I had to somehow kill them, too, and survive. I knew just how to do what I needed. As I came back into consciousness on the floor, I knew it was back to the lab. I had to make myself a formula that would allow me to live forever. I lifted myself from the floor and made my way to the bathroom. I thought of just how I would finish off the other two. One look in the mirror, and I could see what I wanted. It was blood!

He's been gone entirely too long!

I was losing control, and I knew it. It wasn't until that afternoon that I realized I had two more adversaries to deal with.

Killing these two would be a lot harder than putting AJ and Cheryl to rest for good. I knew that when I wasn't in the driver's seat, things were always different when I came back. The clothes I wore, my hair. I always had to fix myself back up from scratch whenever I woke up. I never fully understood that until those other two bitches showed up.

I was at a loss as to how strong they actually were. I also had to guess about how much they knew about me. Given the circumstances, maybe they knew as much about me as I knew about them. There was a chance, though, that they knew very little. Armed with that information, I knew that I would have to be smart about what I did out in the open.

I left the bathroom and looked around the house to see if Jacob had been here. I couldn't remember what I had him doing. I just knew he wasn't here.

"I can't think! Where the hell are you, brother Jacob? Humph."

There was a feeling tugging at my gut. I didn't know what it was, but it turned from a feeling to a pain. It started from somewhere deep within my body, and it grew quickly and moved itself into my head. I could feel the thought so strongly, it was almost as if it were a scream. In fact, I put my hands over my ears. The feeling pierced my temples; I could almost make it out.

What is it?

Then, as clear as the ring from a crystal chandelier, I felt its presence.

Brother. The voice said.

And that was the last that I would remember as I felt that bitch Elizabeth herself take her rightful place in this fucked-up race of musical chairs of the mind.

Brother?

I had always longed for a brother to play with when I was young. Somewhere far off in my mind, there was the notion that that empty pit of a feeling was filled to a well of hope. It was almost as if I were dreaming about how much I had wanted a brother so bad, and all of a sudden, I felt that wish was washed away with a startling feeling of reality.

"I have a brother?" I asked aloud.

I didn't know who I was asking, but the thought was undeniable. I just knew, at that moment, that I had a brother. It was strange. I had always hoped and prayed for a brother when I was young. Now, it was alarming that I felt, all of a sudden, my prayers had been answered. The feeling was too strong to ignore. I had no idea where I was. I was standing in a very red living room. I actually kind of liked it. I never know where I am exactly when I wake up. Most of the time, I'm at home and don't realize it. I looked around and saw the guest bathroom in the front of the house. I walked to the bathroom and looked at my face.

"Oh!"

Blood covered my face. It was dry and caked up, like it had been there for a while. My nose was also bleeding, but that blood was fresh and still trickling. I took a look at my clothes and frowned.

"I'm tired of this!" I felt disgust for the way I was dressed.

The Hate

All of a sudden, I was overcome with a feeling of hate. In my mind I saw flashes of people and places that were horrific in nature. There was death and blood, gunfire and screaming.

"Ahh!" I screamed.

I reached back as I was falling backward. My hands found the top of the toilet, so I sat down on the closed lid.

"My God! What is happening to me?"

The feelings I had just experienced were as real as the ones that told me I had a brother. I could feel myself losing it, but I fought with all my might to stay conscious.

Deep within me, something was halfway between worlds. It was fighting to come to life. There was a force pulling it down, however, and it was much stronger than this thing was going to be able to handle. I could almost feel exactly what was going on. I had problems interpreting what it was, but somehow I knew that there was someone else there, someone else inside me that knew more than I knew.

"I know you're there!" I said out loud.

As I spoke I stood, using my hands on whatever I could to keep my balance. I looked in the mirror and said, "I know what you look like, too! I know where you come from, and I know what you have done."

I was in a trance; I was barely cognizant of what I was saying, but I knew I had to get it out. All of a sudden, I understood.

It's the hate! It's the hate that brought you here. And it's the fear, too. I hated him so much that I didn't know what to do, and I was so scared that I thought every man wanted to hurt me, too.

The memory of that night returned to me for the first time since it happened. I remembered how I was sitting in front of the TV, playing a video game when a pair of hands gripped my shoulders.

"I don't like that!"

I remembered looking back and seeing Sam kneeling there in his underwear. His manhood stood out. I remembered running through the house and up the stairs. I remembered how he cornered me in the room and slammed my little face on the bed. I remembered the pain I felt while he violated me. I remembered using all my strength, kicking, and swinging my arms and head to get him off of me, and I remembered finally I somehow connected with a part of him that made him scream.

I ran out of the door and jumped over the stairway rail. I remembered hitting the back of the soft leather couch and slamming into the large cushions that broke my fall. Then I saw him coming after me, stepping one leg over the rail I had just jumped from. I remembered screaming, "Nooo!" and grabbing the first thing I could find to throw at him to stop him. I grabbed the video console by the cables and swung it towards him like David did the smooth stone that brought down Goliath. The console struck him square on the head as he was bringing his second leg over the rail. The blow caused him to twist and his leg got caught between the stairwell rail bars. Sam screamed a single note as his leg snapped. He was knocked unconscious and left hanging upside down, swinging from the stairs. I remembered starting to run outside, but as soon as the still cold of the outside air hit me, it scared me even more. All I could think to do was run and hide, and run and hide. I did until I heard my mother's voice.

It was the hate that brought you here! I can't hate anymore.

I looked at myself in the mirror and braced myself. I looked at my hair. The way it was pulled back showed all of my face. I was always scared of people looking at me. I could never tell what it was they wanted, so I always wore my hair down over my face to hide behind it.

The clothes I was wearing were way too revealing. I was even more scared of people looking at my body. I couldn't imagine being touched by anyone. I was smart enough to know that my fear was unfounded. I knew that what had happened to me was just a bad experience. I never felt that way until now. It was as if I was given what I had been missing all these years to cope with my tragedy.

"No more!"

I turned on the water in the sink and began to wash the blood off of my face. I was fed up; I had several small cuts and even a bit of glass still stuck in my skin. As I cleaned myself up, I saw for the first time how beautiful I really was.

See, you're beautiful. A thought entered into my mind. It was so prevalent, that it scared me. I heard it as if the actual words were spoken. *I need love.*

Again, I was halfway in a trance, and I felt as if my mind was getting away from me. There seemed to be a part of me that longed for what I had really ignored for myself my entire adult life.

*Love...*There was a desperate feeling inside me that was weak and dying. It was the feeling of desperation that told me that I could not "feel." It had made me become dead inside, ignoring all of the emotions that made me alive.

I looked at myself again in the mirror with a clean face and began to pull at the clothes I was wearing. I wanted them off. They were stained with blood, but that wasn't the reason. I pulled my shirt over my head to reveal a very strong upper body. I realized that I never really looked at myself. I was extremely muscular, and my breasts were large and tight against my body.

I never paid any attention to that part of my body because it was the part that all men wanted. It was a man that hurt me, and I swore to myself that it would never happen again.

But it was one man. It's never happened since then!

I looked back on my life. But I really couldn't remember. All I could remember was my work and school. It was as if I wasn't there half of the time.

I had everything in my life exactly the way I thought I wanted it, and when those times came when I had on the wrong clothes or my hair was wrong, I just fixed them and ignored that they were ever out of place. I could remember now, how, so many times I woke up and realized that I wasn't where I was when I could last remember. There was something inside me that just allowed me to dismiss it all and move on from there.

That is so wrong!

I stripped off the rest of my clothes to see that my body was sculpted. I gazed at myself in the full-length mirror behind the door. I turned the overhead light on and was in awe at the powerful body that was in the mirror's reflection.

"Could this be real? How could I look like this and not know it?"

My body was a symmetrical masterpiece. Every muscle showed its striations. For the first time in my life, I felt good about myself. I was confused, but I had such a clear feeling in my mind that was way too positive for any confusion to trouble me. I turned from the mirror and ran water in the tub. Then I stepped into the shower and felt the cool water refresh my body. The feeling was euphoric. I felt like someone lifted a hot, wet blanket from over me so that now I could breathe fresh air.

After cleaning myself up and getting out of the shower, I walked naked around the house and looked at everything as if seeing things for the first time.

As I walked into the bedroom, I saw that it was immaculate. There wasn't a thing out of place.

This isn't my room!

I know that I couldn't clean a room to save my life. I remembered how my mother used to come in and clean up after me, and I would wonder how she made the room look so clean. I loved it that way, but I could never do it myself. In the master bathroom, I grabbed a huge, plush, red towel from the rack on the wall and wrapped it around me, then walked into the closet. There were all of these nice clothes hanging up with the cleaner's tags still on them.

I looked around and saw a trunk underneath the hanging clothes. Opening it, I became uneasy with what I saw. There were pictures in it, tons of them. I gathered as many as I could in my hands and took them over to the bed. As I looked at the pictures of what seemed to be me posing with a bikini on, showing off all of my muscular body on stage, I was completely taken aback.

It wasn't until this moment that I admitted to myself that I had a problem. I didn't know who I was. These pictures proved it, because I didn't remember taking them. I knew I would never show my body off like that. I was scared to wear a T-shirt without an accompanying sweatshirt (a *large* sweatshirt) or a jacket or coat. I had always wanted to, but there was the fear of people looking at me. I didn't want that type of attention.

These pictures, though, were proof that I led a different life. There were other pictures of me in the gym with another woman, and even more with a T-shirt on with my arms showing and a knot tied in the middle with my name written on a tag with the gym's logo on it.

Only it wasn't my name. Or was it?

Who on earth is Tia?

Deep down, I knew. I had always hated the name Elizabeth. I was named after my grandmother, who had passed years before I was born. I remembered thinking as a child if I were to change my name, it would be Tia, which was a shortened version of my middle name, or Liz.

"Ahh!"

As I thought of the name, it seemed to bellow in my mind.

"It's you!" I said out loud. "Liz! I can feel it when I say it. You want to take my life! I know about you now, and I will stop you!" I had tears in my eyes. I didn't want to be crazy.

I was really scared. I never wanted to know that I had not been in control of my life. It had been made obvious to me by the events that transpired on this day. I got up and looked in a dresser drawer and put on some clothes that fit my mood: Boxers, jeans, and a T-shirt. I looked at myself in the mirror and almost didn't recognize myself. I started to pull my hair back but then stopped.

I wasn't sure what I was looking for, but I walked around the room and then back into the closet. I looked up on the shelf and pulled down a baseball cap. I went back to the mirror and put it on.

This is about as normal as it gets. I liked what I saw.

I went into the kitchen and saw the broken glass and pills on the floor. Reaching down, I picked up one of the pills. I didn't know what it was, but I knew it was bad news. I grabbed a broom and cleaned up the mess, then took some cleaner and wiped up the clotted blood from the floor. After picking up the pills from the pile of glass I swept up, I put them in the garbage disposal. As I did it, I felt extremely lightheaded.

"No, you don't!" I told myself as I quickly turned on the water and splashed it on my face before I fell backward. I didn't know why, but I seemed to remember the feeling that I was passing out, and whenever I had that feeling, I used to let it take over because I was in a situation where I wanted out. Right now, I'm not trying to go anywhere. I needed to be where I was, and I would fight to stay there.

I got up from the freshly cleaned floor and flipped the switch on the disposal. A sharp pain had begun forming at my temple, but it slowly subsided. I looked in the cabinet and found all kinds of vitamins and supplements in bottles. I took them all out and emptied them on the counter. Most of them were what the bottles said they were, but there were some that had the same pills in them that were on the floor. I decided I wasn't taking any chances. I pushed them all into the sink and let the disposal do its work.

Then I looked in the cabinet again to see if there was anything left. I had to get on the counter to see on the second shelf. It was there I saw a supply of pills with a handwritten label on them. I looked in a drawer and found a pen and paper. The writing was mine. The bottle read, "Jacob, take one of these three times a day with pie."

"Who is Jacob?"

I opened the bottle and immediately recognized the drug inside. It was a drug doctors used to keep criminals lethargic so that they couldn't hurt themselves or anyone else.

What was going on here?

I continued to look in the cabinet and pulled out a stack of notebooks. There were detailed notes on drug research for cancer and anecdotal evidence of progress for a cure. That was just too much for the moment, so I put it down. I looked in another book, which described a drug that seemed be a catalyst for isolating a bipolar deficiency. The notes were very well organized. I could tell that the research was questionable when I read about it being administered to a healthy subject and what the implications were.

"This couldn't possibly be legal!"

I put that book down and as I looked through the third and final notebook, I found that it was not research at all. It was someone's journal. There was no name on the front, but what disturbed me most was that it was all in my handwriting. There were names and events on dates that I had no recollection of, and as I read, I knew that I didn't want to remember any of it. But I read on and on and became more horrified as I read.

"I've killed people? It can't be true!"

But it is!

I screamed when I heard the voice, but there was no one here. I immediately grabbed all three books and headed outside, grabbing the keys on the counter as I went. I felt the warmth of the setting sun on my skin, along with the fresh air. I continued to walk and saw the green Jaguar in the driveway. Opening the door, I climbed in.

I looked in the glove compartment and found a makeup bag and some loose papers. As I looked deeper, I found the registration. Jacob Livingston was the owner of the vehicle. I was determined to know who this man was, so I started the car and backed out of the driveway. Looking at the address on the registration, I thought to myself, *This is just as good a place as any to find some answers. I'll get to the bottom of this once and for all.*

Livingston Manor

I drove with a lot on my mind. I didn't realize that I had been so busy in the last two years. I could feel what I had always ignored within me. My life had never been a happy one, not since my ordeal. I never realized how unhappy I was until now. I thought that my life was all me and my mother. Those were the good times. It seemed whenever I would become angry about my mother's situation, I would loose consciousness and "wake up" in some other place. I didn't dismiss it as normal; however, I didn't know what to do about it either.

Sometimes I would dream about the things my alter-self would do. To me, they were never just dreams, though. Every once in a while, there would be evidence that what happened in my dreams was actually true. All the while, I was a puppet being pulled and pushed along by something I couldn't explain. I really didn't have time to worry about the situation that I was in yet. I felt that there would be a time that I would surely have to answer for all the things I might have done. This lay heavy on my mind, but I let it stay in the back of my mind because I had bigger fish to fry. I was on my way to the address on the registration of the green Jaguar. I didn't know whom I'd expected to see, outside of the owner of the car.

I have a brother somewhere. I only hope he's alive and well.

I thought that he might have been in some type of situation, maybe not trouble, but definitely some type of distress. Whenever I thought about the name Jacob, I felt a twinge of an unknown emotion in my stomach. I couldn't interpret it. It was like a mix of jealousy and anger, but with the way I felt about the prospect of having the brother that I'd always wanted, I added a dose of hope to the mix. It all made for a strange mixture for me to have to deal with. I didn't even know what I was going to say when I got there, but I drove until I got to the address on the registration.

I rolled up to the large gate and there was a soft beeping sound coming from above my head. A small black box that resembled a remote control unit was attached to the sun visor. I didn't do anything to it, but the gate opened anyway. I drove the car in and followed the brick road to the front of the house. As

I came up the driveway, I could see a garage door opening automatically. So I drove the car into the garage and shut off the engine, then got out of the car and went to the front door. I could hear the garage door close behind me as I walked to the front door.

"God, this house is big!"

I pushed the button to ring the doorbell and waited. There was no answer. I looked at the keys on the key ring and noticed on the alarm remote there was a button with a house on it. Naturally I pushed the button and a chime like that of a clock rang softly from within the house. The door to the house opened slowly before me.

"Wow! I could live like this! Hello," I said, walking into the house.

Again, there was no answer. I walked cautiously into the foyer of the mansion and saw that it seemed to be abandoned. There were no lights on and some fresh spider webs were forming in the front window.

Somebody would have seen this.

I walked around the beautifully constructed home and was amazed at how large everything was. Coming to the staircase leading upstairs, I decided to go up.

Man, I could walk arm in arm with two other people up these stairs!

This place was a small palace with a down-home feel to it. Someone spent a lot of time making sure that it was perfect. Everything from the hand spun Turkish runner that flowed beneath my feet as I traveled up or down, to the busts of Fredric Douglass and Beethoven that graced the halls of the upper floor. It was a very impressive display.

I looked around and saw a door with a large poster on it. It was a picture of Michael Jordan holding Spike Lee by the head in one hand and a basketball in the other. I opened the door to the room and saw that it was full of gadgets. They were all neatly arranged on shelves and on a large desk in the room, along with model rockets and cars.

A large telescope pointing towards the stars stood in front of the window. I looked over to the far side of the room and saw a picture. I couldn't make out who was in it, but as I stepped toward it, I felt butterflies in my stomach. I forced myself to go on. I got to the shelf where the picture sat and picked it up, just staring at it in awe. It was a photo of a younger guy and an older one; both were clad in tuxedos and smiling for the camera. A handwritten caption at the bottom of the picture read, "My son, the genius, and his father. Jacob II and III—we make a special team!"

"There are *two* Jacobs?"

I walked over to the bed and sat down. "Even the bed is big!"

I lay back on the bed for a second and realized that I was exhausted. I couldn't remember the last time I actually went to sleep. The bed got the best of me. I had about three more minutes' worth of thoughts before the sleep monster pounced on my head and put me out. I needed sleep and couldn't fight the urge. Gently, I faded from the world and went to sleep.

Jacob Makes Plans

I looked at Sheila and could tell that she was in deep thought. I didn't want to put her through the changes that I was about to, but I felt that if I didn't control this situation from beginning to end, I couldn't be sure that the outcome would be the right one. She was much older and much wiser than me, but I had the advantage of my youth and my strong convictions. Most people couldn't get past my convictions. I seemed to be so sure of myself that whatever I said was usually taken as gospel.

"What are you thinking?" I asked Sheila.

"I was just thinking about when my baby was young and carefree. She's been through so much, and she seemed to take it all so well. I had to send her to therapy, but she wouldn't talk to the doctor at all. Yet, she would talk to me without hesitation. When I talked to her, I had to make sure that I asked her all the right questions and covered all of the areas I felt I needed to so that I could make sure that she was okay. I'm no doctor!" she openly complained. "She was such a happy, beautiful child. I took that away from her! I can't fail my baby again!"

"Jacob," she continued, "you have to promise me that we will try and help her!"

I thought for a minute. My main focus was to figure out how to stop her, not so much to help. I did feel that I had to protect the person that was truly at risk. Elizabeth was the victim in all of this. She was a slave to the driving forces of her inner self. Her mind had split in an effort to protect herself from the world.

"She was always a good little girl; however, Elizabeth didn't help herself much to get better. She would have been a lot better if she had participated in her recovery a bit more. She was in a weakened state for a long time after she had come back home. I was so distraught over the fact that Elizabeth's rape was my fault that I couldn't help much. For a very long time, we just both stayed in the house.

"As she got older, she spent a lot of time on her schoolwork. It seemed that she lived with that rape every day of her life. At night, she would try and go over in her mind how she could have changed the situation. She would sometimes dream that she got away completely; other times, she wouldn't get away at all and she had to live through it again. She spent countless hours awake, crying at night, feeling the same pain she felt so long ago.

"Eventually, she must have gotten tired of all the crying and just buried the pain. Whenever she felt the urge to revisit the events of that night, she would concentrate harder on her studies. By the time she graduated from high school, she had gone from a mediocre student to a straight "A" senior, graduating with top honors. She went on to college and did the same thing, graduating in four years and staying on at the university to continue her work on cancer research. I had become sick before her graduation, and it was then that she started to change."

I thought of the possibility of a happy ending out of all of this. I didn't think it was possible for Sheila to be happy, Cheryl to be safe, and Elizabeth not to be harmed in any way. It would take serious planning and precise execution to pull off a stunt like that. Then I would have to think if I wanted to be a part of it all. I had already lost more than anyone else could lose in this endeavor. I had already lost both of my parents and the last two years of my life, and if Liz had her way, I would lose the rest of my life as well. I wasn't about to let that happen.

I didn't consider the possibility of ending her life. I wouldn't know how to do it if I had to, but I did know that she might have the ability to kill me, along with the others that were involved. "I'll do what I can," I told Sheila.

Over the intercom, I heard a soft, familiar voice. "Attention on the floors, visiting hours are now over."

I hadn't realized I had been there for so long. I looked at my watch and saw that it was well past nine o'clock in the evening.

"I have to go, Sheila," I said, standing for the first time in a while. "Elizabeth hasn't seen me all day. What's worse, I haven't seen her all day."

"How often do you see my daughter?"

"I used to see her all the time. She would bring me an apple pie almost everyday."

"My!" Sheila gasped. "She said that she was taking them to friends. I never knew that you two had been so close for so long."

"I wouldn't exactly say that we were close, but I wasn't in a good way in those days."

"Well, what was wrong?" Sheila asked.

"That one will have to wait for another time." I felt that she had been through enough up to that point. "Can I come see you again?"

"Yes, you *have* to come back!"

I only asked that question to be polite. I knew I had to come back, but for now, I had to make plans. I didn't know how I was going to accomplish my tasks, but I knew it would take some serious thought. I left her with a short hug and walked out the door that I walked through hours before. I felt I had accomplished something. Before that afternoon, I knew very little about Elizabeth and her background. Now I knew where Elizabeth came from. An important part of the puzzle was solved. There were still a bunch of loose ends I had to tie up, like telling Sheila more about her daughter. From this point on, Elizabeth and I would have a different relationship.

I didn't know if I could keep up the facade I had been using the last few days. I also didn't know how dangerous it would be, but I was determined that Elizabeth and I would talk for the first time ever.

Maybe I can reach her…

It seemed that Elizabeth had been switching personalities several times a day. I had seen her transition before, so I knew that I would have plenty of warning before she changed. I also knew that Liz was the only person she changed into when she did change.

At least I have something to work with.

Reaching the elevator doors, I pushed the button and thought about the voice over the intercom. I knew it was Stacy, and I wanted to talk to her. She had a few more pieces of the puzzle that I needed, but that could wait for the moment. Elizabeth would keep me busy for a while. If it came down to it, she could probably beat me in a physical match. It wasn't that I was a weakling. It was more-or-less the fact that she was just so much stronger than I was. I had always loved the way that my half-sister and Cheryl looked. I especially loved the way Cheryl looked. I saw the whole show that she and Elizabeth put on the night Cheryl was shown "the way," as Elizabeth called it. Ever since that day, I had a thing for Cheryl.

I had never seen such a show before. Then when I heard her reaction the next day, I thought I could help her. I knew at that point she didn't want to be like Elizabeth. That could have only been a good thing for me. The truth of the matter was, though, they were both extremely strong women, and they could both beat the pulp out of me if they chose. I had the opportunity to talk to Cheryl in my present state; and from what I could tell, she liked what she saw.

Maybe I have a chance. We could be a pretty good team.

I entered the elevator, which took me to the lobby floor, then stepped out to the sight of an empty hallway.

I have to call a cab.

I was wrong, because there was a taxi waiting right outside the door. I thought about the cab ride to the hospital and looked to see if it was the same cab. It wasn't. I got in and told the cabbie the address to where I was headed—home. I then put my head back and almost immediately went to sleep. I had been through a lot that day. From my conversation with AJ that morning to Stacy that afternoon, and on to Sheila that evening. It was a full day's worth of events. I knew I had a big job to do.

This isn't gonna be easy.

With that thought, I was gone to the world while the cab whisked me back to my part of town.

Stacy's Frustration

** Sheila **

I was distraught as I laid my head on the pillow after my evening prayers and thought about the things that Jacob said to me. He really didn't give me as much detail as he could have, but what he did tell me was a lot to take in. I had to figure out a way to save my daughter. I mulled over thoughts in my mind on how I was going to get my daughter treatment for her disorder.

If that young man is correct, there has to be a cure for her mind. I can't believe she would have anything to do with a murder! I have to see how I can help her. When I get out of here, I will get to the bottom of this.

I wonder if I told Jacob that I was leaving in the morning? I'm almost sure I didn't. I don't know how, but I know I will see him again. I can't let Elizabeth know that he has been here. I hate to keep secrets from her, but if she did those things that Jacob said she was involved in, then I have no choice but to get her off of the streets. "Yes, Lord, tomorrow is, indeed, a big day!" With that, I curled up in a ball and waited for sleep to come.

The lights dimmed in the hallway outside of my door. Before I closed my eyes, I could see the dimmed light from the bottom of my still-cracked door. The door open slowly and the night nurse stuck her head in. I raised my head to see a little bit better.

"Good night, Miss Williams," Nurse Caugman whispered.

"Good night, baby," I answered with a smile.

"I'm gonna close the door all the way; is that okay?"

"That's fine," I said as I put my head back down to rest. The crack in the door was actually bothering me deep down, but I didn't want to go through all the trouble of getting up to close it.

** Stacy **

I always made a point to check on Sheila before my shift was up or my rounds were over. It didn't matter if I was working that floor or not. I really cared about my patients. Sometimes, I had problems separating them from my own life, as was the case with Jacob. I took my job very seriously; in fact, for me, this job was my life. I'm the type of person who thinks very little of myself. I need to have something to make me feel important. I take some of my patients on as "projects" so I can have someone to depend on me for certain needs.

New patients would come onto one of my wings and I would immediately introduce myself and assess their mental state. I would sit down with them and just get to know them. I'm a great people person and an outstanding conversationalist. Once I came to the conclusion of what they needed outside of the medical reason for being there, I would take on the job of administering that treatment to them. It could be something as small as taking the time during a patient's busy day of eating and sleeping to just sit there and talk. Other times, it's a bit more tactile. Occasionally, I would have to sit with elderly cancer patients and stroke their hands because their family members seem to have forgotten about them. Then there were those time when I had to pull out my entire arsenal of caring weapons, and that's what happened when I met Jacob.

Jacob was completely helpless when I first saw him. He needed me more than any other patient in the building. He would be the one to affirm my place in life. Jacob became the unwitting sponsor for my self-indulgence. Having no say in the matter, he lay in that hospital bed, far away from the outside world. I took advantage of a need within me to satisfy myself with some kind of possession. I took on Jacob as the ultimate project. I wanted be the one to bring him out of his coma, and when he awoke, he would love me for it.

My interaction with people was one troubling situation moving to another. I can hide my inhibitions well, but to the trained eye, my insecurities are glaring. While I walked down the hall from Sheila's room, I thought about seeing Jacob again after all this time. He was such a big part of my life for so long that I felt empty inside without the focus I use to have on him. For someone whom I'd never had a real conversation with, he was a surprisingly major part of my life back then. When I took the leave of absence after Elizabeth witnessed my moment of weakness, I was momentarily destroyed inside.

"That woman nearly ruined my life!"

I'm frustrated because there's something I want. I haven't felt those feelings in a long time, but they hadn't gone anywhere. They just laid dormant until they were triggered by the only thing that could have awoken them...Jacob.

There hadn't been anyone in my life in the form of a boyfriend. Of course, the truth of the matter is that I am deathly afraid of being hurt. I still tell friends that there is no one who could love someone as much as I would. Unfortunately, I would also tell them that no one could love me as much as I could love them. This meant that I would always get the short end of the stick in a relationship. I felt that in my heart. I want so much to be in a real relationship, but I just can't bring myself to trust anyone enough to get close to me. I know one day I'm going to have to trust someone.

My best friend, Trina, told me that what I was feeling was normal, but until I took that first step to trust someone, I would always be alone. Jacob was the only man I trusted. He never hurt me, he never lied to me, and most of all, when I spoke to him, he listened. This was my rationale for my feelings for him whenever I questioned myself about my motives. No man in my life had ever lived up to my expectations. I ask for too much in a man. For me, truth, respect, love, and honesty—all at the same time—was too much to expect from any man.

I reached the front desk and checked the monitors for each of the ICU rooms. Things were quiet, and that was how I liked it. I am a rock under pressure. That was the reason I was in charge of such a large area of the hospital. Doctors trusted me to administer care to the fullest extent until they got there. I've saved many lives here at the UCLA Med Center. At home, I have award after award stacked up in corners of the house.

I sat down behind the desk and began to close out the logs for the evening. "This life can be so hard. I am not happy!"

"Why not?"

I turned around, jumping upon hearing the voice. It was Rolonda, the other floor nurse on duty. She had come from a room behind the desk.

"Now you know I didn't intend to have you hear me talking to myself. I know my job is an important one. I do it well. I make sure this place runs like a Swiss watch. People like you and me make a difference in those people's lives."

I looked at Rolonda for confirmation that what I was saying was true. She looked at me with a concerned, but patient look.

"So what is the problem?" she asked.

"I…I don't know!" I said, frustrated. "My life is so fulfilled, yet I feel so empty inside!" I stamped my foot.

"You know what I'm going to say," she responded, looking away to avoid my eyes.

Here we go. I shook my head.

"You need a *man!*" she said firmly.

She said it anyway. If I had a dollar for every time we've had this conversation…

"Girl, you've got cobwebs on it—it's been so long!"

"I mean…why does it always have to be about a man?"

"Don't get mad at me," she replied, looking defiantly at me. "That's what your problem is! You've told me the story a million times in a million different ways. You have everything but what you have always wanted. 'Someone to love you as much as you can love them.'" She mocked me, shaking her head in a goofy way, like I was some kind of crybaby.

I just put my head in my hands and took a deep breath, letting it out with a long sigh. I had no idea what to do about my problem. All I know is that I'm miserable. The only man I felt I could love only now knows that I'm alive. I had hopes to let my feelings be known soon, but I had to get to him again. He said he was going out of town.

Rolonda was still talking, but I could barely hear what the she was saying.

If I can just talk to him. He remembers me; I know he does. All I need is a chance to talk with him. He'll like me, and then we'll get to know each other better, and maybe a couple months down the line…

"Stacy!" Rolonda interrupted.

I jumped back into reality. "Huh?" I answered.

"Are you listening to me?"

"What is it? I'm sorry, my mind was somewhere else."

"Well, I figured you were going to tune me out about your man problems, but the least you could do is sign these release papers for Sheila Williams so she can get out of here in the morning."

"Are they back already?"

"Yes, Dr. Colman came by this evening because he said he had a conference to attend in San Francisco tomorrow." She held the papers out for me.

"Good! She has been waiting for so long to get out of this place. This hospital is like a prison to some of the people in here. To others, it's a final resting place. I'm glad she is going home. She deserves the second chance that God has given her."

We continued to talk about the times that we'd spent with Sheila. Since the day she came in to our lives, we had all been enriched by her insight and positive attitude. Everyone who came in touch with her was a better person because of it. The hospital would lose a good friend tomorrow, but Miss Sheila Williams would get her life back and start to live again like so few get to do that start down the road she had come from.

The Gathering

** Jacob **

I could hear the traffic drone away as I fell asleep. When I was completely gone, I fell into a land that resembled Africa. I looked around and saw trees and water-starved grass, the land and the grass was all the same color, a sort of khaki brown. I knew I was dreaming; I always knew. My days of nightmares and dreams where I wasn't in control were long past. It took me years to develop the self-confidence that it took to defeat the monsters in my dreams.

I heard a rumble start from behind me. The sound quickly surrounded me until I found myself running with a group of small antelope. I looked around, but all I could see were more and more of these animals running with me. I seemed to be leading the pack. I heard what would have been a frightening sound anywhere but in a dream, at least for me. It was the sound of a lion on the hunt. Its growls were magnified in my ears. I could feel it in my entire body. I looked back again and above the backs of the other antelope, I saw it! It was closing in on the pack. It was a male, a magnificent beast whose mane shook with each gaining step. I scoffed at the thought in my mind. I knew that male lions were usually too lazy to hunt.

I slowed down and let the rest of the antelope pass me. As they did, they changed from antelope to people. They were all people that I knew, too, or at least had seen before.

They're watching me.

I turned completely around and faced the charging lion. It was still coming at a crazy pace. I had to fight the doubt that always reared its head at a time like this in dreams. I looked the lion straight in the eyes like it was standing in front of me. Then I started running right at it. I looked down and could see my small hooves. I could also feel my rear legs pushing me forward as I jumped from spot to spot.

I stared at the lion, making sure it could see my eyes. As I got closer, its expression changed, like it was making a last-ditch effort to scare me. Then the lion roared a loud, menacing roar. That just pissed me off. As I got closer, the lion seemed to slow down a bit, but it still continued to run right at me. When I was a few feet short of the lion, I reached out and extended my hoof until it changed into a paw. Then along with my hoof, the rest of my body changed from an antelope to an even larger lion than the one that faced me. When I was finally within arm's reach, I stretched out my paw and swatted it to the side, just as I had seen a lion do once on a nature show. When my paw met the face of the other lion, I felt its texture change from fur to skin.

I heard a strange sound as the lion went sprawling off to the side. It sounded like pills in a container being dropped and bouncing in all directions. I looked again and saw that I was in the kitchen of Elizabeth's house. I could see her on the ground, struggling to get up. I wasn't in the kitchen myself, but I could see her very clearly. Even though her face was bloody, I could tell it was her. There was something different about her, but I couldn't explain what it was.

I looked at her again and she was clean, standing before me in a green field of grass. I jumped as she reached out and touched my face. A tear fell down Elizabeth's cheek, like she was seeing me for the first time. She just stood there, holding a picture, clutching it to her chest. Another single tear flowed down her cheek. She looked at me like she didn't know what to say.

While I looked at her, I decided not to speak. Whenever she saw me, she usually had specific instructions for me, as if she were seeing me for the first time after a long corporate meeting of some kind where a decision was made and she was giving me instructions to implement it. This time she said nothing. I decided that I would go with it and not push the issue.

In the distance, I could see what looked like two tornado-like funnels reaching towards the ground. One person was at the bottom of each of the funnels, seemingly riding them down like parachutes. The funnels were brilliantly colored with twists of silvers and blues. As the funnels reached the ground, I could see the limp bodies of the two people in them were almost being gently placed on the grass by the tornados instead of them riding them down. Although they were one, maybe two miles away, I could see them as if they had been placed right in front of me and my silent half-sister.

** AJ **

I woke up to a grassy field beneath me. I could smell the grass and feel the warmth of the sun above me. Then I sat up and looked around. Green grass stretched as far as I could see. When I stood, the blades of grass that had seemed really tall only a moment ago were only inches tall, hardly covering my bare feet. I looked over to my right and saw my friend Cheryl at her desk, working on what looked like a watch.

Cheryl looked up and saw me. "See, boss; I told you, it's as good as new." She was happy to see me. I could tell by the big smile she gave me.

"I thought you had died and gone off to that place where all the good people go."

Cheryl looked up at me. It was like I could see in her mind that she thought she was on the ground, sitting naked in the grass. I realized that just because we appeared to be in the same place, that didn't mean that we saw the same things. I understand that people see what they want to see on the road to the truth. Just as it is in the "real" world, in this place, "real" was as relative as time.

I saw Cheryl as the reliable friend that could fix almost anything. This would be the first thing that would come to my mind in a word association exercise. Cheryl, on the other hand, has a much different view of me. I think I was something that Cheryl really needed in her life. In her time of need, I was exactly what she needed. Whenever we talked about it, Cheryl told me that she felt like sighing a breath of relief. She told me that sometimes she could not believe she was so lucky as to have a friend like me. I really need her as much as she says she needs me. I just don't know how to tell her.

** Jacob **

I was well-versed in dreams like this. Sometimes I couldn't wait to get to sleep so I could see what dreams awaited me in the night. My first thought was to look around to see what my surroundings were. I felt that the purpose of dreams was to tell you to do just that, like the rule was to look around you and see where you stand in this life. So I did just that. When I saw Elizabeth, I knew that I was about to get another piece of the puzzle, possibly a piece that I'd failed to realize in my consciousness.

Choosing not to speak when I saw her was a form of control. I felt I had to not only control the situation, but also to think about my actions before I moved. Things moved much slower here and I knew it, so I had the time to correct for would-be mistakes. I felt, however, that the reason for this was to allow me practice so as not to make mistakes in the real world.

** Elizabeth **

I've spent what seems to be half of my life in this world—the underworld. I know it better than anyone who comes here and briefly visits. Most of all, I know the rules to navigate within the underworld. I've been trapped here for what has seemed like an eternity. It would seem that every so often, I would wake up to the world I knew, the world where I had been born. Those encounters would be brief as I would be so scared of life itself that I would quickly retreat back to the confines, but not necessarily the comfort, of the underworld.

Here I could manipulate things to make them suit my needs. I could spend what would seem like hours with a healthy mamma, talking, laughing, and even playing in the sand like we used to do when I was a little girl.

There were many memories here that I could live over and over again. It wasn't my intention to stay here forever. In fact, I was in training. There was a place here in underworld that scared me to death. In this land, it was a cave. It was dark and windy and only dimly lit. I had to force myself to get through it when I was dropped there the first time. There was nothing but fear and pain in the halls of this cave, where the tunnels of it twist in my mind. Here is where time and time again I fought the beast that held me in this world. It was the man that hurt me as a child. Here it manifests itself as a dark, clingy creature that breathed hot, fiery breath and had large hands and a hairy body. I could smell its scent getting stronger and stronger the deeper I went into that cave.

When I first encountered the beast, I was dropped right in the center of its lair from another dream. I fought many battles with it. Some of the battles I faired better when I took the time to think about what I was doing. Other times, I was bound with the restricting cords of fear, and I had to relive that horrible experience again and again.

Nowadays, I have to find the cave where the tunnel lies. Sometimes I would search for days or until I woke, but my state would often change with the dizziness of the transition back here. Liz would either fade in and then out, or she would immediately get up and live for as long as her seemingly allotted time allowed. Again, I would be stuck back in the world beneath the world we all know during our busy days.

Other times, I would find the cave hiding on the side of a grassy hill or at the base of a cliff on the beach. Either way, I always made my way to the entrance with the sole purpose of getting my life back. The prize for my mortal combat was my soul, as I knew it. It was the very essence of my being. I could feel it as it called to me from deep within the caverns of the tunnel. It was the reason I knew how to navigate the many paths at the end of the long entrance.

I could feel deep within me the fulfillment I would receive as I was reunited with myself. I had to get past the beast before that reunification, and I knew it. Each time I made the journey, it made me stronger. The entrance to the cave was getting harder and harder to find. I didn't know what that meant. I felt that if I didn't finally beat that beast and ensure its death, I could never leave this place.

** Cheryl **

I looked around and smiled at the view. I loved the look and feel of grass. "It just makes you want to golf, doesn't it?" I asked AJ.

I had just looked up, and she was there in her white coat, with notepad in hand. I felt really comfortable and in no hurry at all. Peace encompassed me with my rock, AJ, standing in front of me. AJ just stood there, and it was confusing. I could see through her eyes, or maybe it was her mind. She was looking at me sitting at a desk, working on something with a small screwdriver. As she approached me, the desk began to distort. I'm guessing AJ barely noticed it because she was looking me directly in the eyes.

I wonder what she sees in me?

Her gaze was held there as she walked, and I kept it with her for fear of the scenery changing, as it sometimes does in a dream.

I know from dreaming that one of the rules is that people see what they want to. AJ told me once when the auras of two people in the same dream become too close, they see right into each other when their attention is focused on each other. This can be a very frightening experience sometimes. This is where the truth is really seen. It's one thing to see what you want to in a dream because dreams are subject to interpretation. Dreams, to some, are just pictures painted by emotions expressing themselves. In the event when two people are in the same dream, however, when the circles of their auras coincide with each other, they can see the other person's reason for being there in the first place. They can see the truth in the dream, where the other person can only see what they feel. I don't know where she gets this stuff, but I've found it to be true.

It's like two people standing in front of each other and they are both almost invisible, but neither of them knows this themselves. So the two people can see right into the souls of each other, but they can't see inside themselves. AJ immediately saw my pain, and I saw AJ's dilemma.

How could she know?

The sky changed color as if it were going to rain. Something made AJ look to the horizon. I followed her gaze. It felt like we were looking through the same pair of eyes. We could both see two figures in the distance. The world seemed to spin increasingly beneath our feet. The faster it spun, the closer the figures became.

** Jacob **

I wasn't sure what was going on. I could usually see something like this coming and change my surroundings in a dream. As the world spun, I felt like I was in a ride at the carnival that came to town once a year. It was the ride where the cylinder spun so fast that you stuck to the walls; the ride where you once heard little girls scream as the floor dropped away from you, but you remained stuck to the wall like a fly on that sticky strip of paper hung out on a hot summer day. I saw Elizabeth just stand there with her eyes closed and her hands over her mouth.

When the spinning stopped, there were four of us standing before each other. It was very confusing. With so much energy in one place, it was hard for any of us to see. We all seemed to fade in and out of each other's consciousness like small reminders of each other's existence. Cheryl threw herself to the ground. The sweet smell of grass filled her nostrils. That was what she needed to ground herself. I reached above my head and made a staff appear in my hands. I then thrust it into the ground to help me stand strong. AJ placed her hands at her temples and then moved them outward, pushing the confusion away from her and down until she could open her eyes and see straight. Elizabeth merely stood there with her eyes closed and her hands covering them. Thunder clapped above our heads.

The three of us most prepared looked at each other, and we could see the anchors of confidence residing in ourselves—all except for Elizabeth, who still stood in front of us with her hands covering her face. Suddenly, lightning struck the place where Elizabeth stood, and what happened next shocked us. Her body sort of peeled away from itself from the top to the bottom. What was revealed was very different from the woman that stood before us only moments ago. She looked the same; only her clothes were different. She was a very powerful looking woman. Her arms were very muscular with the veins pushing out from her skin like wires. She wore all black, with her hair pulled back, tied in a single knot. Both Cheryl and I knew this woman well, but the combined auras of all four of us occupying that space in the underworld did not allow for any other interpretations but the truth. This meant that all involved saw and heard the same things.

"Welcome to my world," Liz spoke. "I guess it is your world, too. But I spend more time here; I know I do. I watch you on the other side while you live your lives. The three of you are the same, but you are still three." She looked at all of us. As her eyes glanced over us, she fixed her gaze on Cheryl.

"I'm not the one who pains you."

Cheryl looked at her, speechless. She could see that this person wasn't evil.

"Who are you?" Cheryl finally asked.

"I don't really have a name, but you can call me Liz. I was born from hate, hate kept inside and fed, but buried deep within the ground of this world. Like a seed, it sprung me forth into existence."

"You are powerless here," I said, almost in surprise.

"I am here just as you are."

"But you've been on the other side."

"In your world, I am driven by emotions. I have no control. I do what those things make me do, to satisfy the need."

"What need?" AJ asked, becoming a part of this experience consciously.

"On the other side, there is a pain you feel here," and she placed her hands on her abdomen.

"Hunger?" AJ asked.

"Yes," Liz answered. "Only it is for action and not food. It calls me, and I answer. As I go from this world to yours, I change into a very angry beast. I fill the empty space left by Elizabeth, and I do the biddings of the emotions. The rules here are different than out there. Out there, everything is final, and I have no control over my actions. If Elizabeth doesn't beat her beast soon, one of us will take her place. In truth, it means she will die in here and eventually, we will die with her."

"Who is 'we'?" AJ asked. "You keep saying 'we.'"

"There is another personality," I pointed out. "Her name is Tia."

Again, lightning struck the spot where Liz stood. Cheryl immediately recognized the new person. We could all feel her heart pounding in her chest. She stood up and grabbed the staff from me, swinging it right at Tia's head. I winced because I could imagine the blow as it connected with its intended target, but it wasn't her head.

Tia caught the staff and brought it under her arm where she held it fast. Cheryl opened her eyes to see that she did not hit what she meant to. AJ and I stood there in shock. AJ had never seen Cheryl act like that, and I almost wanted her to strike the blow as much as Cheryl wanted it.

"Why are you trying to hurt me?" Tia asked in the calm voice that Cheryl remembered belonged to her.

"You ruined my life!" Cheryl screamed at her, but as she said it, emptiness overcame her.

"That is what you feel when the truth is forgotten in this place," she said in the same calm voice.

Uh-oh, AJ thought to herself as she knew what was about to happen. I could hear the thought as if she said it aloud.

For the past five years, Cheryl had blamed everything bad that had happened to her on Tia.

"I showed you only what I needed myself," Tia said. "I gave you what you longed for."

"It was wrong!" Cheryl screamed. "It was wrong and you took advantage of me!" she yelled, looking at the ground.

"You were soon to be held prisoner in this world, too, if I hadn't loved you," Tia said to her. "It wouldn't have been much longer that your unhappiness would have killed you."

Cheryl took in a deep breath. AJ was aghast. She could feel what Cheryl was thinking, too.

"Suicide?" AJ said aloud in disbelief.

Cheryl looked away, but no matter where she looked, AJ's gaze of disbelief was there in front of her.

"The day I met you," Cheryl started, "I was coming to see another psychologist." She cried, "I almost couldn't believe when I spoke to you that you were everything that I needed, everything that I prayed for. I almost got to the point where ending my life seemed to be an easy way out. I know I was wrong, but I couldn't think straight. My head was so full of thoughts that I couldn't ever concentrate. I just wanted it all to stop! AJ, I just wanted it to stop!"

She went on to explain that after she made it through that night, she made herself a promise to get help. "And that's how I came to meet you," she said with tears in her eyes. Only they were tears of happiness, and we could all feel it.

"I have seen these two personalities at different times," I said, "but what about the third one? I've never met her."

"She *is* Elizabeth, and she is in danger," Tia started.

She told us about how the three of them existed in a world where only one of them belonged. "She must be set free from the thing that keeps her here, and she must do it alone, or she will never make it back," Tia stated.

Cheryl looked over at me. *He really is fine!*

At the same time, I felt those thoughts without realizing they came from her. I looked up and saw her staring at me. I knew in my mind that this was a dream, albeit a strange one, a dream nonetheless. I stood up and walked over to her. Then I took my staff from the grasp of both Cheryl and Tia, stared Tia in the eyes, and said, "I don't really know you on the other side, but I do know your other half. When it comes down to it, there may only be three standing in the end. But three may die in the process."

I turned around and kissed Cheryl hard on the lips. Cheryl was stunned, but she welcomed my lips like water on a thirsty day—for Cheryl, a *very* thirsty day.

"There is your love," Tia said to Cheryl, "but that is only in here." She continued, "You will still have to deal with me on the other side."

The wind started to kick up, and it seemed like we were all being pulled apart. I knew it was time to go so I took my staff and walked away. Although I seemed to float away from them, I could see and hear everything like I had only moved above them. Cheryl sat on the ground and lay back so she could go to sleep as she had learned to do in dreams. It was the only way she knew how to wake up. AJ, on the other hand, was not done. Lightning had struck like it had done twice before and left a weakened Elizabeth on the ground in the fetal position. AJ knelt beside her and pulled Elizabeth's hands from her face.

"So this is all about you, huh?" AJ asked.

Elizabeth sat up and crossed her legs.

"I can stop them, but I need time. If I can find the cave this time, I can beat him for good."

"Beat who?"

Elizabeth took both of her hands and placed them in AJ's. Immediately AJ saw the monster, which, to her, was a man. From Elizabeth's eyes, AJ could see what had happened that night her mother left her with Sam. AJ screamed as Elizabeth had when it happened. She could see everything Elizabeth saw, and most of all, she could feel everything Elizabeth felt. AJ snatched her hands away because it became too much to bear.

"I live with that feeling every day," Elizabeth said. "It is what keeps me here. Until I finally beat him for good, I will be lost. This is my last chance. I don't know how long it will take me to find the cave this time, but when I do, I must be prepared."

AJ knew exactly what she meant. Elizabeth had to come to terms with what happened to her and conquer the fear that kept her trapped in this cage like a prisoner.

"Do you believe in God?" AJ asked her.

"God?" Elizabeth repeated. "God will not help me while I am in here," Elizabeth answered.

"But you do believe in Him?" AJ asked again.

"Believe?" Elizabeth repeated again. "You must not understand," she said in disbelief. "In here, you can walk from person to person, from body to body. You can go right up to anyone and merge with them. You can see the things that they see and have seen, and most of all, you can know the things that they know. Haven't you ever sworn that you knew someone you had never met before or seen someplace you had never been before?" she asked AJ.

"Well, yes."

"This is where that all happens," she told AJ. "And God is right here."

AJ thought for a minute. "You're saying He won't help you unless you help yourself, right?" she asked.

"That's exactly what I am saying, but you are ignoring the point. I said God is…"

BOOM! There was a loud clap of thunder, and I couldn't hear what Elizabeth was saying. The sky turned dark once again, and the wind was kicking up. *BOOM!* Another clap of thunder.

Lost in Reality

** AJ **

I was shaken awake by the sound of thunder. Slowly I opened my eyes to the hospital room, and the dull ache returned to my entire body.

"Must be one of those freak summer storms," a voice said from behind the drawn curtain around my bed.

I could feel that I was missing something, but I didn't know what it was. I thought I may have been dreaming, but I could never tell because I was always waking up. That much I knew.

** Cheryl **

Where am I? I feel like I was just in a fight. I can't remember…I need to sleep. I don't even care what's going on. I'm just so tired and drowsy. I…I…

Homecoming

** Jacob **

When we were finally across town, the cabbie woke me up when he reached the familiar gate to my real home. I slept pretty good. I had been dreaming about lions in Africa. *That little rest won't stop me from sleeping when I get in the house, though.*

"Thanks for the ride," I said as I paid the cab driver.

"Anytime for this neighborhood!"

He brought the money that I paid him to his mouth and kissed it in mock triumph. I watched as he drove away into the night.

When the large iron gate closed behind the cab, I turned to open the front door.

This door looks larger than it use to.

I never really noticed how massive the large oak door was. I had very seldom used the front entrance. As a kid, I either came or left from the side of the house where my bike was. I reached into my pocket and realized that I had no keys. I usually opened the door with a remote that was on my key ring. I looked on the wall and saw the familiar keypad that I'd been accustomed to using whenever I had come from around the house without my keys, or when I used to go to the gate to get the newspaper or mail and I let the door close behind me.

*Hmm...*the code for the lock escaped me for a moment.

"Oh, yeah!"

I promptly punched in the code.

"Two bottles of 409 works just fine in troubled times."

I took myself through the rhyme I made up to remember the code. Then I went into the house and closed the door behind me. As I walked through from the end of the entrance way to the foyer, I noticed a faint but familiar smell. I checked my clothes, thinking that it may have been perfume from Elizabeth's mother, but it wasn't. I was sure of the smell, though, and I could just catch traces of it lingering in the air.

I looked around. The house didn't seem to be disturbed. I hadn't been there in quite some time. Elizabeth had kept me so busy in the past few weeks, she had not taken me here. Since I left the hospital, the only time I came here was with Elizabeth. This was actually the first time I had been here alone since then. I was exhausted from the day's events.

"I'm hungry."

I walked through the foyer to the back part of the house and went through the swinging doors of the kitchen.

My mother had taken a traditional checkered, black-and-white motif and spiced it up a bit with a lot of dark woods, stainless steel, and black appliances. I love this kitchen. I didn't cook very often, but I was no stranger to the large kitchen. When I was younger, my mother would steal me from the grasp of mathematics and my dad and use me to help her make dinner. She would cook elaborate meals that I just loved to be a part of. It was from that experience that I'd learned to cook myself. I never really *had* to do it. When I went to college, I just rode right down the street to a friend's and we drove to our homes together. So there were no dorm cook-ins or -outs, for that matter. Just home, and that's the way I liked it.

I looked in the refrigerator, but there was nothing in it that suited my needs.

"I'm too tired to eat anyway."

I walked out of the kitchen and looked around a bit more. There was an eerie silence that bothered me. I reasoned with myself, concluding it was because I was in the house alone. I needed sleep, and I knew it. I felt if I didn't make it upstairs to my bed, I would just have to flop down on the floor and sleep right there on the spot. I walked past the closet that the coat my mother asked me to find still hung in and made my way up the stairs. My legs felt weak, but I wouldn't allow my mind to wander in that direction. I climbed the stairs slowly.

As I got up to the top, I placed my hand on the familiar bust of Beethoven that had been there as long as I could remember. I had always thought of it as a woman with a stone head until I learned about Beethoven's history. Then it became one of my most favorite things in the house. I loved to learn as a child, and that bust reminded me of everything I'd learned about the marble representation of the musical genius. I passed the other bust of Fredrick Douglass and then stopped in my tracks. I saw the poster of Michael Jordan my father got for me at a Bulls game some years back.

The door to my room was open.

There goes that smell again!

Not being able to put a finger on it was frustrating! I moved forward cautiously. I wasn't sure why, but I was spooked. When I reached the doorway, I looked inside and my heart stopped. The sweet smell was coming from a woman! My mind raced. I didn't know whether to stay or run. All I could think about was that there was no way anyone could have known I was coming here. Elizabeth had left long before I did, and she hadn't seen me all day. I knew that she was smart, but even this would have been too much for the genius of my half-sister. I took a deep breath and calmed down a bit. I couldn't tell who she was because she had a hat on and her hair was covering her face.

She had a picture in her hands that I recognized by the frame. It was a picture that my father and I took at an awards banquet a year prior to his passing. I could feel a huge wave of emotion working its way from the pit of my stomach. I fought it as best I could. I leaned against the doorframe and let my face rest on the inside wall. I welcomed the cool texture of the wall surface.

I miss you dad…

A single tear managed its way from the corner of my left eye down my cheek. I quickly wiped it away and the feeling with it.

Focus!

I looked again at the woman asleep on the bed. She had on jeans and a white T-shirt. I moved closer to my king-size bed. My hand was stretched out before me as if I wanted to be as far away as possible in case I had to run. I had no intention of running, but the situation made me very tense, and I wasn't in complete control like I preferred to be. When my hand was but inches from her, I stopped. I looked at the only exposed skin I could see…

"Oh, my God!" I nearly shrieked, but barely managed to keep it to myself. With the little bit of exposed skin I saw, I recognized…

Muscle!

Fear, anticipation, and disappointment all rifled through me at the same time.

It's her!

I realized that maybe she was as smart as I hadn't previously given her credit for.

"Mmm…" she moaned as she moved in her sleep.

I nearly lost my mind. Again, I didn't know which direction I was going in. I managed to stay completely still while my thoughts raced. As the woman on the bed moved, the bill of the hat she was wearing got caught on the picture frame and the hat came off to reveal the face of my half-sister. I could see that she had scratches on one side of her face. I looked at her and felt that she just looked so at peace.

She looks so different!

I had never seen her with what I would call "regular" clothes on. On top of that, she never wore her hair down or even wore hats, for that matter.

I realized that I had been standing in that spot for quite some time, and I needed to move or to do something besides just stand there. My mind must have had enough because before I knew it, I was reaching for her shoulder to shake her gently. At least that was the thought that entered my mind. The moment my hand squeezed Elizabeth's shoulder, her eyes popped open. Her sleep still had most of her, though, because she squinted from the light coming from the hallway.

"J…Jacob?" she murmured.

Her voice was soft and unsure. I was both intrigued and shocked at the same time. The Elizabeth I knew was anything but unsure. As she came to her senses, Elizabeth realized that she was not alone. She quickly scrambled to the furthest corner of the bed where the headboard was.

I was startled but I quickly said, "Wait! I'm not gonna hurt you!"

Elizabeth looked at me in awe. "It really is you!" she said, unable to hide her surprise.

She came out of the protective stance or, for lack of a better explanation, she unraveled herself from the ball she was curled into and stared at me with loving eyes. I was caught in that gaze for what seemed like an eternity. The woman I knew as Elizabeth had never received me like that. My Elizabeth was mean and nasty, and she was very direct and self-assured.

I never realized that the woman I knew as Elizabeth was a puppet with a master named Liz. When she was with me, she referred to herself as Elizabeth and that is who I always knew her as. Liz was as smart as a whip. She knew how to manipulate people, but the woman who sat on the bed before me was not the same one that I knew.

Elizabeth continued to look at me in awe. She had no idea who I was. She looked back at the picture of me and my father—our father. This was a time in my life that I would have been waiting for if I had only known it was possible. I could remember since I was young that if I'd had a brother or sister, my life would have been so different. I never really wanted a sister, but really, any sibling would have done. I had always wished for someone else in my life, and now it seemed she was real.

I returned her stare for a short while because I just didn't know what to say. I felt for a moment that she was scared, but I saw that it was only because she had just awoken. I had never seen her in that state because I made a point to stay on the other side of the house. I never really knew how I'd gotten in that house to begin with, but I did know to stay as far away from her as I could.

"Who are you?" I asked.

I figured I would start slow so that I could gather all of the information from her that I could. She looked at the bed as she went to return an answer.

"I…I'm Elizabeth. Elizabeth Livingston. This is my father." She pointed at the elder Jacob in the picture, still keeping her head down. "And I think, well, I'm sure that you are my brother."

She looked up at me with hope in her eyes that I wouldn't say anything that would contradict her short statements. I smiled at her and at the same time, relaxed, because I realized that this woman had no idea of the ordeal we had been through.

"Your mother, what can you tell me about her?" I asked.

"Well, my mother has been sick for a long time. She has been fighting cancer for months now. I've done what I could to save her, but I don't know how well it has done."

"It?"

"Yes, well, I have been studying not only chemistry, but also cell therapy for a long time as well, and I had been experimenting with several treatments that I thought would work. Even as I'm saying it, I know it sounds kind of strange or even wrong that I would use my mother as a guinea pig for untested drugs and treatments, but I was so sure that the course I was on was right.

"The formula I used basically told the cells that were cancerous to turn off and the healthy cells that replaced them were immune to what was causing the others to mutate. There was even some tissue regeneration. I didn't have time to study the long-term effects because my mother was dying. I don't know if it did any good. I can't even remember if I made it to the hospital to administer the drip that I prepared for her."

"I saw your mother a short time ago."

Elizabeth looked at me with both excitement and disbelief.

"How do you know my mother? Wait! Before you answer that, how is she?" she asked quickly.

"She is getting discharged tomorrow," I smiled.

"Discharged?" she said inquisitively. "How is that possible?" She was stunned.

"Apparently someone was sneaking a cocktail in her IV bag, and it completely cured her of all the cancer that was in her. They are talking about her all over the hospital," I said proudly as I spoke. "I think you did it."

Elizabeth sat there, still in awe as yet more good news permeated her soul. It looked as if the burden of all those years that weighed on her mind lifted, and it made her feel lightheaded. She was overjoyed, but at the same time, she looked concerned.

"I...I can't remember doing it," she said. "I'm just so happy she's okay; I can't believe it!" She reached forward and moved across the bed on her knees.

Elizabeth grabbed me and hugged me with what I would have thought was all her might. I literally couldn't breath. She finally let go when she saw the pain on my face. It was the hug, coupled with the fact that it was so sincere. I could remember the times when she came to see me in the hospital and she would hug me in front of my doctors. The hugs were so fake, and then she would add that little pat on the back that most people know means that it isn't real. This time, however, I felt real joy coming from her. I didn't know if I'd ever felt that before, at least from anyone but my mother.

"Well, it appears that no one saw you do it, no one but your mother, that is," I told her.

Elizabeth looked at me with a worried look on her face. "I didn't hurt you, did I?" she asked.

"No, but you aren't the weakest woman in the world."

She looked down at her body and at her very large arms.

"I have no idea how I got like these." She had a sad look on her face. "I would wake up sometimes and would be in so much pain. Not really bad pain, but just sore all over. Sometimes it was my legs, and sometimes my chest and back. I never could...I was never..."

She couldn't finish what she was saying for fear of saying too much. I had a clear idea that when she was in the gym, she was anyone but who she was sitting before me.

"It's okay!" I said as I grabbed her hand.

I couldn't believe I was doing it, but it just seemed so natural. "I know a thing or two about you, but they can wait, if you don't mind."

"Will you promise to tell me everything you know?"

"I will. But it will be difficult, do you hear me?" I looked her square in the eyes.

I'm sure Elizabeth knew that there was a lot behind the look I gave her. She looked tempted to ask me what I meant, but she didn't. She'll find out in time.

"Back to your mother—she knows a lot about you as well; in fact, she is aware that you are the one who was treating her cancer while the other doctors were merely practicing medicine. She also knows that you have another issue that we will talk about for sure before too long."

My stomach was rumbling. "Are you hungry at all?"

She thought about it and said, "You know, I can't remember the last time I actually ate. Usually I feel so bad, eating is the last thing that I want to do, but now that you have mentioned it, that is all I want to do."

"Good! Let's go see what's in the kitchen."

I pulled on her hand to get her off of the bed. As she stood on the floor, she held onto my hand as I tried to let go.

"You don't mind do you? I have this feeling you are going to slip away if I let go," she said with a hesitant smile. I felt a little awkward, but it was okay. We walked out of my room into the bright hallway, and she pulled at my hand to get my attention.

"You were saying something about issues?" she halfway asked.

"It can wait; for now."

In the back of my mind, I realized that I didn't know how long I would have this opportunity. I've seen her change in front of me once without even knowing who she was. It happened to me when I awoke from my coma. I didn't want to loose this opportunity to find out everything she could tell me. I was convinced, though, that she didn't know much, if anything, about the other two I'd had to deal with.

We moved down the hallway of the house that I grew up in. As we passed by the busts at the top of the stairs, I couldn't help it. I placed my hand on the top of Beethoven's head and rubbed it for good luck, as if it were on stage at the Apollo Theater. Then we moved on down to the kitchen, and I turned the lights on. The décor shone brightly under its luminance. The house had been cleaned up a great deal after Liz and her band of domestic terrorists went through it. There were many things replaced in the house that were either stolen or destroyed. I didn't have anything to do with the restoration, though. It was the insurance company, coupled with the help of some of my mother's friends. I hadn't been to the house in a little while. In fact, I wasn't aware of actually how long it had been. The truth is, Liz had plans to use it for her own purposes, so she had a local grocer deliver a large amount of food that she ordered from them over the Internet. She met the delivery people at the house only a week before to put the food where it belonged. It didn't take long afterwards for the cobwebs that she tore down at the front entrance to get rebuilt. It seems that the little creatures of this world never know when their presence will be tolerated.

"Tell me something," Elizabeth said as we made it to the checkered floor in the kitchen.

"Hmm?" I sort of murmured.

"How long have you known about me? You haven't been surprised a bit at this whole situation. You know, or at least know about, my mother, and you say you know things about me that give hints that they are things I am not aware of. So...how long have you known about me?" The look on her face was intense.

I pulled my hand away from her gently, partly because it was getting sweaty and also because I needed to exercise one of the many nervous reactions that I had catalogued that many people in the world do. I immediately scratched the back of my head right behind my ear and then placed a balled up hand in front of my mouth, pressing my lips against my thumb and index finger.

"Hmmm."

I wasn't quite sure I knew how to answer that question. As I thought about the answer, Elizabeth pressed on.

"How long, Jacob?" she said, placing a hand on my shoulder.

I looked at her and said, "C'mon" as I led her to the dining room to have a seat. I was really tired and didn't have the energy to start playing any kind of game with her. As I had thought before, I didn't know how long I had her to myself, so I knew I needed to get a lot out of her and get back as much from her as I possibly could.

I had a theory about people with multiple personalities. I felt that one only existed because of something that the other wouldn't do. I realized that one of the first things I needed to do was get to the bottom of why she had the problem to begin with. I understood the trauma that could have caused it, but it was everything else that made the change I needed to understand. I didn't know how long I had left to do it, but I knew it had to be done. The woman trailing behind me that may have killed my parents was a good-natured (buff, mind you), beautiful person it seemed, but she had a wicked secret hiding within her.

"Sit down."

I pulled out a chair for her. She sat and I took a seat opposite her at the corner of the table.

"I don't really know where to start, but to answer your question, I have known *you* since the time you woke up with me looking at you."

She looked at me with confusion as I'd expected. I squirmed in my chair, moving closer, and then backing up as I had gotten too close and was almost on top of her. This time, the nervous reaction I chose was to rub my hand back and forth on the top of my head, while looking at the ground. I recovered quickly, a little disturbed and disappointed in myself for not being more "Jacob-like" in this endeavor. You know, like in control.

Elizabeth waited, not really patiently, but for lack of anything real to say, she just kept quiet and looked at me, expecting my answer.

"I met Elizabeth the day I awoke in the hospital from a coma." I didn't know if I was prepared to go the distance with my explanation, but I was determined to try.

"You were in a coma?" she asked, although the look on her face showed she felt she could have kept that question to herself since I had just stated the answer.

"It's a long story; I was in a coma for six weeks following a…um…a…well, for lack of any better thing to say, my family was attacked in this house and…and…"

My eyes began to well up. I hadn't cried in a long time, and I wasn't about to now. But the thought of explaining what happened again was a tough proposition. I took a deep breath and sniffed back the obligatory running nose one gets whenever tears are present. Elizabeth took both of my hands in hers, but she didn't realize that *she* could not console me. I looked her in the eyes and continued as I reminded myself that the question was about her.

"I was here when it happened and was hurt during what the police called a robbery by a well trained gang. I never saw them." I continued slowly. "I was in a closet where, somehow, I suffered a head injury. I believe you were there, too, but I don't know that for sure."

I paused for a second to see her reaction. Judging from the looks of it, I felt that she was feeling fear for what happened to me. It looked as if she was dreading what almost could have happened to her, as if she was almost a victim as well.

From the neutral look on my face, Elizabeth could not draw any conclusion as to what I meant, but she held back the urge to ask how we (as in she and I) got out alive. I calmed myself and continued.

"I lost my mother and father that day, which was roughly two years ago. When I woke up in the hospital, the first thing…"

I stopped for a moment because that was exactly what I meant, but I didn't want to refer to this Elizabeth as a "thing" because she, at least, appeared to be far from that person of whom I was referring.

"The first person I saw was…" I swallowed hard as I spoke. "It was Elizabeth," I said finally, leaving enough out there so that she had to ask further questions, giving me time to calm myself.

Like clockwork, Elizabeth looked directly at me.

"Another Elizabeth?"

"Yes," I answered.

Elizabeth thought about it for a minute and smiled. "I have a twin!"

I'm guessing she felt that would have answered for her the major questions she had.

"Not exactly…"

I spoke up loud enough to take away some of her enthusiasm.

"Well, then, who was she *exactly?*" Elizabeth asked.

"Well, she was you," I answered as I prepared to respond to her questions more fully.

"So why did you refer to her as if she were someone other than me?" her tone became serious.

"Okay, here goes," I said as I rubbed my hands together. Yet a third nervous reaction, and I hadn't been seated ten minutes yet. I hadn't used that many reactions in ten years.

"The person I awoke to in that hospital was you…physically," I started. "But you can't tell me that you were there, can you?" I asked.

"I wasn't there," she answered defiantly.

"And you can't tell me why you're built like a tank either, can you?" I asked.

"I already answered that question—no," she answered a little frustrated as the look on her face turned to a worried one.

"What else can't you remember?" I said as I craftily handed off the baton to her.

Elizabeth reflected on the question and was almost in tears. She picked her head up from the shameful position it was in and looked at me as she spoke. "Sometimes, I wake up in places I have no business being in. I am wearing clothes that I would never normally wear; and although I have no evidence of it, I have felt I have done things I couldn't possibly speak about. I could never hurt another person—I know it! At least, I know I could never do it knowingly." She stopped all of a sudden in horrid surprise.

She started shaking as she was trying to hold back tears that were forcing their way through the ducts for which they were made. I thought for a second that she was changing, so I scooted closer to her and placed her head on my chest. I felt I had to keep her calm in case something we talked about triggered the change in her.

"You said I was there!" Elizabeth said as she moved back to look at me. "What did you mean, 'I was there'?" she said in tears.

By now, she was almost hysterical, and I was mentally planning on an escape. If she were to change right before me, I would have to transform into the Jacob that she knew. I was used to acting the part out now, but it wasn't completely an act when I was doing it. I really did feel less than whole before when I was doing it, but now, I didn't know how convincing I would be, having interacted with people as normally as I had been lately.

"Calm down," I said to her, reaching for her hand.

Elizabeth pulled away from me completely. She wanted an answer. I was troubled. As Liz, I could easily (but carefully) berate this woman and let her know my absolute hate for her. It would be easy for me to release all of my frustration on her. But I knew that she knew nothing of the things that Liz did. The thought had crossed my mind that she may have been acting the innocent Elizabeth role. I took a step out on faith that she was a victim herself, and for at least now, she needed help.

"What did you mean?" she shouted. She didn't want to know what I couldn't even tell her.

"Okay!" I said to calm her, and it worked because her mouth shut and her eyes were planted on me as she awaited my answer.

"I was knocked out, either by the closet door or a trunk on the closet floor that day. But I came to and when I did, I heard a voice." I paused.

"A voice?" she echoed a little calmer.

Damn, gee! You took that mothafucka's head clean off! I see you got the bitch, too. All right, take everything you can find. There ain't nothing in this house that don't cost a lot. What you can't take, tear the shit out of. It played over in my mind like a bad recording.

"A voice," I continued. "It was the voice of a woman, a woman I have come to know as Liz."

"Liz, as in Elizabeth," she stated.

"Yes."

"And what did she say?" she pressed.

"She was barking orders to the rest of the people, or thugs, whatever they were, telling them to take everything in the house. She also made a reference to what one of them did to my mother…" I sobbed. "An…and my father!"

"And this woman was…"

"You!" I interrupted in tears.

I got up and turned my back to her. "It was you," I said more calmly.

** Elizabeth **

I was broken at this point. Although I knew it was possible he would say something that would shock me, I had no idea of what it was he was going to say and what it would do to me once he said it. I completely lost it. I got up and ran out of the kitchen. I had no idea where I was going, but I wound up in a guest bathroom on the bottom floor. I couldn't control the tears or the jerking sobs that wracked my body.

I switched the light on and turned on the water in the sink. Then I just cried with my face in the sink and my hands covering my eyes. My hair was getting soaked. As I sobbed openly, my tears were lost in the rushing water. I looked up at myself. I could barely see as my hair was in my eyes and it was dripping all over me. I grabbed a hand towel off of the wall and began to dry my face and hair. I put my hands on my head and then on the wall, like I felt dizzy. I had a terrible headache! I turned the water off and dabbed my shirt the best I could.

Behind the mirror was a medicine cabinet. I opened it and found a single bottle that had two words written on it: "for headaches." I thought it was odd that the handwriting looked like mine. At the moment, I didn't care to ask any questions and, for the time being, it seemed that a bottle with "for headaches" written on it was a godsend, so I opened it up and took two of whatever was in it. Next, I sat down on the closed lid of the toilet and held my head as the pain got worse.

"Ahhh!"

I reached for the lock on the door. I didn't want anyone to see me like this. I had no idea what was happening to me. I could barely see. I thought it was my wet hair matted to my face, but when I went to reach for it, I couldn't feel my hands move. I was fading…

Oh, God! Not again…

The Underworld

I woke up on the cold ground, wondering what was about to happen. I knew where I was immediately when my head lifted up to look around.

This is it!

I knew that this could be my last chance to finally defeat the creature that held me here in this world. I looked around. The gloomy purple sky mocked me with streaks of brightly lined, sinister-looking clouds that were as dark and purple as everything else around me.

"I have to do this!"

I was trying to motivate myself to get up and do what I knew had to be done. Previously when I had gone through this, there was always a big maze to follow. In the beginning, I used to walk around aimlessly until I either fell into the lair of the creature that haunted me or I would be snatched and would find myself face-to-face with it. I never looked it in the eyes, however; I was always much too scared. Instead, I would cower or run as fast as this place would let me. Sometimes, I would try to run, but something inside this place wouldn't let me. It felt like I was being pulled backward, like I had some invisible force holding onto me and all the while making my legs feel weaker.

There were times in more recent visits to this place where I didn't do so badly. I would sometimes get in several blows that appeared to inflict pain. There were other times when I would find a weapon, and I was able to strike it in the head, allowing me to get away. Each time I decided to fight this monster, I gained a little piece of myself back. I had no idea how long I had been fighting it, but I had fought it enough times to know that one day, I would beat it. As soon as I beat it, I was sure I'd be free forever.

I'm still scared to death of this place. It's a part of me. I know the feelings that it evokes in me well. I know that it is a place that I created. I stood to my feet and tried to brush my clothes off. While patting myself down to get the dirt off, I realized that I wasn't wearing anything normal. I ran my hands up and down the body suit that I was wearing. It seemed to be made of some kind of rubber. I was amazed at the texture of the suit. I couldn't feel anything underneath the suit.

Wow, body armor!

This made me feel a lot more confident. Now I was beginning to think that I had some help. There was a warm, comforting feeling rising from my stomach that spread throughout my body. I yawned and stretched out my arms with my elbows pointing out on either side of me. Then I moved my head from side to side, letting the satisfying crack of the bones in my neck sound off, signifying my defiance to the fear that I once felt. After that, I squinted my eyes and slowly nodded my head.

"It's time…It's time for me to get my life back! I'm so tired of being alone and of being scared. I've had enough! I'm not running anymore!"

I was slowly becoming enraged at the fact that my life was being run by two "people," my creations because of my cowardice.

"Where are you?" I screamed aloud. "Show yourself!"

There was no answer, only the echo of my voice carrying through the twisted landscape.

"So, it's like that, huh?"

I stepped off on a journey that I would most likely never forget. The ground seemed to give in an odd way when I walked. The harder I stepped, the more it seemed to reach out and meet my feet before they should have met the ground beneath them. After what seemed like a few minutes, I looked back to see that I was moving uphill. I could see the trail that I was leaving, and it lagged way behind me, as if I had been walking for hours in a desolate, desert terrain. I could see my steps for miles behind me.

I didn't have time to worry about this frivolous detail so I moved on, determined to get to wherever this was going to take me. I looked up ahead and saw a group of rocks.

My legs feel a bit worn-out.

I headed in the direction of the rocks in order to sit down for a minute. The rocks were pretty large, and I couldn't see behind them. As I walked up to them and reached the other side, I could not believe my eyes.

"Hey, sister!" a woman spoke.

I was stunned for a second. Standing before me were both Liz and Tia. They looked as if they were just working out, and they were pumped up, as if it were competition day.

I was never really sure about these two. I didn't really know them like they knew me. All I knew was that on occasion, I would dream about the adventures that they would take my body through. I didn't fear them, but I knew that there was something very wrong about them both as they stood before me. I looked at them, marveling at their size. I then looked down at myself and realized that I looked the same as my two "sisters." I had seen it once before in the mirror in my bedroom. I found it amazing how I could have gone so long without realizing the workouts I was "put" through.

Looking back at Tia and Liz, I could remember talking with them before. My memory was vague, but I knew that there had been a confrontation between us. They didn't seem as if they were ready for any kind of fight at the moment, though, and I felt at ease standing there with them.

I just stood there for a minute and took it all in. Tia decided that she would break the silence of the awkward moment and put my mind at ease.

"You've come a long way."

She reached out and gave me a warm hug. The feeling was amazing! I couldn't understand it, but when Tia put her arms around me, I felt almost "whole." It was like a piece of me that had been missing my whole life was just added.

The embrace didn't last long, but I wished it would have lasted forever. I understood now that these two were a part of me, and that they were separated for some reason. I remembered thinking that it was the hate that I had for Jacob's father for what he did to Mamma. There was something else, though. I barely remembered the letter that I found in Mamma's closet. I didn't know if I was in control at the time.

I never get that angry.

"That's because it's my job to hate," Liz finally broke in.

I was a bit startled by her voice. It was so rich and very powerful. Although the three of us resembled each other, there were considerable differences between us that were very noticeable. The way I saw Liz was much different than the impression that I was feeling. I was scared of her because to me, she signified a lack of control. I understood now that Liz was born out of anger. She was born from anger that ultimately placed me in the predicament that I'm in now. I figured that I had to be cautious when dealing with her because I could never predict what she would do.

Liz walked up to me, and I took a step back. I wasn't going to let her intimidate me, but I was cautious at the same time. I looked her right in the eyes while saying absolutely nothing. Liz held out her hand in a gesture for me to take it in her own. As she did it, Tia stepped forward and took Liz's other hand and reached for me also. I wasn't sure what was going on, but I trusted Tia and followed suit, taking both of their hands in mine.

As our fingers tightened around each other's hands, I felt a very powerful emotional surge, like I was an empty one-gallon milk jug and was being filled with cool, refreshing water on a hot summer day. The feeling was empowering and as it surged through my body, it gave me purpose, compassion, confidence, and a feeling of tenacity that I had never felt before.

I felt Liz's hand tighten around mine, to the point where it was becoming uncomfortable. With this new feeling that I felt, I instinctively squeezed harder to counteract the pain that she was causing me. I was only partially coherent while I was going through this process, but I was slowly beginning to focus as the water jug filled to the top. Tia let go of my hand and Liz's as well. Suddenly, I realized that I was locked in a struggle with Liz. Liz relaxed her grip momentarily so she could change grips altogether. Before I realized it, I was standing in front of the group of rocks with my hands locked tight in a sort of unsupported arm wrestling match.

I looked at Liz with contempt, while at the same time she looked at me with wondering eyes.

She's sizing me up.

Liz continued to stare me in the face. Her eyes gleamed and there was a partial smile on her face. She pulled harder while I pulled as well. The muscles on both of us were bulging under the strain they were being put under.

"You're gonna need that attitude!" Liz finally spoke.

I still wasn't sure of her motives. I just kept staring at her, amazed at her likeness. I decided that I liked the way that Liz looked. It was striking. To me, it signified power and strength. I wasn't afraid anymore. I was just beginning to believe that Liz was there to help me, until all of a sudden, Liz lunged and threw me to the ground. I was both stunned and amazed at the quickness in which I wound up on my back.

"You have a weakness! I despise weakness, and when you don't return because the bad man beats you for the last time, I will be here to take your place."

I was convinced that I had to kill the thing that haunted me for so many years. I got up from the ground and just as I got to my feet, Liz came at me again, only this time, I was ready. As she came forward, I reached out and grabbed her by her straining neck. I could tell immediately that she was not going down easily. Liz reached out before I could straighten my arm out completely and grabbed ahold of my neck as well. Once again, we were at a battle stance, staring at each other. I had no idea that I was that fast, but Liz was faster.

"You heard what I said!" Then she removed her hand from my neck and slapped my arm down, making me release the hold I had on her.

Liz backed up and turned around. She then jumped up on top of one of the shorter rocks and sat down, almost posing. Not only could I see the strength and attitude in her face, but in her body as well.

"Let's take a walk," Tia spoke softly, taking my hand and pulling me forward.

Very little conversation had passed between the three of us since I first encountered them on the rocks. I sort of just felt my way through the situation, believing that there was really nothing to be said by me. I didn't want to show any emotion at all by allowing the other two to know how I felt about them through my speech.

"I don't completely understand what is going on," I said calmly.

"She's testing you," Tia said. "You must be aware of your strengths and weaknesses; you have been kept here for a long time. It is not hard to forget who you really are. You have lived in this place away from others much too long. You are in a dangerous situation. If you lose, you could be stuck here forever. Liz and I are not supposed to be. Liz, you and I are supposed to be one. There are rules here that govern what we can and can't do. You are not subject to those rules because you do not belong here. This is a place of learning; it is a place of growth. You come here to solidify the thoughts of your mind and to dream the next steps in your life. You have been stuck in the same time here for years. This place will eventually change you so that you will not be allowed to go back."

As Tia spoke, I listened very carefully. I understood now that turning into myself and shutting out the rest of the world had put me here. I know I needed to leave this place of dreams and nightmares where I have been living for most of my life. Up until now, I lacked the strength I needed to not only assure myself that I could regain control of my life, but also the strength to kill the thing that has kept me here for so long.

"You will be in for the battle for you life," Tia said as she finished explaining to me my current situation.

She then explained that the people that I was dealing with on the other side were bonded in a special way. Furthermore, that only once in thousands of years did such a bond occur. I was not aware of the similarities between me and my half-brother. Nor was I aware of the connection between Cheryl, AJ, and her twin brother.

All of us were born on the same day in the same hour and nearly the same minute. AJ was born seven minutes after her brother, and I was born nearly two minutes before her. Cheryl was born only a few seconds after me and nearly took her first breath at the same exact time as Jacob. In this world, we were all winds flowing effortlessly as one part of the same jet stream of consciousness. Fate brought us together in the world of the living for us to continue the harmony that once only existed in this underworld.

Tia said that everyone has a soul mate in the world of the living. This world would have one know, however, that all souls are mated in one way or another. As they pass through the individual consciousness of each other, they trade the secrets of the world as they discover the vast treasures of knowledge in their journeys. The soul is the key to all of our existence. It is fed by forces known only by God himself. Each of us has a journey to make in the world of the living. Each of our souls are prepared with the questions that elude us for the answers that stand before us. They taunt us in our everyday quest for absolution. We have a responsibility to the living world, and when we leave it for our own purposes, the consequences will only be that of difficulty and hardship in coping with those who continue to flow in the mix of company.

We continued to walk and I was having difficulty with the concept of "enjoying" the serenity of a good ole stroll and conversation. I did feel pretty good, though, despite the problems I was having with it. I asked a lot of questions about how Tia and Liz came to be. The answers all seemed to be tied into the fact that I just stopped living. I had no friends. The only people I had ever interacted with were my professors and the people behind the counter in my labs from whom I had to sign out equipment.

I was sad about the way my life turned out; however, Tia explained to me that my life was not over, and that I had a lot of life left to experience. She cautioned me also that if I were to continue on the path that I had been on, that I wouldn't make it.

"This is as far as I go," Tia said. She stopped just before a bend in the path that we were walking on.

"How do I know what to do?" I asked.

"Just follow your heart. It will always tell you the truth."

I hated answers like that. There were times when I felt my mother was following her heart, and it led to nothing but heartache and pain for her. Since I've been in this place, I realized that you have to differentiate your wants from your needs. Your heart will tell you what it needs, but it leaves much to interpret as it gives you no directions on how to get it. It is all a part of this life we live and how things come together in such a spastic way. One plus one may equal two, but there are an infinite number of ways to get to that same number.

I've learned that the trick is to stick to the facts, as you know them, and the decisions you make will be the best for you, given the circumstances you are in.

I said my goodbyes to Tia. She left me with the notion that when we saw each other again, we would be much closer. I was also left with the impression that if I failed, I would be cursed to live in this lonely place forever.

I continued my journey up the path, thinking about the life that I never lived. I wondered how I could have let all of this happen to me. I didn't feel that it was entirely my fault. There had to be some things I had no real control over. As smart as I was, I just couldn't figure out how I had let my life slip away from my control. I did have one consolation, however, and that was my determination to set it all back straight.

I continued to walk and think to myself and ahead, I saw what appeared to be two people in the distance. I quickened my steps, thinking that there were potential answers ahead. As I drew nearer, I could see that it was a middle-aged man and a woman, both about the same age. They had a distinguished look about them. I was clueless about who they were, and as I came up, they seemed to smile at each other and just gaze in one another's eyes.

"It's good to finally see you," the gentleman spoke.

I didn't know what to say. I figured he may have meant that he was trying to look and see who I was from a distance.

"Who are you?" I asked.

Right when I finished the question, I had an almost blinding flashback that took me back to Jacob's room. I remembered that there were two of them. There were two Jacobs—Big Jacob and Jacob the son. I felt slightly dizzy as the thoughts of my mother's letters and all of the emotion I felt overwhelmed me. I couldn't bring myself to a point where I could hold onto any one emotion. They just shot through my body as if to remind me only briefly of a past moment in time.

I thought of Mamma and how sick she was. I also remembered that I could not have done for Mamma what I did had it not been for this man. This was why I hated him so much. I could not stand the fact that the man whom I felt was responsible for Mamma's condition actually helped me take care of her.

I looked at the man as he stared at the woman in his arms. His stare then shifted to me. I looked at him and realized that his eyes were very kind. There was an overwhelming sad feeling rising from within me. It was taking over my entire body.

I'm so tired of these changes!

Everything around me seemed to dim, and I felt sick.

I could see the man and woman release each other from their embrace from beneath my squinting eyes. The wind picked up and was now swirling around me, blowing dust everywhere. Suddenly there was a very large *BANG!* I saw the woman fly backward, as if she were pulled by something violently from behind her. The wind continued to swirl around me as I raised my arm up to my forehead in an effort to block the flying dust from the path of my vision. The man, still standing there, was unaffected by the huge gusts. He stood there with a look of sadness on his face. I reached out for him as I thought I would, at any moment, be blown away by the wind. He reached out with both hands, and as his hands touched mine, the gusts of wind abruptly disappeared. Sunlight washed over everything around us. I looked into the eyes of the man and could see tears forming beneath his warm, brown gaze.

I felt ashamed. I remembered something that brought goose bumps to my skin.

"You are my father," I whispered aloud. "And you are Jacob's father, too!"

Mr. Livingston smiled and hugged me.

"I am truly sorry for the way things turned out."

I needed to hear that, but it wasn't going to be enough to fix all the pain I felt all of those years.

"You nearly killed my mother!"

"How is that so?" he asked with a look of surprise on his face.

"She was so sick from the way you treated her that she developed cancer," I spouted.

"That is simply not true," he frowned. "Your mother had a fight with cancer before you were born; in fact, she had it even before she started school. She had a partial scholarship from the Cancer Research Foundation for recovering cancer patients. It was there long before me."

I felt a crushing blow to my stomach.

"It's not true…" I said weakly.

But it was. I saw in my mind Mamma with short hair coming home from the hospital with friends. I could see scenes of her smiling first in a bed, and then outside in a park. I saw a young Mamma at a banquet, where she was being presented with a check to further her education. I saw Mamma working at a bar to help pay the rest of her bills while she was in school.

I felt really sick now. I was so driven by the thought that my father made Mamma so sick. I could feel the hate that I had felt then rushing though me. The feeling became stronger, and I pushed away from him. The second he let go, the winds returned with a vengeance. I could barely make his face out as his mouth made the words, "I'm sorry." Then there was an even louder explosion than before and I saw his head disappear in a flash and his body fall limp to the ground.

"Noooo!" I cried out.

Tears streamed down my face as I fell to my knees. I saw the bodies of my father and his beloved wife picked up in a whirlwind and carried off into the distance of a purple sky. As they faded into the horizon, the wind faded with them. I lay there, crying uncontrollably from what I saw. I didn't understand completely, but the sight of a man's head exploding after he made me realize that my whole life I was perpetuating an angry lie was way too much for me. I cried hard while lying on the ground. I called out for my Mamma. I couldn't take it anymore. All I could think about was Jacob and the stories he told me and the things that I saw in the house that just didn't make sense. I gripped my stomach as the jerking sobs riffled through me. I couldn't feel much of anything through the material of the suit that I was wearing, and that made me feel in even less control.

The pain of my life seemed to just take over my body. I was racked with fear, loneliness, and the pain of my recollection. Suddenly, I felt the ground give beneath me. My condition worsened to the point where I barely noticed the ground move, until in one shake of the earth, the only thing above ground was my head and arms. I screamed again with everything I had, and with the sound of my shrieking voice, the ground swallowed me whole, silencing what became a wail in the distance of the world I was trapped in.

One of Many

** Jacob **

I sat in the kitchen, knowing that I didn't have long until Elizabeth came back. I heard the screams from the guest bathroom in the front as I had heard many times before. I never knew who would show up after it was over. I guessed that Liz was around most of the time because of her demeanor. Liz was always mean to me, always putting me down. Tia, on the other hand, was always nice and cordial. Needless to say, she wasn't around much.

I realize now that sometimes, there was probably a mix of the three, but none of them was in any kind of control. I figured that the one piece that was missing was the reason that the real Elizabeth did not know who I was. Until I had awaken her on my bed earlier, I had never spoken to her before nor had she ever spoken to me. This was another one of those things that I would have to take time afterwards to figure out.

I have to get back and see her mother.

I was worn out, but this wasn't the time to sleep. My body didn't agree, though, because I was slowly but surely losing strength in my neck as my head flopped back and forth. It was late, and I couldn't hold on. It was against my better judgment, but I moved toward the stairwell in the front of the house. As I climbed the stairs, I looked back at the door to the bathroom where Elizabeth had entered. I could see the light from under the door, but there wasn't any movement. Deep down, I wondered if she was okay. The thought would have to wait, however, because I was barely coherent as I placed my hand on top of old Beethoven's head to balance myself. I made my way to my room and thought that I shouldn't go to sleep. Again, however, my body had other plans in mind as I placed a knee on the bed to boost myself up on the raised California king sleeper. By the time my head hit the pillow, I was already gone to the world of the living. Tomorrow was a new day. Only God, Himself, knew what I would have to deal with. For now, sleep was the only thing that was important.

* * *

I dreamt of rain. It came down harder and harder upon me as I stood on an empty city street. Looking around, I was barely able to see anything resembling some kind of shelter. Then I saw a woman standing beneath an awning across the street. So I headed toward her, and as I did, she walked into the building she stood in front of.

Sometimes I hated the rain. It got in between my neck and my clothes and ran down my back, making me shiver. I was miserable and needed to get out of the pouring rain. As I got to the awning, I took cover and turned to see where I had come from. The street was turned into a vast river by the rushing water. The rain fell harder, but I stood protected for now since the awning served as my umbrella.

"What does this mean?"

I could see trash and property floating down the street in the rushing stream. I saw a newspaper dispenser floating on its side. It bobbed up and down as it went by me. I read the headline very clearly as it passed:

MAN AND WOMAN FOUND MURDERED IN HOME; NO SUSPECTS FOUND.

My stomach began to turn. *I have to deal with this.*

I never really had the chance to deal with my parents' death. The trauma of the events I was going through began to take precedence in my mind. I am a very strong person mentally. My mind knew how to protect itself, though, so I was not always in complete control of everything I went through. It seemed that subtly, my mind was trying to bring me back into the present. I took a break from reality for a long time. It wasn't as drastic as the complete separation of my half-sister, but I did live in a world that was very confusing to me. I was as obedient as a puppy and as playful, too. Elizabeth had me wrapped around her finger with the regimen of drugs she gave me. I had no choice but to follow her lead in my condition.

Ever since the day Elizabeth left town to get some hardware for a job her crew was going to do and she left me the wrong medication, I started on the road to a complete recovery. I had still not been given ample time to realize what I'd been through, and now my mind would "wake" me in my sleep to start the mourning process that I suppose will strengthen me for my new life to come.

I turned my head and reflected for a moment. I could still feel the pain that I felt that day when my parents were murdered. I stood strong, however, realizing that it was two years ago. I really missed my mother and father, but I felt I was here for a different reason. I turned the rest of my body toward the doors of the building with the intent to find the woman I saw from across the street. I reached out for the handle of the glass door and pulled on it. The door gave and as it opened, I was washed with a bright light. I moved forward and stepped inside to a large, brightly lit lobby, where I could see that I was in some type of office building. However, I didn't recognize anything around me.

I continued to walk and saw a large water fountain in the center of the lobby. The rushing water was loud, but the sound was very soothing. I walked toward it and when I got there, I sat on the edge and looked into the water. I could see my reflection clearly, but it was strange. The reflection was mirror-like, as if I were looking at a sheet of glass. The water moved in an odd way. I got up while keeping an eye on the spot where my reflection was. As I moved further back, my reflection became more and more real. I was soon looking at myself face to face.

Now, I had never had a dream where I'd seen myself with the ability to interact. It was too strange for me, so I tried a trick that usually worked when I was dreaming. I closed my eyes and imagined myself being somewhere else. I confidently opened my eyes again and was shocked to see that I was still in the same place, looking at what appeared to be myself.

"Not this time," he laughed.

"What's the deal?" I asked.

"You're in pretty deep."

I wasn't sure what he was talking about. He could have meant deep as in this dream, or deep as in I was the proverbial fox and I was looking at the front end of a farmer's shotgun. Like he was saying that I was caught deep in the hen house. Either way, the other me's tone signified that I was in trouble.

"Come on," the new Jacob said to me as he turned to walk toward the rear of the lobby.

I never planned on there being a Jacob IV…

I was amazed. I had been used to being in control of my dreams for so long that I was happy to "follow" some directions for once. Dreams, for me, had always been nighttime entertainment. I was always in total control. Sometimes I would revisit the events of the day and actually change things I did to see if the outcomes were more favorable. There were other times when I would just have the whole world at my fingertips, and I would fly around and enjoy it for as long as it lasted. I'd had affairs, I drove futuristic cars, and I'd been to other planets and visited other civilizations.

My dreams were the best thing in life to me. I couldn't get enough of them. Just like most other people, though, I usually couldn't remember what I dreamed about once I woke. I tried to keep a dream book by my bed, but for the most part, I would be able to retain an idea or a solution to a problem, but not the details that brought about that solution. Somehow those details were always lost in the cloudiness of the trip back to consciousness.

I followed the other me to the back and could see that we were headed for a group of elevators. As the other Jacob neared the first of them, the door opened and he walked in. I followed obediently, just waiting to see what would happen. I noticed that the elevators were the same as the ones in the hospital.

"Don't get ahead of yourself," he scoffed.

I understood what he meant as soon as he said it. I figured that this other "me" was two steps ahead of my every thought. I was thinking that we were going upstairs to the cancer ward of UCLA Med. Apparently, that wasn't the case. Wherever we were going was to be a complete mystery to me. So I decided to take it all with a grain of salt and enjoy the trip.

The new Jacob leaned against the back door of the elevator and looked at me. "Hmmm," he sort of mumbled. "Not much going on up in that noggin of yours, huh? I've always liked that about us—we are always quick to figure out a situation."

"Us?" I looked back at him, sizing him up.

"Yeah, us," he repeated. "Give me a good guess. How many Jacobs do you think there are down here?"

"*Down here*?" I was looking for some kind of confirmation as to just what or where "down" and "here" was.

"Always on the job, huh?" he laughed. "Yeah, just where is down here? We have been here enough times, you should know. As a matter of fact, we spent a great deal of time down here after our skull got cracked, but you were separated from us at the time. Something about a really naked girl with really big eyes frolicking in a field of brilliant colors had your particular attention. There is another part of you that knows her quite well," he snickered. "Only her dreams would reveal how nasty you can really be." He was laughing harder now.

Wow…What do I say to that? I can't mess with this guy.

I was truly embarrassed. I could imagine that if all of the different aspects of me were down here, I'd hate to admit what part of me was doing with her.

"It's okay, tough guy," the other Jacob taunted. "There was another part of you that wanted to hand her a slide rule, but she wasn't having it. She wanted to slide with a different rule." He was bent almost completely over from laughing.

He gained his composure quickly and slammed his hand against the emergency stop button on the wall. The elevator came to a sudden, screeching halt. I had to hold onto the rail on the wall in order to keep from falling.

"But seriously now, folks."

It took me a minute, but I realized that this was the cynical side of me I was talking to.

"Back to the question at hand." The dead quiet of the elevator echoed his voice in my ears. "How many?" he quizzed.

I thought for a minute. I figured I had at least one personality for every mood I could ever be in. He looked at me and just started laughing hard and uncontrollably. It was difficult for me not to be irritated by his actions, but he tried really hard to concentrate on the question. I gave up and just threw a number out there. "Ten."

I couldn't have been any more unsure about the answer. I had to just stand there with a hopeful look on my face. He looked at me and his face lit up like a Christmas tree. He then went into complete hysterics. He had to hold his stomach with both arms wrapped around himself, as if his insides were going to burst out of his clothing. I was getting very frustrated as the other me actively hopped up and down, using every bit of space he could in the elevator, sometimes stepping on and bumping into me.

I had no idea what part of me this was. I wished I *could* laugh that much at anything. I didn't have much of a sense of humor, at least none that I would share with anyone else. All I had was my cynicism, which I kept to myself most of the time as part of the private joke collection I had about the world. I could imagine, though, that if the world knew what I was thinking, sometimes they would feel about like I did at the moment—left out and the butt of the joke.

The other me just kept on laughing as he pulled the emergency stop button back out. The elevator did not continue to move. I didn't know if we were going up or down to begin with, but there was a soft *ding* that elevators sometime have and the door opened behind the now calmed down, me look-alike.

From the vantage point I had at the front of the elevator, I could tell that there was no hall that this door led to.

"Come on," he said, very excited. "Take a look." He looked as if he were fighting back another fit of laughter.

I didn't think I could take anymore of that, so I stepped forward and looked down into what appeared to be a valley with a wide-open space in the middle. A few hundred people appeared to be gathered in what looked to me like an all-grassy area.

"Here; have a better look."

He pushed me out of the elevator. His hands were cold against my back, which was still wet from the rain. I was scared to death because I wasn't expecting anything so drastic coming from the other me. I fell for what seemed like forever and quickly discovered that I had none of the controls that I was accustomed to having in my dreams, namely, the ability to fly. The ground came rushing up before me, and I landed hard. I was both scared and confused. This was too real for me. I felt pain as I lay there in the deep green grass.

I had to lie there for a moment as the pain took its time to subside. I managed to get to my knees and from that position, I could see the large gathering just up ahead about a hundred or so yards. Somehow, I managed to get to my feet and as I did, the sun became very bright all at once. I felt like I did when I first walked into the building out of the rain, being washed with light. As the light passed, there was an accompanying dryness that affected the once-wet clothes I was wearing.

"Ah ha! Wash and wear, huh?"

I whirled around to find my pusher standing there with a broad smile on his face.

"Hurt, didn't it?"

I was furious. I thought if I knew how, I'd beat the crap out of this character. I wasn't a fighter, though. I avoided physical confrontation like the plague. I would have dreams sometimes when I would have to fight and my hands wouldn't move or I would move in slow motion, rendering my ass kicked if the dream lasted long enough. I always felt out of control in situations like that.

Very few times in my youth could I overcome the disabling feeling I got whenever I tried to fight someone in my dreams. It wasn't until I got older that I would turn myself into things that could do the fighting for me, and I would use my attitude to help me win. Not too long ago, I had a dream where I faced a lion that was pretty big! By the time I was done, I was a bigger lion with not much to worry about.

This situation didn't present that opportunity for me, so I simply did my best to calm down before I wound up feeling more pain at the hands of my alter-self. The other Jacob just looked at me and brushed by me as he began to walk toward the crowd. I obediently followed his lead. The pain that I felt from that fall was belittling. I did not want to feel anything like that again.

We trampled through high grass, one behind the other. I was bringing up the rear until we got to much lower blades, where we walked comfortably, me as comfortably as I could until we were only a few yards away.

"How many?" he said as he stopped and turned to speak to me.

At this point, I had been walking with my head down, sort of looking at the feet of the other me as he walked. Then I looked up, and my jaw dropped. I gasped aloud.

"Good Lord!"

I opened my mouth to speak, but I had to take a hard swallow first, like I was about to give my first speech at sixth-grade graduation. "There must be hundreds of them!"

"Of *them*—you mean of *us*!" he blurted.

"I guess thoughts to myself are out of the question, huh?"

He just placed his arm around my shoulder and pulled me closer, holding his fist in the air in mock triumph. The crowd of nearly three hundred Jacob personalities cheered as they all looked back at us.

"Each of them was born from your evasive pretentiousness," the second of the nearly three hundred Jacob personalities spoke as he hugged me tighter with mock pride.

Ordinarily, I would have thought that seeing the other parts of myself would have been an intriguing idea. Somehow, I was sort of embarrassed at the thought. I realized in my attempts to get along with the world since I was a kid, I'd reinvented myself many times until I realized that it was okay to be "just me." I didn't know why I wanted to change. I was the most confident person that I knew. I didn't mind the way I looked, especially when I had on a suit and tie. I felt that I could hold my own in practically any conversation. There was, however, one thing missing in my life.

I envied the people in the world who dared not to have a care in the world. I was jealous of their supposed ignorance. That was all I could have figured that it was. I felt that there were too many things in the world to consider at a given time before any decision was made. Well, in that thought, I felt if there were decisions to be made and I had to make them, I would not be accountable myself if the decision were a bad one. I made a point of "becoming" someone other than myself in times where I felt that my true self would be compromised.

I thought about the comment the other me in the elevator made about the *other* Jacob that was doing things with the girl in dreams that I had only dreamed of. I am a normal guy in my twenties, and, of course, it was only natural that I have those types of feelings for a woman, right? My only problem was that I just couldn't bump into the right one. Things like that just didn't happen to me. I could tutor women and see how grateful they were, and I could help a woman do just about anything, but when it came to dealing with the wash of emotional turmoil that overcame me whenever I wanted to get closer to someone (that *special* someone), I would rather not deal with the lack of control my body experienced.

That was only one of the many problems I seemed to have with the world that prompted me to change my personality when I saw fit. I liked to have myself to myself, and I didn't see how that could have ever been a problem until now.

"Why don't they go away when I'm done with them?" I asked.

"That question makes about as much sense as why am I still there when I open and close my eyes in front of a mirror," he answered. "Where are they going to go? You create another part of us every so often, and then, every once in a while, you call upon that new part and you use us as you please. When you have no further use for us, we are here, using the skills and personality you gave us. You should see the stuff that goes on down here."

"Stuff like what?" I was curious. It's not often that you get to see yourself in action.

"Take a look over there," the other Jacob said, as he pointed off to the side.

I looked and had to walk closer because I couldn't believe my eyes. I saw myself and a really big lion wrestling in the grass a few yards away.

"Those are both us!" he said excitedly. "Let's see who's winning."

I looked on as one of them (the human one) used a large staff which he had underneath the lion's front legs, cradling the staff with both of his arms so that the lion's legs were up in the air. The other Jacob was standing behind it with his hands locked behind the lion's head in a full nelson. I couldn't believe what I was seeing, but then I remembered what the first new Jacob said to me.

I understood that I was wrestling with myself as a lion. I remembered using that lion in a dream at least once. I also remembered that I would use that staff to beat anything that I came across in my dreams. It was strange to me that both of what I would call protection mechanisms would be in the same dream at the same time. It was like a video game, where I could grab the weapon of my choice, only this time, the option was two weapons. It didn't make sense to me because I would never use them that way.

"Why would I fight myself?"

"Well, that answer is not so simple," the other Jacob answered. "There isn't much to do down here sometimes, so we have to stay occupied."

"Say 'uncle'!"

I looked in amazement at the two that were wrestling. I wasn't sure which one had spoken. But I saw who needed to. The human Jacob had the lion on the ground, wrapped up. To my disbelief, the lion tapped on the ground three times with its huge paws and said,

"I give up! Uncle! Uncle!"

"Awe, this is just way too much!"

I could only laugh because it was hilarious to see, or at least hear, the lion give up. I didn't try to figure out the meaning behind it. I just looked at it for the pure entertainment value of it.

"That was too much!" I smiled. We walked on to see many more things, like two Jacobs playing chess.

"They've been there forever."

We also saw many Jacobs reading, writing, painting, and riding horses. I saw a few of them floating above the ground and even flying in the air. I was sort of comforted by the sights of me doing the things that I'd apparently only dreamed of doing.

"You're gonna need a few of us before you go."

Right away I understood. Before I even had a chance to look around to take my pick, there were already several forming a line just in front of me.

"Last one in is a nerd! Oops, that would be you already!" he cackled.

Before I realized what was going on, the ones who were lined up ran straight at me, and as they hit me, they were absorbed into my body. Each time one of them struck me, I could feel his strengths and personality and all the feelings and emotions that came with him. They seemed to go on forever, hitting me from all sides.

I finally felt a pause as the last one hit me hard enough to knock me off of my feet. I slowly stood back up and saw one more Jacob walking unhurriedly toward me. I looked at him with wondering eyes. This Jacob was swollen with muscles. He wasn't huge, but I liked the way his body just commanded attention. The way he walked was kind of lewd to me and with him walking toward me that way, it made me kind of nervous. As he reached me, he placed his hand over on one of my shoulders and circled behind me. I just stood still. I wasn't scared because as the larger Jacob placed his hands on me, all I could think about was the girl in my dreams back when I was in a coma. Once behind me, the larger Jacob placed his other hand on my free shoulder and pulled his way into me. I was overcome with a feeling I would never admit to in any court of law (or anyplace else, for that matter). Just before his head sunk in to mine, he whispered in my ear, "No more slide rules, you know what I mean?"

And then he was gone, but that feeling lasted for a minute. I felt warm all over and had a strange feeling emanating from my mid section that I think most would describe as a warm and fuzzy.

"Well, we won't be seeing you again!" the other me shouted.

He jumped up high in the air. I was amazed. It was unnatural for any person to jump that high. I saw him rise way up in the air, and then I realized that he was coming back down quickly. Before I could get out of the way, I heard him scream, "Geronimoooooo!" and he landed right on top of me, being the last to absorb himself back into the Jacob fold.

Closure

** Cheryl **

I thought to myself about how important my family was to me. I never really told them, but it really was true. There were many times I'd said harsh things to my sisters and to my mom. I wished bad things when things were not so good at home. It was now I regret not saying what my heart felt at that last goodbye. My mother has passed since then. It tore at my insides that I was not able to say goodbye. I was too stubborn to call home on Mother's Day or on Christmas when most families were together.

I felt regret, and I felt pain. I knew that wouldn't bring her back. It made me sick inside whenever it surfaced. I kept the pain buried deep inside. My mother died of a heart attack coming home on the bus one day.

"It happened so fast, she just wasn't there anymore!" Ki Ki told me on the phone after it happened.

I had finally decided to call, and my mother had passed that very day. My younger sister, Jazz, would hold it against me forever, but Ki Ki understood. "Come home, Cheryl," she told me. "Come home and make your peace."

"That was so long ago. I always loved you, Mommy! You were just so hard on me! If you would have just told me you loved me, just once so I could have known, I would have never left you like I did." I ignored the tears falling from my cheeks…

I awoke with tears in my eyes. I couldn't remember why, but I was sad. I looked around the enclosed space that I was in and realized where I was. It was dark, but I recognized the sounds of the machinery in the background. I tried to move my legs, but realized that they were immobilized. I squeezed both my hands together one at a time. I was relieved to feel my nails digging into my hands. Slowly, I brought my hands to my face. I could feel the bandage that covered most of it. I also felt the crust of what could be nothing but blood, dried and matted in my hair.

It's a miracle I'm alive.

The sight of the oncoming car played on over and over in my mind. "Lord, if I make it through this in one piece, I will make the change that I've been talking about for so long," I prayed.

And then I thought of my friend AJ; I laid very still for a moment, scared to even think. If anything had happened to AJ, I would never forgive myself. I loved AJ like a sister. No one understood me the way AJ did. Now, because of my past catching up with me, AJ has suffered God knew what at the hands of my past. I tried to open my mouth to call out her name, but the pain in my face was too great. I laid there and cried silent tears, not knowing what had become of her.

"I will never do it again, Mamma. I let you leave this world without telling you I loved you. I won't do it again to someone I really care about. I still love you, Mamma, and I love AJ, too. I know you are with God's angels, but please help me, help me make this right," I cried.

I drifted back to sleep and as I passed into the world of dreams, I kept the same frame of mind and it was clear. AJ taught me that oftentimes after a painful event, the residual thought tends to be that of "why"—"Why did I do it?," "Why am I here?," "Why was this done to me?" She said it isn't a particularly loud thought, but it is a calling one that is interpreted by individuals differently. I was feeling my entire existence. I wondered why I had been dealt the hand that I had been given for this life. I felt as if I have always been a good person. I was honest, friendly, and most of all, I was very spiritual. In the midst of my life, the thoughts that echo in the back of my mind reminded me that I was one of the "good ones."

Even as a kid, I knew that I didn't deserve to be treated badly; but I knew that if there were someone else getting picked on, I would be glad that there was a chance that someone would share in the pain.

I should have loved myself more.

It wasn't easy for me to be the person that I was led to believe I was. (Ugly and undesirable.) I believed those things because I had been inundated with name calling and jeering from other kids for most of my childhood. I was feeling that "if only" feeling that allowed me to pity part of my existence.

I wasn't smart enough to see through all of the hate I had for those mean kids. If only I knew then what I know now, I believe that I would have been popular, despite my differences.

"You were always a smart girl," a voice said from somewhere within me. Or at least I thought it did.

"Mommy?"

"Yes, baby, I'm here," the voice echoed.

I tried to look, but I couldn't see anything; the murkiness of semi sleep was all I could feel.

"Mommy, where are you?"

I was calm. I didn't know why, but the sereneness of my sleep kept things in their own perspective. I fell deeper into the sleep that allowed me to open my eyes within me. I was back at home, in the house where I grew up. I looked around and realized that the place I was standing in was our old living room. I recognized that old carpet smell that reminded me so much of the days I would sprawl out on the floor and put together the biggest jigsaw puzzles ever. I looked over at the Lazy-Boy chair my mother had gotten from a yard sale when my father was still around. I loved to sit in that chair when no one else was around. I sat down in it and welcomed it's cool, cracked, leather surface.

"You always did love that chair, didn't you?"

This time, I whirled around and there she was. She looked just as I had always remembered her, only she was smiling brightly. That was very uncharacteristic of her. I knew that my mother worked almost nonstop day and night to support her fatherless children. That smile was replacing a look of weariness. Many times she came home from one job, just to take off for the next income opportunity. We had very little back then, but what we did have, we cherished, as if it were a day old from the showroom floor.

"Oh, Mommy, I miss you so much!"

I went to her with tears in my eyes. When I reached her, I threw my arms around her thin frame and instantly felt at home. I was never this close to my mother, but this was what I always wanted. My mother wanted to be there for me, but paying the house note and trying to keep the lights on were what came first. Although I knew the reason, I still held it against her for never being there when I needed some girly advice. She wasn't there when I thought I should go to the prom. She wasn't there to see her little girl grow up before her eyes. Instead, I became the head of the household. I was an extension of what my mother wanted to be. For the times that she wanted to be there for her children, I had to be the substitute.

I didn't mind that much. As far as I was concerned, I didn't have a life to speak of. There were no after-school plays for me. There wasn't any basketball or volleyball practice. There was just the constant stare from kids that didn't know me or understand me. There was one thing, however, that no one could hold against me. My grades and my school work were both excellent and always very original. That brought on, yet, another set of problems for my mother. There were many times when her presence was requested for parent/teacher nights. My teachers were very interested in speaking to her about the possibilities of college in my near future. But she was never able to make it; it's not that she didn't want to. She just couldn't afford to. In her mind, the future of her family depended on getting them out of the neighborhood and away from the life they were in.

The classes that I wanted, I got on my own merit. There were many road-blocks in my way because I didn't have anyone to speak up for me. All I had were my grades to stand on—every one of them an "A" and every one of them earned quietly. I didn't bring any extra attention to myself. I didn't want to be singled out for not having turned in an assignment or for wrongly answering any question on a test. So I studied diligently. It wasn't my intent to outdo any-one. I actually found the work easy, and it gave me something to concentrate on. If it had not been for my schoolwork, I would have gone crazy worrying about all of the other things that went on around me.

Despite the lack of help from outside sources, I scored well on my SAT, earning myself a full academic scholarship to the University of Southern California. I studied computer and information sciences because I was fasci-nated by the fields. I loved the fact that computers only did what I told them and nothing more. They didn't talk back, and they didn't call me names. Most importantly, they didn't make me feel less than who or what I was. What they did do was give me an avenue to express myself. I drew pictures, created music, and created many ways to both entertain and to make everyday tasks easier and more efficient. I created a world that I got along with, as well as one that got along with me.

"You seem troubled."

"I think I've been hurt, Mommy, really bad."

"Your mind is strong, Cheryl, baby." Her voice was very soothing, very reassuring.

"Why am I here?"

"You don't always know the reason for things. Sometimes we are brought to places to remind us of where we came from, other times, to remind us of where we've gone. Either way, you pay attention to how you feel, you hear me? Don't worry so much about what you see. You have a gift, little girl; one that is shared by only a few people at this time. It will allow you to see things a lot of people don't know even exist. But you have to be careful because your gift won't tell you what to do with what it shows you. Only you can take the things you learn and apply them to your life. It's easy to lead yourself down the wrong path. You have to be strong for yourself, just as you always have."

I thought about what she said. I didn't feel as if I had any special gift. The only significant thing I felt about myself that was out of the ordinary was that

I dreamt a lot. I had very vivid dreams that seemed so real to me that I couldn't tell the difference between the dreams and real situations sometimes.

"Mommy…" I began, thinking about the life I led since she had died. "How much…I mean, do you know about my life? Can you see me every day?" I turned my back because I was ashamed and didn't want to see the look on her face when she answered.

"Yes, child!"

I opened my eyes to see that she was in front of me. The look of disappointment that I had been expecting was not there. Instead, she gazed upon me with loving eyes.

If only you would have looked at me like that when I was young…

"I was young once myself, little girl."

I thought about that. My mother didn't have a chance to live the life she had wanted. She had me at an early age and two more kids not long after. From the time I was born, all my mother knew was work to support her kids.

"I'm not a…" I stopped in the midst of my words. I was about to tell her that I was no longer a little girl, and that those issues no longer existed for me. But as I looked up to speak those words, I glanced just past where she was standing and saw my reflection in the mirror. I got out of the chair and went toward the mirror. I was amazed at what I saw. Tears instantly welled in my eyes. I saw myself as I was, maybe twenty years ago. I stared at my reflection as if it was the first time I had ever seen it.

"I was so beautiful!" Tears rolled down my cheeks.

The little girl in the mirror was smiling independently of me on the other side. I reached toward the mirror to touch the shiny glass surface. The little girl on the other side moved as I did, stretching her hand toward me. As my hand reached the glass, instead of the cool, mirrored texture of glass, I felt the grasp of small, long fingers. I let them intertwine with mine. The little girl released her fingers and placed her hand within mine.

I looked at the little girl and said to her, "I love you."

She beamed with apparent delight. I thought I had never seen anyone so happy. She returned a loving look to me and mouthed the words, "Thank you." I saw the little girl back up in the mirror. Our hands parted, and the mirror started to distort. The next thing I knew, the little girl was gone, and her reflection was replaced by my mother's.

"Life can seem cruel at times, little girl," her reflection said to me. The voice carried in my mind. It was as if she was all around me. "Remember that nothing is merely as it seems. There is always a reason for the way things are.

Listen to your heart, and most of all, listen to your feelings. They will lead you to truth."

As she spoke those last words, the entire room started to fade and I found myself between worlds in the blackness of my subconscious. As she faded with the vividness of the dream, I whispered, "I love you, Mamma, and I always will."

Reunited

** AJ **

I looked around at the floor; it was the only thing I could see clearly from behind the drawn curtain that surrounded my bed. I was still in a haze, but I knew something was wrong.

My phone! My phone is in my desk with my purse! No one could possibly know that I'm here.

The soft beep of machinery was still steadily sounding off in the distance. I checked myself to see the extent of my injuries. I was still a bit shaky, but it was nowhere like the way it was before. I felt weak because my body was working overtime to rid itself of the drugs I was given, or over administered, as one could put it. I was soaked head to toe from sweat as my body did its job in waste removal. I wanted to get out of that bed and see just where I was.

There wasn't much light in the room, but I could see well enough to know where I wanted to go. My leg was in a Velcro splint, and it hurt to move it, but I was determined to find out what I wanted to know. I slid my hurt leg over the side of the bed and the pressure from the angle became too much. As quickly as I could, I gently slid my entire body up until the foot of the cast gently touched the ground. I paused for a moment while a head rush passed. I nearly fainted as I rocked back and forth uncontrollably until my blood pressure equalized. I still had an IV attached to me with the bag hanging on a hanger of sorts that was attached to the bed. I had to make a choice between removing the IV or taking the bag with me. I opted to take it with me since there was a pole on wheels by my bedside. I winced as I reached up and detached the bag from the hanger on the bed and pulled the rolling hanger to me with the foot on my good leg.

"Whew!"

When I got the bag on the pole, I used the whole thing to get myself on my feet. I was still a bit groggy from the drugs that were given to me, but I was well enough to do what I was doing. I managed to get on my feet, but had to hold onto the pole for dear life. I was in a lot of pain, more pain than I probably knew. The drugs that I was given were still hard at work in my system, despite my body's attempts to rid itself of them. While holding onto the pole and keeping my balance, I reached out and pulled the curtain open. It made a loud whirring sound as it did, to reveal the rest of the room's interior.

"Hello?"

The voice came from behind another curtain. I wasn't feeling very cordial because I was on a mission. I was a bit preoccupied with my efforts to pay attention to whoever it was calling out. I moved slowly, but deliberately across the room, inches at a time. I had to stop and rest every few steps because of the amount of energy that it took for me to move.

** Cheryl **

I was beginning to get scared trying to figure out what was going on outside of the curtain surrounding my bed. I could hear something moving, and it was getting closer to my bed. I didn't know what it was, and I was on the verge of tears. I could remember a few times when the nurse came in during the night, but she was always quiet. The movements that I heard were deliberate, to the point where I could figure out what the nurse was doing. Sometimes I could hear the buttons on the machines she was pushing and the curtain moving back and forth, but this time the sounds were spooky.

I had heard something in my sleep that woke me up, thinking that someone had opened the curtain around my bed. But when I looked up, I didn't see anything, so I figured I was just dreaming. When I put my head back down, I heard another noise that sounded like a squeaky wheel on a shopping cart. It sounded like it was coming directly toward me!

Okay, girl. Whatever it is, there is a rational explanation for it. Don't start acting all timid.

"Hello?"

I thought there was a pause, as if it were a reaction to me calling out, but very soon after, I heard the noise again. There was a squeaking noise and then a shuffling sound right after it, as if someone were dragging himself across the ground.

This place is giving me the creeps.

I was getting frustrated. I felt my body betraying me as my breathing quickened; I felt it difficult to stay calm.

Oh my God! It struck me. *It couldn't be!* The feeling wouldn't go away.

"AJ?"

I spoke in pain because my face was still very swollen and it hurt to talk.

** AJ **

I stopped dead in my tracks when I heard my name called. Instantly I remembered.

"Cheryl, girl, is that you?"

Slowly I made my way to the opening of the curtain surrounding Cheryl's bed.

"AJ!"

I could see the relief on her face when she saw that it truly was me. She was overwhelmed with emotion and eagerly anticipated the curtain moving back so she could see for sure. I reached the opening of the curtain and pulled on it. The curtain whirred back and I saw my best friend in bandages.

"Wait!"

I turned toward the entrance of the room and moved much faster toward it despite the pain that followed each step. Reaching out, I found what I was looking for and flipped on all of the light switches. The room came alive with light. I then turned around and looked with both excitement and sorrow as I saw my friend battered and bruised, lying in the bed with her feet raised on pillows.

Cheryl just looked at me as I approached in the light, tears soaking her bandaged face.

"Oh, AJ, I'm so sorry."

She did her best to reach out for me. I went to her open arms and despite the strength I usually displayed, I cried in Cheryl's arms. I didn't really know whether it was that I needed to be consoled, or if it was just the situation itself and I was happy that my friend was okay. As I lay in Cheryl's arms, I began to cramp up in my bad leg so I had to pull away from my bent over position. This may have been a good thing for me because it allowed me to step back into some sort of reality.

"Look at me; I'm a mess," I said, managing a smile on my swollen face.

Cheryl just started crying. She tried to speak, but every time she opened her mouth, the emotion just took her over and a fresh bout of tears came pushing through.

I said, "Hold on for a second," looking for a chair to prop my leg up on. There was already a chair next to Cheryl's bed. I just needed another one so I could elevate the leg in the splint. I found a chair by the front entrance. It took me a second to get behind it with the IV pole tethered to my arm, but I managed to get in the right position to kind of push sideways since I couldn't move forward with a broken leg propped out in front of me.

Cheryl just watched me in tears, but seeing me struggle brought a smile to her face. She knows that I would never let any simple obstacle get in my way. She watched as I maneuvered the chair in front of the one by her bedside and then moved the IV pole behind the first chair. Then I scooted sideways in between the two and used all of my strength to lift my splinted leg onto the cushioned chair. When I was done, I was sweating from head to toe.

"Okay, I'm here!"

I plopped my head down as close to Cheryl as I could. She reached over as best as she could and stroked my matted hair.

"You are just so wonderful. You are always here when I need you. I would kiss you, but I can't tell my lips from my cheeks," she managed to squeak out like it was still a little difficult to breath.

I smiled when I realized that even under the circumstances we were in, Cheryl was able to keep her sense of humor. She looked me in the eyes.

"Do you remember what happened?"

When I heard the question, I winced slightly as I had almost forgotten why we were both here. I never saw what happened, so I had no recollection of the accident. All I could remember was that I was in and out of a bunch of difficult dreams.

I could remember the nurse and those horrible Narcan treatments. I could remember my veins being on fire as the antinarcotic did its work. I remembered feeling helpless and open, like the whole world could just look inside of me and see all of the things that I kept hidden from them. My eyes saw reds and oranges and blacks, like I was in some kind of hell you could see illustrated in a book. I could now remember the faces in the walls of the fiery tunnel I was in. The faces that revealed to me everything I had ever had a question about. I could understand the way of the world for all of a few seconds, and then it was as if my mind was gently clouded again as the faces turned back into the walls of fire.

That was real! All of that was real. If I didn't know better, I…I stopped my thoughts as I realized that Cheryl had asked me a question.

"What did happen?" I asked, after the less than short pause that I took to reflect.

She took a deep breath and looked at me with worried eyes. "Where do you want me to start?"

I looked back at her, understanding that this would take a minute. I remembered that just before we took off for lunch, I realized that Cheryl had a secret and if I had only paid attention, I would have recognized it long before Cheryl's breakdown. The look that Cheryl gave me when she asked where she should start made me believe, all of a sudden, that our predicament was not one we were in by chance.

"You know me," I said softly.

I was trying hard not to tip my hand to Cheryl. I was afraid of letting her know the fear I had growing in the pit of my stomach. "Start from the beginning. It's always the best place to start." Then I sat back and put myself in a more comfortable position to listen to what she had to say.

True Confession

** Cheryl **

I didn't really know what I wanted to tell AJ first. I had so much that I'd always wanted to tell her about me but I always refrained because of the bad feelings I had about my childhood and early adult years. I didn't really realize that I hadn't gotten over the events of my past. I let time bury them so that consciously I didn't feel them haunt my daily life. I told AJ the story, and now I felt it was an opportunity for closure. I went over everything that made a difference in my life—my family, those mean children, and most recently, my ordeal with Tia.

I spoke for what seemed like countless hours as AJ listened to me quietly but intently. As much as it really hurt to talk, I went on until my story brought us to the present. It was three hours later when I was done. Neither of us really felt the time go by as we were both somewhat still sedated, or at least under the influence of some kind of painkillers. I finished my story, and AJ seemed in deep thought. I looked at her quietly as I finished.

"There, that is the whole thing…except there is one other thing I failed to mention."

She looked back at me, realizing that there was something in my voice that held a different meaning. It was a deliberate tone that I'm sure made her believe that something big was about to happen.

AJ, looking sympathetic, kept silent as I spoke. I had suffered a loss within myself and for me, it was defeating. I did just as any normal person would have done and that is, coped with it the only way I knew how. There was a feeling deep within me that told me since the incident with Tia happened, that I had been ruined to some extent. I could never say, "I would never do that." Or I could never stand in confidence and say there is no way I could be with another woman.

That kind of thing is a source of pride in a lot of women. The values that we hold inside as our own are solid, and we generally stick to our guns when it comes to situations that are foreign to us. I've seen women together, I mean, that sort of thing finds its way in front of us at some point in time in our lives. It's in the movies and all around us. I had seen on a few occasions two women together on screen and it bothered me. To me, at the time, it was unnatural. I didn't understand why people of the same sex would want to be with each other. It was like they ignored a part of themselves that told them that it was wrong.

Years later, I found myself in the same predicament. I ignored plenty that was going on inside my mind and my body. There was a part of me that made me feel that I was dammed to hell. It made me feel as if I were the walking dead. It was like I had been bitten by a vampire and no matter what I did in this life, I would be considered evil by most. All except for those that were like me; others would never accept me. So I migrated slowly into that life, one which for me caused me to give in to my dark side. It was always wrong for me, but I lost my will and the sense of choice that we all have. I was weak because I felt unloved by the world and even by God, Himself.

I was breathing hard as the truth about what happened to me was about to come out.

"AJ," I started cautiously. "When you were in with your last client, I received a phone call." I paused for a moment. "It was a woman. A woman I had met only the night before." I stopped again because I had only just realized how hard it was going to be to tell this story to her. "I wound up going home with her after we had a few drinks and it turns out that she knew me. She knew of me through someone else in my past. I knew since I'd gotten up this morning...or whenever it was, that something was wrong.

"Call it a premonition or whatever, but I thought about things then that I hadn't thought of in years. Anyway, there was a woman that I use to train with; her name was Tia. One day she said some things to me as I ran out of her house that I will never forget.

"First of all, I was date raped. She gave me a pill that made me lose all of my inhibitions, and I wound up having sex with her. I had never done, or had ever planned to do, anything like that with a woman! When I woke up on her living room floor the next morning, I lost my mind. I just couldn't believe what she had done to me! She was pleading with me, saying that she could show me "the way" just as it was showed to her. "The way" being the...alternative lifestyle...for women.

"Well, to make a long story short, I told this woman whom I'd met the other night, her name was Gina, I told her that I couldn't do it anymore. I wanted my life back and what I did was a mistake. I didn't want to be...that...anymore.

She didn't take it well. AJ, in fact, she went off the deep end. She dropped the phone; I could tell that she was running around the house. I could hear her screaming, like she was in fear for her life. She picked the phone back up and then started to beg me and plead that I wouldn't break it off between us, and that's when she said it. She said the exact same thing to me that Tia did, about showing me "the way" as it was showed to her.

"But let me back up. On my way to the office, when I got off the elevator, I could have sworn that I saw Tia in the lobby, and if I didn't see her, then I definitely smelled something that just reminded me so much of her. It took me right back to that night, and I swear, I almost lost it for good. It lasted only two good seconds, but it was the most powerful, incapacitating feeling I have ever felt. I was sure it was just my imagination, so I was able to dismiss it long enough to get the food for us.

"I didn't realize that I was actually scared until I got back in the elevator and was headed for the office. AJ, I couldn't get here fast enough. That is what was wrong with me when I came to you, crying. I had a rough time dealing with what happened to me all those years ago. There was a time when I rationalized the whole incident and blamed it on myself. I felt like it was all I was worth since there were no men in my life I could trust. Somehow, I wound up in that situation again and then again, and I closed my eyes to what I was doing. I can't explain it, but I just kept on doing it despite how I knew I felt deep down."

I needed to get this part of the story out as well, but in truth, I was stalling. I knew at some point, I would have to tell AJ what really happened, but I was scared to death of what it could do to our relationship.

"The car that hit us…" I started. As soon as I opened my mouth, it seemed that my throat closed and all of the moisture left my mouth. I swallowed hard and continued. "Gina was driving that car, AJ!" I was barely able to make the words come out. "I did this to you, and I'm sorry!"

I sobbed hard and long. I had to gasp for air because the sobs were so strong, they stopped me from taking short breaths.

** AJ **

I understood Cheryl's dilemma for the first time. Of course, I didn't share her sentiment. I knew that the choices we make in life always affect the people around us. I wouldn't have blamed her for what happened, no matter what the circumstances.

"Cheryl, girl, you didn't do this to me. You were riding along side of me, not in the car that hit us!"

"You know what I mean!" Cheryl said, obviously not trying to be let off the hook.

"That's enough of that!" I nearly snapped back. I loved Cheryl too much to let her place an emotional wedge in between us. "I won't let you do this! You didn't control the actions of those people. Not the one that hurt you or the one that came into your life at any point after."

Cheryl winced at the lash that I gave her. Strangely enough, it made her forget her sorrow for the moment and she looked angry. The feeling must not have lasted, but it was there long enough to make her think. Several thoughts may have been going through her mind, judging from that look—"I already feel bad; why is she yelling at me?" to "I hate you, too, for the tone of your voice. I hate you!"

The thoughts, I'm sure, were not aimed at me in particular, but they were there like a little devil perched in her mind trying to get her to react to them.

Cheryl looked at me and understood what I meant. She knew that I wouldn't let her use self-pity in any form when it came to the both of us. She also knew that she could trust me and maybe that was what scared her most.

"I…I…" Cheryl started between sobs.

"Listen!" I said to Cheryl. "I know you might feel responsible, but I'm going to make it a point to take that away from you. You did not do this to me! Do you understand me?" I softened my tone.

"I do," Cheryl answered. "But I feel so bad. I wanted to tell you a long time ago that my life was running itself. You don't have any idea how much you've helped me since I met you." She cried harder. "AJ, I was thinking about ending my life until I met you!"

I was shaken inside upon hearing those words. But somehow, I felt I'd heard them before.

"Well, I'm glad you didn't go through with it," I said flatly. "I would have been all alone with that talking computer of yours," I had a look of love on my face.

I wanted to see Cheryl smile despite the seriousness of the situation we were in.

Cheryl just looked back with an endearing smile. I felt as if I had known her all of my life. She seemed to always have the right thing to say.

"I can't figure out for the life of me why I never came clean to you with the story of my life before! I believed, at first, that just being around you would bring me to the point where I could have the strength to take charge of my life and deal with my problems. I mean, I could have dispensed with a lot of pain and heartache, and possibly avoided this situation completely if I had just trusted you with the knowledge of my life…" Cheryl threw her hands up.

"So, we have come to a new point in our lives, haven't we Cheryl?"

"I guess you can say that,"

"We have been through a lot together since we have known each other."

"Yes, we have!"

"Well, I have finally heard the life story of my best friend in the whole world, next to my brother, that is, but he's a man so you have one up on him."

** Cheryl **

I laughed when she said that, remembering the conversation we had a while back about men not wanting to ask for directions and taking credit for all they had accomplished.

"Men aren't so bad," I said in a thoughtful tone.

"Really?" AJ said, a little astonished.

"Yeah," I said flatly. "I was trying to tell you that I was working on a real change in my life. The thing that happened to me with that woman was a freak…well, not an accident, but I just didn't see it coming. Somehow I understand how it all happened, but I wasn't given either the choice or the opportunity to make a decision one way or the other. Looking back on it, I can truly say that I would have preferred not to have gone through it…at least, the way that it happened."

I took a pause and looked at her to see how she was receiving what I was telling her. I know, deep down, that I did not want to go through life as a homosexualor a lesbian, or even as a bi-sexual! I didn't want to be anything but a normal person! I gave in to my sexual frustration by allowing someone to let me "feel" for once. The fact that I was pretty much drugged and date raped to get to that point in my life was the biggest problem. I never knew any women who preferred other women. I felt if I had, I was never aware of it. To think that someone out there looked at me in any other way than I looked at myself was difficult for me to deal with.

My self-esteem was at a low point in my life, as it seemed to me it had always been from the time I grew up dealing with those mean kids to the day I decided I wasn't going to take it anymore. I never really received the one thing that would have solidified my progress in life. I needed positive affirmation that I was as special as I really was. Because I never let on to AJ about my feelings, she never realized I had a problem. I just sort of fed off of her energy, and AJ, in turn, fed off of mine. Together, we made the best of friends.

"So you're saying that it wasn't all bad?" AJ asked cautiously.

"Well…I got something that I needed out of it, only I never knew I needed it until I got it. If that makes any sense."

"It does in a way," AJ reasoned.

"I needed for someone to want me; not only that, but to love me!" I was getting a little exited. "No one has ever given me what I needed to believe in myself my entire life until I met you."

AJ looked like she was blushing. This was clearly "props" that made her feel all mushy inside.

"You *are* a very special person, Cheryl."

"I always thought so, but how come it took so long for anyone else to realize it?" I pouted.

"Sometimes it takes a significant emotional event in life for one to stop and realize it himself, then he or she can almost demand that other people recognize just who they are."

"That's not good enough, AJ; I can't believe that I 'had' to go through what I did in order for me to realize who I am."

"I can't say that you had to go through it, but can you say that if it hadn't happened, you would have come as far as you did given the time that you did it in?" AJ asked.

I thought about that question. I wasn't sure what the answer was. I was just so dead set against admitting that I had to go through what I did. What's worse, I had to admit to myself that I knew (not even deep down) that I liked it. There was a terrible dilemma twisting my insides. All my life I believed that things were supposed to be a certain way. I had always been open-minded, but when it came to women being with other women, it just wasn't for me all the while I was growing up. When I had my first experience, I was drugged! I felt that was my best defense. How and why I eventually fell into that lifestyle is still partially a mystery to me.

Deep down, I knew the truth, though. I needed to be needed. I wanted to be wanted. There is that primal feeling within all of us that just wants to be satisfied.

"I never asked to be a homosexual! I am not a homosexual!"

It seemed that this is what I had been trying to say all along. There was that nagging contradiction within me that was driving me mad inside. It said to me that I knew I liked it; I just felt it was wrong. Where do you go from there?

"Who are you trying to convince?" AJ asked.

Again, I thought about the question. If I just flatly answered it, then it would seem that I *was* a homosexual, but I just didn't want to be. I knew that was wrong, though I just didn't know quite how to express it.

"First of all…it is not a matter of anyone being convinced." I stopped abruptly and looked at AJ so I could at least make sure that this particular point had gotten across to her.

AJ looked back at me, apparently agreeing to the statement.

"I am trying to come to terms with just what I am."

"What you are in terms of what?" AJ asked patiently.

"Homo- or heterosexual," I said a little frustrated.

"Well, do you think you are homosexual?" AJ asked.

"No!" I almost shouted. "I know I'm not."

"Well, just what makes a person a homosexual?"

Damn! Once again, I thought about the question. I felt I could say that it was someone who enjoyed having sexual relations with someone of the same sex, but that would be a nail in a coffin for me! I also thought I could say someone who was born with something different about them, which made them go in that direction. This was a safer explanation for me, and it was the one that I went with.

"Someone who was born with an affliction."

"An affliction?" AJ repeated. "So you believe that there is something wrong with the homosexual population of the world."

"Well, it's a sin, isn't it?"

"That really wasn't the question, and although I have been through my Bible a few times in my life, the one thing that I have learned is that I am not the judge, so if it is a sin, I am not the one to declare it."

"Wow! That was the most political thing I have ever heard you say, AJ."

"You somehow want me to either exonerate you or to let you know that you have sinned, and that is not my place," AJ stated defiantly. "In dealing with all of the clients I have seen in my years in this business, I have learned not to judge as I have been taught since I was a child. I will tell you, Cheryl, this has helped me in many ways cope with the differences in the people of this world.

"What is right and wrong? I have my ideas on the terms of each, but there is a line I draw when it comes to preferences that do not necessarily harm anyone. There was a point when I could not for the life of me understand why anyone would want to be with anyone else of the same sex, but think about the people in this world who have been abused by others. Women that have been raped oftentimes can't bring themselves to get close to a man.

"Sometimes the trauma of the rape distorts their ability to reason as they would have prior to the experience. This, somehow, allows them to be subjugated by thoughts that are intended to cure the problems that they are having, like loneliness and having no love in their lives. Then there are those who have felt as if that was how they were always meant to be.

"Maybe there is a gene that dictates which way a person goes, and the gene malfunctions or gets placed in the wrong DNA. Those answers I don't have. I will tell you, however, that people are who or what they are for a reason. Whether it be they had it forced upon them, or they just simply are that way because they have always known themselves to be like that. That is how and who they are. You can either accept them or leave them be to their own existence," AJ finished with a long breath.

I listened to AJ's speech with tender ears. I had to take everything that she was saying personally. But I just didn't know how to get satisfaction out of any answer I got. AJ apparently could sense this so she took one more step to bring the most important point home.

"If nothing else, Cheryl, girl, you need to remember this." AJ looked dead in my eyes. "I love you with all there is in the world to love you with. I believe you are in my life for a reason, and I have never been as fulfilled since before I met you. When I say you are special, I really mean it. There is something about you that puts my mind at ease and gives me energy at the same time."

Cheryl had an amusing thought despite the desperate feelings she was experiencing and had to let it out. "Well, maybe *you* are a homosexual!" she said smiling.

I caught AJ a little off guard with that one but because she caught the look on my face, she was instantly put at ease. Although she could emphatically deny it, she didn't want to get into a debate about the reasons why because it could undermine everything she had just explained with so much confidence to me.

"Yeah, right!" AJ came back, smiling at the joke. "I may not have a man, but I *can* have one," she said in a sheepish tone. "You are a beautiful person, Cheryl, and that is all that matters to me. That should be all that matters to you as well."

"Thank you, boss. I really needed to hear that. Well, speaking of men, what do you think about the guy who came to see you before we left...Whenever that was."

Fresh Revelations

** AJ **

I was stunned instantly when Cheryl spoke. How could I have forgotten?

"Cheryl!"

"What is it?" she answered, almost panicking.

"The guy! He...He..."

"AJ, what is it? You're scaring me."

I took a second to go back over in my mind everything that Jacob told me. I couldn't believe that I sat there listening to Cheryl tell her story and that whole experience did not dawn on me. I must have been traumatized and was not thinking straight. How am I going to tell her in a way that won't confuse her? I was confused myself as to how I just forgot about it. "That makes absolutely no sense!"

"Boss, can you please tell me what you are talking about?" Cheryl pleaded.

I stood my ground for a second. I had to get my thoughts straight before I said anything else. I felt as if I was in the twilight zone or some wickedly strange déjà vu. It had been at least a couple of days that I had that conversation with Jacob, or had it? I wondered. I actually had no idea. It seemed so long ago to me.

"AJ!" Cheryl pushed.

I snapped out of it and looked at my friend. Cheryl could tell the difficulty that I was having, but she couldn't possibly fathom what it was all about.

I gathered myself and began to speak. Cheryl sat up as best she could and was all ears. "Okay, girl," I spoke slowly. "Where do I start?"

"You know what you always tell me," Cheryl chimed in.

"The guy..." I continued again. "His name is Jacob, Jacob Livingston III." I looked at Cheryl as I spoke to see if any of the preliminary stuff would mean anything to her.

She just looked on as the name meant nothing to her.

"The woman that you spoke about before..."

"Her name was Tia," Cheryl stated.

"Actually, her name is Elizabeth," I corrected her.

Cheryl was thrown hard. She felt like her whole world was about to end all of a sudden. It wasn't because of the name; she'd never heard of it, either. It was the confidence in which I spoke. She looked like she was about to be let in on the joke that was her life, and I carried the punch line.

"How would you know something like that?" Cheryl asked as she tried hard to stop from shaking. "I only told you that story a few hours ago."

"The guy," I said holding back tears in my eyes. "His name was Jacob Livin—"

"I heard you the first time!" Cheryl nearly yelled.

"Her name is Elizabeth Tianna Livingston!" I shouted back.

"No!" Cheryl said as her head slammed back into her pillow. "It can't be!" she cried.

"Tia is the shorten form of her middle name," AJ said.

"What did he want?" Cheryl moaned as she stared at the ceiling.

"Listen!" I said trying to calm her down. "He's a good guy; his sister…"

"Sister?" Cheryl interrupted.

"Yes, actually his half-sister. She's a very sick person. She suffers from a multiple personality disorder."

"She's crazy as fuck!" Cheryl shouted.

"Jacob told me a very long, drawn-out story about how his parents were killed, and how he thought she had something to do with it. He said she was a brilliant chemist, and she kept him in a sedated state for years, maybe so she could figure out a way to get all of his family's money. He also told me the story of when she took you to her house and drugged you and you wound up…well, you know. He said you got up the next morning screaming and running around the house. Then he said she use to have you followed everywhere you went so she could keep tabs on you. She had a plan to get you back in her life. He said if her plan didn't work, she was probably going to kill you, but he wasn't sure of that part. He came to me to warn me that you were in danger!"

"Is that what was wrong with you in your office?" Cheryl asked.

"Yes! I had no idea what to do." I began to cry. "That's when I said let's go to lunch so I could get you out of there and figure out what to do next."

Cheryl was stunned. She didn't know what to say. On one hand, she probably felt better because she knew now that someone else had confirmed her story and she was recognized as a victim. On the other hand, I'm sure she couldn't figure out why when she was telling me the story earlier, I didn't let her know then that I knew. Cheryl was confused and looked at me for the first time with a bit of distrust.

"How could you have not remembered that?" Cheryl asked in disbelief.

"Did you not hear me asking myself the same question?" I pleaded. "I don't know! I just don't know," I said in tears. "Oh, Cheryl, baby, I'm so sorry. I just can't explain how it happened, but I have told you all I know, except for the things he told me about himself." I couldn't stop the tears from flowing down my face.

I went on to explain all of the details that Jacob told me. There was such a thing as client privilege, but in this case, it was out the door. I loved Cheryl too much to keep any of this in the dark.

"We'll figure this thing out, Cheryl, together; but first, we have to let someone know that we're here." I looked around. There were no phones in the room.

There was a disturbance behind me which took me off guard for a moment. The door to the room was pushed open slowly and a very surprised nurse emerged through the doorway.

Busted

** Stacy **

"What is going on here?" I said, half smiling and with half a look of genuine concern. I looked at Lucky and her jerry-rigged chair set up and the other one with her hair a mess.

"Hi," Lucky said to me for lack of anything else to say as she wiped some very obvious tears from her face.

"Hello," the other one said to match her friend's salutation.

"Don't even look at me like you all know who I am. I'm just a stranger to you. I'm just someone who has been taking care of you for the last few days. My name is Stacy, and I would love to know just who you two young ladies are…"

I was so relieved that they seemed to be okay. Before I screamed at Lucky to get her butt back in that bed of hers, I needed to take advantage of the fact that they were conscious enough to answer questions about who they were.

"My name is AJ."

"And mine is Cheryl."

They both replied right after one another.

"Well, up to now, your name has been Lucky. You have been through quite an ordeal. And you, Ms. Cheryl, you…You weren't trying to make it for a minute. I'm glad you decided to stay with us." I was so happy, I was beaming!

I was really emotional about their situation. I truly cared about the patients under my care. I also really felt the need to get to the bottom of their situation. Both Cheryl and AJ had pieces to the puzzle that I was not aware of. In the back of my mind, Jacob loomed as something else I needed to resolve.

"We need a phone!" Cheryl piped up all of a sudden. "No one knows that we're here!"

"Really, I need to call my brother, Alonzo; he will tell my mom I'm lost after a while, and the whole world will never rest again!"

"Of course!" I said. "I put out APBs all over the United States and no one has come to claim you. How is it possible that you two managed to get in here without the least bit of identification?"

"Well, that's a bit of a longer story than I'm willing to tell at the moment," AJ said. "But, Cheryl, you had your purse with you, didn't you?"

"Yeah! I'm sure of it. You were the one who left your purse, not me. Awe, man! Can you believe, I have to replace all of that stuff!" she complained. "Anyway, I'll take care of that mess later. AJ, you have a phone call to make."

"Okay!" I said interrupting. "I will get you a phone as soon as I can get you back in that bed where you belong. And if you're really nice about it, I'll even set you two side by side so you won't be tempted to make this journey again. You two are restricted to the bed, do you hear me? The only reason you should be getting up is to use the bathroom, and even then, you should consider calling me first."

I helped AJ to her feet and moved the chairs to the side to provide a clear path to the bed from which she had escaped.

"Now comes the fun part," I said as I helped her maneuver the IV pole around the chair and walk to her bed.

AJ was still in a bit of pain. The drugs that we gave her before were wearing off and she began to whimper with each step.

Journey of No Return

** Elizabeth **

I woke with a snort. It was much easier for me to take over now that Elizabeth was occupied by fear. I got up from sitting on a toilet and looked at my face. The remnants of blood from earlier were still visible. I could barely see the cuts as they had already started healing. I washed my face and unlocked the bathroom door. I had no idea why I was here at the Livingston place. I turned around again and looked in the mirror at the shirt I had on.

"Oh, fuck, no!"

I took the bottom of the shirt and tied it into a knot just below my breast line. I posed for a second in the mirror so I could see the knots that protruded from my abdomen.

"Better!"

Then I reached into the pocket of the jeans I would never have put on and pulled out the keys to the Jag. When I stepped out of the bathroom, I went straight out the front door of the house, opened the garage, and got back in the car. I was on a mission, and this time, I would not be stopped.

** Jacob **

I thought I heard the gate closing as I woke from a deep slumber. What a night!

I got out of my bed and stepped quietly into the hall, making my way downstairs. As soon as I reached the landing, I saw what I'd feared.

She's gone!

I didn't know who, however. I could only think the worst and count on Liz being back in control. I turned around and went back upstairs. When I got to my room, I realized that half of the day was already gone.

"I have to get out of here. There's too much I still have to do."

I decided to hop in the shower and make a plan to finish this entire thing now! After I finished getting cleaned up, I found some clothes to put on and some house shoes. Then I went back downstairs to fill the void in my stomach. I was hungry when I first came in the house a day and a half ago and had yet to eat anything in all of that time.

I went to the refrigerator just as I'd done before and was still unimpressed with what it held for me to eat. I knew I had to eat, however, so I looked deeper and pulled out the ingredients for an omelet and closed the door.

"This isn't going to do!"

I looked around for something else to make. In the pantry, I found a box of pancake mix and figured that would do. I didn't see any syrup immediately so I turned to go back into the pantry and noticed the cabinet door above the sink. It struck me as odd. I couldn't remember what was in that cabinet, or if I'd even seen it before. I stepped closer to it and my mind began to blur. I couldn't concentrate. Somehow, I managed to keep walking, although my mind seemed to force me away from the thought of the cabinet. I had the strangest craving for a piece of pie. I didn't understand what was going on, but I was determined to concentrate on the matter at hand. I was angry at the fact that I couldn't clear my mind.

When I reached the cabinet, I felt as if I was going to pass out. I grabbed ahold of the cabinet frame on the inside of the door, making the door swing wide open. I was literally sick to my stomach. As I held onto the cabinet frame, I became delirious! No matter what, I was not going to let go of that frame. I hung on and held my head over the sink, feeling that my empty stomach was going to heave up whatever it could muster. I became faint, and my mind began to wander. I could see pictures in my mind of Elizabeth swinging a shiny object in front of my face. I could hear her voice saying,

"Whenever you see this cabinet, you will think of pie. You will not go near this cabinet."

She kept repeating it over and over in my mind. I was struggling to stay conscious. I used everything in my power to try and make myself concentrate. It was only just working. Bit by bit, I fought between the realms of consciousness and the dizzy, chaotic frenzy my mind was in. I seemed to be making ground as clear thoughts pierced through the cloud of confusion. I could feel my mind fighting to beat the post-hypnotic suggestion embedded in my subconscious by my half-sister. I felt as if my mind was going to snap. I fought the urge to let go and just collapse on the floor. All of a sudden, it was over. I fell forward like I was the victim of a tug-of-war, where the other side abruptly let go of the rope.

My mind was instantly clear; it was *too* clear. The transition from one state to the other was like violent silence. Slowly I got to the point where I could stand on my own, but I still kept my hand in place, holding onto the frame of the cabinet.

"Wow, she really did a number on me."

I could remember everything now, including all of the times I went toward that cabinet and wound up in a corner of a room, eating a piece of pie. But it wasn't this particular cabinet. It was the one I used to see her put stuff in all the time at the other house. There were times when I had a whole pie in my hands with a fork and evidence all around my mouth. I could also remember seeing Elizabeth take small plastic bags full of pills and a set of books out of the cabinet from time to time, as well as putting those same items back on occasion.

I looked into the cabinet and swept my hand to the very back on the top shelf. "Empty."

I wasn't sure how long it had been that way, but I was almost sure that Elizabeth had recently cleaned it out. I thought of the possibilities of what could be in those books. I had walked up behind her while she was working on a formula once before. She looked like she was asleep in the chair. I looked over her shoulder to see what she was working on and to me, it seemed to be some kind of mind-altering drug judging from the ingredients.

She had several books about drugs around her and had bookmarked and highlighted pages in all of them. I was there for one minute too long because when she turned to look at me, she gave me a look and a berating that I will never forget. Elizabeth as Liz could be very cruel when she needed to. It would seem that the brunt of her intellect, as borrowed from her host, was utilized specifically for anger and no good.

"It's empty! She always seems to be one step ahead of me."

I raised myself up onto the sink so that I could see the entire cabinet, including the very rear of the top shelf, and was met with even more disappointment. The cabinet was completely empty. I let myself down and turned my back to the sink and leaned against it. I needed a small victory in this ordeal to give me the strength to follow through with my plans. At this point, I didn't know what the next step was. All I really knew was that I needed to get back to the hospital to talk to Elizabeth's mother. She would be able to help me figure out what to do next.

I was still torn between helping Elizabeth and making sure she paid for her role in my parents' death. I didn't know for sure that she actually had anything to do with it. There was some doubt in my mind that she could have done what had been described to me as a massacre in my home. I felt that I had to explore every possibility and that I could leave no options out when it came to deciding what to do about my situation. I had to move on with my life at some point. Elizabeth had been in control of me for a long time and that, in itself, was a reason to put her away. Her motives were unclear, but I was sure that she was after my family's money. In her "normal" state, however, I felt that she was not capable of doing wrong, and if given the opportunity, she could be someone I could come to love as the sister I never had.

The whole situation was very hard for me to deal with, but I gave myself no choice. I was determined to see this through to the end. At this point, I couldn't say how it would all turn out. I would have to just take it all one step at a time.

"Food!" I said to myself as I went back to the pantry, looking for more ingredients. I found a few more items to prepare and then started on my way to making myself a good breakfast. Half an hour later, I was sitting at the table, leaning back in the chair, ready to take another nap because I'd eaten so much.

I got up from the table and removed the empty plate and silverware. I then went to the sink and washed them immediately. I hated seeing dishes in the sink. My mother had always taught me to clean as I went, so the pots and pans and all of the utensils I used to cook with were already drying in the dish rack when I finished my meal. I put the plate and the silverware in the drying rack and then went into the study, where I could sit down and concentrate on my plan for the next day.

I knew talking to Sheila was a must. What I didn't know was what I needed from her. I really wanted to believe that deep down, Elizabeth was a good person. I believed that her mother was the key to finding that information out. If she did cure her mother's cancer, there was no way I could just let her become a part of the prison mental health system. She could be an asset to society if, in fact, she wasn't crazy.

I sat down behind the large oak desk that once served as my father's workplace, where he spent many an hour working. Looking in the middle drawer, I pulled out a legal pad, grabbed a pen out of the holder on the desk, and began to formulate a step-by-step plan of how I was to either help my sister or put her crazy other half behind bars. If it came down to it, I decided that I would put her away forever. I even felt that if I had to, I would end her life. I had no earthly idea how I would do it, but I believed that if I had to do it, that I wouldn't hesitate a second to save the life of another.

I put the pen down for a moment and thought about what I was going to do. I felt that maybe if she knew that her mother had spoken to me, that it might buy me some more time.

"No, that won't work!" I would have to do too much explaining as to how I came to be at the hospital and how the meeting came to be.

"There must be something!" I was at a loss at the moment. I needed to figure out a way to talk to the real Elizabeth, possibly at the same time I spoke to her mother. I thought that maybe the presence of her mother would keep her other personalities at bay. "Now that's an idea!"

Although I wondered how I could arrange such a meeting, there was no telling if I would even see the real Elizabeth again. Out of all the times I'd seen my half-sister, I had only known her evil half and Tia on rare occasions. I was only barely aware of Tia because she only came out when she was dealing directly with Cheryl.

"Hmmmm…There has got to be a way."

I decided if I was given the opportunity to talk to the real Elizabeth again, the very second I saw her, I would try to arrange a meeting with her and her mother. Then I would try and get all of the answers at once. I knew that it was a risky plan because Elizabeth may not be prepared for the things that I planned to talk about. I would have to take her back to the day that she was raped and that, in itself, could end my plans to get any further with her.

For now, I would leave it as a contingency. If I got the opportunity to talk to her again, I would be very careful, but I would get as much done as I possibly could for as long as I could. I figured if I pushed her, she would probably end up in another bathroom, screaming, only to come out as someone I did not want to see.

The one thing I had going for me was that Liz had no idea that I was well. I had to make sure that it stayed that way. Deep down, I was worried that Liz had me fooled and she may have led me to believe that I was talking to the real Elizabeth. I figured that it was a chance that I would have to take. If she didn't know, then all was well until the next time we met. If she did know, then she would very likely be prepared for me the next time we met. This put a good amount of fear in me, but I subdued the fear to the point where I knew I would be able to react when the time came. If there was one thing I recognized, it was that I would have to be ready for anything. If I allowed her to fool me, there was a lot that could ultimately happen because of my mistake.

I decided that I'd had enough sitting behind that desk trying to plan for a situation that I realized I had no control over. I went back upstairs again and gathered my things. I decided that I was going to see Sheila after all. I felt that I should have waited at one point, but now I couldn't justify the reasons why. Every reason I had was dependant on some other factor that I couldn't predict.

So as a rule, I went with the most obvious choice, which was to execute what I had control over and let the situation itself determine the next steps to take.

It was a beautiful day outside. Although I was used to walking, taking a cab, or using public transportation, I decided that today I would drive. It wasn't anything new for me to be driving instead of the other alternatives, but it had been years since I'd done it with any frequency. In fact, I hadn't driven alone since I'd gotten out of the hospital. The fact that I could concentrate and that I was myself gave me the confidence to get back behind the wheel.

The decision to drive again came at a cost. I knew that as soon as Elizabeth saw that a car was missing from the garage, she would come after me. She would know that I was more in control than she was willing for me to be. I would be at risk of her doing something to me that could render me useless to the rest of the world. I decided that if I was going to do this, I would be starting on a journey that was a one-way trip. Either it would work out in a positive way, or I could very well wind up dead. I didn't know that she could actually kill me, but whatever the alternative, it would be anything less than desirable for me.

I went into the kitchen briefly and looked in a drawer by the sink where my father kept the spare keys to almost everything. It only took a few seconds to identify a set of car keys that would do. I grabbed the keys and headed out the front door and made a beeline for the garage. Then I opened the far right door. I hopped in my father's black Ferrari. The last time I saw this car was when I put the new registration stickers on the license plate. The registrations came in the mail, and I knew to put them on the cars as soon as I got them so they didn't get lost in the shuffle of thoughts in my mind.

After putting the key in the ignition and turning it, the engine came to life with the wind of the turbine sounding off in the garage. To my dad, it was like music to his ears. He bought that car to add some youth to his life. I always thought it was ironic that my father thought adding youth was more beneficial than staving off old age. The idea of a good diet and exercise was so far beyond him as a means of "adding youth" to his life. He would rather look young, sit in a sleek car, and wear clothes to match.

I backed the car out of the garage and drove carefully down the driveway toward the iron gate. One might think it odd that the day I decided to become reacquainted with driving, I would pick such a vehicle to do it with. It was my choice, though, and I was going to succeed in getting to my destination regardless of what the horsepower was. My father used to tell me, "Son, if you are going to do anything, you might as well do it in style."

I didn't necessarily agree, but even I had to admit to myself that I really liked this car. I left the gate behind me with a screech of the tires. I wasn't showing off; I just wasn't used to the way the Ferrari handled yet. I figured that once I got on the highway, I would be fine. I looked around cautiously as I drove down the street. If I saw the green Jaguar pass me from the other direction, I would have to make plans to not go back to the Livingston Manor. But it didn't seem to me that I would be seeing my father's favorite ride any time soon. Lately, I had scarcely seen Elizabeth when I wasn't actively looking for her.

The sign for the highway came up, and I breathed a sigh of relief. I maneuvered the Ferrari into the right lane and entered the highway smoothly.

"Just like falling off a bike."

I was much more comfortable behind the wheel of the car now than when I started. In fact, it was like second nature to me. I zipped in and out of traffic until I found a comfortable spot in the fast lane. From then on, I just kept with the flow of traffic and proceeded on the journey to the hospital. I wasn't thinking about what I was going to say any longer. I figured that this time, Elizabeth's mother would have a lot more to say to me. I believed that she might answer my questions even before I'd gotten a chance to ask them. I really hoped that this was true, because if it was, it would make it much easier to realize what I had to do next.

Waiting for the Cause

** Jacob**

As I rolled into the hospital parking lot, my heart started beating faster. I knew that I was at the point of no return. My fate, along with that of my half-sister, was about to be determined shortly. I got lucky and found a parking spot close to the front entrance of the hospital, got out quickly, and headed to the doors.

While I walked, I was reminded of the time just a few days ago when I did this the first time, stepping out of a cab as I followed Elizabeth. I also thought about Stacy and my initial meeting her. I told her that I had to go out of town on business and that I would call her when I got back. I figured if I ran into her, I could say that I had plans to come see her, which was not far from the truth.

I felt that while I did need to talk to Sheila to get more information about Elizabeth, I also needed to talk to Stacy so I could learn a few things about myself. No one had ever taken the time to explain to me what I had gone through during my stay upstairs. When I spoke to Stacy the last time I was here, I learned more than I'd ever known about my hospitalization. I was right about at the spot where she called my name before, and I halfway expected to hear it again. In truth, I hesitated to look around in case she may have been standing somewhere in the lobby and might see me. This struck me as odd and slightly annoyed me. These were not the actions of Jacob Livingston III. I never used to avoid situations that could result in a tad bit of awkwardness. I wondered what happened to me and vowed to make some changes as soon as I had the time to think about what was different about me.

I made my way to the elevators and continued to feel like I was going back in time and was retracing my steps as I went. I pushed the button on the wall and the doors opened immediately. Then I stepped into the elevator and had the strange sense that I was just here, talking to some guy that I knew from a long time ago. I couldn't figure out what it was, but I was sure that it happened.

The elevator began to move after I pushed the button for the ninth floor and the doors closed. I looked into the lobby as the doors shut and thought about how interesting it would be to have the doors shut on this world and move on to the next to have a different life before me as the doors opened to the next world. I laughed silently to myself because thoughts like that often crossed my mind years before all of this happened. I took it as a good sign that things were becoming normal once more. My confidence stemmed from being surrounded by things that I created for myself as comfort items. The thoughts that went through my mind were a big part of that comfort zone, and I made sure that I stayed in control of them.

The elevator went straight to the ninth floor without stopping. I was kind of glad because I wanted to get the first few minutes of this reunion over so that I could concentrate and not have to deal with the anxious feelings I had. I actually had butterflies in my stomach as I took my first steps out of the elevator. I tried my best to ignore them, but they were going to be there until they were ready to go themselves. I figured I would just have to deal with them for the time being. I came to the crotchet name plate on the wall that said Sheila Williams and knocked on the door. Then I waited patiently as the door pulled back to reveal the smiling face of a young nurse.

"Hello," she greeted me warmly.

"Hi. I'm here to see Sheila Williams."

"Miss Sheila, you have a caller," she said as she pulled the door open wider for me to pass. "And he's cute!" she said while pushing past me to get out of the doorway. "I'll talk with you later," she said to Sheila as she disappeared behind the door.

"Jacob!" Sheila said as she finally saw who it was coming to see her. She stood up from her seat on the bed and reached for me, giving me a hug.

I was still a bit unnerved at the greetings I got from her. I didn't really know why she would be so happy to see me, but I put the thought aside as I hugged her.

"I have been thinking a lot since we last saw each other," she said, smiling.

"I didn't think you would be so happy to see me."

"Well, I get out of this place today."

"Oh, well, that explains a great deal."

"Sit down, young man; make yourself comfortable."

She guided me to the same spot on the bed where I sat the previous visit and stared at the picture of Sheila and her daughter. I inadvertently started looking for the picture so I could focus on the reason I was here. I could see that none of the things that were previously displayed were here this time. The room looked a lot less comfortable and more like the patient's room that it was. Sheila noticed me looking around and told me that she had packed everything up the night before in anticipation of her daughter showing up some time this morning.

"I thought she would have been by here already, but it's okay because I have a good number of people to say goodbye to and they have been coming by all morning."

"I haven't seen her since yesterday."

"I'm still amazed at how you two know each other!"

"Well, it's not quite like you may be thinking. Do you remember what we talked about the last time we spoke?"

"Yes, I do."

"Well, let me give you an update on what I've learned about Elizabeth." I relaxed a bit and prepared myself to tell the story.

"When I came home from here a few days ago, I went to my actual home where I grew up. I was staying with Elizabeth in a house over in Watts for some time. I don't know how long I'd actually been living there, but my guess is that it had been quite a while."

Sheila looked at me intensely as I spoke. She wasn't sure what I was going to say, but she looked like she needed to prepare herself for some kind of disturbing news. So far, everything I was saying was okay and she relaxed slowly, but not completely.

"Anyway, as I made my way up to my room, I could smell her perfume throughout the house, but I figured that it was from the nurse, um…Stacy that I'd met earlier that day. When I got to my room, there was someone sleeping in my bed, holding a picture of me and my father. She was wearing a hat and her hair was covering her face, and I didn't know who it was until I reached out to shake her. When I saw the muscles in her arms, I knew it was at least part of her."

I paused for a minute to see if Sheila was paying attention. She was; not only that, she was hanging onto my every word.

"What do you mean, 'at least part of her'?" she asked as she braced herself for more news she wasn't ready for.

"Well, remember when I told you that your daughter might be suffering from a multiple personality disorder?"

"Yes, I do remember it."

"Well, when she woke, she jumped and scooted herself to the top of the bed as far as she could get away from me. That was not the Elizabeth that I know. The Elizabeth that I know has a personality to match the muscles that she has. She is as tough as nails and fears nothing. This woman, however, was genuinely frightened until she saw who I was. Then she was speaking to me as if we'd met for the first time. Honestly, we were meeting for the first time because I had no idea who I was talking to. I asked her if she was hungry, so we both went downstairs to find something to eat. She was holding my hand the whole time.

"That is nothing like the Elizabeth I know. We sat down and started talking about you for a minute. She asked me how I came to know you and I kind of stepped around the answer. Then she asked me why I wasn't as surprised about meeting her as she was about seeing me for the first time. I told her that it wasn't the first time I'd met her. I also told her that I had some things to tell her that she might not like.

"I started with the story about how my parents died, and I told her that I thought that she was there. It didn't faze her as I thought it would. She thought that she was there and that her life was in danger, too. She asked me some questions about how I really came to know her and I told her about how when I woke up in the hospital from my coma, the first person that I saw was Elizabeth. She asked me if she had a twin because she didn't remember anything about seeing me in the hospital. I said no, that she didn't have a twin. Then she said that if she didn't have a twin and I said that it was Elizabeth that I saw, what was I trying to tell her.

"That's when I told her the rest of the story about what I believe I heard her say when I was laying on the floor in the closet. She didn't handle it well and took off running through the house, screaming. Usually when she does that, shortly thereafter, I see the Elizabeth that I know, the one who calls herself Liz."

I took a long breath after telling that part of the story. Sheila looked at me with worried eyes.

"Well, that was the last time I saw her. This morning when I woke up, she was gone. As I said before, that was the first time I'd ever talked to that Elizabeth and I don't know if I'll ever get the opportunity to do it again."

Sheila looked at me with tired eyes.

"I knew that there was something different about her. There were times when I would lay here half asleep and Elizabeth was here, and she did seem different. She always put her hands to the sides of her head, like she had a bad headache, and paused for a moment before she spoke. Thinking back on it, I could believe that I saw her change right before my eyes on more than one occasion. What was she wearing when you saw her?"

"She was wearing jeans and a T-shirt with a hat on and her hair down," I answered.

"Hmmm..." she replied. "She always wore her hair down to cover her face. She didn't like people looking at her, especially men."

I could understand that. I felt that if I had been through what she had, I wouldn't want anyone looking at me either.

"As far as the jeans," Sheila began again, "Elizabeth never wore them. She mostly wore long, summer-like dresses that were kind of baggy. They were cute, but they covered her up well. She usually would stay away from anything that accentuated any part of her body. I say usually because I have seen her in some outfits that I would dare say it was not my daughter in them. There was a time she came home with what I called an all-black cat woman suit on with a big red sash around her waist. She walked right past me without speaking and had this look of hate on her face that scared me."

"Now that would be Liz!" I said quickly. "She wore stuff like that all the time. It was like she wanted everyone to look at her."

"I agree!" Sheila said. "When I saw her, it was the first time I realized that she was so big. It wasn't much longer after that that I began passing out from time to time and that's when I started my stay here."

"So we know what we're dealing with?"

"It would appear so," she answered me. "But I can't begin to say what we can do about it."

"I have an idea, but the situation has to be just right in order for it to work. I believe now that as long as you are here to speak to her that we may be able to keep her true personality around long enough to learn how much she knows about her actions."

I didn't take it as a long shot, but I did believe that my plan could backfire and she might try and protect her mother from me if she felt threatened.

"She's bound to be here sooner or later, so I'll just hang around, if that's okay with you," I said, looking over at Sheila.

"That's fine," Sheila said, "as long as you don't mind a visitor or two."

I spent the next few hours with Sheila, talking about various things from Elizabeth's childhood to how much she knew about my father. There were things I had to come to terms with and her affair with my father was one of them. I was astonished to find out that my mother knew about my father's infidelity. She checked the mail at the post office one day and found that she had the wrong keys. My father had gotten a post office box right next to the one that they both normally used. When her key didn't fit into the correct one, she became a bit confused about the number and tried the one next to it. She didn't think twice when it opened, but she was almost sure that it was the incorrect box. That is, until she saw the contents of the box that she opened. It had obviously been a while since he'd checked it. Sheila told me that there were several letters written by her in the box.

My mother went to the counter and had the clerk verify that the box was, indeed, registered to my father, and it was. She also verified that the box that wouldn't open was the correct one and had the clerk retrieve the mail from it for her. My mother answered the letters herself, understanding that Sheila was a victim in this situation, and she intended to make sure that her husband's wrongdoing would not make anyone suffer. Sheila told my mom that she would not accept any money for herself, but she would be grateful if she made sure that her daughter, the illegitimate daughter of my father, would be taken care of. My mother agreed, and she went far beyond what Sheila had asked for.

She set up a trust for Elizabeth to be used for her education. It was not only for college, but for all of her needs through every year of school she would have. That was how Elizabeth came to attend private schools and why she had the resources to do so much. She was actually double dipping between accounts that were set up by both of my parents, without the other's knowledge.

I had no idea how she could pull such a thing off but my mother was a very shrewd person and it was obvious that she was not to be thought of as anything but that. I really admired her. I also looked up to my father, too. I was really disappointed at the thought that he could have done such a thing to my mom, but I had learned that there was little respect for marriage in most families. I also learned that to some extent, everyone seemed to have to go through something like that to validate the strength of their relationships. I didn't see why my family had to be any different. It was just one of those things that I could have gone through life never knowing, and it wouldn't have bothered me a bit.

Driving to Destiny

** Elizabeth **

I was now speeding toward the hospital, having completed my errands and was ready for the meeting with my long lost training partner. All I could think about was the great time I had dancing with her to the sounds of Johnny Gill and showing her oh so willing body "the way" as it was shown to me. I had never felt more connected to anyone in my life. I felt it was the key to my survival to get back what I lost. I love her so much. I can't understand why she's been so lost to me for so long.

She will be happy to see me; she has to be. Everyone needs love in their life, and it's up to me to show her that she can have love too…

** Alonzo **

Riiing! The phone sitting next to me rang, startling my already unnerved frame. The caller ID listed the caller as the Los Angeles Police Department.

"Hello?"

"Mr. Taylor?" a man's voice said over the phone.

"Yes."

"We may have a good lead on what happened to your sister."

"Outstanding!" I replied, trying not to leave myself vulnerable to bad news.

"I thought you'd feel that way. Anyway, we did a routine check of car rental places since a lot of times when there is foul play involved, the victims' credit cards are often used for a variety of things," the voice stated.

"Victim?" I said, almost in tears.

"Let me finish," the voice interrupted. "Your sister's car is over at the dealership where she bought it. It's being serviced right now. The dealership rented her a car a few days ago because they knew it would take some time to get her car back to her. Well, the rental car company reported one of it's cars had been in an accident about three days ago, and your sister's name is on the contract for the car." He paused.

"Oh, my God!" I was quickly losing hope.

"The day of the accident, two women were taken to the UCLA Medical Center who were the victims of what is called a TA Rollover. In plain terms, what this means is a traffic accident in which one or more of the vehicles involved was overturned."

The man on the phone was driving me crazy. It was as if he were delaying a point that my entire life depended on.

"Can you get to the point, please!" I stated impatiently.

"I was just trying to be thorough, sir," the man at the other end said in a slightly offended tone. "We here at LAPD take our work very seriously, and we like to pass on all of the hard-earned information to the people who file the reports with us."

"What is your name?" I asked at the end of my rope.

"Oh, I apologize. My name is Inspector Guthrie, Hal Guthrie."

"Inspector Guthrie," I said slowly. "Is my sister okay?" I waited patiently for an answer.

"Well, we are not sure. I haven't received word from the hospital yet."

"So you are not sure if it is my sister at that hospital?" I asked.

"As I said, we are still waiting for an answer."

My cell phone began to vibrate at that moment. I was both worried and irritated and didn't want to be bothered by anyone at that time. I was trying to turn my attention back to the inspector on the phone, but I instinctively snapped the phone from its clip on my side and looked at the number. My heart nearly jumped out of my chest. I looked at the house phone and just hung it up with the voice on the other end still rambling. Then I quickly answered my cell phone, fumbling to push the right button to answer the call.

"Hello?" I said quietly.

"Big brother, is that you?" a familiar voice said on the other end.

"Angie! Where the hell are you?" I asked, but I already knew the answer to the question. The caller ID on my phone read UCLA Medical Ctr. "Sis, I have been going crazy trying to find you for like forever!" I trembled as I spoke.

"I'm okay, big brother. I was in an accident. I'm not sure how long I have been here, but I know that it's been a while. How is Mamma doin'?"

"She's not as bad as I am. I didn't let her know that I felt anything was wrong. But she is a little disappointed that she didn't get her phone call."

"Oh, I'm so sorry! I can't call her from here, Lonzo. You have to tell her and let her know that I'm kinda okay and then go and get her on your way here," she said in a coaxing way.

"What do you mean, 'kinda'?" I asked, preparing myself.

"Well, it hurts to talk, and I've got some pretty bad bumps and bruises. But you'll see all of that when you get here."

"Man, you don't have any idea how worried I was. You never called me back and I forgot I had even talked to you until a whole day later."

"Yeah, I know, big bro. I told you that job would consume you. You can't even think outside of that job. All you have to do is walk in the door and you're lost," AJ paused. "My entire face is on fire. I never thought I would say this, but I need something to kill the pain. Listen, I have to go, but you need to go and get Mamma, tell her the story, and, Lonzo, start the whole thing with, 'I'm okay.' Okay?"

"Sure, sis. I'll call her as soon as I get off of the phone with you."

The MRI

** Cheryl **

I sat back in my bed and listened to my friend say goodbye to her brother. I felt good about the fact that she and her family were so close. AJ had something that I had never had. The Taylor family had always been so good to me. There were times when AJ's mother was the closest thing to what I wished I'd had as a child. That didn't take anything away from how I felt about my own mother. It was just that after she passed away, I was really lost in the world. I felt that loss contributed to a lot of my bad decisions in life.

I've learned that everyone seems to wish at some point in time that they had their mother or father to lean on once they are gone. Even if they had passed on years before, that lingering thought that everything is gonna be okay with a hug, or that kiss on the forehead that just made everything better happens to most people.

Growing up is just so hard to do sometimes.

Stacy came back in the door and told me that I had to take a trip. "Let's go, sister; we have an appointment with a really big magnet."

"Huh?" I uttered, slightly confused.

"We have you scheduled for an MRI," Stacy explained. "There are some things that we have to take a better look at so that we can make sure we don't let you out of here with something that will cause you further complications."

"That makes sense," I said.

"Not that you are leaving any time soon," she added.

"How much longer do you think we'll be in here?" AJ asked as she put the phone down.

"Well, that depends on how much you all cooperate. I can't have you two traipsing around the hospital like you own the place. I need you two right there where you are, in those beds until I don't need you there anymore. But to answer your question, it shouldn't be but a few more days. The real doctors show up after the weekend, so when the surgeon gets back from whatever golf resort he flew to this weekend and the rest of the staff shows up, he can take a look at your films and your charts and he will be the one to ultimately make a decision. You guys have been through a lot. We need to make sure that we take care of you the best that we can."

As Stacy spoke, she straightened out my bed and got it ready to move. AJ just looked on as she listened to the lengthy answer Stacy gave her. I'm sure AJ didn't want to be here any longer than she had to, and I didn't want to leave until I knew I didn't have to come back for a good while. I never liked hospitals. My motivation to take care of myself came from my dislike for places like this. I always felt that if I didn't take care of myself, I would wind up like the people who were in our office everyday. That was just an unbearable thought for me.

"I know that's right!" I said as I prepared myself for the move through the hospital.

"You guys are leaving me all by myself?" AJ whimpered.

"Oh, girl, please, after all you've been through, I don't think there is much you can't handle all by yourself," Stacy stated. "I'm really proud of you, Lucky…I mean, Miss AJ. You were really strong to handle all of the treatment you got the way you did. Sometimes I hate this job because of what it makes people have to endure, but it's the ones like you that make it all worth it."

AJ was touched, I could tell. She was almost brought to the point of tears. I really liked this nurse. She cared about her work, and that's what made our situation just that much better.

"Thank you!" AJ told Stacy. "Those were really kind words. I'm so glad it was you here to help me get through all of this. That one over there is usually the one who bails me out of trouble, but I guess we both needed a hand this time."

"Okay, woman, say your farewells. It's time to go for a ride," Stacy told Cheryl. "We won't be much more than an hour," she told AJ. "Just turn on the boob tube and before you know it, we'll be on our way right back through this door."

With that, Stacy propped the door open and released the brakes from my wheeled bed. As we got out of the door, I waved a taped up hand to my friend as I said goodbye. Stacy kicked the doorstop, and the door closed behind us.

** AJ **

As the door shut, I felt the loneliness of the hospital room I was in. Being here alone would be a tough one, but I decided to be strong as I reached for the remote for the television. Last night had been a long night; my eyes were already getting heavy. I needed sleep, and that was the intent of my mind and body for the time being.

Mamma

** Alonzo **

I picked up all of my belongings I needed to take the relatively short trip over to Mamma's. The phone was ringing behind me as I closed the door to the house and turned toward the car in the driveway. *Can you believe that guy?* I thought. I assumed that it was good ol' Inspector Guthrie calling me back. "Sorry, Inspector, I'm not available for your banter."

I got in, started the car, and backed it out of the driveway. I couldn't believe the amount of stress I had been under since the last time I'd spoken to AJ. There was the multimillion dollar deal I had on the table, which almost went off without a hitch. There was some discrepancy in the money that slightly irritated the communications company executive, but between his lawyers and my quick thinking, they managed to give up even more money than they'd originally intended because of a simple change of wording. I felt like the guy just wanted to be in control. Granted he did run one of the largest companies in Europe, but he didn't have a clue about the internal workings of the business. I wound up selling him more support and services, at a higher price than originally quoted, all because the man kept saying that he wanted certain capabilities built in that he could have very well done himself. Me being a fair person, I tried to let him know what he was asking for, but the man just would not listen. So I had to make a few more million from him that could easily have been written off as compensation for services rendered by his own company. This would mean an incredible bonus for me when all was said and done.

I thought about all of the times my sister had been there for me. I couldn't remember one time when she'd forgotten about me. How I came to forget about her after such an event in her life that had shaken her, I will never know.

I wonder what it was?

I never did find out what it was that had her so upset. I'll have to ask her as soon as I see her.

Judging from the sound of her voice, I was sure that things were much worse than she let on over the phone. AJ was smart. She knew if things were bad, if she had Mamma come to the hospital thinking that she was just a little banged up, she would handle it a lot better. Then Mamma wouldn't have a chance to worry as much. Mamma was a strong person. But when it came to her children, however, she couldn't control her emotions.

I hit the highway and connected my cell phone to the plug in the car, then placed it in the holder so I didn't run the risk of being too distracted while I was driving. After that, I punched the speed dial buttons for Mamma's number.

"Hi, Ma!" I said as she answered the phone.

"Hi, yourself."

"I'm on my way over there; put some clothes on; we're taking a trip."

"A trip, huh? Where are we going?" she pushed.

"I'll be there in twenty minutes."

"You're not going to tell me where we're going?"

"Can you be ready in twenty minutes?"

"I'll see you when you get here."

"Bye, Ma," I said to her.

"All right," she said as she hung up the phone.

I sped along the highway and thought about just how I was going to tell Mamma about where AJ was. I knew from the way AJ told me that I would have to be very careful with my wording. She wasn't really aware that anything was wrong. In her mind, she was always amazed at how AJ was so punctual with her phone calls home. She probably figured that there would be times when she might just forget or have something better to do.

I approached the exit to get off the highway. By then, I had assured myself that I had the right things to say locked down in my mind. A short time later, I was pulling into the driveway and all of a sudden, I couldn't remember a thing. When I called, she seemed to be in a pretty good mood, so I figured now that maybe she would take the news better if I just got her out of the house and briefly mentioned it to her on the way.

I parked the car and got out, heading straight for the front door. Just as I was about to reach for the doorknob, the door opened and Mamma came pushing out with a light coat in her hand, nearly knocking me over.

"How could you not tell me!" she said as she pulled me along with her to the car.

I was shocked, but it didn't last for long. She always seemed to be at least three steps ahead of her children. Since as long as I could remember, she always seemed to just know everything before it happened.

"So how did you find out?" I asked as we both strapped in.

"The rental car company called me. AJ left my number as a point of contact on the rental agreement."

Way to go, sis!

"I can't believe you would try and keep something like this from me!" she complained.

"Ma! Get over it. I came all the way over here to get you, didn't I?"

"So, when were you going to tell me—when we were in the hospital already? Good Lord, you think you raise your kids right, and this is how they repay you!" she said, throwing her hands up.

I knew just to keep quiet from this point on. No matter what I said, it would be an opportunity for her to turn it into something else that I should have done, but didn't do. It was a much longer ride to the hospital than it was to get to the house. It would be a lot longer if I allowed myself to be sucked into a long discussion about how and why I hadn't told her this or that. She went on and on about seemingly nothing in particular. I just drove carefully down the highway, trying my best not to give her anything more to talk about.

No Loose Ends

** Elizabeth **

After driving around for what seemed like forever, I just pulled over to the side of the road and stopped. I was barely coherent and driving like that was a miraculous stunt. My head was throbbing, and I was nauseous. As soon as I stopped the car, it was as if I ceased to exist. I placed my hands on the sides of my head and screamed.

"Where the fuck am I now? Humph…It doesn't matter. I have some loose ends to tie up!"

I smoothed back my hair and tied it into a knot. I was inside the car again, and my ears were ringing.

I pulled out into traffic, deciding to head to Gina's house, where I had seen the news about the accident.

"I need supplies."

About thirty minutes later, I made a phone call from the house, calling the leader of my boys. I told him to assemble the entire group at a house they used for a hideaway from time to time. The gang had used it often for a hangout, so he said that it was no problem getting there.

"Make sure you are all there!" I let him know.

He knows better than to fuck with me, so he acknowledged and hung up. I gave him three good hours to get them together. I figured that was enough time for me to assemble what I needed and to get over there in time for the meeting. I looked around the house and shook my head.

"Fuckin' Gina, I'm sure you did your best."

I went into the back room and started gathering things that I would need before I met my boys.

"Sorry motherfuckers! This will be a day a lot of motherfuckers will remember!"

I packed a black duffle bag until I had everything I needed from that house. Come to find out, I had everything I needed right here. I took the bag into the kitchen and placed the things I needed on the table. After I inventoried the contents on the table, I quickly got to work.

"We have to do this just right," I said to myself as I worked carefully but rapidly. "If everything works out right, there will only be one more fuckin' thing to do."

Elizabeth down under

"Oh, Lord, I'm going to go crazy down here!"

After seeing the death of Jacob's father up close, all of my sanity went out the door. The more I screamed, the deeper I sunk into the ground until suddenly, I was falling. At this point, I just wanted to be dead. I couldn't take anymore of this torture. I landed hard on the rocky surface of a familiar ground.

I let out a final cry in pain from the landing. Somewhere in the distance, I heard a loud moan and it silenced me faster than death could have. I knew exactly where I was. I had to remind myself why I was there. Slowly, my courage labored itself to the surface.

I picked myself off of the ground and ignored the pain I felt from my fall. I wiped off my arms and was comforted with the feel of the suit that I was still wearing. I turned my head from side to side until I felt the satisfying crack of the bones in my neck. Then I was ready. I stood tall in defiance of the thing I was there to kill. I knew that I would either walk out of this dark place a winner, or that I would surely die here if I failed.

There was just enough light for me to see without me having to peer through the maze to make out where I was going. The creature moaned again, and I honed in on the sound. It seemed as if it was far away, but I wasn't going to take any chances.

Just ahead, there was a narrow pass and I would have to be careful because it didn't seem too sturdy. I took a confident step forward, but it proved to be the last I would take on that pass. The ground gave way beneath me, and I began to fall. I hit the side of the cave wall and began to tumble down a slope. I did my best to keep from screaming and just concentrated on the landing. Quickly I covered up my head so I wouldn't strike it on a cave wall. When I finally came to a stop, I stood to my feet as fast as I could in anticipation of the creature's pounce.

I had been over this seemingly a thousand times, and I was well rehearsed. I would not be caught off guard as I had been so many times before. I felt that was the key to me getting the upper hand. Too many times before I was blind-sided or snatched from behind, and I started out losing.

"That's not gonna happen this time! Do you hear me? That's not gonna happen!"

** Liz **

"That's not gonna happen!" I repeated over and over. I had no idea why I was saying what I was. I barely realized the words came out of my mouth. I just concentrated on the job at hand as I mixed and assembled the items on the table.

By the time I was done, two good hours had gone by. I put my finished project in the duffle bag and padded it with a special material. I got myself together and went into the back room to find some real clothes. When I was done, I looked in the mirror in the bathroom and admired myself. I loved being alive and in control. I turned from the mirror and it seemed like the reflection stayed there for a second. I turned back around and I saw me as I was when I walked into the house earlier, dressed in jeans and a T-shirt. I looked harder and the reflection in the mirror mouthed, "I'm coming for you."

I didn't know what the fuck that was all about, but I'm taking it to mean I'm coming for you, Cheryl. I felt no fear, so I didn't think that the reflection was the true owner of the body I hijacked. That bitch, Elizabeth, was warning me that my days were numbered.

I turned away from the mirror again and walked out to the living room, where I carefully picked up the bag and then walked out the front door. Placing the bag in the backseat of the Jag, I got in. I would be right on time when I got to the spot.

A short time later, I rolled by the front of the house, but parked the car a little bit down the street. I got out of the car, grabbed the duffle bag, and headed to the front door. After ringing the doorbell, I walked in. As I did so, I heard the familiar snap of a bolt being cocked back on an automatic handgun.

"Whoa!" the owner of the gun said. "I didn't know it was you. Not too many people ring that doorbell."

"Is everyone here?" I asked as I looked around the living room.

"Yep! Dey all right here," he answered.

I could see that there were the right number of bodies and the right faces all sitting around the living room. Then I placed the duffle bag on the floor in the middle of them and said, "Don't move."

I turned around and walked out the front door, gently pulling it behind me, but not so hard that it would close. The intent was for them to think I was coming right back. As I got into the car, I pulled a remote from my waistband, started the car, and drove off.

"Perfect!"

I looked around and there was no one outside in the neighborhood. With that, I pushed a button on the remote as I turned the corner and the next thing that happened looked like something out of World War III. There was a violent explosion. I know one of those cats had to be nosy! It would be the last thing he would remember in this life! The heat from that blast vaporized him and everything else in that room.

No evidence!

I smiled as I drove down the busy main street. "Another loose end tied up. Only one more thing to do. Here I come, Cheryl, ready or not. You have a choice to make and not much time to make it…"

When I got to the house, I was there for all of about fifteen minutes. I couldn't stand the fact that Cheryl was someplace and not know what she was thinking, what she was doing, or how she was doing, for that matter. I put a suit on as if I was going to a business meeting of some kind. But I was going to see Cheryl, for what could be the last time. I decided that if Cheryl didn't want to be with me, then she would just have to die. Her fucking boss was written into that plan, too. It was going to be up to Cheryl whether she or her boss live or die after today.

I was on the road again, anxious because I didn't know what was going to happen in the next few hours. I was very confused and seemed to be fading in and out. I would look up and realize that I was driving. When I looked up again, I would be in a different place. As hard as I tried to hold on, on I couldn't. I was determined to get close to Cheryl to find out whether she would be with me.

I finally arrived at the hospital entrance and placed a handicapped placard on the rear view mirror, parking right next to the entrance. Next, I got out of the car and straightened out my clothes. I thought to myself that I had to look good for this meeting. I made a beeline for the elevators and caught a ride with several other people, all there for different reasons. Some were patients, some were hospital staff, and the rest were visiting relatives, coming to see their loved ones.

I hate you all!

I looked at all of them in disgust, but made an effort not to carry that look on my face. I simply looked ahead at the elevator doors and waited for them to open. The doors opened to the floor I was looking for, so I stepped out and immediately began to feel a bit lightheaded. I still didn't know where I was going, but I'd been in that hospital enough times to start looking in the right place. I walked down to the nursing station with my hand on my right temple, trying to massage out a headache that was quickly forming there. When I got to the station, I asked the nurse about the accident and the two women that were involved. I didn't know the nurse behind the counter, and that was a good thing to me since it could complicate matters if someone recognized me too soon. The nurse told me that they were in the same room down the hall and that I would have to stop by the nurse's station on the other side before I went there. I smiled and thanked her, assuring her that I would head straight to the nurses station. I then turned to find the room down the hall. I had to make a stop in the restroom first, so I headed to the door marked with the men/women's placard on it and closed the door behind me. As soon as the door closed, I nearly fainted from the pain in my head. I locked the door and sat on the closed lid of the toilet while I held on for the painful ride.

Why am I here? And where am I this time? I can feel Cheryl all in my mind. She's hurt…She's been in an accident. I have to find her!

I sat there for a good ten minutes until I finally realized that I was where I was supposed to be.

I never worried about how I got places. I just seemed to know why I was there. I knew that I was in the hospital and that for the first time in a very long time, I was going to have the opportunity to talk with the woman with whom I was so in love. I stood up in the restroom and checked myself in the mirror. I liked what I saw. I was dressed for a power meeting with an executive. That's how I felt, and I was there to pitch for a second chance with the one I loved.

The Meeting

** AJ **

I was sitting in the room going stir-crazy. Cheryl was only supposed to be gone for an hour, but Stacy came back and said that complications with the machine set the time schedule back a bit, so she had to wait for another patient needing an MRI first. I flipped through the channels on the television and wondered what my mother was going to do when she showed up. I would have thought that Alonzo and Mamma would have been here by now.

I took a deep breath and sighed. I wondered just how I wound up where I was. I looked at my life as if everything I did was representative of the things that happened to me. I searched my mind for a reason that would explain why I had to be in a hospital with broken bones and tubes attached to me.

I could never express those feelings out loud because it would completely contradict the tools I used in my profession. I could easily debunk the notion that all things happen for a reason for someone else. I couldn't, however, shake the "why me?" feeling that permeated my thought process. I finally just wrote it all off as just another thing I had to go through in order for me to empathize with someone else that had just gone through it.

There was a knock at the door. I was still for a moment, and then I instinctively said, "Come in."

The door opened and a beautiful woman walked through it with a curious look on her face. I looked at her and thought that she looked like some kind of lawyer or someone who obviously carried a very large presence with her.

"Hello?" I managed from the back of the room.

"Hi," the woman answered. "Maybe I'm in the wrong place..."

"Who are you looking for?" I asked politely.

"Well, I'm not sure," the woman said. "What I mean to say is that I'm not sure she's here. You see, a friend of mine has been missing for a few days, and I was wondering if she was here. Her name is Cheryl, and she may have been involved in a car accident. It was all over the news and I...I'm hoping that it isn't her here, but at the same time, maybe I'm hoping that it is. Do you know what I mean?"

I was just amazed at the way that this woman looked. I couldn't figure out what it was, but she just did not look like anyone else I had ever encountered before. Jacob told me about how he had names for the different types of people that there were in the world. He subscribed to the theory that there were very few in terms of categories. I wondered what name he would have for this woman because she was clearly different. I could see it in just the few seconds since her arrival.

In my awe, I somewhat lost my bearing and let slip that Cheryl was, indeed, here without so much as asking the woman who she was. I realized I made the mistake, but was placated when the woman reached out and began to introduce herself. Everything from that point on seemed to happen in slow motion. I could hear the woman speaking and, at the same time, reaching out to shake hands, but there was something wrong.

"Well, hi," the woman started. "My name is Tia," she said as she shook my hand. I barely had time to react to the name because I had another problem to deal with. As I shook hands with her right hand, she reached out with her left and stuck me with a hypodermic in the same arm I was welcoming her with. The drug took affect the very second it hit my bloodstream. I could see her place a hand up to her temple like she had a headache.

** Elizabeth **

I have to get her out of the picture for the moment! I can't concentrate. Get the needle in her quick! I have to sedate her so that my time with Cheryl will be uninterrupted...

The drug I chose was untraceable in the bloodstream, but as I pushed it in, the door opened with a bang behind me, forcing me to pull the needle out prematurely and put it away.

** Stacy **

"All right, Miss AJ, we are back and all in one piece. Oh! I see we have company."

When I saw the woman standing by AJ, at first I didn't recognize her because she was dressed so differently and her hair covered a good portion of her face. A few seconds passed before I realized who I was talking to. Instantly I was taken back to the day when I kissed Jacob and told him that I loved him. Cheryl saw the look of fear on my face, but she couldn't see why because she came in the door head first and she couldn't see behind her.

"What are you doing here?" I finally asked Liz.

I asked with a slightly cordial tone because I was scared to death of the woman. I knew that she could easily cost me this job that meant so much to me. I continued to push Cheryl forward until we were all the way in the room.

** Cheryl **

I came riding up along side of a sight that I never expected to behold. With tears in my eyes, I did the only thing I could think of on such short notice…scream.

Mamma

** Alonzo**

Mamma never let up the entire trip to the hospital. My mind was numb by the time we found a parking spot near the rear entrance. I got out of the car and out of the corner of my eye realized that Mamma didn't budge. With a sigh I calmly walked around the car and opened her door. She wouldn't even look at me as she stepped out.

"Mamma..."

I stood behind her with my arms out. I know my mother well and both AJ and I can tell you that she will not be deprived of her emotions. She would do everything in her power to go back in time and feel everything she believes she should have felt up to now! I believe she felt all of the last few days she didn't know to worry in the relatively short trip we took to the hospital.

Mamma turned around and stepped into my arms. She couldn't hold back her tears any longer.

"Lord you think you raise your children right!" She sobbed.

"I know Mamma I just didn't want to worry you."

"She's my child Alonzo it's my right to worry!"

"I'm sorry Mamma I just didn't know how to tell you. She says she's okay but she told me not to let you worry. Let's go inside and see what's going on."

After a final squeeze she let go and cleaned up her face. We began to walk and she took my arm in hers. Mamma is as strong a woman as they come, but she has a weakness for her children that's for sure.

"We have to stop by the gift shop." She reached in her purse to look for some cash.

I wasn't about to argue, I was just happy we were continuing to walk. I needed to really se how AJ was doing. This wasn't over yet for me. We finally reached the entrance and I held the door open for Mamma. She walked in slowly. The flower shop was right ahead of us down the corridor. You would think that we would be in and out in a minute. I think Mamma was stalling to prepare herself for whatever was about to happen once we made it upstairs.

She moved through the gift shop and I saw the expression on her face change. She made a beeline to the very rear of the shop. I couldn't see what it was until she turned around with a smile on her face. She had picked up a teddy bear holding onto some small foil balloons tightly. The balloons swayed back and forth like they were trying to free themselves from its grasp.

"Let's go Mamma AJ is waiting."

She quickly paid the lady at the counter and we headed to the Information Desk. I almost didn't know how to begin but Mamma took over in her usual business like way.

"My daughter was in an accident and she's been here a few days..." she started.

"Is you daughter's name AJ?" The attendant asked.

"How did you know?" Mamma looked surprised.

"We were put on alert to ask." He said politely. "Head up those elevators to the seventh floor, turn right and see the nurse at the desk. She will take care of you."

"Thank you so much!" Mamma walked and talked at the same time making another beeline to the elevators.

"Thank you." I said to him as I tried to keep up with her. She was already stepping into the elevator when I reached her. She pushed the button for the seventh floor and we rode quietly as the elevator made two stops before we made it there.

** Jacob **

I was glad that my encounter with Elizabeth's mother had worked out so well. As she sat with me, we talked for a long time, learning a lot from each other. The topic of conversation at this point was about Nurse Caugman. Sheila told me that she used to talk about me all the time to her. I was amazed at how small the world seemed to be. I had plans to talk to Stacy while I was here, but I didn't know how long that would take until Sheila suggested that we go down the hall to find her. I agreed to walk with her, and we both got up from the bed. Both Sheila and I had to stretch from sitting in awkward positions for so long. We both walked down the hall to the nurse's station. The nurse I had met at the door when I first knocked smiled when we walked up. She said that Nurse Caugman was two floors down. Sheila asked if I could escort her to the nurse's station downstairs just to say goodbye since she may not get the opportunity to see her before she left.

The nurse said that it was okay because Sheila was just about out of there, but that she still had to sign out of the nurse's station with her daughter. Sheila said that was fine with her and asked that the nurse let her daughter know where she went in case she showed up and we weren't there. The nurse nodded her head in compliance, and both Sheila and I went on our way.

I felt a little strange as I walked side by side with Sheila down the hallway to the elevators. We didn't say much; we just sort of enjoyed the new scenery as we walked. As we reached the elevators, I pushed the button on the wall and it lit up a bright green. A few moments, later a soft *ding* sounded, and the doors opened. I politely let Sheila pass before me, and she nodded in thanks as she took her place at the back of the elevator. I followed behind her and pushed the button for the floor that we were headed for.

It took almost no time at all for the elevator to reach the seventh floor. As the doors opened, we both remarked about how fast we got there. We exited the elevator and headed in the direction of the nurse's station. I looked and thought I saw Stacy at the end of the hall.

"Is that her right there?" I asked Sheila.

"I can't see a thing without my glasses," she answered. "Although I do see much better than I used to..."

I was pretty sure it was Stacy I saw pushing a patient through a door at the end of the hall. I decided that it was and suggested that we wait for her at the nurse's station midway down the hall. Sheila agreed, so we walked to the station and waited.

** Cheryl **

After I screamed, the calm and collected woman who called herself Tia came unraveled and took a few steps back, holding her head as she went. Stacy jumped as she heard the sound coming from my mouth. She didn't know what to do. Most of all, she didn't know why I screamed. Tia stepped forward and caught Stacy by the neck, pushing her forward and all the way to the other side of the room. She was stopped abruptly by the wall as she came into contact with it, hitting her head. Tia opened the door to the room and pushed Stacy hard out into the hall.

I was a mess lying strapped into the bed unable to move. I managed to free my arm so that I could wipe the tears from my face. Tia came back to the bed, holding her head again.

"Cheryl, baby, what's the matter?"

I wanted to scream again, but I calmed down a bit.

"What do you want from me?" I asked in frustration.

"You just left the house that day and disappeared. You made me feel terrible. I didn't know what happened to you, girl; I was so scared."

I wasn't buying that shit! In my mind, I went back over the story that AJ had told me earlier. This bitch was dangerous, and I wanted nothing to do with her.

As Tia spoke to me, she placed her hand in her pocket. I was already paranoid while I was looking around, trying to figure out what to do when I saw her reach into her pocket as she leaned closer. I thought quickly and felt I had one chance.

"But you didn't ask me," I said to Tia. I spoke in a timid, yet welcoming tone.

"You had to be shown," Tia insisted.

"And you showed me," I interrupted. "But you didn't give me the choice! You took advantage of me, Tia."

I made sure I kept eye contact with her as I spoke. I could see that Tia seemed a bit more relaxed. She continued to move her face closer to mine.

"I didn't know how else to give you what you needed," Tia said softly.

"There was a better way," I said, keeping her gaze. "I didn't know what I wanted then. I know what I want now."

"What do you want?" Tia asked. Her face was now inches from mine.

I paused to really look at my adversary. Then I moved my face closer to Tia's and started to whisper.

"I want…" I said softly as I balled my fist up and swung as hard as I could hitting Tia square on her chin. "I want you out of my freaking life!"

Tia flew backward with the force of the blow and hit her head on the hard linoleum floor of the hospital room. She let out a feminine yelp and her eyes disappeared inside of her head.

** Elizabeth **

Out of nowhere, I was struck by something that I didn't see in the dimly lit cave. I hit the ground hard, but got back up on my knees as quickly as I could. I worked my jaw back and forth as whatever it was that hit me caught me right on the chin. I was pissed by now, and I stood to my feet, screaming, "Where are you!"

Taking it to the Beast

** Jacob **

I said hi to an orderly as he emerged from the rear of the nursing station. He was a pretty big guy, and it made me wonder why he chose that particular profession. There was a disturbance down the hall that made us both look in that direction. Sheila and I both gasped as we saw Stacy come flying out of the room and sliding along the floor until she hit the wall in the hallway with a loud thump. The orderly quickly jumped over the counter and ran down the hall with both of us trailing behind him.

Stacy moaned as she came to after about a minute of the orderly shaking her.

"Are you okay?" he said to her as he patted her face lightly.

"Stop her!" Stacy yelled as best she could, pointing at the door she came flying out of.

The orderly let her head down lightly and turned to investigate what was happening behind the door.

** Alonzo**

The doors to the elevator opened and as Mamma and me walked out we saw someone fly out of a door and slide across the hall floor hitting her head on the wall.

"What on earth?" Mamma gasped.

I saw a big guy in white jump over the counter at the Nurses Station and two other people standing there followed him. I couldn't tell what was going on but I could see now that the person that was on the ground was a nurse. She pointed to the door and all three people went running into the room. I rushed down to where the nurse was pulling Mamma with me and knelt down to see if she was okay.

"That was quite a tumble!" I told her, "are you okay?"

"I'll be okay but I need to get in there."

"Okay hold on for two seconds." I put my hands on her shoulder.

She looked up at me and the expression on her face went from pain to one that was hard to describe. This was one fine woman! I couldn't stop looking at her. She just returned my stare until all of a sudden she scooted back against the wall and began to fix her hair.

"Shh Shhh…I hushed. Let's get you on your feet.

"There's quite a commotion going on in there" Mamma sort of warned.

"I have to get in there!" The nurse said as I got her to her feet. We followed her as she pushed the swinging door open.

** Cheryl **

Tia recovered from the blow and quickly got to her feet, screaming, "Where are you?" She was looking around wildly. She found a metal trash can and grabbed it, lifting it over her head and turning toward me. As she did this, the door to the room opened and a very large man clad in white came bursting through the door. He had to jump over my bed to stop her from bashing me over the head with the trash can. Tia grit her teeth as she saw the orderly come flying over the bed, tackling her and landing on top of her.

** Elizabeth **

I looked around wildly for some kind of weapon to use against the beast. I found a rock and lifted it over my head. Out of nowhere, something hit me head on and I went flying backward. I didn't see it coming, but the creature came at me with blazing speed. I found myself on my back once again with the creature breathing heavily on top of me. I panicked immediately and screamed as I was taken right back to the night I was raped. I quickly gathered my thoughts and pushed the creature off of me with all of my might. The beast was thrown backward, and I got to my feet. It drained my energy as it came in contact with me. I shook off the fear that I was feeling and concentrated on the confidence building from the times I thought about beating this thing.

I crouched down to lower my center of gravity and faced the enemy before me. We circled each other and waited for one another to make a move. I was tired of dealing with this thing so I lunged forward and reached out for its throat. It was much too fast for me as it dodged my move and swept my feet from under me. I hit the ground hard and as the creature came at me again, I caught it in the midsection with the heel of my foot. It howled in pain and rolled away from me long enough to recover from the blow.

The creature let out a voracious roar. I felt the sound vibrate to my very core. It reminded me of the past fights I lost to this thing. I had no intention of losing this time because I felt that I would not survive if I did. My mind flashed and I saw a man in white in its place, holding his stomach like I kicked him instead of the creature. As soon as I let my guard down, he turned right back into the beast and lunged back at me, thrusting his clawed hands around my throat.

I struggled, trying to remove his hands from my throat. He was choking me, and I was slowly losing consciousness. I struggled on the floor of the cave as the creature had me pinned down, and it was squeezing my throat shut. The longer it remained in contact with me, the less energy I had. I could feel the strength leaving my arms as they began to feel like rubber. I was beginning to believe that I could not beat this thing. I had let it control my life for much too long, and it seemed that now it would kill me. In my mind, I thought about the mother I was leaving behind. I loved my mother tremendously. She was the only light in my world of darkness. Now it seemed as I was failing myself, I was failing my mother as well.

I wept silently in my mind as I weakened even further. I could feel the last of the will that I used to beckon the creature slowly melt away. I wondered now if that was such a good idea as the life left my body. I had all but given up when a voice from somewhere sounded off near me.

"Hey!" a woman shouted, standing above me.

I looked up and saw Liz standing on a rock, looking down at me. She looked me in the eyes and threw something to me. I couldn't tell what it was, but it hit just within my reach. I felt around with my hand and found the slender object, closing my hand on it. All at once, my confidence returned as I flipped open the butterfly knife Liz threw to me like it was second nature. The creature took one of its hands and felt down my body, violating me once again as the man my mother trusted did long ago. As it went to turn me over, I plunged the knife in its side and it let out a deafening howl. I twisted the knife from side to side, widening the wound as the creature scrambled to get away. I held on and drove the knife in further. The more I twisted, the more it screamed and sounded more humanlike. I looked up at the monster and realized that it wasn't a monster at all. As I looked at it, I could see that it was now just a man. It was a weak, feeble man. As it weakened, I threw it off of me and slowly backed myself away.

"He's dead now!" Liz said as she stepped down from the rock she was standing on.

"You have done us proud," she said as Tia came from behind her. "You no longer have a use for us. It's time to go back to your world and live. Had you died here, we could not have survived. You have finally beaten what has kept you here for so long."

Tia reached out to me with a powerful arm. I took her hand and pulled myself to my feet.

"What will happen to you?" I asked her.

"Part of us will remain with you as you learn how to deal with your world again. We will always be a part of you. We are your love and your strength. Use us wisely," Tia said as she hugged me tightly. "Goodbye," she said as she disappeared into my body.

Liz just looked at me and stepped forward with her hand extended toward me. There was a strong slapping grip that followed as we held each other by the forearm in a barbarian-style handshake. With a final look, Liz's gripping hand dissolved into me and the rest of her followed suit until she was gone.

I looked around and was suddenly overwhelmed with the thought that it was all over. I dropped to the floor and pulled my knees to my chest and sobbed openly in relief as I rocked back and forth.

"It's over," I said to myself. "It's over..."

It's Over...

** Jacob **

"Let her go!" Sheila yelled at the orderly who was so angry by now, he didn't realize that he was choking Elizabeth and she had stopped fighting back. When he realized it, he let go and Elizabeth took her final attempt at a breath with relative ease. She scooted herself back into a corner, holding her knees to her chest and began to rock back and forth. She was whispering something to herself that was barely audible by the rest of us.

To me, it sounded like, "It's over." She kept repeating it over and over again as tears streamed down her cheeks. I let out a sigh of relief because the person I saw on the floor huddled in a corner was the same that I woke up in my bed the night before. For me, it was just beginning. Soon I would have to make a decision about her. The irony of this situation was almost prophetic.

As I looked around the room, the whole story sort of came to me like some kind of sick, reverse tale. I just then realized that it was Cheryl on the bed and looking across the room, I could see AJ moving her head back and forth as if she, too, was trying to wake from a bad dream.

Sheila went to her daughter and sat down next to her. As Elizabeth opened her eyes, she reached out and hugged her mother as a child would when lightning struck and the thunder that always followed it boomed. Sheila held her daughter and comforted her as they both rocked back and forth.

"Mamma!"

"It's okay, baby, I'm here," she said to her daughter. "I may not have been there when you needed me before, but I'm here now."

The orderly was as confused as everyone else in the room as the two of them carried on in the corner. He wasn't sure what was going on, and he looked at Nurse Caugman to clear things up for him. By this time, she had just pushed her way back into the room with a man and a woman following behind her. We were all in the room in awe of the entire situation.

"I think everything is okay now," I said to Stacy I motioned to her to let me handle it from there.

She looked at the orderly and pulled him off to the side. After whispering something in his ear she told him to go and get himself cleaned up and thanked him for his help. He told her if she needed him, he would be behind the desk.

Stacy acknowledged what he said with a nod and he walked out, wondering if all that beef was for show or that was just one hell of a strong chick.

** Mamma Taylor**

"AJ!"

I rushed over to my daughter and looked her up and down. I was afraid to touch her. She looked drugged out of her mind! Oh my poor baby!

"Mamma?" she slurred.

The nurse came over to us and looked her in the eyes. "I'm not sure what's wrong with her. She was much more coherent a little while ago. Let me look her over."

** Cheryl **

I looked at Jacob but stayed quiet. I was not over the trauma of the events that had just passed. I couldn't see Tia in the corner, crying in her mother's arms, but I could hear what was going on. It was only then that I realized that Tia was not in complete control of her life. I knew how that felt, but I couldn't imagine what it would be like to have absolutely no control over my actions. I actually felt sorry for Tia or Elizabeth, as I learned that was her name.

I felt safer now that Jacob was here, even though it was the orderly that saved the day. I knew now in my mind and now in my everyday presence that my life would be changed forever. It was a good change that would allow me to smile and feel free. I believed that's all most people wanted in life. I thought to myself that AJ would agree. Life is worth living! This was to be my new motivation. Indecision would be the death of me if it came back into my life. Knowing what I wanted gave me all the energy I needed to cruise through the days as it was God's will for me to do so.

"Jacob," I called to him.

He came to me and got close because I was almost whispering.

"So, how do you feel about cripples?" I smiled as I displayed myself with a wave of my hand across my body.

** Jacob **

I prayed that no one was looking, but I was very discrete as I kissed Cheryl on the lips and said, "I like you just fine."

** Stacy **

I saw the kiss from the corner as I tended to AJ. My heart sank, but I was happy for him. I hoped that one day there would be someone for me, but for now, I figured I had my job and it was fulfillment enough.

Two Years Later...

"Girl, I couldn't believe it when that man came flying across the room and tackled you. It was like something from a Raiders game, and you didn't score!" Cheryl laughed while she made more room on her plate for the greens that Jacob made.

"I can't believe it was so long ago! You all have been so good to me, despite what I've done to you. I could never repay you for the help you have given me."

"Enough already with the thank yous," AJ said. "This is a barbeque! Let's eat!"

"You all had better put those forks down before you give thanks to the Lord for what He allowed you to have!" Sheila scolded lightly.

As we all gathered around the table, Cheryl, AJ, Jacob, Alonzo, Sheila, Elizabeth, and me, Mamma Taylor, joined hands and gave thanks for the meal we were about to take part in. Each of us said a small bit of the thanks for the life we were living. AJ thanked God for her success as a psychologist. Jacob gave thanks for his new wife, Cheryl, and the joy she brought him. Cheryl gave thanks for her unborn child and prayed that he or she would be healthy and be loved by all. Sheila gave thanks for her daughter and the second chance she, herself, was given in this life. Elizabeth gave thanks for her mother and for the ability to help science by working out a cure for certain kinds of cancer. Alonzo lightly squeezed the hand of his bride to be as the diamond on Stacy's hand sparkled brilliantly in the noon sun. He thanked the Lord for a Love at last. She thanked the Lord for her man, and asked for a love that lasts. Lastly, I gave thanks to the Lord for patience and understanding and the ability to do good despite the crazy circumstances we encounter in this life.

All of our lives had been touched by something other than our acquaintances. We were touched by something much bigger than all of us, a force that few are aware of in the world. Elizabeth was still with us, thanks to a lot of prayer and Jacob coming to her aid. We really don't know the extent of her involvement with Jacob's parent's death. Jacob made her promise to see AJ weekly for the first year to make sure there were no re-occurrences of her problems. There weren't any and now we all pray together as a family, and watch each others back. We all learned a lesson about life from this experience. As Jacob would say, "Life will go on, with or without you. So get on board…"

978-0-595-38187-6
0-595-38187-1

Printed in the United States
52750LVS00003B/22

9 780595 381876

HANDBOOKS

GEORGIA

IM MOREKIS

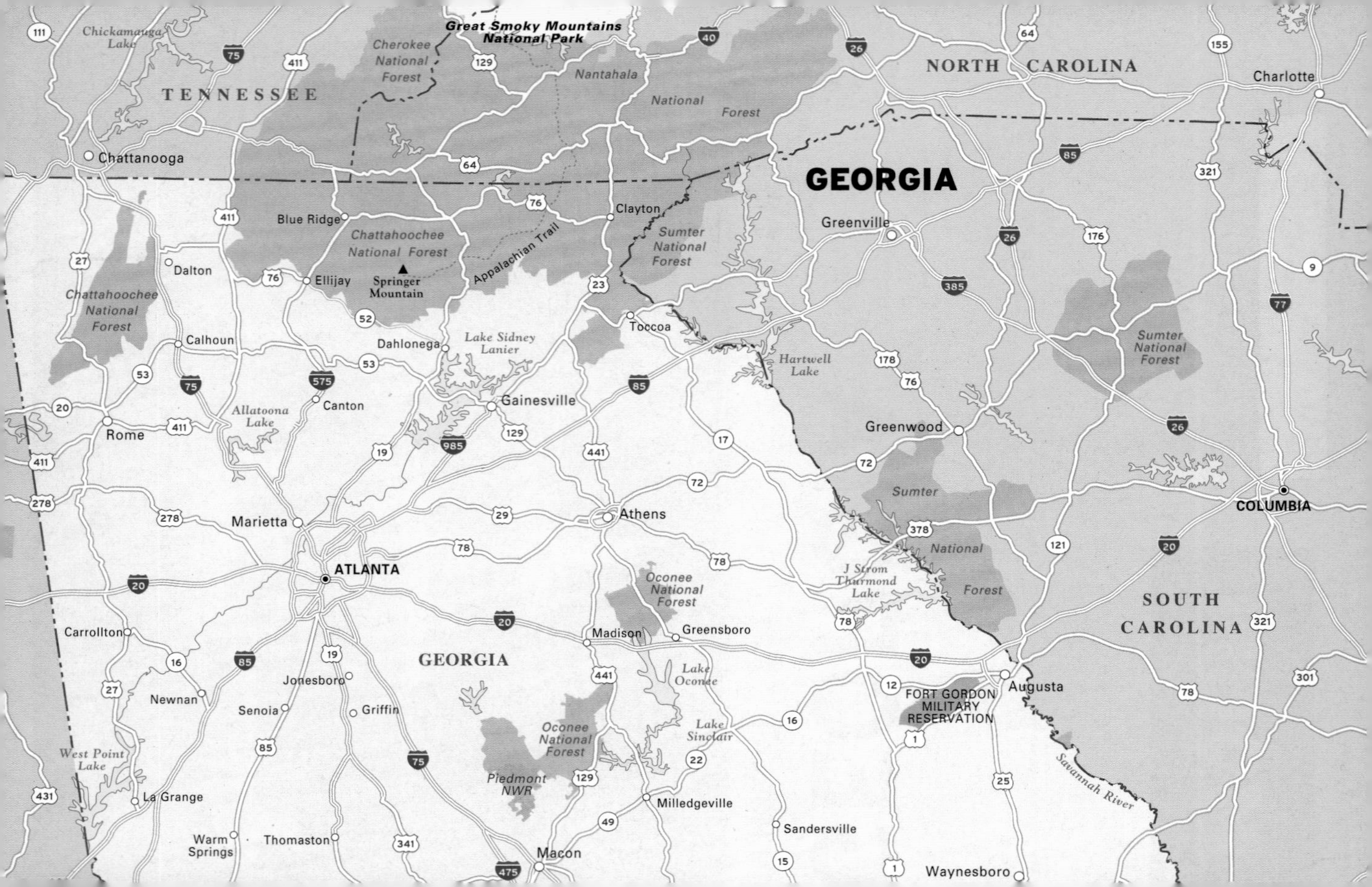
Great Smoky Mountains National Park
TENNESSEE
NORTH CAROLINA
GEORGIA
SOUTH CAROLINA
Chickamauga Lake
Chattanooga
Cherokee National Forest
Nantahala National Forest
Chattahoochee National Forest
Sumter National Forest
Oconee National Forest
Piedmont NWR
Appalachian Trail
Springer Mountain
Lake Sidney Lanier
Allatoona Lake
Hartwell Lake
J Strom Thurmond Lake
Lake Oconee
Lake Sinclair
West Point Lake
Savannah River
FORT GORDON MILITARY RESERVATION
Charlotte
Greenville
Greenwood
COLUMBIA
Augusta
Waynesboro
Blue Ridge
Clayton
Toccoa
Dalton
Ellijay
Calhoun
Dahlonega
Canton
Gainesville
Rome
Marietta
Athens
ATLANTA
Carrollton
Madison
Greensboro
Jonesboro
Newnan
Senoia
Griffin
La Grange
Milledgeville
Sandersville
Warm Springs
Thomaston
Macon

Columbus
FORT BENNING MILITARY RESERVATION
ALABAMA
Walter F George Reservoir
Chattahoochee River
Dothan
Perry
Statesboro
Eastman
Vidalia
Americus
Plains
McRae
Cordele
Lake Blackshear
Savannah
FORT STEWART MILITARY RESERVATION
Dawson
Fitzgerald
Pridgen
Baxley
Jesup
Albany
Tifton
Alma
Sapelo Island
Colquitt
Moultrie
Waycross
St Simons Island
Brunswick
Jekyll Island
Homerville
Okefenokee Swamp
Okefenokee National Wildlife Refuge
Bainbridge
Thomasville
Valdosta
Folkston
Cumberland Island National Seashore
St. Marys
Lake Seminole
Fargo
TALLAHASSEE
Jacksonville
Osceola National Forest
Apalachicola National Forest
FLORIDA
St. Marks National Wildlife Refuge
St. Johns River
0 30 mi
0 30 km
© AVALON TRAVEL

Contents